Praise for Elin Hilderbrand's

What Happens in Paradise

"Once again, Hilderbrand demonstrates her mastery of immersive escapism with a carefully deployed pineapple-banana smoothie or the blue tile of an outdoor shower... The absolute pleasure of the reading experience combined with a cliff-hanger ending will have readers anxiously awaiting the conclusion to the trilogy."

—*Booklist* (starred review)

"Expect romance, drama, and some holiday touches—just don't hold your breath for any snow in this island escape of a novel."

—Rebecca Renner, *Real Simple*

"Captivating...Those who want a sweet page-turner that's more than just beach fare will want to take a look...The book ends on a cliff hanger, setting readers up eagerly for the next book."

—*Publishers Weekly*

"You'll be counting the days until you can return to the Virgin Islands with these characters in the concluding volume of the trilogy. Print the bumper sticker—I'D RATHER BE LIVING IN AN ELIN HILDERBRAND NOVEL."

—*Kirkus Reviews* (starred review)

What Happens in Paradise

What Happens in Paradise

A Novel

Elin Hilderbrand

Little, Brown and Company
New York   Boston   London

Copyright © 2019 by Elin Hilderbrand
Excerpt from *Troubles in Paradise* copyright © 2020 by Elin Hilderbrand

Little, Brown and Company
Hachette Book Group
1290 Avenue of the Americas, New York, NY 10104
littlebrown.com

Originally published in hardcover by Little, Brown and Company, October 2019
First Little, Brown and Company mass market edition, August 2021

Little, Brown and Company is a division of Hachette Book Group, Inc. The Little, Brown name and logo are trademarks of Hachette Book Group, Inc.

ISBN 978-0-316-43557-4 (hardcover) / 978-0-316-42607-7 (large print) / 978-0-316-53651-6 (Canadian) / 978-0-316-42807-1 (signed) / 978-0-316-42808-8 (Barnes & Noble signed) / 978-0-316-42809-5 (Barnes & Noble signed Black Friday) / 978-0-316-43554-3 (paperback) / 978-0-316-43555-0 (mass market)

10 9 8 7 6 5 4 3 2 1

Printed in the United States of America

ATTENTION CORPORATIONS AND ORGANIZATIONS:
Most Hachette Book Group books are available at quantity discounts with bulk purchase for educational, business, or sales promotional use. For information, please call or write:
Special Markets Department, Hachette Book Group
1290 Avenue of the Americas, New York, NY 10104
Telephone: 1-800-222-6747 Fax: 1-800-477-5925

This novel is for St. John, U.S. Virgin Islands—the island itself and everyone who lives there.

Thank you for the revelry, and thank you for the refuge.

AUTHOR'S NOTE

What Happens in Paradise is the second book in a planned trilogy. While this book can, most certainly, be read as a stand-alone, a richer and more textured reading experience will be had by starting with book one, *Winter in Paradise*.

In the author's note in *Winter in Paradise,* I explained that the St. John portrayed in the novel is the one that existed before September of 2017, when Hurricanes Irma and Maria created such widespread devastation. There are businesses and restaurants mentioned in both books that now exist only on my fictional St. John. Thank you.

PART ONE

A Rooster and Two Hens

IRENE

She wakes up facedown on a beach. Someone is calling her name.

"Irene!"

She lifts her head and feels her cheek and lips dusted with sand so white and fine, it might be powdered sugar. Irene can sense impending clouds. As the sun disappears, it gains a white-hot intensity; it's like a laser cutting through her. The next instant she feels the lightest sprinkling of rain.

"Irene!"

She sits up. The beach is unfamiliar, but it's tropical—there's turquoise water before her, lush vegetation behind, a rooster and two hens strutting around. She must be back on St. John.

How did she get here?

"Irene!"

A man is calling her name. She can see a figure moving toward her. The rain starts to fall harder now, with intention; the tops of the palm trees sway. Irene dashes for the cover of the tree canopy and wishes for a towel to wrap around her naked body.

Naked?

That's right; she forgot to pack a swimsuit.

The man is getting closer, still calling her name. *"Irene! Irene!"* She doesn't want him to see her. She tries to cover up her nakedness by hunching over and crossing her arms strategically; it feels like an impossible yoga pose. She's shivering now. Her hair is wet; her braid hangs like a soggy rope down her back.

The man is waving his arms as if he's drowning. Irene scans the beach; someone else will have to help him because she certainly can't. But there's no one around, no boats on the horizon, and even the chickens are gone. There will be a confrontation, she supposes, so she needs to prepare. She studies the approaching figure.

Irene opens her mouth and tries to scream. Does she scream? If so, she can't hear herself.

It's Russ.

She wipes the rain out of her eyes. Russell Steele, her husband of thirty-five years, is slogging toward her through the wet sand, looking as though he has something urgent to tell her.

"Irene!"

He's close enough now for her to see him clearly—the silvering hair, the brown eyes. He has a suntan. He's had a constant tan since he started working for Todd Croft at Ascension, thirteen years ago. Their friends used to tease Russ about it, but Irene barely noticed, much less questioned it. He was on business in Florida and Texas; the tan seemed logical. She had chalked it up to lunch meetings at outdoor restaurants, endless rounds of golf. How many times had

Russ told her he would be unreachable because he'd be playing golf with clients?

Now, of course, Irene knows better.

"Irene," he says. His voice frightens her; she digs her heels into the sand. Russ's white tuxedo shirt is so soaked that she can see the flesh tone of his skin beneath. His khaki pants are split up one leg. He looks like he's survived a shipwreck.

No, Irene thinks. *Not a shipwreck. A plane crash. A* helicopter crash, *that's it.*

"Russ?" she says. He's getting pummeled by rain, and Irene flashes back twenty years to a Little League game of Baker's that was suspended due to a violent midwestern thunderstorm. All the parents huddled in the dugout with the kids, but Russ, in a show of gallantry, ran out onto the field to collect the equipment. Another father, Steve Sonnet (Irene had always rather disliked Steve Sonnet), said, *Reckless of him, picking up those metal bats. He's going to get himself killed.*

There was another time she remembers Russ soaking wet, a wedding in Atlanta. The Dunns' daughter Maisy was marrying an executive at Delta Airlines. This was five or six years ago, back when Irene and Russ found themselves attending more weddings than they had even when they were young. The reception was held at Rhodes Hall, and when she and Russ emerged from the strobe-lit dance floor and martini bar, it was to a downpour. Again, Russ insisted on playing the hero by tenting his tuxedo jacket over his head and dashing across the parking lot to their rental car. When he'd pulled up to the entrance a few moments later, his shirt had been soaked through, just like this one is now.

"The storm," Russ says, "is coming."

Well, yes, Irene thinks. *That much is obvious.* It's a proper deluge now, and the darkest clouds are still moving toward them. "I thought you were dead," she says. "They told me…" She stops. She's speaking, but she can't hear herself. It's frustrating. "They told me you were dead."

"It will be a bad storm," Russ says. "Destructive."

"Where should we go?" Irene asks. She turns to face the trees. *Where do the chickens hide from the rain?* she wonders. Because she would like to hide there too.

At eight o'clock on the dot, Irene wakes Cash. He has started calling her Mother Alarm Clock.

"I had another dream," she says.

Cash props himself up on his elbows in bed. His blond hair is messy and he's growing a beard; he hasn't shaved since they left the island. Irene has put him in the grandest of her five guest rooms, the Excelsior suite, she calls it. It has dark, raised-panel walls with a decorative beveled edge at the chair rail and an enormous Eastlake bed with a fringed canopy. There's also a stained-glass transom window that Irene got for a steal at a tiny antiques shop in Solon, Iowa, and a silk Persian rug in burgundy and cream that she purchased from a licensed dealer in Chicago. (She'd thought Russ might veto a five-figure rug, but he told her to go ahead, get it, whatever made her happy.) Irene's favorite piece in the room is a wrought-iron washstand that holds a ceramic bowl edged in gold leaf; above it hangs a photograph of Russ's mother, Milly, as a young girl in Erie, Pennsylvania, in 1928. Irene remembers the joy and pride she'd felt in refurbishing this room—every room in the house, really—but at this instant, she can't understand why. The Victorian style seems so heavy, so overdone, so tragic.

Irene has abandoned the master bedroom; she will never be able to sleep there again. Since she returned from St. John, she's been using the smallest guest room, originally meant to be quarters for a governess. It's up on the third floor, across from the attic. The attic is crammed with the bargains Irene scored at flea markets but couldn't find a place for in the house along with all the furniture from their former home, since Russ refused to let her take it to Goodwill. Russ had remarked many times that he would have been just as happy staying in their modest ranch on Clover Street, and Irene had thought him crazy. Of course, that was before she realized that Russ had a second life elsewhere.

The governess's room had been all but neglected in the renovation. Irene had simply painted the walls sky blue and furnished it with a white daybed and a small Shaker dresser. Now she appreciates the room's simplicity and its isolation. She feels safe there—although she can't seem to hide from these dreams.

"Dad was alive?" Cash asks.

"Alive," Irene says. This is the third such dream she's had since returning from St. John. Irene and Cash and Irene's older son, Baker, all traveled down to the Virgin Islands upon receiving the news that Russ had been killed in a helicopter crash off the coast of Virgin Gorda. He had been flying from a private helipad on St. John to the remote British island Anegada with a West Indian woman named Rosie Small. Irene then discovered that Rosie was Russ's lover and that Russ had left behind a fifteen-million-dollar villa and a twelve-year-old daughter named Maia. It was a surreal and traumatizing trip for Irene and her sons, and yet now, a week later, all of these shocking facts have been woven into the tapestry of Irene's reality. It was incredible, really, what the brain could assimilate. "He was talking about a storm. A bad storm, he said. Destructive."

"Maybe he meant the lightning storm," Cash says.

"Maybe," Irene says. The helicopter had been struck by lightning. "Or maybe it's what lies ahead."

"The investigation," Cash says.

"Yes." The week before, only a couple days after they'd arrived home from St. John, an FBI agent named Colette Vasco called Irene, Cash, and Baker to let them know that the Virgin Islands Search and Rescue team had contacted the Bureau with suspicions that there might be more to the helicopter crash than met the eye.

What does that mean, *exactly?* Irene had asked.

The damage to the helicopter doesn't match up with a typical lightning strike, Agent Vasco said. *There was lightning in the area, but the damage to the helicopter seems to have been caused by an explosive device.*

An explosive device, Irene said.

We're investigating further, Agent Vasco said. *What can you tell me about a man named Todd Croft?*

Next to nothing, Irene had said. She went on to explain that she had tried any number of ways to reach Todd Croft, to no avail. *I probably want to find him more than you do,* Irene said. She gave Agent Vasco the number that Todd Croft's secretary, Marilyn Monroe, had called Irene from. Agent Vasco had thanked her and said she'd be back in touch.

More to the helicopter crash than met the eye. An explosive device. This was turning into something from a movie, Irene thought. Yet she suspected that it was only a matter of time before the next dark door into her husband's secret life opened.

"Also, there were chickens in the dream," Irene says to Cash. "A rooster and two hens."

Cash clears his throat. "Well, yeah."

Well, yeah? Then Irene gets it: Russ is the rooster, Irene and Rosie the two hens.

Other than Cash and Baker, no one here in Iowa City knows that Russ is dead; Irene hasn't told anyone, which feels like a huge deception, as though she stuffed Russ's corpse into one of the house's nineteen closets and now it's starting to stink. Irene quiets her conscience by telling herself it's her own private business. Besides, no one has asked! This isn't strictly true—Dot, the nurse at the Brown Deer Retirement Community, asked where Russ was, and, in a moment of sheer panic, Irene lied and told Dot he was on a business trip in the Caribbean.

And he couldn't get away? Dot asked. *Even for this?* Dot was fond of Russ; she cooed over him at his every visit as though he had forded rivers and climbed mountains to get there, although she took Irene's daily presence at Brown Deer for granted. Irene perversely enjoyed watching the shadow of disillusionment cross Dot's face when she learned that Russ had put work before his own dying mother.

Russ's footprint in Iowa City all but disappeared after he took the job with Ascension thirteen years ago. Russ used to know everybody in town. He worked for the Corn Refiners Association and was a social creature by nature. He would drop off Baker and Cash at school and then go to Pearson's drugstore on Linn Street for a cup of coffee with "the boys"—the four or five retired gentlemen known as the Midwestern Mafia, who ran Iowa City. Russ's coffee break with the boys was sacred. They were the ones who had encouraged him to run for the Iowa City school board, and they'd suggested he join the Rotary Club, where he eventually became vice president.

All of the boys were now dead, and Russ hadn't been involved with local politics or the Rotary Club in over a decade. Irene occasionally bumped into someone from that previous life—Cherie Werner, for example, wife of the former superintendent of schools. Cherie (or whoever) would ask after Russ and then add, "We always knew he would make it big someday," as though Russ were a movie star or the starting quarterback for the Chicago Bears.

But who from Iowa City remained in Russ's everyday life? No one, really.

Now that the business of Milly's death has been handled—her body delivered to the funeral home, her personal effects collected, the probate attorney from Brown Deer enlisted to settle her estate—Irene has no choice but to face the daunting task of contacting the family attorney, Ed Sorley, to tell him about Russ.

"Irene!" Ed says. His voice contains cheerful curiosity. "I didn't expect to hear from you again so soon. Everything okay?"

Irene is in the amethyst-hued parlor, pacing a Persian rug that the same Chicago carpet dealer who'd sold her the Excelsior-suite rug had described as "Queen Victoria's jewel box, overturned." (Irene had bought it immediately despite the fact that it cost even more than the other rug.)

"No, Ed," Irene says. "It's not." She pauses. Russ has been dead for ten days and this is the first time she's going to say the words out loud to someone other than her sons. "Russ is dead."

There is a beat of silence. Two beats.

"What?" Ed says. "Irene, what?"

"He was killed in a helicopter crash on New Year's Day," Irene says. "Down in the Virgin Islands." She doesn't wait for Ed to ask the obvious follow-up question: What was Russ doing on a helicopter in the Virgin Islands? Or maybe: Where *are* the Virgin Islands? "When I called you last week to ask about Russ's will, he was already dead. I should have told you then. I'm sorry. It's just…I was still processing the news myself."

"Oh, jeez, Irene," Ed says. "I'm so, so sorry. Russ…" There's a lengthy pause. "Man…Anita is going to be *devastated*. You know how she adored Russ. You might not have realized how all the wives in our little group way back when thought Russ was an all-star husband. Anita used to ask me why I couldn't be more like him." Ed stops abruptly and Irene can tell he's fighting back emotion.

Anita should be glad you weren't more like him, Irene wants to say. Anita and Ed Sorley were part of a group of friends Irene and Russ had made when the kids were small—and yes, Anita had been transparently smitten with Russ. She had always laughed at his jokes and was the most envious on Irene's fiftieth birthday when Russ hired an airplane to pull a banner declaring his love.

"I need help, Ed," Irene says. "You're the first person I've told other than my kids. The boys and I flew down to the Caribbean last week. Russ's body had been cremated and we scattered the ashes."

"You *did?*" Ed says. "So are you planning a memorial, then, instead of a funeral?"

"No memorial," Irene says. "At least not yet." She knows this will sound strange. "I can't face everyone with so many unanswered questions. And I need to ask you, Ed, as my attorney, to please keep this news quiet. I don't even want you to tell Anita."

There was another significant pause. "I'll honor your wishes, Irene," Ed says. "But you can't keep it a secret forever. Are you going to submit an obituary to the *Press-Citizen*? Or, I don't know, post something on Facebook, maybe?"

"Facebook?" Irene says. The mere notion is appalling. "Do I have a legal obligation to tell people?"

"Legal?" Ed says. "No, but I mean . . . wow. You must still be in shock. I'm in shock myself, I get it. What was . . . why . . ."

"Ed," Irene says. "I called you to find out what legal steps I need to take."

There's an audible breath from Ed. He's flustered. Irene imagines going through this ninety or a hundred more times with every single one of their friends and neighbors. Maybe she *should* publish an obituary. But what would she say? Two hours after the papers landed on people's doorsteps, she would have well-intentioned hordes arriving with casseroles and questions. She can't bear the thought.

"When I called you before, Ed, you said Russ signed a new will in September." Irene had shoved this piece of information to a remote corner of her mind, but now it's front and center. Why the hell did Russ *sign a new will* without Irene and, more saliently, without *telling* Irene? There could be only one reason. "You said he included a new life insurance policy? For three million dollars?" She swallows. "The life insurance policy...who's the beneficiary?" *Here is the moment when the god-awful truth is revealed,* she thinks. Russ must have made Rosie the beneficiary. Or maybe, if he was too skittish to do that, he made a trust the beneficiary, a trust that would lead back to Rosie and Maia.

"You, of course," Ed says. "The beneficiary is you."

"Me?" Irene says. She feels...she feels...

Ed says, "Who else would it be? The boys? I think Russ was concerned about Cash's ability to manage money." Ed coughs. "Russ did make one other change. After you called me last week, I checked my notes."

"What was the other change?"

"Well, you'll remember that back when you and Russ signed your wills in 2012, you made Russ the executor of your will and Russ made his boss, Todd Croft, the executor of his. In my notes, I wrote that Russ said his finances were becoming too complex for, as he put it, a 'mere mortal' to deal with and he didn't want to burden you with that responsibility. He said Todd would be better able to deal with the fine print. Do you remember that?"

Does Irene remember that? She closes her eyes and tries to put herself in Ed Sorley's office with Russ. She definitely remembers the meeting about the real estate closing—she had been so excited—but the day that they signed their wills is lost. It had probably seemed like an onerous chore, akin to getting the oil changed in her Lexus. She knew it had to be done but she paid little attention to it because she and Russ were in perfect health. They were finally hitting their stride—a new job for Russ, a new house, money.

No, she does not remember. She doubts she would have objected to Russ making Todd Croft the executor of his will. Back then, Todd had seemed like a savior. *Todd the God.*

"So Todd was the executor," Irene says.

"And when Russ came in to sign the new will this past September, he changed it," Ed says. "He made you the executor."

"He did?" Irene says.

"Didn't he tell you?" Ed says.

"No," Irene says. Then she wonders if that's right. "You know what, Ed, he might have told me and I just forgot." *Or I wasn't listening,* she thinks. It's entirely possible that back in September, Russ said one night at dinner, *I saw Ed Sorley today, signed a new will with extra life insurance protection, and I made you executor.* And it's entirely possible that Irene said, *Okay, great.* Back in September, this information would have seemed unremarkable, even dull. Life insurance; executor. Who cared! It was all preparation for an event, Russ's death, that was, if not exactly inconceivable, then very, very far in the future.

Now, of course, the will has red-hot urgency. Irene is the beneficiary of the life insurance policy and she's the executor of the will. This is good news, right?

"I have something else in my notes," Ed says, and he sounds on the verge of getting choked up again. "When I asked Russ if he was concerned that being executor might be a burden for you, considering the complicated nature of his finances, he said, 'Irene is the only person I trust to do the right thing.'" Ed pauses. "Those were his exact words. I wrote them down."

Irene is the only person I trust to do the right thing. That seemingly simple sentence has a lot to unpack. Russ didn't trust Todd Croft to do the right thing—no surprise there. Had Russ assumed that Irene would find out about Rosie, Maia, the villa in St. John? And if the answer was yes, did he expect that Irene would have enough forgiveness in her heart to make sure that Rosie and Maia were taken care of financially? If again the answer was yes, he had given her a lot of credit.

Irene sighed. Russ was right. Rosie is no longer an issue, but Irene most certainly plans on providing for Maia.

"What do I do from here, Ed?" Irene asks.

"I'll need at least ten copies of the death certificate," Ed says. "I'd like one as soon as possible so I can start the probate process."

"Where do I get a death certificate?" Irene asks.

"Um...no one provided one for you? You should have been issued one from the state where Russ died."

"He died in the British Virgin Islands," Irene reminds him. "Between Virgin Gorda and Anegada."

There's silence from Ed. She might as well have named two moons of Jupiter.

"Baker was in charge of figuring out exactly who claimed the body," she tells Ed. "And who performed the cremation. He had some trouble. It's apparently very hard to get a body back from another country, and it was over the holidays. The regular people were on vacation."

"I'm not going to lie to you, Irene," Ed says. "My experience with this is limited. But you're saying you didn't get a death certificate while you were down there?"

"We didn't," Irene says. "Baker called the Brits, who directed him to the Americans, who sent him back to the Brits. Todd Croft had someone go down and identify the body—that was before we arrived—and he ordered the cremation without even asking me."

"What?" Ed says.

Irene has opened the proverbial can of worms now; she may as well keep going. "Todd Croft has, essentially, vanished. I can't reach him or his secretary, and the Ascension web page is down."

"Jeez, Irene," Ed says. "This is like something out of a movie."

"Ed," Irene says. "You didn't know anything about Russ's owning property in the Caribbean, did you?"

"In the Caribbean?" Ed says. "Heck no!"

"How much did you understand about his job?" Irene asks. "Did the two of you ever discuss it?"

"He worked for Croft's hedge fund, right?" Ed says. "He was the front man?"

"Right," Irene says. She relaxes a little. The way Russ had described it to her, the Ascension clients were investing such large amounts of money in such a high-risk environment, they needed a dedicated person just to put them at ease, and that person was Russ. Up until this very second, Irene wondered if maybe Ed Sorley was in on the whole mess, but now it's clear from his earnest tone that he's just as bewildered as she is. Ed wears sweater-vests. He handles wills, trusts, real estate closings, and the occasional dispute over property lines for the farmers of Johnson County. Russ and Irene hired him for their legal matters because he's their longtime friend. Irene realizes Russ must have had a second lawyer, one provided for him by Ascension.

Real estate, though.

"I'll call our bank, obviously," Irene says. They used to keep a checking and savings account at First Iowa Savings and Loan, where their friend Jerry Kinsey was the president. But shortly after Russ started working at Ascension, they switched to the behemoth Federal Republic Bank because Russ insisted that that bank was better equipped to handle Russ and Irene's "change of circumstance." Irene recalls pushing back on this. Just because Russ had a shiny new job didn't mean they had to change their small-town ways, did it?

Russ had looked at her like she was naive and Irene had capitulated. They opened a joint brokerage account at Federal Republic, although Irene defiantly kept a smaller account at First Iowa in her own name; that was where her paychecks from the magazine were deposited.

Now that Irene thinks about it, she realizes she never saw a balance of more than fifty thousand dollars in the Federal Republic account. They have several million invested, or so Irene has been led to believe, and the amount in the Federal Republic account was obviously replenished by Russ's paychecks and bonuses. So there should be a money trail that leads to Todd Croft and Ascension. Irene never delved into the particulars of their new financial situation because, quite frankly, she had done her share of worrying—creating budgets, stretching their meager resources—for a long time, and it was a relief just to know that there was money now, so much money that Irene could take a bath in French champagne every night if she wanted.

Back when Irene was renovating the house, Russ had transferred money into an account dedicated solely to paying the contractors and estate-sale managers and rug dealers. But that account had been closed for a while now. "We bought the house and the lot here on Church Street outright," Irene says. "That money was wired to our Federal Republic account from somewhere else. Would you look into it?"

"I can certainly do that," Ed says. "It was seven years ago? We've gotten a whole new computer system since then, but we must still have the paperwork in a box in the attic. I'll go upstairs and check."

"Thank you, Ed," Irene says.

"Aw, Irene," Ed says. "It's the least I can do."

"Please don't say anything to Anita," Irene says again. "I'll tell people when I'm ready."

"You have my word," Ed says. "Your job is to get a certified copy of the death certificate. Without that, Russ is technically still alive."

Still alive, Irene thinks. Just like in her dreams.

Irene's next move is a trip to Federal Republic. There's a branch in Coralville, although she has never set foot in it. She manages to find the most recent statement, which shows a balance of $46,270.32. There was a deposit of $7,500 on Monday, December 10, and another deposit of $7,500 on Monday, December 24, at eleven o'clock in the morning. The withdrawals are automatic payments for the household bills—electricity, cable, heating oil. There's a $3,200 payment to Citibank—that's Irene's credit card— an amount that was a little higher than normal due to Christmas.

Irene approaches the teller with trepidation, even though she has never seen the young woman before. She's Asian and far younger than either Cash or Baker, which is good. Irene craves anonymity. The last thing she wants is to deal with someone who knows her family, even slightly. Irene checks the woman's name plate: JOSEPHINE.

"Good afternoon, Josephine," Irene says. She stretches

her face into a smile, but she suspects it looks like a grimace. "I have some questions about my account."

"Certainly," Josephine says. She accepts the statement from Irene, then starts tapping at her computer keyboard. "Let me just bring this up on my screen." She pauses. Her eyes grow wide.

What? Irene thinks. She's worried she's going to be exposed on the spot. She'd have to say, *I'm here because my husband died under mysterious circumstances. I've just discovered he had a second life but I was never suspicious because, honestly, Josephine, I paid very little attention to him. And I know next to nothing about our current financial situation.*

"You're a valued and trusted account holder here at Federal Republic," Josephine says. "With us since 2006?"

"Yes," Irene says. She points to the amounts she underlined on the statement. "I was wondering if you could tell me where these two amounts were wired from? I don't see any other account number or the name of the bank."

Josephine checks the amounts on the statement, then blinks at her screen. "You're referring to the seventy-five-hundred-dollar deposit on Monday, December tenth, and the seventy-five-hundred-dollar deposit on Monday, December twenty-fourth?" Josephine's voice is very loud, Irene thinks. She seems to be intentionally drawing attention to her teller window. Irene quickly casts a glance around the bank. She lives in mortal fear of seeing someone she knows.

"Yes," Irene whispers, trying to telegraph the delicate nature of the situation.

"Those deposits were made in cash," Josephine announces brightly.

"Cash?" Irene says. She nearly adds: *You mean to tell me Russ walked in here with seventy-five hundred dollars on his person and then did it again two weeks later?*

"Yes, cash!" Josephine says with such gusto that Irene thinks, *Why not just broadcast over the bank's PA system that Russell Steele was a drug dealer?*

"Okay," Irene says. "Thank you. One more quick question." She leans in, locking eyes with Josephine, hoping that Josephine will finally understand the need for discretion. "Are there any other accounts at this bank under my name or my husband's name?"

Josephine pulls back a couple of inches. "Do you have the account numbers?"

"I don't," Irene says. She's trying to choose her words carefully here, though really what she's tempted to do is tell young Josephine a cautionary tale: *I let my husband take over our finances and now I don't know what I do or don't have!* "I think I may have a second account here, one I haven't been keeping close tabs on. Would you be able to check using my name or my husband's name, our address, or our Social Security numbers?" Here, Irene slides Josephine a piece of paper with both Socials clearly labeled. "I can't find any paperwork on our other accounts but it's a new year, so one resolution I made was to figure this out."

Josephine presses her lips together in a way that lets Irene know she's growing suspicious. Still, her fingers fly across the keyboard. She slows to punch the Social Security numbers in carefully, then waits for the results. Blood pulses in Irene's ears, and her shearling coat feels like it's made of lead.

"I don't see another account under either name or Social," Josephine says. "Nothing's coming up. Would you like me to call over my branch manager?"

"No, thank you, that's okay," Irene says. "For all I know, the account I'm thinking of could be at a different bank altogether."

Josephine tilts her head. "A different *bank?*"

Irene backs toward the door. She can't get out of there fast enough. "Well, like I said, it's my New Year's resolution to get organized."

"All righty!" Josephine says. "Good luck with that."

AYERS

Huck has asked Ayers to help him go through the things in Rosie's bedroom during the week, while Maia is at school. Ayers doesn't make it up to the house on Jacob's Ladder until the Thursday before the Martin Luther King Day weekend.

"I'm sorry I didn't come sooner," Ayers says. "My life just got really busy all of a sudden."

"Don't apologize," Huck says. "You have two jobs, and now that you're back with Mick, I'm sure he wants your attention as well."

Ayers sighs. She *is* back with Mick and he *does* want her attention. He admitted that seeing her with Baker (Mick calls him "Banker") drove him crazy with jealousy, and he vowed not to let anything—or anyone—get between them again. Since they've been back together, Mick has stopped by La Tapa at the end of Ayers's shift each night and walked her to her truck before heading back to Beach Bar until closing. He's abandoned his usual ritual of late-night drinks at the Quiet Mon and instead drives straight to Ayers's apartment in Fish Bay, where he spends the night. When Ayers works on *Treasure Island,* he meets her at the customs dock at four o'clock with a pineapple-banana smoothie from Our Market. On the one day off they've had together so far, Mick borrowed his boss's boat and they cruised all the way up the north shore to snorkel at Waterlemon Cay. They spotted three basking sharks and two spotted eagle rays. Mick is as much of a snorkel-nerd as Ayers. When they saw the second spotted eagle ray rippling along the sandy bottom, Mick dived down and undulated right along top of it. When he and Ayers surfaced a few moments later, he pulled off his mask and grinned like a kid with a shiny new bike, and Ayers felt a wave of the familiar adoration. This was her guy.

They'd left Waterlemon and headed to Gibney for an hour on the beach. When Ayers's stomach started to rumble, they climbed back into the boat and tied up to the dock at Caneel Bay. They strolled hand in hand, salty and sandy, to the Beach Bar, where Mick ordered a bottle of Moët, the conch fritters, and four sushi rolls.

Ayers had craned her neck to ogle the hotel rooms that

lined the beach, each of them as luxurious and appealing as pearls on a string.

"I'm dying to stay here," she said, then instantly regretted it. The champagne had gone right to her head.

"Guess you'll have to wait for your banker to come back," Mick said.

"Guess so," she said lightly. Mick dipped a fritter in aioli and let the topic go. Maybe he was consciously avoiding a fight or maybe he wasn't as jealous as he'd claimed to be. Maybe he was content to let the past be the past. Maybe he thought Baker Steele would never return to St. John. Maybe he thought he and Ayers could just continue their relationship where they'd left off, as though neither Baker nor Brigid had ever existed.

Ayers wasn't so sure.

Huck leads Ayers to Rosie's room and opens the door. Ayers has been in Rosie's room only twice before, both times years ago. The first time was when they swung by after work so Rosie could change before they went dancing at Castaways. The other time, Rosie was at work and Ayers was off and Rosie had texted Ayers and begged her to grab her bottle of Percocet—she had just had all four wisdom teeth removed and was crying in pain. But that was it. They were grown women; they hung out in bars, not in each other's bedrooms.

Ayers remembers, however, that while the rest of the house looked like it was shared by the protagonist of *The Old Man and the Sea* and the Little Mermaid (Huck and

Maia), Rosie's room was a sanctuary, cool and elegant, and it still is. The wallpaper is printed with pink hibiscus blossoms, and the hibiscus theme is echoed by a bush outside the open window. The queen-size bed has at least a dozen pillows artfully arranged against the rattan headboard. Rosie was a fastidious bed-maker, whereas Ayers sleeps in a tangle of sheets every night and sees absolutely no point in making a bed that she's only going to climb right back into the next night. (Ayers gets a sudden vision of Rosie folding napkins at La Tapa. She was careful and precise in the task, like she was doing origami.)

Against the wall is a large teak bureau; over it hangs a giant, round silver-framed mirror. The door to the closet is closed tight. The only personal touches that Ayers can see are a trio of framed photographs in one corner and a copy of *Jane Eyre* on the nightstand. Rosie was a sucker for the classics, especially the novels of Edith Wharton, George Eliot, and the Brontë sisters, and it was nearly impossible to get her to read anything contemporary, though she and Ayers had made a deal: Ayers would read *Middlemarch* if Rosie would read *Eat, Pray, Love*. (Ayers hadn't kept her end of the bargain, which she feels awful about now.)

Huck asked Ayers to "help" him go through Rosie's things, but it's clear he hasn't been in here even once, and Ayers suspects Maia hasn't either. The room is undisturbed, as if Rosie might walk back in at any moment, straw market bag over her shoulder, singing Aretha Franklin.

That, probably, is the point. If they go through everything and sort out what to keep and what to throw away, they're admitting Rosie is gone.

"I'll get started, I guess," Ayers says to Huck. "I'll make four piles—to keep, to give away, to throw away, and undecided."

"Ayers," Huck says.

She turns to him. She's afraid he's going to break down, and if *he* breaks down, she will too. They both vowed to be strong for Maia, and they have been, but this hasn't left a lot of time for them to tend to their own grief. Ayers can practically hear the texture and timbre of Rosie's voice: *You make me feel like a nat-u-ral wo-man!*

"Last Friday," Huck says, "the FBI called."

Ayers snaps back to reality.

"Virgin Islands Search and Rescue contacted them about the wreckage. The agent I spoke to said it looks like there might have been foul play."

Ayers nods but says nothing. After she and Mick had left Caneel Bay and returned the inflatable dinghy, they'd continued on to Joe's Rum Hut for happy hour, then they stopped at Woody's for a drink, then they strolled down to Morgan's Mango to have dinner. By that time, Mick was drunk enough to engage in some pretty wild theorizing. *The bird Rosie was on did not go down by accident,* Mick had said. *I guarantee you that.*

"Turns out the damage to the helicopter wasn't consistent with a lightning strike," Huck says. "They think there might have been a bomb aboard or that maybe someone tampered with the wiring to cause an explosion."

Ayers blinks.

"I just thought you should know," Huck says. "They're still investigating."

"Maia?"

"I didn't tell her," Huck says. "The less she thinks about the actual crash, the better."

"Agreed," Ayers says. "What about...I mean, do we know if..." She swallows. "Have you heard from Irene?"

"I made her promise she would text me once she made it home," Huck says. "And she did. Then a day or two later, she texted to let me know that her mother-in-law, Russ's mother, had passed away. Which I guess was something of a blessing. Though I don't know...that's a lot of loss for one week. I sent my condolences, then decided I'd leave her be for a while. So I'm not sure if she knows about this. Though I assume so. Have you heard from the boys?"

Ayers has not, which bothers her more than it probably should. Especially since she told both Baker and Cash to leave her alone. She was disappointed that they had lied to her about who they were, and besides that, she was back together with Mick. There was no reason for either of them to reach out to her, but their silence chafes nonetheless. They had both claimed to have feelings for her. Baker used the phrase "love at first sight," and Cash said he thought he was in love with her. But now that they're back in America, living their lives, Ayers has been forgotten.

Which is why she never dates tourists.

She is especially peeved at Cash because she had texted him the day before with a link to a job opening on *Treasure Island*. Wade, the first mate, was moving back to the States to manage a marijuana dispensary outside of Boston, and they needed to hire a replacement before he left in two weeks. Skip, the bartender at La Tapa, had expressed interest, but Ayers didn't think she could handle dealing with Skip at both of her places of employment, and she suspects that James, the captain, would throw Skip overboard before they made it into British waters. The problem is that everyone on St. John already has a job, and anyone who's not on St. John doesn't have housing. Then Ayers thought of Cash. He had been a big help on that trip to Virgin Gorda. And he'd had years of experience as a ski instructor, which, as he pointed out, was exactly the same thing, only completely different. He's probably certified in CPR. He would have to get his lifesaving certificate, take a marine-safety class, and, literally, learn the ropes. But all of that stuff is easy. The most attractive thing about Cash, other than his charm and love of the outdoors, is that he has a place to live.

Maybe it was a bit of a stretch to imagine that Cash would drop everything and move to the Virgin Islands in order to crew on *Treasure Island*. Maybe he thought Ayers was teasing him or taunting him, but if so, wouldn't he have shot back a snappy response?

"Not a word," Ayers tells Huck. She tries to make this sound like a good thing, but he must know better, because he pats her shoulder.

"Holler when you get hungry," Huck says. "I'll bring you some lunch."

"Great," Ayers says weakly. She thinks of the awful fish sandwiches on buttered Wonder Bread that Huck packs for Maia.

"I'm picking up barbecue from Candi's," he says, and Ayers perks up. "Thank you for doing this." He casts his eyes upward. "I'm sure Rosie would prefer to have you discovering her secrets rather than me."

Discovering her secrets makes the work sound intriguing when in fact it's merely heartbreaking.

Ayers starts with the closet. Rosie loved to wear white; it made her skin look luminous. The clothes in the right half of the closet are all white. Shades of eggshell, ivory, ecru, and pearl mix with the most blinding of whites. Everything is crisp and ironed, even her jeans. The clothes in the left half of the closet are full of color—Rosie's bright printed handkerchief halters, her bohemian blouses, her simple cotton tank dresses. Nobody rocked a jersey patio dress like Rosie Small. Ayers's favorite is a ribbed cotton racerback in brilliant marigold. She fingers it, remembering some special occasion at Chateau Bordeaux. The two of them had gone for cocktails to enjoy the spectacular view over Coral Bay, and Rosie had been wearing that dress.

Beneath the clothes are shoes—sandals, wedges, and the pair of black Dansko clogs marked with green tape that Rosie wore when she waited tables at La Tapa.

Ayers inhales through her nose, trying to stave off the tears. Everyone at La Tapa wore black clogs, and on Ayers's very first day of work, Rosie had advised making hers distinguishable in some way. She showed Ayers the green tape. *Looks like we wear about the same size,* Rosie said. *But if I ever see these on your feet, I'll cut you. Hear?*

Ayers could take the clogs now, of course, and wear them as a tribute—but is she worthy? Rosie was hands down the best server at La Tapa, the best server on the island, period. The guests clamored for her; her name was mentioned something like a hundred and seventeen times on TripAdvisor. Ayers would also like the marigold dress and all of the pristine white jeans. The handkerchief halters are so quintessentially *Rosie* that Ayers can only imagine giving them to Maia to wear when she's older. Much older.

Ayers throws herself down on the bed. She'd look awful in the yellow dress. But maybe she'll take it anyway and hang it in her closet, a reminder of her beautiful friend.

Foul play. The FBI. Russell Steele was into something illegal. He had enemies. Someone wanted him dead, and Rosie was collateral damage.

Ayers pushes herself up and goes to the corner to study the photographs. The top is a photo of Rosie with LeeAnn and Huck. Rosie is wearing a white cap and gown; it's her graduation from the University of the Virgin Islands on St. Thomas. Huck looks pretty much the same as he does now, maybe a few pounds lighter then with a bit more red in his beard. Ayers studies LeeAnn, Rosie's mother. She was tall and statuesque and wore her reddish-brown hair in a braided topknot. Ayers had heard all about the glamorous LeeAnn—that she had modeled as a teenager and gotten as far away as the fashion shows in Milan but had come home to marry her childhood sweetheart, Levi Small, who'd ended up leaving the island for good shortly after Rosie was born. LeeAnn had then gone to school to become a nurse practitioner. To hear some people tell it, LeeAnn was the most qualified caregiver at the Myrah

Keating Smith Community Health Center, even better than the doctors. Ayers had found LeeAnn intimidating—initially, anyway. She exuded competence as well as something Ayers could only describe as a regal bearing. When LeeAnn first met Ayers, she'd seemed disapproving that Ayers had no college degree and no way to support herself other than the hand-to-mouth existence that waiting tables afforded. *Don't your parents want more for you?* LeeAnn had asked. Ayers had tried to explain that her parents were wanderers without a home, without possessions, really, and that they counted wealth by life experiences. LeeAnn had met this news with a skeptical arched eyebrow. *Don't you want more for yourself?* LeeAnn asked. Ayers had shrugged; she was twenty-two years old at the time. But it was LeeAnn Powers's questions that led Ayers to get her second, slightly more professional job on *Treasure Island.* After that, LeeAnn's opinion of her had seemed to improve. *Learn everything you can about the business,* LeeAnn said. *Then save your money and buy it.*

LeeAnn had been even tougher when dealing with Rosie. The worst insult LeeAnn could dish out was to say that Rosie took after her Small relatives. That look in Rosie's eyes, for example, that fire, that defiance, was pure Small, LeeAnn said, and it had to be contained or the girl would ruin herself.

What would LeeAnn have made of the Invisible Man? Nothing good, Ayers guesses.

Ayers hasn't said this out loud to anyone but she doesn't think it's a coincidence that Russell Steele, the "Invisible Man," reappeared in Rosie's life just after LeeAnn died. A few weeks ago, Ayers had learned that Russ was Maia's father, meaning he had been in Rosie's life a lot longer than anyone knew.

Oh, how Ayers longs to ask Rosie herself. *You could have told me everything,* Ayers thinks. *I was a safe place for you.*

The center photo is of Maia, taken outside the Gifft Hill School. She's very small, wearing a backpack that is nearly as big as she is, and in the photo she's on her tiptoes, reaching for the latched gate of the fence to let herself in. The picture is precious and Ayers can imagine Rosie in the parking lot, possibly crouched down between two cars so Maia wouldn't see her, capturing this early expression of independence.

Maia's relationship with Rosie had been less contentious than Rosie's with LeeAnn, but that's not to say it was all milk and cookies after school and snuggles and stories at bedtime. There was a ferocity that ran through the female line of that family—maybe LeeAnn, Rosie, and Maia were all too similar—and Ayers had seen Rosie and Maia butt heads again and again. When Ayers was called on to referee, she usually sided with Maia, causing Maia to utter the famous line that Ayers was like a mother to her but better, because she wasn't her mother.

The third photograph is of Rosie and Ayers on Oppenheimer Beach, back when the tire swing still hung from the crooked palm that stretched out over the water. The tire swing was more fun to look at than actually ride on, as Ayers had learned the hard way, but this picture of the two of them in bikinis is the best picture of them ever taken. Ayers keeps the same photo on her phone as her screen saver, and she will never replace it.

She feels honored that she has earned a spot on Rosie's bedroom wall. It seems to mean that Rosie considered her family.

Ayers can't help but notice that there is no picture of Russell Steele on the wall.

If there are secrets to discover, Ayers predicts she'll find them in the top drawer of the dresser. That's where people put intimate things, right? Women their lingerie and men their condoms. Rosie's top drawer holds the expected collection of bras and panties, some functional, some recreational, as well as teddies and slips, cotton socks, a box of tampons, two full carousels of birth control pills, and a plastic bag containing six tightly rolled joints, which Ayers slips right into her purse. Rosie would definitely want Ayers to take those so Maia doesn't find them and get thoughts about experimenting.

The middle drawer is a jumble of bikinis, nearly all of which Ayers recognizes; at least half a dozen are white. The rest are black, red, blue gingham, kelly green with hot-pink piping. There's a pink smocked top that Ayers loves, and then she remembers a supercool turquoise crocheted bikini that Rosie got from Letarte. Ayers digs for it, but it's not there—maybe Rosie wore it to Anegada? A sobering thought. Then Ayers finds something intriguing. Beneath the bikinis is a layer of clothbound books. But they're not books, Ayers realizes when she opens one and sees Rosie's handwriting. They're journals.

Ayers extracts the journals like she's unearthing the

bones of ancient peoples on an archaeological dig. She reads from the one on top.

January 1, 2000

It's not only a new century but a new millennium. I, Rosalie Veronica Small, am seventeen years old, a senior at Charlotte Amalie High School. I'm in love with Oscar Cobb and nothing my mother or Huck can say will keep us from getting married on my eighteenth birthday.

Ayers shuts that journal and scrambles for one closer to the bottom of the pile, from 2015. Her breathing is shallow.

January 1, 2015

R. has stayed in Iowa through the holidays because his older son is visiting from Houston with his new baby. I wanted to text him a picture of me and Ayers doing tequila slammers up at the Banana Deck but of course the rule is "no texting."

Ayers closes the journal, then her eyes. Tequila slammers at the Banana Deck, New Year's Eve four years earlier. Yes; they had stopped there after the end of service at La Tapa but before they went to the Beach Bar to dance to Miss Fairchild. It had been a fun night, recklessly wild. They had closed the Beach Bar, gotten high, skinny-dipped in Frank Bay, then crashed a party all the way out on Ironwood Road in Coral Bay and stayed up to watch the sun rise. Ayers knew then about the Invisible Man, but he was just some guy who showed up every now and then to wine and dine Rosie and give her lavish presents. If Ayers is remembering correctly, it was right after that New Year's that Rosie got a new Jeep, a four-door Wrangler in stingray gray with all the bells and whistles.

Whose is that? Ayers had asked when Rosie pulled up in it.

Mine, Rosie said without another word of explanation. Ayers had known then that it was from the lover, the Invisible Man, and that was when Ayers started to wonder just how serious that relationship was.

Ayers turns around to make sure the bedroom door is closed. How is she going to smuggle the journals out of there? If there's any question as to whether she's the right person to read them first, she pushes it aside. God only knows what kind of details they contain; Ayers can't risk letting Maia read them before she does. And Huck made his feelings clear.

Despite this, Ayers doesn't want to tell Huck she's found them.

Why?

Well, she's not sure why. It's just a gut instinct. What if curiosity or ego gets the best of Huck and he decides to read them himself?

Ayers can practically hear Rosie saying, *Noooooooooo!*

Ayers looks under the bed and on the floor of the closet for a duffel or a suitcase but finds nothing. Then she hears a car and peeks out the window to see Huck pulling out of the driveway. He must be on his way to get lunch from Candi's—perfect. Ayers heads out to the kitchen and pulls a reusable shopping bag off the hook next to the sink. She loads the journals up and hurries them out to Edith, her truck. She throws a beach towel over them for good measure.

She goes back to Rosie's room, replaces all the bikinis, and shuts the drawer. She sits on the floor. She's short of breath. She has discovered all of Rosie's secrets. They're waiting like a time bomb in Ayers's truck.

A few minutes later, Ayers hears the front door open and then Huck calling out, "Grub! Come and get it!"

Ayers is too keyed up to eat. She wants to get home and read the journals! She's going to have to hide them somewhere Mick won't find them or see her reading them.

Huck knocks on the bedroom door and swings it open just as Ayers pulls out the third dresser drawer, so they both see what's inside at exactly the same time.

Ayers shrieks.

Huck says, "What the hell is that?"

It's money. The bottom drawer is filled with money.

CASH

He's having dinner with his mother at the Pullman Bar and Diner when she asks the question he's been dreading.

"So what's next for you? Back to the mountains?"

"Trying to get rid of me already?" he says.

"Not at all," Irene says. "It's just that I thought this"—she indicates the restaurant and their server, Ryan, whom she seems to be on pretty familiar terms with—"was the stuff of your nightmares. Stuck in Iowa City, eating the early-bird special with your mother."

"It's been only five days," Cash says. "And Milly—"

"Milly is handled," Irene says. "I don't mean to make your grandmother sound like a loathsome errand. But I also want you to know that you don't need to stay here on my account. Surely you have better things to do than listen to me describe my crazy dreams."

His mother is right. Cash should load Winnie into his truck and return to Denver to clean up what's left of his life there before he heads to Breckenridge for the remainder of the winter. But what had seemed so appealing before he got Irene's phone call informing him his father was dead has lost its luster. He received no fewer than ten panicked voicemails from Dylan, the manager of Cash's Belmar store, asking why there are chains on the door and why no one is answering the phone at the Cherry Creek store. (Cash finally responded: *Business went under. I would offer you a reference but I know you've been skimming from the register. Sorry, bro, good luck out there.*) Cash is two payments behind on his truck so he needs a job right away. But because it's already January, all of the positions at the ski school have been filled. Cash called his buddy Jay, and he said Cash could sleep on his sofa for a week but that would be all his new girlfriend would tolerate and finding other housing at this point would be tricky, especially with a dog.

"You might want to cool your heels there," Jay said. "And try coming out in March when everyone else gets cabin fever and leaves."

Cool his heels in Iowa for *two months?* In winter? There's no way he can do it, can he? And yet, what choice does he have? Living with his mother is free, the house is comfortable and plenty big enough, and she gives him twenties and fifties every time he goes out. She would probably make his car payment in exchange for him doing some simple handyman work.

But would his morale survive? He fears not. Earlier that day, his mother pressed two hundred dollars into his hand and sent him to the Hy-Vee for groceries, which he didn't object to as he needed dog food for Winnie and some shaving cream for himself. And who should he run into at the deli counter but his high-school girlfriend Claire Bellows, the one who went to Northwestern and promptly slept with Baker?

"Cash?" Claire said, blinking like he was an apparition. "Cash *Steele,* is that you?"

Cash forced a smile while he cursed his truly terrible luck. And yet, this was what happened when you returned to your hometown: you bumped into the people you used to know. Claire Bellows looked basically the same, maybe a little older, maybe a little washed out; her face was wan, her hair colorless and pulled back into a sad little bun. She was pushing a cart that held two children, a toddler who was standing up among the groceries—his left foot perilously close to a carton of eggs—and a baby in a bucket seat that snapped onto the front of the cart. The toddler was a boy;

the baby was swaddled in a pink fleece sack, her face obscured.

"Hey, Claire." Cash said it casually, as though he'd just seen her the week before. He *felt* like he'd just seen her the week before because he and Baker had spent so much time talking about her. The good news was that the bad mojo of Claire Bellows had been exorcised. Cash felt nothing when he looked at her. He leaned in to kiss her cheek. "How are you?"

"This is like that song!" Claire exclaimed. *"Met my old lover in the grocery store, the snow was falling Christmas Eve!"*

Cash nodded along, trying to be a good sport. The lyrics rang a distant bell—Gordon Lightfoot, maybe? Simon and Garfunkel? Cash was reminded that Claire used to be a lyrics wizard, especially when it came to the music of their parents' era, because Claire's mother, Adrienne Bellows, was a disc jockey on the local easy-listening station. When Cash and Claire were in high school, Adrienne worked the evening six-to-ten shift; she was eastern Iowa's answer to Delilah. While Adrienne Bellows was comforting the heartbroken and lovelorn who called in with their requests and sappy dedications, Cash and Claire were making out and, eventually, having sex in Claire's bedroom.

"And who do we have here?" Cash asked in an attempt to be gallant. He was trying, he really was.

Claire looked confused until she realized he meant the children. "Oh!" she said. "This is Eugene and the baby is Mabel."

Cash tried not to grimace. Claire had followed the trend of naming her children as though they'd been born a hundred and twenty years ago. "Nice," he said. "Hi, guys." The toddler turned to look at Cash, missing the eggs by a fraction of an inch, and Cash couldn't help himself—he moved the carton to safety. "So you're back in Iowa City?"

"Temporarily," Claire said. "For the next five or six years. My husband is doing a fellowship in endocrinology at the university."

Cash nearly said, *And you?* But he was afraid Claire would tell him that she'd given up her job as a marketing executive with Colgate-Palmolive in Chicago in order to follow her husband back to Iowa and then add that she was "okay" with it or else openly express bitterness. To extract himself from that awkward topic, Cash would then ask about her mother, and Claire, realizing that she was doing all the talking, would take the reins and say, *What about you? Why are you in town?* Cash could then say he was visiting his parents, which would be half a lie, although lying would be preferable to telling Claire that Russ was dead. Claire had loved Russ. She and Russ had had a thing where they told each other knock-knock jokes, which Cash had found annoying even at the height of his passion for Claire.

> *Knock-knock.*
> *Who's there?*
> *A broken pencil.*
> *A broken pencil who?*
> *Never mind, it's pointless.*

He might be able to successfully evade the topic of his parents but there would undoubtedly be follow-up questions about where he was living and what he was doing—and then finally, as if it had just occurred to her for no particular reason, Claire would ask about Baker.

To avoid that inevitable moment, Cash smiled at Claire and said, "Well, at least Iowa City is a good place to raise kids. We learned that firsthand. See you later, Claire."

"But—wait," Claire said.

Cash did not wait. He sacrificed the half a pound of sliced turkey on Irene's list and sauntered off in the direction of the bakery. Claire had always been socially awkward in a sweet way. When Baker hit on her at that frat party at Northwestern, it must have been like taking candy from a baby.

But, really, what did Cash care? He was over it.

Thinking about it now in the Pullman Diner, he can't imagine spending two to three months here in Iowa City dodging land mines like his ex-girlfriend Claire.

To Irene he says, "I'm going to stay a few days longer. At least."

She gives him a tight smile and Cash wonders if maybe she *wants* him gone.

"Let's order," she says.

He's nearly asleep, sprawled across the massive acreage of the guest-room bed, when he gets a text on his phone.

Who would be texting him so late? Cash figures it must be Dylan again, telling Cash that he left his one-hitter behind the counter or complaining because he's still owed for a day and a half of work. The first thing Cash notices when he picks up his phone is the time. It's not late at all; it's only ten o'clock. It just feels late because it gets dark at four thirty in the afternoon and there's nothing to do in this town after the dinner hour. The second thing Cash notices is that the text is from Ayers.

Ayers.

Cash stares at the phone, wondering if it's a trick. Did Baker somehow figure out a way to send Cash a text that looks like it's from Ayers? Cash hesitates a moment, then swipes to open. The text isn't a text but rather a link, and when Cash clicks on the link, it opens to the website for Treasure Island Cruises—*Day Trips to the BVIs, St. Thomas, Water Island, and Beyond!*

Beyond? Cash thinks. *Beyond* must be that place you visit in your mind after nine or ten painkillers.

This section of the website starts with *Join the* Treasure Island *crew!* In smaller print beneath that is *We are currently seeking a first mate for our BVI routes. Must possess strong administrative skills and CPR and lifesaving certification; must enjoy working with people. Valid passport required, boating experience preferred. To apply, contact Ayers Wilson, ayers@treasureislandcruisesvi.com.*

Did Ayers send this to him for a reason? Cash wonders. Does she think he should…apply? He has been boating exactly once in the past ten years—when he went on *Treasure Island* as Ayers's guest. Yes, he'd enjoyed it, and yes, Ayers had asked him if he wanted a job. But that had been a joke. Right? And yet now, apparently, they were looking for someone.

CPR certification he has; lifesaving, not a chance—unless you considered avalanche-rescue certification "lifesaving." Well, it was, but it wouldn't help him save someone who was drowning. Cash is an okay swimmer and he does have years of experience working with people, but in his heart, he's a mountain boy.

His thumbs hover over the keypad. It doesn't matter why Ayers sent this; it only matters that she's reaching out. She's thinking of him.

He lies back in bed and tries to lasso his bucking bronco of a heart. Ayers had been so angry the last time he saw her, so indignant that two people she'd befriended had deceived her about who they were and what they were doing on St. John. In retrospect, Cash doesn't blame her. They—meaning Baker—should have told Ayers who they were at Rosie's funeral lunch. But okay, let's say that would have been in poor taste. Fine. Cash should have told her who he was when he bumped into her on the Reef Bay Trail. No excuses; he should have and he hadn't, and then once he'd spent the day with her aboard *Treasure Island,* he'd become infatuated with her and didn't want to ruin his chances. The same had been true for Baker. And guess what—they both lost out. Ayers told them she had gotten back together with her old boyfriend, Mick.

Cash reads the link she'd texted him again. She must have sent it to him because she thought it would be a good fit. Right? *Right?* Or maybe it was a joke. For all Ayers knows, Cash is back in Colorado, skiing the bowl on Peak 8.

But he's not. He's in Iowa City without a job, without prospects. He closes his eyes and tries to imagine a life on the water.

With Ayers. He would agree to live in the space station if it was with Ayers.

He decides not to respond to the text right away. He wants to sleep on it.

In the morning, the text is still there and Cash is proud of himself for exercising restraint and not sending a knee-jerk response.

Winnie is asleep at the foot of the bed. When she feels Cash stir, she lifts her head.

"You liked St. John, right?" Cash asks. "Wanna go back?"

Of course, it's not Winnie's permission that he needs. Cash pads down to the kitchen in his pajama bottoms and a decade-old Social Distortion T-shirt he found in the bureau in his room. Irene is juicing oranges the old-fashioned way—by crushing the hell out of the buggers with a galvanized-steel juicer that had belonged to her own mother. Cash watches her as she presses and twists the orange under her palms. All of that energy for a dribble of juice. Though it's probably not the worst way to release pent-up frustration.

"Mom," he says. "I'm not going back to Colorado."

"You're not?" she says, relaxing her death grip on the orange in her hand and then tossing the rind in the sink.

"With your permission…" he says. His voice sticks. Asking her this is harder than he thought it would be. "I'd like to go back down."

"Down?" she says, though he can tell she understands.

"To St. John," Cash says. He clears his throat. "I have a lead on a job there. And I was hoping I could just stay in the villa."

Irene abandons the juice project altogether in order to stare at him. He can't tell what she's thinking, but then, his mother's expressions have always been inscrutable. Against all odds, they had both sort of fallen in love with St. John— at least, Cash did. He knows Irene had warmed to it as well; she went out fishing with Huck once in an attempt to get information, but she also took a second boat trip with him before she and Cash left. He supposes it's possible that her feelings have changed since they've been back home and now the whole Caribbean represents an enormous, ugly deception that she doesn't want to revisit. And maybe she'd prefer that Cash not revisit it either.

It's the idea that Irene might say no, might ask him nicely not to go or forbid him to stay in the villa, that makes Cash realize how badly he wants to return and give life down there a shot. He won't stay forever. Maybe just until summer.

"Is this about the girl?" Irene asks.

"What?" Cash says. He can feel his face turning red. "No, of course not."

"Oh," Irene says. "That's too bad. I like her for you, you know."

"So…is it okay?" Cash asks.

"Yes, honey," Irene says. "It's fine. The villa is just sitting there empty. Someone should use it. Let me buy your plane ticket and give you some money to get started."

Cash wants to tell her she doesn't have to—he's too old to be taking handouts from his mother—but the fact is, he's flat broke. Broker than broke.

"Thank you, Mom," he says. "Thank you so much."

Irene gives him a sad smile. "I'm jealous," she says.

HUCK

One hundred and twenty-five thousand dollars; this is how much cash Huck and Ayers discover in the bottom drawer of Rosie's dresser. It's all banded up in neat bricks, just like in the movies. After they count the bricks, they count them again, announcing the amounts out loud as they go so they don't lose track. Then Huck says, "Come into the kitchen."

"I don't think I can eat," Ayers says.

"I'm not talking about barbecue," Huck says. "I'm talking about rum."

Ayers shuts the drawer, and the blue Benjamins disappear; Huck ushers her down the hall. In the kitchen, he takes two shot glasses out of the cabinet and brings his trusty bottle of eighteen-year-old Flor de Caña—useful in most emergencies—down from the shelf.

He pours two shots and gives one to Ayers. "I don't know what to say," he admits, raising his own glass.

"Me either."

They clink glasses and drink. He notices Ayers eyeing the barbecue spread out across the counter. She grabs a drumstick dripping with comeback sauce. Huck follows suit. No matter what the circumstances, Candi's is too tempting to resist.

After Ayers leaves, taking one yellow dress and three pairs of white jeans with her—the rest of the clothes they should let Maia go through, Ayers said, as soon as she's old enough—Huck picks up the money, armful by armful, and stashes it under his bed. He's aware that it has remained undetected in Rosie's room, but he figures it's only a matter of time before Maia goes snooping. Maia will never voluntarily enter Huck's room. He's messy, and Maia has declared on numerous occasions that, despite Huck's valiant effort with the laundry, his room smells like fish guts, *rotten* fish guts.

After the money is beneath the bed, he stacks all the issues of *Field and Stream* and *National Geographic* that he's collected over the past twenty years around the bed so that if Maia does come poking around, she will see only that Huck is a packrat.

Money hidden, he feels a little better. He drives to Gifft Hill to pick up Maia from school.

A hundred and twenty-five grand. In cash. In a dresser drawer.

It's a lot of money, but it's not enough to kill two people over; that's Huck's thought as he pulls into the school parking lot.

Maia is lingering by the gate with her friend Joanie and two boys Huck recognizes but can't put names to. All four kids have their phones out and they're laughing at something on the screen. Huck knows Maia sees him and he also knows enough to be patient and not tap the horn or, God forbid, call out to her. That would be *so embarrassing*.

Maia runs over to his window and he cranks it down.

"Hello there," he says. His voice sounds normal to his own ears, gruff, grandfatherly. All of his internal panic about having so much cash hidden under his bed is, he thinks, undetectable. "Are you not getting in?"

Maia bites her lip. "Would you take me and my friends into town so we can walk around?"

"Walk around and do what?" Huck asks. Cruz Bay is a small town consisting mostly of bars. Three o'clock is when happy hour at Woody's starts, luring people off the beaches in the name of good, cheap rum punch, and at four o'clock, all of the excursion boats pull in and disgorge people who have been drinking all day, most of whom are interested in continuing their drinking on land. This is all well and good for the island economy—Cruz Bay in the late afternoons is one of the most festive places on earth—but it's not exactly a wholesome environment for a bunch of twelve-year-olds.

Maia shrugs. "Get ice cream at Scoops, walk around Mongoose, maybe listen to the guitar player at the Sun Dog. He knows some Drake songs."

Huck is pretty cool for a grandpa; he, too, knows some Drake songs. "All right. Pile in, I guess. What time should I plan to pick you up?"

"Joanie's mom will bring us home," Maia says.

"Fine," Huck says. If Julie is on board with the kids going into town, then Huck figures it must be all right. Joanie climbs into the truck, giving Huck a fist bump, but the boys offer him scared sideways looks, like he's Lurch from *The Addams Family*. This actually cheers Huck up a bit.

"Hey, fellas," he says. "I'm Captain Huck. Remind me of your names."

"Colton," says one.

"Bright," says the other.

Colton and Bright—Huck has definitely heard both names before, so that's good. The four kids wedge themselves into the back seat of the truck's cab, leaving Huck to feel like very much the chauffeur. He nearly asks Maia to move up front, but he doesn't want to embarrass her and he supposes that part of the fun is being smushed up against a boy. This is how it all starts, Huck thinks. One minute you're leg to leg with a boy in your grandpa's truck during a ride into town, and the next minute you're hiding a hundred and twenty-five thousand of that boy's illegally gotten dollars in your dresser drawer.

Huck heads up the hill to Myrah Keating, then takes a left on the Centerline Road. At every curve and dip, the kids hoot as though the thrill of the ride is brand-new, even though they've all grown up driving on this crazy road. When they descend to the roundabout and Huck signals to go right toward Mongoose Junction, Maia says, "Actually,

Gramps, can you drop us off at Powell Park? We're waiting for some Antilles kids to get off the ferry."

"*Antilles* kids?" Huck says. Antilles is the private school over on St. Thomas. "Not *those* rascals."

One of the boys guffaws and Huck can practically hear Maia rolling her eyes. Waiting for the Antilles kids is fine, Huck supposes. Powell Park attracts a colorful cast of characters but it's perfectly safe to hang out there in the midafternoon. So why does Huck feel uneasy? He knew these days were coming; Maia wasn't going to stay a child forever. But he's not ready. He should probably acknowledge that he'll never be ready. He needs Rosie back from the dead; he needs LeeAnn. Ayers has offered to serve as a surrogate mother but she has her own life, two jobs and a boyfriend, so how much can he really ask of her?

Huck has gotten used to the solo life, but right now he could really use a partner.

Irene? He immediately chastises himself for the thought. He must be out of his mind.

That night, after Maia shows Huck her completed homework and then goes into her room to FaceTime Joanie and giggle about God knows what—probably Colton and Bright or possibly a boy who goes to Antilles—Huck climbs into bed with his Michael Connelly novel. He's been reading this book since before Rosie died, which is an addling thought. When he first cracked open *The Late Show* a couple weeks ago, his life was one way, and now that he's on page 223, it's completely another. Now

Rosie is dead—*dead!*—and he's hiding a hundred and twenty-five grand under his bed. The book does the trick, though—keeps him engrossed for a few chapters until his eyelids start to feel heavy. He closes the book and turns off the light.

Sleep, he thinks.

But he can't sleep. He might as well have a pile of uranium under the bed; the money feels radioactive.

A hundred and twenty-five thousand dollars. In cash.

Why?

Eventually, he drifts off; when he's awakened by his alarm, his head aches and he's in a foul mood. In his day, this was known as getting up on the wrong side of the bed.

"Let's go!" he calls out to Maia. "I have a charter at nine. A bachelor party."

Maia emerges from her room wearing a pink jean skirt, a black tank top, and black Chuck Taylors. She looks older, as though she aged three years overnight.

"I thought you hated bachelor parties," she says.

"Put on something else," Huck says. "That top is too revealing and that skirt is too short."

"What are you talking about?" Maia says. "I wear this outfit all the time."

"You do?" Huck says. He has to admit, he doesn't usually notice what Maia is wearing and he has never commented on it before. "I guess maybe you're growing, because it looks too small."

"Maybe you need new glasses," Maia says with a grin. She peers into the frying pan, where he's scrambling eggs. "Cut the heat. They're perfect now."

Huck snaps the burner off. It's an ongoing joke that Huck tends to overcook the eggs, and Maia feels about dry eggs the way that Huck feels about dry fish. No *bueno*.

"Serve them up yourself," Huck says. "And make your own toast. I have to get ready."

Maia stares at him. "Is this about yesterday?"

Huck stops in his tracks. He's facing the refrigerator, where he's about to grab Maia's lunch box—packed with a peanut butter and jelly as per her request because all of a sudden sandwiches made from freshly caught fish aren't good enough. "Yesterday?"

"Taking my friends to town," Maia says. "You've been in a weird mood since then."

She's intuitive, he'll give her that. He can't very well tell her the truth—that what has put him in a "weird mood" is the hundred and twenty-five grand he found in her mother's room—but neither does he want her to think that he minds driving her and her friends around. If she believes that, she'll start asking someone else for rides, and he'll lose his window into her world.

"That's not it," Huck says. "I enjoyed taking you to town."

"Oh," Maia says. "What is it, then? Is it Irene?"

At this, Huck does turn around. "Irene?"

"You miss her, right? That's why you're grumpy?"

Huck opens his mouth but for the life of him, he can't think of how to respond. The night following Irene's departure, he made the mistake of drinking a couple of shots of Flor de Caña and saying some things to Maia that he should have kept private. What exactly did he say? Maybe something as innocuous as *I've never seen a woman fish like that before.* Maybe something more revealing. But did he say he had *feelings* for Irene? No. Did he ever say he'd *miss* her? No.

Huck nearly snaps, *I'm not grumpy!* But he is, and it's not Maia's fault.

"Sorry, Nut," he says. "I'm just tired, I'm missing your mom—and your grandma too, for good measure—and I'm dreading this bachelor party."

Maia opens her arms to give Huck a hug, which he gratefully accepts. He loves this child to distraction, she's all he has left, and he'll be damned if he's going to let whatever mess Rosie was involved in affect her.

"Eat your breakfast," he says.

Adam is late getting to the boat, which normally ticks Huck off, but today, he's grateful. He has to think. What does he do about the money? He's a human being, so part of him fantasizes about keeping it and slipping five hundred here and three hundred there into Maia's college fund. He's not rich, he might not even qualify as "comfortable," but his house is paid off and so is the boat. He has money saved for a new truck once his old one finally dies and he has a fund for boat repairs. The money, if he kept it, would be a cushion. A really soft cushion.

He can't keep it. He has to report it. But to whom? He'll call Agent Vasco, he decides. He'll call her today, after the charter.

But maybe he'll call Irene first.

A dinghy putters up to the *Mississippi*. It's Keegan, the first mate from *What a Catch!*, a friendly-rival fishing boat, dropping off Adam.

"Sorry, Cap," Adam says, climbing aboard.

"He was up late talking to Marissa," Keegan says.

Huck pretends not to hear this last comment, as though ignoring it might make the situation go away. Marissa is the daughter of Dan and Mrs. Dan, the Albany couple from Huck's charter on New Year's Eve. Marissa is the girl who did not cast a line, the one who barely took her eyes off her phone's screen the entire time they were out on the water. Adam asked the girl out for New Year's Eve, an act of desperation if Huck had ever seen one. But the date must have been a humdinger because after that, they'd been inseparable until Marissa left a few days ago.

The day before yesterday, Huck said to Adam, "Why pick a girl who doesn't like to fish?"

Adam scoffed. "You know how hard it is to meet a chick who actually *enjoys* fishing?"

Huck nearly spoke up about Irene—the woman seemed to have taken up permanent residence in the front of his mind and on the tip of his tongue—but instead he said, "Maia likes to fish."

Adam said, "Maia is twelve. She'll grow out of it."

Keegan putters away in the dinghy. Adam removes his visor, runs a hand through his hair, and gazes in the direction of St. Thomas, where they both see an airplane taking off, probably going back to the States.

"Head in the game," Huck says. "Check the lines."

"I have to talk to you, Cap," Adam says.

Huck shakes his head. "Afterward, please. We have a bachelor party today, and you know how I feel about bachelor parties."

Huck hates bachelor parties. Nine times out of ten, if someone calls looking to book the *Mississippi* for one, Huck will tell the person his boat is unavailable for the foreseeable future. With bachelor parties, something bad always happens. Huck keeps one case of Red Stripe on ice at all times—and one case only. Bachelor parties often bring an additional thirty-pack of Bud Light (undrinkable, in Huck's opinion) as well as rum or tequila or sometimes punch in a plastic gallon jug. Huck gives extra alcohol the side-eye, but he has never flat-out forbidden it—that would be a fatal move for his TripAdvisor ratings—although he thinks to himself that what these kids really want is a booze cruise, not a fishing trip. He nearly always ends up with one participant completely jack-wagon drunk, puking off the back. He's had guys fall off the boat, and he's had fistfights. Huck never gets involved in the fistfights; he just turns the boat around and drops the group at the National Park Service dock without a word, regardless of whether they've caught any fish.

Huck agreed to book this bachelor party because he has been all but ignoring his business since Rosie died and he needs to get back into some kind of groove.

He pulls up to the National Park Service dock at ten minutes to nine but the only people waiting are four gentlemen, Huck's age or maybe older. They're in proper fishing shirts and visors and they have bags from the North Shore Deli, home of a roasted pork and broccoli rabe sandwich that Huck dreams about. He wonders if these guys are waiting for *What a Catch!* and feels a stab of envy.

Huck gives them a wave as he ties up and considers just poaching this foursome and letting Keegan and Captain Chris from *What a Catch!* handle the bachelor-party guys—who, Huck guesses, will show up late and hung over after a raucous night at the Dog House Pub.

One of the gentlemen, full head of snowy white hair, steps forward. "Captain Huck?" he says. "I'm Kyle Maguire."

Kyle Maguire? That's the name of Huck's guy. These four geezers *are* the bachelor party! Huck laughs with relief. He'd been expecting Millennials with their hashtags and their GoPros and their swim trunks printed with watermelon margaritas.

"Welcome aboard!" Huck says.

It's the charter of Huck's dreams. The four geezers—Kyle Maguire, his brother Harry, and Grover and Ahmed, childhood friends from Worcester, Massachusetts—are in their sixties, like Huck, and Huck can tell right away that they are *good* guys. They grin with just the right amount of eager enthusiasm as they kick off their shoes without being asked, shake Huck's hand, and climb aboard the boat.

Kyle, the groom-to-be, tells Huck he's a hospital administrator at Mass General and that he has a home on Nantucket, where he goes fishing two or three times a summer. "Up there, it's striped bass, bluefish, maybe bonito and false albacore if you're lucky."

Harry is a lawyer, Ahmed a retired ophthalmologist, and Grover a professor of business at the Kellogg School at Northwestern. Grover asks Huck about his USMC hat and Huck talks about his tour in Vietnam. Turns out, Grover was over there around the same time.

"Are you gentlemen okay with going offshore?" Huck asks.

"Let's do it!" Kyle says.

Huck decides to take the boat out to the spot that he and Irene fished, what the hell, why not give it a try. The day is sunny and the water is flat; the men relax with beers, Ahmed chats with Adam, and Huck plays music—the Doors, Led Zeppelin, the Rolling Stones. They reach the coordinates where they found the school of mahi before and start trolling.

C'mon, fish! Huck thinks. Maybe the luck he had with Irene will repeat itself.

Kyle gets a bite first. He reels it in as Huck stands alongside in case he needs any help. It's a barracuda; they all gather around to admire it, then Huck throws it back. After that, it's quiet for a while, which is when some people on these trips grow antsy. Often, that's when Huck has to tell them, "That's why it's called *fishing*, not *catching*." Huck nearly describes to these four men the day that he and Irene had out here—seventeen mahi!—but he holds his tongue because it doesn't seem like history will repeat itself.

"So you're getting married," Huck says. "Is this your first time?"

"No," Kyle says. "Been married twice before. First

time to my college sweetheart. I have two boys from that marriage, but we split after five years. Then I met Jennifer and we were married for twenty-two years. She died in 2014."

This story eerily parallels Huck's own. He'd married his first wife, Kimberly, when he got home from Vietnam, and they divorced six years later, after her second unsuccessful stint in rehab. Then he met LeeAnn and they'd spent twenty blissful years together before she died in 2014.

"So who's the new gal?" Huck asks. He knows that Maia would likely object to his use of the word *gal,* finding it old-fashioned or, possibly, offensive.

"Her name is Sheila," Kyle says. He gives Huck a sheepish grin. "We met on the internet. Match dot com."

"Really?" Huck says. Rosie used to encourage Huck to try one of those dating services, but to him it was utterly pointless. Who was going to want to move to St. John? A week's visit, sure, two weeks maybe, but that didn't make a life together. And no way was Huck moving back to the States. He didn't care if Christie Brinkley came calling.

"Yep," Kyle says. "She's a civil engineer. She builds bridges in the Bay Area, the kind of bridges that can withstand earthquakes. Her husband died of Lou Gehrig's disease two years ago. She has one son, grown up, who lives near me outside of Boston, so Sheila is moving east from Oakland and we're tying the knot."

"If you don't mind my asking, how long have you been dating?"

"Nine months," Kyle says. He waves his beer can in the direction of his friends. "They all thought I was rushing into things when I bought the ring after only six months. I can't describe it. We just clicked. I flew out there one weekend, she came to see me on Nantucket a couple weeks later, then we went to Chicago, where she met Grover and he approved, then we did a week in Napa. At Thanksgiving she came to Boston and I introduced her to my kids. They loved her right away. I proposed when I dropped her off at the airport."

"Are you worried about her moving in with you?" Huck asks. A week in Napa is one thing, he thinks; sharing closet space is another.

"I know it's a gamble," Kyle says. "But I'm sixty-four years old and life gave me another chance to be happy. Only an idiot would say no to that out of fear."

Huck stares over the turquoise sheet of the water toward the verdant hills of St. John. Kyle must sense that his words have stirred something up in Huck because he claps Huck on the shoulder and says, "You hungry? We got enough sandwiches for everyone."

They catch another barracuda, then Adam suggests heading over toward Little St. James and Huck agrees; the spot he picked has lost its magic, apparently. In the next place they troll, Ahmed catches a decent-size tuna, then Harry brings in a wahoo big enough to serve as dinner and Huck relaxes. He cracks open a Coke and turns up the Who's "Baba O'Riley" and casts a line himself. He gets a fish on almost instantly and hands the line over to Grover, who reels in a second wahoo, bigger than the first. Then Kyle catches a tuna. Ahmed takes a nap in the shade. Huck overhears Adam talking to Grover about business school, and suddenly Huck knows what Adam wants to tell him—but he won't let it ruin the afternoon.

At quarter past two, it's time to turn the boat back. Kyle passes out Romeo y Julietas and Huck gratefully accepts one. He loves Cuban cigars. LeeAnn absolutely forbade them, so Huck can't light up without feeling like he's indulging in a guilty pleasure.

How does Irene feel about them? he wonders.

Life gave me another chance to be happy. Only an idiot would say no to that out of fear.

Huck thinks of the first time he saw Irene, her chestnut braid draped over one shoulder as she marched down the dock calling him "Mr. Powers." Now that he knows her a little better, he realizes she doesn't mess around nor suffer fools—but still, it was impressive, the way she talked herself onto his boat.

We just clicked.

Had Huck and Irene *clicked?* He would have a hard time saying they hadn't.

Angler Cupcake.

There's nothing like the wisdom of a twelve-year-old, Huck thinks. Maia was right. Huck misses Irene and that's why he's grumpy.

When they tie up back at the dock, Adam fillets the fish for the gentlemen and Kyle pours a shot of tequila for everyone. They clink glasses and throw back the shots. Kyle thanks Huck profusely and slips him a generous tip, which Huck nearly refuses because the guy has given Huck so much already. If nothing else, he has changed Huck's mind about bachelor parties.

Temporarily, anyway.

They shake hands and say their goodbyes and Huck says maybe he'll see them in town over the next few days, it's not impossible, although Huck hasn't been out since Rosie died.

"They were terrific!" Huck says to Adam once they're gone. He slips Adam one of the hundreds that Kyle gave him. Those are the kind of men Huck would have as friends, if he had time for friends.

Adam stuffs the hundred in his pocket. "Cap," he says. The boy looks green around the gills, downright seasick, as though *he* will be the one to upchuck off the back of the boat. And just like that, Huck is snapped out of the golden reverie that a good day out on the water provides. He's back to real life: the money under his bed, the FBI, and whatever Adam has to tell him.

Huck decides to cut the kid a break and do the hard part for him. "You're leaving me?" he says.

Adam nods morosely. "I'm moving to upstate New York to be with Marissa."

Upstate New York? Huck thinks. What did this girl Marissa *do* to him?

"It's cold in upstate New York," Huck says. "It snows. A lot. And there's no ocean."

"I love her," Adam says, and he swallows. "I'm in love with her."

Huck nods. He yearns to tell Adam that, more than half the time, love dies, and it probably dies quicker in places like Oneida and Oneonta. But Huck won't be that curmudgeonly skeptic today.

"They have lakes," Huck says. "*Great* lakes. You can fly-fish."

Adam looks so relieved that Huck's afraid the boy might try to kiss him. "Yeah, that's what I thought I'd do," he says. "In the summer."

Huck lights a cigarette and inhales deeply. "So you'll leave in May, then? Or June?"

"A week from Tuesday," Adam says.

A week from Tuesday, Huck thinks.

"Oneonta in January," Huck says. "Must be love."

That night after dinner—fresh, perfectly grilled wahoo that even Maia agrees is sublime—Huck heads out to the deck with his pack of Camel Lights and his cell phone.

Agent Vasco or Irene? He decides on one, then changes his mind and decides on the other. Then back, then back again.

Irene.

He's almost more nervous about calling her than about calling the FBI. He *is* more nervous about calling her because he has no idea how the conversation will go.

She answers on the first ring. "Oh, Huck, is that you?"

Her voice stirs something in him. He exhales smoke. "It's me." He pauses. He had planned to say, *I'm calling to check on you.* Or *I'm calling to see how you're doing.* But instead the words that fly out of his mouth are "I have a business proposition. My first mate, Adam, quit on me today and I can't properly run my charter without a mate. So I'm calling to offer you a job."

There's a pause long enough for Huck to take a drag off his cigarette, consider the lights of the Westin below and the cruise ship headed to St. Croix in the distance, and castigate himself for acting like a fool. He should have gone with *How've you been?*

"What does it pay?" Irene asks.

He grins and tells her the truth. "Hundred bucks for a half day, two hundred for a full day," he says. "Plus tips." He clears his throat. "Plus fish."

"That sounds fair," she says. "When do I start?"

He has to rein in the joy in his voice before he makes the second call. He clears his throat, takes a cleansing breath, lights another cigarette, and dials.

"Colette Vasco."

"Agent Vasco, this is Sam Powers calling from St. John. I'm Rosie's—"

"Yes, hello, Captain Powers," Agent Vasco says. "I'm sorry, I don't have any further news—"

"*I* have news," Huck says. He lowers his voice in case Maia happens to pop out of her room in search of some Ben and Jerry's Brownie Batter Core. "I found a hundred and twenty-five thousand dollars hidden in a dresser drawer in Rosie's room. I thought you would want to know."

"Yes," Agent Vasco says. "Yes, you're certainly right about that. What would be a good time tomorrow for me to stop by?"

BAKER

When he tells his "school wives"—Wendy, Becky, Debbie, and Ellen—that Anna has asked him to get a sitter for Floyd so that she and Louisa can take Baker to dinner at Indigo and "civilly discuss arrangements," they all start talking at once.

"Don't let them railroad you," Wendy says. "Ask for full custody if that's what you want."

Debbie slides a business card across the table: Perla Piuggi, Esq. "My divorce attorney," she says. "Pitbull."

"We've agreed to do mediation," Baker says.

"Using words like *civilly* and *mediation* nearly always means an ambush is coming," Becky says.

Baker slips the card into his pocket.

"I'm dying to eat at Indigo," Ellen says. "Their tasting menus are the talk of the city. It's neo–soul food."

"I'm in," Wendy says. "Let's book a table the same night." She cackles. "That way if things go south, you can come sit with us."

"I thought Anna ate only pizza," Debbie says. "Didn't you tell me Anna hated going out to fancy places?"

"She was always too tired," Baker says.

"But not anymore," Ellen says with an eye roll.

"Call the lawyer," Debbie says.

"And report back," Wendy says.

"Also, take a picture if you can," Becky says.

Debbie swats her hand. "We sound like a pack of catty teenagers."

"I want to see if Anna looks happy," Becky says. "I want to see if she has that glow."

"Imagine," Wendy says. "Anna, happy."

Ellen wasn't wrong; Indigo is a unique experience with its own set of rules and a robust social conscience—which must be why Louisa picked it (Baker assumes that Louisa picked it, since what Debbie said is true—Anna eats only pizza). There are only thirteen seats at a horseshoe-shaped bar, making for a communal experience, which Baker figures is both good and bad. On the one hand, things can't possibly get too ugly in such a controlled environment, but on the other, their civil discussion of arrangements might become a group-therapy session. They are, blessedly, placed at the far side of the horseshoe with Baker agreeing to take the seat on the end, in a relatively dim corner. Louisa is next to him, Anna on the other side of Louisa. This feels weird and wrong—shouldn't he be sitting next to Anna so they can talk about Floyd? And yet, it's also symbolic; Louisa is, in fact, the person who came between Baker and Anna, as the seating now illustrates.

They're asked to select their tasting menu; they can choose carnivore, omnivore, or pescatarian-chordate.

Pescatarian means fish, Baker knows. He hasn't a clue about *chordate,* but listed underneath is the word *amphib-*

ian, which probably means frogs' legs, but it's too risky to chance it. Baker chooses carnivore with a first course called Turtlenecks and Do-Rags, and the ladies—women!—choose omnivore and will enjoy a first course called Descendants of Igbo, which is apparently yams with marshmallows.

This place is truly an alternate universe, but at least it serves as a distraction.

Anna, not one for small talk, leans forward and says, "Louisa was offered a position in the neonatal cardiothoracic surgery department at the Cleveland Clinic and she's going to take it, and she persuaded them that two heart surgeons are better than one, so they've offered me a job as well."

"Turns out, they're even more excited to get the great Anna Schaffer than they are to get me," Louisa says, and she covers Anna's hand with her own.

Baker gazes at the two of them. They seem like strangers to him, like people he's met at jury duty. Anna is wearing her hair down and it looks lovely, like a dark velvet curtain. Louisa's hair used to be dark and long like Anna's—Baker has known her long enough to remember this—but now she has cut it very short and dyed it platinum blond. They're both glowing; they're both happy. It's obvious that they're in love, that they're a couple. None of the other ten diners tonight would ever guess that Baker and Anna are the people who are married.

Immediately after making this observation, he processes the words *Cleveland Clinic.* They're both taking positions at the Cleveland Clinic, which, if Baker isn't mistaken, is in Cleveland.

He feels like he has to double-check. Hospitals all have satellite campuses these days.

"Are you talking about the Cleveland Clinic in... Cleveland?" he asks.

Louisa's head bobs and he notices her grip on Anna's hand tighten. "Yes, Baker," she says. It's probably not her intent to speak to him like he's a moron but that's pretty much what she's doing. "We're relocating to Cleveland."

"Not with Floyd," Baker says. "You aren't taking my son to Cleveland."

"That's what we wanted to talk to you about," Anna says. "There's more than one way to look at this."

"Oh, really," Baker says. He runs his eyes along the horseshoe to the opposite side, hoping that he will see his four friends eating amphibians. He needs them now because it's becoming clear that this *is* an ambush. Anna and Louisa have accepted positions at the Cleveland Clinic. They're moving to Cleveland, Ohio!

"Yes, really," Anna says. The server arrives with Anna's and Louisa's Descendants (yams) and Baker's Turtlenecks and Do-Rags, which appears to be a crab dish (not actual turtles' necks). Louisa and Anna dig in, but Baker can't even remember how to use his cutlery. "Our first choice would be for you and Floyd to come to Cleveland."

"What?" Baker says.

"You can do your job from anywhere," Anna says. "You don't have to be in Houston."

"But...we have a house, Floyd has school, we have friends in Houston. A community. A life."

Anna scrapes yams out of the bowl. "The deepest roots

we have in Houston are mine, at the hospital. And I'm willing to pull those up for this opportunity."

Baker stares at his crab, fervently wishing that Wendy, Becky, Debbie, and Ellen were here so he could inform them that his friendship with them is, according to Anna, shallow—or at least, not as deep as Anna's career. The woman is so *cold,* so dispassionate, Baker can't believe he ever decided to marry her. Good luck to Louisa!

"You and Louisa go to Cleveland," Baker says. "Floyd and I will stay here. I'll send him up to you on his vacations."

"That's our third choice," Louisa says. "A distant third, because we'd obviously like to remain a cohesive family unit." Baker very much resents her chiming in at all. She stole Baker's wife and now she's dragging her to Ohio. It's clear that Louisa is maintaining some kind of utopian vision of the three of them as the parents in this "cohesive family unit," with Anna and Louisa as the breadwinners and Baker as Floyd's primary caregiver. "But we want to keep the transition as harmonious as possible, for Floyd's sake. So we can try that option for the first year if you insist upon it. You and Floyd stay here and we'll set up a realistic visitation schedule—holidays and summers."

"Great," Baker says. "You can be the Disneyland parents." This is Debbie's term. Her ex-husband, Jaybee, takes her kids only three weeks per year—to Martha's Vineyard over the summer, to Aspen at Christmas, and to a different European city each spring. Baker considers the two very serious, accomplished women—people!—on his left. Sorry to say, they are no one's idea of Disneyland parents.

And yet, this plan works for Baker. Because he is *not* moving to Cleveland.

"You should also know..." Anna says, and for the first time during this unpleasant and confusing dinner, she seems ill at ease.

"That I'm planning on getting pregnant," Louisa finishes. She considers the yams and marshmallows on the end of her fork. "Using a sperm donor."

The words *sperm donor* should never be uttered during dinner, Baker thinks. He has just lost his appetite.

Their server takes advantage of the pause in their conversation to whisk away their first-course dishes—Baker's untouched—and set down the Homogenization of Mandingos (venison sausage with beets) for Baker and the Belly of the Beast (boar ribs) for the ladies. Women. People. Baker has some other words to describe them at this point, words that don't fall in the category of "civilly discussing arrangements."

"So Floyd will have a half brother or half sister, in a sense, and we obviously want them to have a relationship," Anna says.

"Cohesive family unit," Louisa says again. Those are her buzzwords, and it takes all of Baker's willpower to keep from shouting at her that Anna, Baker, and Floyd are—were—the family unit. Louisa is the interloper. The homewrecker!

Baker reaches for his beer, which he's been too distracted to drink. He takes a long sip, buying himself time. Anna has left herself wide open here.

"I thought you said you didn't want any more children," Baker says. "You were adamant about it, in fact. And now you're talking about a baby."

"Louisa will have the baby," Anna says.

"And yet you want a cohesive family unit," Baker says. "So you'll be co-parents."

"Of course," Anna says, shrugging. She doesn't meet Baker's eyes because, very likely, she doesn't want to provoke him into describing what having Dr. Anna Schaffer as a co-parent was like. It was like…having no co-parent at all! But Baker decides he *won't* tell Louisa this; he'll let her find out on her own. Two busy surgeons at the Cleveland Clinic, one baby—what could go wrong?

"Well," Baker says. "Congratulations." He picks up his fork. Suddenly, the whole situation seems amusing—and maybe even fortunate? Anna and Louisa are leaving town. Floyd will see them for vacations and holidays, which on the surface appears sad and pathetic. He's a four-year-old boy; he needs his mother. But Baker is in a position to know that Floyd *doesn't* need Anna. He's been fine this long without her. Maybe Anna will be more engaged as a parent when the job is taken in small bites.

Anna smiles at him; her glow returns. "Thank you for being so understanding," she says. "And please know that whatever financial resources you want, we'll provide. You can keep the house; there will be support for Floyd and support for you as well."

He's being paid off, but he doesn't care. He cuts into his venison sausage. He can't wait to get home and call his friends.

* * *

He starts with Ellen because, really, theirs is the closest relationship, and Ellen is a single mother by choice, so she is savvy and resourceful by nature.

He tells her *everything*—including the esoteric menu items at dinner—and with each new revelation, she gasps.

Louisa offered job at Cleveland Clinic.

Anna offered job at Cleveland Clinic.

Louisa and Anna moving to Cleveland.

Louisa and Anna offering to move Baker and Floyd to Cleveland.

Louisa and Anna offering to take on the role of Disneyland parents while Baker keeps Floyd in Houston.

Louisa having a baby with sperm donor, Anna agreeing to co-parent. Anna and Louisa promising to support Baker and Floyd financially.

At the end, Ellen says, "On the surface, this sounds… great for you. Really *great*. Anna and Louisa are out of your hair, you get to keep Floyd and the house, *and* they're going to pay you…"

"But?" Baker says.

"Doesn't it seem too good to be true?" Ellen says. "Like something doesn't add up? I know Anna isn't the most hands-on mother, but is she really going to move twelve hundred miles away from her son and see him only at Christmas?"

"And summers," Baker says weakly. He, too, feels uneasy now, but he can't tell if it's because he thinks Anna is going to renege and possibly sue him for custody—which is what it would take for her to get Floyd—or if he's just embarrassed about marrying a woman who really just *isn't* maternal. At all. "Listen, I know it sounds unconventional, but think about Anna. This scenario is perfect for her. She doesn't have *time* to parent. I'm concerned about Floyd spending the entire summer with her because you and I both know that means he'll have a full-time nanny. He's better off with me."

"Agreed," Ellen says. She takes a sip of what he can only assume is 8th Wonder IPA (she's a craft-beer *fanatic*) and says, "So my brilliant-best-friend mind now wonders why you would even stay in Houston. With Anna leaving, you're free to go wherever you want."

Ellen's tone is heavy with innuendo. She's the only one in the group that he's told about his father dying *in the Caribbean,* the fifteen-million-dollar villa, and... Ayers. She's the only one he's told about Ayers.

That night, the carnivore tasting menu churns in Baker's stomach as he scrolls through every reason why he *shouldn't* leave Houston for good and move down to St. John. He starts with the reasons he gave Anna.

They have a house here.

Well, the house is a house. He can sell it or rent it or leave it be until he sees how things work out down in the islands. He and Anna bought it outright when they moved from Chicago, so there's no mortgage, only taxes, insurance, and maintenance.

Floyd has school. They have friends, a community, a life.

Floyd is four. He goes to Montessori. He's not a sophomore in high school; he's not even in middle school. If they leave Houston now, it's possible Floyd won't have any memories of the place, much less feel resentful about moving. Floyd can already read and count to a hundred. Baker should investigate the schools in St. John, make sure there's somewhere suitable.

Friends. Community. Baker is chairperson of the Children's Cottage annual benefit auction, which is in two weeks. Baker's work on the auction is basically done; all of the items have been solicited. He bought a table for three thousand dollars and invited all his school wives. He should really attend.

But it's not necessarily a reason to *stay*. The auction will happen, the school will make money, the auction will be over.

Would Anna object to Floyd living in the Virgin Islands? She's seen the villa; she knows it's comfortable. She'd be concerned about the schools. Baker will look into it first thing in the morning. Maia goes to school. Maia is…Floyd's *aunt*. Okay, that's a little weird. But maybe not. It's late, Baker is tired, everything seems weird.

Louisa wants to have a baby, essentially a half brother or half sister for Floyd.

Baker would love to have more kids.

Ayers. Baker knew the instant he saw her that he wanted to marry her. They'd ended on bad terms—really bad—and she said she was back with Mick. *That means she's having sex with Mick,* Baker thinks, *maybe even this very second,* which is enough to make him sick. But he needs to think realistically about sex. Sex is ephemeral. Once it's over, it's over. Sex is not a lasting connection; it's only real while it's happening. It's not love.

Besides, Mick cheated on Ayers, and once a cheater, always a cheater. If Baker is confident of anything, it's that Mick will blow it and Baker will be there to show Ayers how she deserves to be treated.

Ayers hadn't wanted to get serious about Baker because he was a tourist.

If Baker moves into his father's villa, he will be a tourist no longer.

Bright and early the next morning, Baker books two tickets to St. Thomas with a return flight in two weeks so that he and Floyd will arrive back the day before the auction. Then, assuming all goes well on St. John, after the auction they will move back permanently. This trip will be an exploratory mission, a toe dipped in to test the waters.

He calls Paulette Vickers to let her know that he and Floyd will be down on Saturday to stay at the villa for a couple of weeks, and might she be able to meet him at the dock with the keys?

"Certainly, Mr. Steele," she says. "I'm happy to know you're using it. A beautiful villa like that shouldn't sit empty. I asked your mother if she wanted me to rent it and she said to hold off for the time being."

"My mother is overwhelmed," Baker says. "She doesn't need more to worry about. I'll handle all things relating to the villa from now on." He wonders if he's overstepping, but all of the goodwill he's put in with Paulette is paying off because she doesn't question it.

"Very good," she says. "I'll meet you at the ferry dock on Saturday with the keys."

Baker hangs up and feels an elation so strong he could levitate. The only string tying him to earth is . . . Irene. Baker should call her and tell her his plans.

But . . . what he just told Paulette is true—Irene *is* overwhelmed. She doesn't need one more thing to worry about. She doesn't need to fret about Baker and Floyd on St. John or about Anna relocating.

Then again, Irene had been perfectly clear that she would not tolerate any more secrets. Secrets are lies, Irene said.

Baker's trip to St. John isn't a *secret*. Of course it's not a secret. Paulette knows he's coming, and before he and Floyd leave, Baker will have to tell Anna.

Once Baker is down there and settled in, he'll call Irene. This will give her a few more days of relative peace. That's the kind thing to do.

ROSIE

February 21, 2006

My life is a house that has been ransacked. My heart, which I had so recently reclaimed as my own, has been stolen again. Some might say I'm being careless with it.

Friday afternoon was the start of Presidents' Day week-end, which brings nearly as many tourists as Christmas and Easter now because schools in the Northeast—Massachusetts, New York, and a few of those other densely packed states—give their students a winter break. The problem with the visitors who can afford to come when the weather is the most inhospitable at home is that they tend to be demanding. They want their Caribbean experience to be just so—the sky must be clear, the mangos ripe, the cocktails strong and delivered right away.

Caneel Bay was at maximum capacity. Every room was booked at high-season rates, and along the front row on Honeymoon Bay, it was all return guests, the ones Estella calls "the patronage": Mr. and Mrs. Very Important of Park Avenue, the Big Deal Family from Lake Forest, Illinois, the New Moneys from La Jolla. I recognized them (and yes, I called them by their real names: Mr. and Mrs. Vikram, the Caruso family, the Burlingames). Their eyes lit up when they saw me but I always reintroduce myself, just in case.

"Oh, yes, Rosie, how are you! Wonderful to see you again! How has your year been?"

I said my year had been good, though nothing was further from the truth. But there was no way I could tell the New Moneys about my excruciating breakup with Oscar and how disappointing that had been because he'd promised me that once he got out of jail he would work in a legitimate business, maybe even get a job alongside me at Caneel, but instead he was back to selling drugs to people on the cruise ships. I didn't complain that I was still living at home with my mother and Huck. The returning guests, the patronage, loved coming back and seeing a familiar face because it made Caneel feel like home; it made it feel like a private club where they were members. For me, it was primarily a business relationship. The tips were double what they would have been with complete strangers.

In most cases, anyway.

The guests at Caneel are 95 percent white. There are a few Japanese here and there, a couple of rich South American businessmen (rum, casinos), and the occasional black American couple or Indian family, so when Oscar came in for drinks with Borneo and Little Jay, they stuck out. They wore baseball hats on backward, heavy gold chains, those ridiculous jeans that drooped in the ass.

Estella saw Oscar first. She came over while I was at the bar getting cocktails for a trio of pasty-white gentlemen who had just anchored their enormous yacht out in front of the resort, and she said, "Oscar here, Rosie-girl, with his clownish friends."

"Send him away," I said.

"I wish I could, Rosie-girl, but they're paying customers just like the rest."

"Keep them out of my section."

"Oscar asked for you."

"All the more reason."

"Okay, I'll give them to Tessie."

I loathed Tessie, so this was killing two birds.

I dropped the drinks off with the yacht gentlemen. Yacht Gentleman One was tall and bald with a posh English accent and what I knew to be a forty-thousand-dollar Patek Philippe (I'd picked up some useless knowledge on this job). Yacht

Gentleman Two had dark, slicked-back hair and such distracting good looks that I nicknamed him "James Bond" in my mind. Yacht Gentleman Three was a doughy midwesterner with silvering hair. I knew he was midwestern because he stood up and introduced himself.

"Russell Steele," he said. "Iowa City."

His manners caught me off guard. Normally, men like the ones he was with either ignored me, made a pass at me, or snapped their fingers so I would move faster. They did not stand up and offer their names like they were crashing a party and I was the hostess. And thank goodness they didn't—on an average holiday-weekend night, I had over a hundred customers. How could I possibly remember them all?

"Rosie Small," I said. "Pleasure." I had already forgotten his last name, but I did retain his first name, Russell, and Iowa City, because the place sounded so…American, or what I always thought of as American. Iowa City evoked cows in pastures, silos, corner drugstores where kids bought malted milkshakes, church socials, marching bands, and grown men wearing overalls. "Enjoy your drinks. Let me know if you're interested in ordering food. The conch fritters are very good."

"Conch fritters, then," Russell from Iowa City said. "I'm not sure what they are but if you say they're good, I'm up for trying them. In fact, bring two orders. That okay with you guys?"

The other two gentlemen were poring over a sheaf of papers printed with columns of figures. James Bond looked up. "Yeah, yeah, Russ, get whatever you want. Bring some sushi too, you pick. Enough for three, please." James Bond handed me his AmEx Centurion Card and said, "Start us a tab, doll."

I wanted to tell James Bond that I was not a doll, I was a person, but I figured I'd get back at him by ordering the most expensive sushi on the menu—sashimi, tuna tataki, hamachi, unagi. I could see poor Russell looking very uncomfortable, like he wanted to stick up for me but didn't know how. He was, quite clearly, low man on the totem pole of this partic-ular triumvirate as he had neither the flashy watch nor the movie-star good looks (nor the Centurion Card). He might have been the brother-in-law of one or the other, a sister's husband whom they had brought along to the Caribbean as a favor or because they lost a bet.

He didn't know what conch fritters *were!*

I went to the register to put in an order for the fritters and two hundred dollars' worth of sushi—I could have dou-bled that; James Bond wasn't the kind of man to complain about his bill or even check it—and studied the name on the Centurion Card.

Todd Croft. *It was a solid, whitewashed name, symmet-rical and masculine, like the real name of a secret superhero—Clark Kent, Peter Parker. I wondered if it was made up. I didn't care as long as the card worked, which it did.*

I kept tabs on Oscar out of my peripheral vision. He or-dered a bottle of Dom Pérignon, which Tessie made a big production of carrying out in front of her, label displayed, like she was one of those chicks on a game show giving away the grand prize. The pop of the cork cut through all the chatter and the restaurant quieted so that I could clearly hear Harry Belafonte singing, "Yes, we have no bananas." People whis-pered and sneaked glances at Oscar and I yearned to tell them to stop. Couldn't they see that was what he was after?

I then watched the Big Deal Family's daughter, Lucinda Caruso, who has made sure to tell me every year for the past three years that she "recently graduated from Harvard" (which I take to mean that she has yet to find a job, a theory reinforced by the fact that she signed every charge to her father's room), approach Oscar's table and proceed to take the fourth seat. Lucinda was wearing a very short, sequined cocktail dress that would have been better at an event where she remained standing. I overheard her say, "Are you guys rap stars?" *I rolled my eyes, not only because Lucinda was feeding the beast but also because she probably couldn't imagine a black man having the money to order Dom unless he was a rap star or a professional athlete. I could have shut her up by telling her the truth.* He sells drugs, Lucinda! *But it was none of my business.*

The yacht gentlemen's food was up. I set one order of conch fritters—piping hot, golden brown, and fragrant, served with a papaya-cayenne aioli—in front of Russell from Iowa City. This is my favorite part of the job, other than the money, introducing the Caribbean to people who have never experienced it. I plunked the tower of sushi—the way Chef had arranged it was quite impressive, and the fish was so plump and fresh, it looked like art—in front of Todd Croft.

"There you go, doll," I said. "Enjoy."

Russell from Iowa City barked out a laugh so surprised and genuine that I gave him a wink.

The night progressed. It was busy. I kept one eye on the yacht men—after all that, they barely touched the sushi—and one eye on Oscar and his friends. Lucinda stayed at the table; they ordered another bottle of Dom. Mr. and Mrs. Big Deal stopped by the table and tried to entice Lucinda to go with them to the Chateau Bordeaux, but she refused to leave, and the second her parents were out the door, she rose from her chair and sat on Oscar's lap.

At that point, I turned away. I knew Oscar was show-boating just to goad me into reconsidering my decision, but I hadn't done all my soul-searching only to cave because I couldn't stand to see him with a silly rich girl on his lap.

I tended to my other tables. I was even nice to Tessie. When I saw her heading out with a third bottle of Dom, I said, "Tonight is your lucky night. Oscar is an excellent tipper."

Around ten, things started to quiet down. Two of the yacht men—Todd Croft and the tall, bald Brit—left, and Russell from Iowa City moved to the bar and planted himself in front of the television to watch a basketball game. When I checked the screen, I saw Iowa was playing Northwestern. I went up to him because I had a minute and also because Todd Croft had left an even five hundred dollars for a three-hundred-and-twenty-dollar check.

"You're rooting for Iowa?" I asked.

"Northwestern, actually," he said. "My alma mater."

"Ah." I knew more about football than basketball, and nearly all my basketball knowledge was limited to the San Antonio Spurs in general and Tim Duncan in particular because he hailed from St. Croix and some of my Small cousins had actually played a pickup game with him once on the courts in Contant. But it was best I change the subject. "So, your friends left you behind?"

"They went into Cruz Bay," Russell said. "Looking for women." He held up his left hand. "I'm married, with two boys."

"Well, your wife is a very lucky woman," I said, and I patted his shoulder. "Your next drink is on me. How did you like the conch fritters?"

"I loved them!" he said. "I was meaning to ask if you knew a place I could get some real Caribbean food. I have the day to myself tomorrow and I want to explore."

"Well," I said, "if you want local flavor, go to the East End. There's a place called Vie's on Hansen Bay."

He took a pen out of his shirt pocket and pulled a cocktail napkin off the stack. "Vie's?"

"She makes some mean garlic chicken and the best johnnycakes," I said. "For a few dollars, you can rent a chaise on her beach."

"Is there shade?" Russell from Iowa City asked. He held out a pale, freckled arm and I thought, This poor guy. God bless him.

"There's shade," I said. "Here, I'll draw you a map."

I clocked out at eleven, sorted my tips, marveling at my windfall from Todd Croft, and decided that I would stop by the Ocean Grill at Mongoose for a drink on my way home. I headed past the Sugar Mill on my way to the parking lot and stopped to say hello to my wild donkeys, Stop, Drop, and Roll. They always looked a little eerie at night, more like ghost horses than white donkeys, and the backdrop of the stone ruins of the sugar mill only heightened the otherworldly effect. But I thought of these three like pets—they rarely wandered off the grounds of Caneel—and I couldn't ignore them.

In retrospect, I should have realized that Oscar knew this. He jumped out of the shadows and grabbed my arm.

"Baby."

I gasped, though I wasn't exactly surprised. A part of me knew there was no way he'd left. I had already planned to turn on the flashlight of my phone and sweep the back of my car before I climbed in. "Let me go, Oscar."

He held tight. I checked behind him for Borneo or Little Jay or even Lucinda Caruso, but there was no one on the path in either direction. If I screamed, Woodrow or one of the other security guards would hear me and escort Oscar off the property but the last thing I wanted was everyone all up in my business. As soon as it got out that Oscar had shown up at the restaurant and made trouble, my mother would hear about it and somehow twist it into being my fault. She would say that I had led Oscar on or had acted recklessly by walking to my car by myself.

Oscar didn't let go. He pulled me to him so close that I could smell the champagne on his breath. "I need you to come back, baby."

I said, "We've been over this, Oscar. I'm not changing my mind."

"You got another man, then? That brother from Christiansted?"

He was talking about Bryson, a guy I'd gone out with a few times in college. Bryson lived on St. Croix.

"It's none of your business, Oscar." I succeeded in reclaiming my arm. "I'm tired, I'm going home, good night." I turned around. "And you know that if you come anywhere near the house, LeeAnn will call the police and you'll go right back to jail."

Oscar said, "I'm going to Christiansted tomorrow to kill that brother."

I stopped in my tracks. Had anyone else said something like that, I would have scoffed, but what had landed Oscar in jail was stabbing his friend Leon for borrowing his Ducati without permission.

"You'll do no such thing," I said.

"Try me," Oscar said. Then he suddenly dropped the tough-guy act and sounded like himself. "Rosie. Try me."

"Why can't you just leave me alone?" I said. "Why do you come here when you know I'm working? There are ten other places you and your friends can hang out. Why come to Caneel? Because you want me to know you have the money to order Dom Pérignon? I don't care! You want me to see that girls throw themselves at you? I care even less! I loved you when I was a girl—fifteen, sixteen, seventeen. But I'm a woman now, Oscar, and I'm moving on."

"Baby," Oscar said, and he grabbed the strap of my purse.

"Get off me!" I said. I put a hand against the unyielding muscles of his chest.

"Stop bothering the lady!"

Both Oscar and I turned to see who jogging toward us? Russell from Iowa City, that's who.

Oscar laughed and I thought, Oh, dear Lord, no. It was probably a midwestern thing to defend a woman's honor but it would end in disaster for Russell from Iowa City. I would have to call out for Woodrow after all.

"What you gonna do about it?" Oscar said. He kissed his teeth. "You gonna stop me?"

To his credit, Russell from Iowa City did not appear even a little afraid. He looked serious and disappointed, as though he were an assistant principal who had found his favorite student misbehaving and a suspension was coming.

"Yes," Russell said coolly. "I'm going to stop you. Rosie, are you heading home? Can I escort you to your car?"

I tried to give him a look that said he didn't have to defend me and he shouldn't defend me because the consequences would be dire. Oscar would beat him to a pulp, or maybe just hit him once, or maybe just humiliate him, but whatever course of action Oscar took, it wouldn't be worth it. I could handle Oscar; Russell from Iowa City most certainly could not.

Russell held out his arm like an old-fashioned gentleman caller. I sighed and hoped that maybe, just maybe, Oscar would be more afraid of violating his parole than of being shown up. I linked my arm through Russell's.

From there, things happened fast. Oscar pushed Russell from behind and Russell let go of my arm and grabbed the front of Oscar's shirt and they tussled while I searched the shadows for Woodrow on his golf cart—where was he?—and then, the next thing I knew, Russell from Iowa City had Oscar in a death grip and Oscar was gasping for air. It looked like Russell was about to snap his neck and I found myself fearing that Russell was going to kill Oscar instead of vice versa.

"Now," Russell said in a calm-but-disappointed-assistant-principal voice, "I'm going to let you go. But you are to leave Rosie alone. Do you understand me?"

Oscar choked out an affirmative and Russell tightened his grip so that Oscar squeaked like a chew toy.

"It's okay," I said. "Thank you."

Russell let Oscar go. Oscar buckled at the knees, stumbled a few yards away, and bent over in the grass, turning his neck to be sure it still worked.

Russell offered me his arm again.

"Where did you learn to do that?" I asked him once we were safely at my car.

"My father was a navy man," Russell said.

I stood on my tiptoes and kissed his cheek. "My hero," I said.

The next day, almost without thinking, I drove to the East End to Miss Vie's at Hansen Bay. I was like a woman possessed because there was no good reason to go all the way out to that side of the island; normally, if I wanted to go to the beach, I parked at the National Park Service sign and hiked down to Salomon Bay. But I somehow convinced myself that, on the Saturday of the holiday weekend, even Salomon would be overrun and that the only way to escape the crowds would be to go to Hansen Bay. Besides which, now that it was in my head, I couldn't shake my craving for Miss Vie's garlic chicken and johnnycakes.

I told myself it had nothing to do with Russell from Iowa City. I wasn't attracted to him, or I hadn't been until the incident with Oscar—but having one's honor defended is a mighty aphrodisiac. Still, Russell was old enough to be my father (I now know he's forty-five, double my age), but that, in a way,

*was also attractive because what I was looking for was someone
older, someone responsible and stable,* someone adult. Oscar
*was older than me by seven years but emotionally he was a lit-
tle boy who had a bone to pick with everyone.*

*I wore my white bikini and a white T-shirt knotted at
the midriff and a pair of white denim shorts. White is my
color.*

*There was a line of cars, all rentals, parked along the
road near Vie's. There was no telling if one of them was Russell's or if he'd taken a taxi or if he was even there at all. The
East End was a hike from everywhere and he might have decided to go fishing with his buddies or cruise over to the BVIs
for lunch at Foxy's. The second I stepped onto the beach and
scanned the chaises in the shade, I saw him, settled back with
a rum punch in hand.*

When he spotted me, he smiled, and by smiled, *I mean
he* beamed *like I was the only person in the world he wanted
to see.*

"Rosie!" he said.

*We hugged and he kissed my cheek and it was like seeing
a friend, even though I barely knew him. He called over
Flora, whom he already knew by name, and said he would
pay for a second chaise and Flora waved a hand and said,
"Rosie don't need to pay, she's family." Which was actually
true; Flora and Vie were second cousins of my father, Levi
Small, and for that reason, they didn't speak to my mother,
so I didn't need to worry about news of me visiting a white
gentleman out at Hansen Bay getting back to her.*

*I ordered a Coke because I had to work at five and
Russ ordered another rum punch and then together we or-*

dered garlic chicken with rice and beans and johnnycakes. We stuffed our faces and we talked. I told Russ the long story of my relationship with Oscar and then he told me that he was down in the Virgin Islands because he had been offered a job with a hedge fund that was owned and operated by Todd Croft, whom he had known during his college years.

"At Northwestern?" I said, proud of myself for remembering.

"Todd flunked out freshman year but he hung around Winnetka and we had some business dealings."

I laughed. "Business dealings? At eighteen?"

Russ sighed. "I haven't even told my wife this story…"

"What?"

"Todd had a contact who wanted to sell alcohol to underclassmen in the dorm. My sophomore year, I was an RA— resident adviser—and in exchange for me looking the other way, Todd gave me a cut of his profits."

"Russ!" I said. "I wouldn't have pegged you as a criminal."

"We never got caught," Russ said. "I have a trustworthy face, I guess."

"So I take it Todd has moved on from the smuggling business?" I said.

"High finance," Russ said. "And I mean high. Todd is an impressive guy, though. He got a job working in one of those boiler rooms, calling people cold and encouraging them to invest money…and now his hedge fund is worth nearly three billion dollars."

"No wonder you're going to work for him," I said. "What an opportunity."

"For the past seventeen years, I've worked for the Corn Refiners Association," Russ said. "But the pay is peanuts and my wife, Irene, is unhappy. She keeps a stiff upper lip. She's from some pretty hardy Scandinavian stock, but I can tell she thinks I'm a failure. And most days I'm pretty sure she thinks about leaving me."

"Oh my God," I said. "She would have to be crazy to think about leaving you."

He stared at me a second with a look of utter amazement and something changed between us then. I felt equal parts terrible and triumphant about it, but terrible won out and I didn't even stay for a swim. I plunked down ten bucks for the food, offered Russ my hand, and said, "I wish all visitors to our fair island were like you, Russ. Thank you for your help with Oscar. I will forever be grateful."

Russ held my hand and said, "Stay a little longer, can you?"

"Sorry," I said. "I have some things to take care of before work." My words were rushed and I tripped over a tree root as I hurried off the beach but I had to get out of there before I crossed a line. Though I knew a line had already been crossed. I had sought him out, worn my sexiest outfit, and said the words that I knew he needed to hear. I would like to say this was unwitting, but working in the service industry has given me keen people skills. I could tell that Russell from Iowa City was a people-pleaser and that his wife, Irene, made him feel like a disappointment and that hearing me say he was the opposite would all but make him fall in love.

He was married. Irene was waiting for him back home in

Iowa. There were women on St. John—Tessie among them—who thought nothing of sleeping with men who were here on vacation. Tessie routinely had one-night stands with gentlemen who were staying at Caneel by themselves; that was one of the reasons I disliked her.

I was not going to sleep with Russell from Iowa City.

And yet, when I got to work at five o'clock and noticed the yacht was gone, I felt something like sorrow. My hero had left, and I couldn't remember his last name. I would never see him again.

So imagine my surprise when, at seven o'clock, as the hibiscus-pink ball of the sun was sinking into the water and Lucinda Caruso was shooting me a smug glance from the table where her Harvard-educated ass was sitting with her Big Deal parents—a look that I could only assume meant that she had slept with Oscar after all, poor girl—Russ walked across the beach and into the restaurant. I blinked, wondering if it was a trick of the blinding light of the sun just before it set, but then he waved at me and I hurried over. "I thought you left," I said. "The yacht—"

"Todd and Stephen headed over to Virgin Gorda," Russ said. "They have business. I told them I wanted to stay here and mull over their offer. They're coming back Monday to pick me up."

"Stay here on St. John?" I said. I was so happy that he wasn't gone forever that I wasn't quite following.

"At Caneel," Russ said. He pulled a key out of his pocket. "Honeymoon 718."

"How did you manage that?" I asked. "I thought we were full."

"I put the general manager in a headlock," he said.

We laughed. I said, "I'd put you in my section but you'll probably be more comfortable at the bar."

He said, "Bar is fine but I'll miss you bringing me my conch fritters."

I said, "If you think I'm going to let someone else bring you your conch fritters, you're crazy."

He gave me a look then that was so long and deep, my legs grew weak and my face grew hot and never in my life had I been more aware that I was a human being—powerful and fallible.

PART TWO

Lawyers, Guns, and Money

IRENE

She drives Cash and Winnie to the airport in Cedar Rapids. From Cedar Rapids, they will fly to Chicago, and from Chicago to St. Thomas. Irene is tempted to tell Cash that she received her own job offer on St. John but he's so excited about getting back down there that Irene decides not to steal his thunder or distract from his anticipation.

Besides, she isn't at all sure Huck was serious.

Still, it was nice to hear his voice.

Cash's departure turns out to be the impetus Irene needs to get things done. On the way home from Cedar Rapids, she calls Ed Sorley.

"Oh, Irene," he says. "You must have read my mind. I just dug up a photocopy of the check that Russ gave me when we closed on the Church Street house. Turns out, it was a cashier's check drawn on a bank called SGMT in the Cayman Islands."

"The *Cayman* Islands?" Irene says. "Not the Virgin Islands?"

"The Cayman Islands," Ed says. "I double-checked that myself."

"But it cleared, right?" Irene says. "We did actually pay for the house?"

"Yes, yes," Ed says. "I'll try to see if maybe this SGMT has a phone number or a website, but even if it does, it might be difficult to track down. It's a cashier's check, which is almost like Russ showed up at the bank with six hundred grand in cash... but that's obviously impossible."

Is it, though? Irene wonders.

"He might have an account at this bank," Ed says. "I'll try to figure it out."

"Thank you, Ed," Irene says.

She hangs up and calls Paulette Vickers. Paulette is out of the office—is Paulette ever *in* the office? Irene wonders—and so Irene leaves a voicemail.

"Paulette, it's Irene Steele," she says. "I need a copy of Russ's death certificate. I can't do anything without it. My attorney said that until it's issued, Russ is technically still alive." Irene gives a weak laugh and flashes back to her dream about the chickens. "So if you would please send me a certified copy, I would greatly appreciate it. That's apparently what I need. You have my address and if there's a fee, I'm happy to send a check, or maybe you can take it out of your operating account for the villa." Irene pauses. "Thank you, Paulette. If this is an issue, please call me back."

Irene hangs up and thinks, *Please don't call me back. Just send the death certificate.* Paulette's husband, Douglas Vickers, was the one who identified Russ's body and delivered his ashes to Irene. He's her only hope of getting this documentation.

She feels a small sense of accomplishment—*really* small, because she has learned nothing except that Russ apparently had a relationship with a bank in the Cayman Islands. Irene doesn't have the foggiest idea where the Cayman Islands are. If she were to visit, would she find that Russ also has a mistress and child there? She laughs at the absurdity of the thought—and yet, it's not out of the question!

The road home from the airport brings Irene perilously close to the offices of the magazine *Heartland Home and Style,* her place of employment. Irene hasn't been to work in three weeks. She has two voicemails from Mavis Key on her cell phone; in the second of these, Mavis announced that she "did a little detective work" and learned that Milly had passed away—which, Mavis assumed, was the reason for Irene's "extended absence." Mavis offered her condolences, then asked if Irene would prefer the magazine to send flowers or donate to a particular cause.

Irene had ignored the message. She didn't want to think about work.

But she can't ignore it forever. Impulsively, Irene turns into the parking lot of the magazine and pulls into her spot. Already the signage has been changed to read EXECUTIVE EDITOR. She cuts the engine and checks her appearance in the rearview. Her hair is braided, her bangs long but not ratty. She's not wearing any makeup but she still has a little bit of color on her nose and across her cheeks from the sun in St. John.

In she goes.

The first person she sees is the magazine's receptionist, Jayne. Jayne decorates the reception desk herself using the magazine's small slush fund; she follows the lead of all the major retailers and really gets a jump on things. Now that Christmas and New Year's are behind them, Jayne has her area decked out for Valentine's Day. There's an arrangement of red and white carnations on the desk and, next to that, an enormous bowl of candy hearts.

"Irene!" Jayne shrieks. She leaps out of her chair and comes running to give Irene a maternal embrace; Jayne has five children, seventeen grandchildren, a pillowy bosom, and soft downy cheeks.

Irene allows herself to be swallowed up in Jayne's arms and soon the rest of the staff—bored or easily distracted, even though they should be hard at work on the April issue—come trooping out, all filled with joy (or maybe just relief) at Irene's unexpected return.

Happy New Year, we've missed you, is everything okay, we've been so worried, it's not like you to take unscheduled time off, we knew something must be wrong, we heard about your promotion, and then Mavis gave us the news about Milly. God bless you, Irene, she was so lucky to have a daughter-in-law like you.

Bets, from advertising, says, "How's Russ handling it?"

At this, Irene separates herself by an arm's length. She can't lie, but neither can she tell them the truth.

She says, "Is Mavis in her office? I really need to talk with her."

Yes, yes, Mavis is in her office. Jayne takes it upon herself to personally escort Irene up the half-flight of stairs to Mavis's office, which happens to be right next door to Irene's own office, the door of which is shut tight.

Jayne raps on Mavis's door, then swings it open and announces, "Irene is here!" As though Irene is the First Lady of Iowa.

Irene steps in. Mavis is on the phone. Jayne whispers, "Mavis is always on the phone." As if this is Irene's first time in the office, her first time meeting Mavis. "She shouldn't be long. I'll give you two your privacy." And she closes the door.

Mavis is wearing a silk pantsuit in what must be considered winter white. She's not wearing a blouse under the blazer, though Irene spies a peek of lacy camisole. In an office where most of the employees are women and most of those women wear embroidered sweaters or Eileen Fisher *schmattas*, Mavis is a curiosity indeed.

Mavis raises a finger (*One minute!*), then lowers a palm (*Please sit!*). She has decorated her office in eggshell suede and black leather, an aesthetic previously frowned upon as "modern" and "urban" by the executives at *Heartland Home and Style*. Irene helps herself to one of the Italian sparkling waters in Mavis's glass-fronted minifridge. Why not enjoy the pretensions that are on offer?

She decides to remain standing.

Mavis says, "Thanks for your help with this, Bernie. I'll circle back next week." She hangs up. "Irene?"

"Mavis," Irene says. She turns back to make sure that the office door is closed and that Jayne isn't stationed outside with her ear to the glass. "I need to talk to you. Can I trust you to keep what we say confidential?"

The question is rhetorical. Mavis doesn't trade on gossip like the other people in the office because Mavis has invested only her head here, not her heart. She was hired to be a problem-solver and a moneymaker. She's an ice queen, which, under the present circumstances, is a tremendous asset.

Irene lets it all out as concisely as possible: Russ has been killed in a helicopter crash in the Virgin Islands; Irene's trip down to St. John with the boys revealed evidence of a second life—an expensive villa, a mistress (also dead), a twelve-year-old daughter. Russ's body was identified and cremated before Irene arrived. Russ's boss, Todd Croft, the apparent puppet master of this whole grotesque theater, can't be reached, and the business's website is down.

"I'm...I'm speechless," Mavis says. "Your *husband* is dead? He had a secret *life?*"

Irene blinks.

"I'm sure you don't want to go into the gritty details. Who can blame you. But...wow. I thought maybe you were angry about your new role here."

"Oh, I was," Irene says. "But then all this happened and..." She studies the bottle of fancy water in her hands because it gives her something to do other than cry.

"Irene," Mavis says. "What can I do to help?"

"I'm giving you my notice," Irene says. "I can't come back to work. I thought maybe, with time...but no." Irene sighs. "I'm not even sure I'll stay in Iowa City."

"What?" Mavis says. "What about your house?"

Irene shrugs. Three weeks ago, leaving behind the house would have been *unthinkable*. That house took six years of her life to complete; it's a work of art. Now, of course, Irene sees how blindly devoted she was to the project, how she sweated over the details and completely ignored her marriage. It's entirely possible that Irene had been standing at her workspace in the kitchen poring over four choices of wallpaper for the third upstairs bath and Russ had come to her and said, *Honey, I have a lover in the Virgin Islands and I've fathered a daughter,* and Irene had said, *That's great, honey.*

What Russ did was wrong. But Irene is not blameless.

"You know, I've been to St. John," Mavis says. "I stayed at the Westin with my parents. It's beautiful."

"I'd like you to pass my resignation on to Joseph," Irene says. "I'll call him myself eventually, but right now..."

Mavis waves a hand. "I got it. Consider it handled."

"And would you smooth things over with the rest of the staff?"

"I certainly will," Mavis says. "They'll all miss you, of course. And they'll assume it's my fault you're leaving. The good news is I don't think they can hate me any more than they already do."

"They're midwesterners," Irene says. "A bit resistant to change."

"You think?" Mavis says. "I tried to win them over with team building—lunches at Formosa, happy hour at the Clinton Street Social Club—but I'm pretty sure they talk about me behind my back the second I pick up the check."

"At least they see you," Irene says.

Mavis cocks her head. She's not pretty, exactly, but she's young, strong, and vibrant. She has presence. But someday, Mavis Key, too, will find herself leaving less of an impression. She'll be overlooked, shuffled aside, forgotten.

Or maybe Irene is just bitter. She tries to regain the feeling she had as she stood on the bow of Huck's boat, but it's gone. She wants to go back down to the islands, she realizes then, if only so she can feel *seen* again.

"I'll come back for my things another time," Irene says. "On a Saturday. Or after hours."

Mavis says, "Whatever you need, Irene. Please ask me." She opens her arms and Irene allows herself to be hugged. "I hope you figure this out."

"Me too," Irene says.

Back at home, Irene sits at the kitchen table with her list in front of her. *Death certificates*—being pursued. *Resignation*—tendered.

Obituary. Irene flips to the next page of her notebook and writes, *Russell Steele died Tuesday, January 1. He is survived by his wife of thirty-five years, Irene Hagen Steele, and his sons, Baker and Cashman Steele.*

Is that all? Irene can't mention his job at Ascension. She could maybe say that he worked for the Corn Refiners Association for two decades. She could mention Rotary Club and his years of service to the Iowa City school board.

She drops her pen, picks up her phone. She sends a text to her best friend, Dr. Lydia Christensen.

Lydia, the first text says.

Irene feels like she's falling backward in one of those

Outward Bound games where you're supposed to trust your comrades to catch you.

Russ is dead. He died on New Year's Day but I didn't find out until I got home from our dinner. The circumstances were so extraordinary and, honestly, so baffling that I didn't know how to tell you or anyone else. I'll call you later, I promise.

Irene presses Send.

Okay, she thinks. It's officially out in the world. Unlike Mavis, Lydia is not a vault.

A little while later, the doorbell rings. The doorbell is an antique, salvaged from a convent in Vicenza, Italy, and it makes quite a formal sound, somewhere between a gong and cathedral bells. Irene hurries down the hallway, hoping and praying it's FedEx with the death certificates but knowing that, unless Paulette read Irene's mind before she left the voicemail, that's logistically impossible. It might be Lydia, though Lydia normally flings open the door and walks right in. Maybe Lydia called the Dunns and the Kinseys and this is the start of the onslaught. Bobbi Kinsey will have pulled a casserole from her freezer or stopped by the Hy-Vee for a deli tray.

Irene pauses before opening the door and takes a sustaining breath. She'll tell people the truth—helicopter crash, Virgin Islands, work, but leave out the villa, the mistress, and Maia.

Strong, beautiful Maia.

Irene opens the door. It's not Lydia, and it's not Bobbi. It's four men in dark suits, trench coats, and impractical shoes for the weather. The man in front—African-American, tall and broad, with a grim facial expression—flashes a badge.

"Irene Steele?" he says.

Irene is so stunned, she can't speak. Is she being arrested?

"Are you Irene Steele?" the man says. "Is this the Steele residence?" He glances above the door frame, then down toward the corner of Linn. "Thirty Church Street?"

Irene nods. "Yes, it is. I am."

"Agent Kenneth Beckett, FBI, white-collar crime division. We have a search warrant for this address. If you'll kindly step aside."

White-collar crime. Irene steps aside.

Three of the agents start searching the house. Irene's instinct is to follow them—not to hide anything but to make sure they're careful with her things. However, Agent Beckett wants to talk to Irene in private. She leads him to the amethyst parlor. It's chilly and she offers to lay a fire.

"Just please sit down, Mrs. Steele," Agent Beckett says. He's stern and serious, like an FBI agent on television. Irene notices a black and gold knit cap sticking out of his briefcase.

"Iowa grad?" she asks. "I'm the class of '84."

"Class of '91," Beckett says. For a second, his eyes smile. "Go Hawks."

"They aren't going to break anything, are they?" Irene asks. "This house...well, it took me six years to renovate and the antiques are real. There's a mural in the dining room; the moldings and trim have all been restored to period. The carpets..." She stares down at Beckett's wet and icy wingtips on the Queen Victoria jewel-box carpet. "They'll be careful, right? Respectful?"

Quick nod. "We're professionals."

"Of course."

"Your husband was Russell Steele?" Beckett says. "Died January first in a helicopter crash off the coast of Virgin Gorda?"

"Yes."

"And what did your husband do for a living, Mrs. Steele?"

Irene briefly wonders if she needs a lawyer present. She tries to imagine Ed Sorley in his sweater-vest dealing with these gentlemen. The idea is nearly laughable.

The fact is, *Irene* has done nothing wrong. *Irene* has nothing to hide.

"He worked for a hedge fund called Ascension," Irene says.

"What was his position there?"

"My understanding was that he was in customer relations."

Beckett looks up. "Customer relations."

"Not like he answered the phone and took complaints," Irene says. "He wined and dined the clients, played golf, a lot of golf, made them comfortable. Russ was a very...*nice* guy. Nonthreatening, friendly, engaging. He told a lot of corny jokes, asked to see pictures of your kids, remembered their names." Irene had been jealous, at times, of how good with people Russ was, how generous with his attention. All of their friends and acquaintances liked Russ better than her. And that was fine, Irene understood; they had their roles. Irene let Russ do the talking because he liked it and she didn't. She enjoyed quieter things—reading novels, cooking, nurturing one-on-one friendships, achieving goals in a timely and organized fashion, whether it was renovating a room in this house or putting an issue of the magazine to bed. She enjoyed fishing, the peace of being out on the water with a single simple mission.

Why is she thinking about fishing?

Well, she knows why.

"And where is this company, Ascension, based?" Beckett asks.

"Miami?" Irene says. "I'm not sure, though. Russ did a lot of traveling for work. He told me he was in Florida, Texas…"

"*Told* you?" Beckett says.

"Yes," Irene says. "But I now have reason to believe he spent most of his time in the Virgin Islands. In St. John."

Beckett scratches down a note.

"You know my husband owns property in St. John."

"Yes," Beckett says. "Federal agents are searching that house now."

"Oh, dear," Irene says.

Beckett looks up. "What?"

"I put my son Cash on a plane to St. Thomas this morning," Irene says. "He'll arrive at the house in St. John sometime tonight."

Beckett nods. "They should be finished with the search by then."

"But if they're not?"

"They'll let him know and he can make other arrangements."

Huck, Irene thinks. *Maybe he can stay with Huck for a*

night or two. Which is a crazy thought. Huck isn't *family;* he's merely a sort of friend.

"I guess I'm confused about what you're after. Is this part of the investigation about the helicopter?"

"Possibly related," Beckett says. "Do you know a man named Todd Croft?"

"Russ's boss," Irene says. "I met him once, December 2005, in the lobby of the Drake Hotel in Chicago. That was right before he offered Russ the job at Ascension. They knew each other at Northwestern. Or at least, that's what Russ said."

"Do you have contact information for Mr. Croft?" Beckett asks.

"I don't. Mr. Croft's secretary, Marilyn Monroe, called here on the night of January first to tell me Russ had died. I've tried calling her back since then but that number has been disconnected and the Ascension website is down."

Beckett says, "Your husband made quite a good living, isn't that right?"

"Yes," Irene says. "After he took the job with Ascension."

"This house must have been expensive to renovate."

"It was."

"And how did you think your husband was earning so much money?"

"He worked at a hedge fund," Irene says. "And I thought that provided a good salary. I didn't know about St. John. I didn't know about the other house…"

"You went down there recently, though? After he died?"

"Yes. That was my first time. We went for a week and returned home last Friday. My mother-in-law, Russ's mother, was failing. Now she's passed away so I have that to deal with."

"I'm sorry," Beckett says. He looks at her again, this time more sympathetically.

"Would you like some tea, Agent Beckett?"

"No, but thank you."

"*I'd* like some tea," Irene says. "Is it all right if we go into the kitchen so I can make some? I mean, I'm free to move around the house, right?"

"Just stay where we can see you," Agent Beckett says. He rests his hands on his thighs and pushes himself to a stand. "Actually, some tea might warm me up."

Irene makes a pot of Lady Grey, and while she's at it, she prepares a tray of sandwiches and rinses two bunches of grapes. Agent Beckett accepts a ham and cheese and a cup of tea. An agent who looks like Tom Selleck pops into the kitchen to report that they have found nothing.

"Did you remove or destroy any of your husband's papers or personal belongings after he died?" Beckett asks.

"I did not," Irene says. "I searched through both this house and the house on St. John, looking for clues."

"Clues?"

"What he was into," Irene says. "Certainly, Agent Beckett, you realize that I think all this is suspicious as well. My husband was killed in a place I didn't know he was visiting, then I found out he *lived* there. He owned *property* there. I was looking for answers."

"What did you find?"

A mistress, Irene thinks. *A love child.* "Nothing," she says.

The youngest agent—a baby-faced ginger—pokes his head into the kitchen. "Nothing in the master bed or bath," he says. He eyes the tray of sandwiches. "Are those for everyone?"

"Help yourself," Irene says. Then she thinks of something! A hiding place! She looks at Beckett, who is reviewing his notes as he eats his ham and cheese.

No, she won't tell them. Maybe they'll find it. Maybe they won't.

Irene wonders if this investigation can work both ways. "I called my real estate contact in St. John to request a death certificate." She blows across the surface of her tea. "My family attorney here says that until I produce it, Russ is technically still alive." She pauses, waiting for a reaction, but none comes. "Which would be quite something, because we've already scattered the ashes. Or what we thought were Russ's ashes. I never saw the body and I wasn't consulted about the cremation until after it was a done deal. Is there any chance...I mean, do you think my husband might still be alive?"

Beckett stands up to secure the door to the hallway and then the door to the dining room. "You've been very accommodating," he says. "And we appreciate it. I'm sure you realize that we're here because we have reason to believe your husband had illegal business dealings. The one thing I *can* assure you"—Agent Beckett holds Irene's gaze—"is that your husband is dead."

"He is," Irene says. Yes, he is, she knows this. She has been processing this news for over two weeks. And yet hearing Beckett say the words comes as a fresh shock. Irene's eyes sting with tears. The dreams were just that— dreams—but Irene must have been hanging on to a thread of hope. None of this added up. From the beginning, it felt like a hoax. The person who told Irene that Russ was dead—Marilyn Monroe—wasn't someone Irene had ever met face to face. Paulette had been professional to the point of seeming insensitive, nearly as if she was just going through the motions because she knew Russ would turn up eventually. "You're sure?"

"Yes," Beckett says. He must have definitive proof, Irene thinks, but he isn't sharing it. "We're going to need your cell phone and your computer. They'll both be re- turned to you."

"Yes, of course," Irene says. She pulls her cell phone out of her purse just as it lights up and starts chiming with a call from Lydia. Of course it's Lydia. Irene hits De- cline and hands it over. She nods at her laptop on the desk in the corner. "When you say my husband had il- legal business dealings, you mean *Ascension* had illegal business dealings, right? *Todd Croft* had illegal business dealings. I can tell you right now that Russ just wasn't the kind of person who would—" She notices the expression on Agent Beckett's face and stops talking. Russ wasn't the kind of person who would…what? Have a mistress, a secret daughter, and a nine-bedroom villa down in the Caribbean? It's pretty clear that Irene doesn't know what kind of person Russ was. She is as clueless as Ruth Madoff was. Irene remembers back when that news story broke. She had thought, *Of course the wife knew her husband was running a bazillion-dollar Ponzi scheme. How could she* not *know?* But now that Irene is in a similar situation, she's certain Mrs. Madoff had no idea what was going on. She probably spent all her time at the club lunching with her friends and meeting with her personal shopper. And if Ruth Madoff—or Irene—had asked her husband questions about his business, who's to say either woman would have been told the truth?

Irene, for one, hadn't asked any questions. She had happily accepted the money Russ deposited into her renovation account and turned her attention to wallpaper and crown molding. "Are you looking for Todd Croft?"

Barely a nod from Beckett. "Not at liberty to say."

Yes; the answer was yes. "He's drinking a daiquiri on some remote island without a name," Irene says.

"That actually happens less than one would imagine," Beckett says. "Men like Todd Croft can't just drop out of society. They're too power hungry." Beckett pops the last bite of sandwich into his mouth and polishes off his tea. "Don't worry. He'll turn up."

"I did learn two things on my own," Irene says, "that you might find helpful." She's hesitant to hand over what she knows, but Russ's words have taken root inside of her. *Irene is the only person I trust to do the right thing.* He probably meant the right thing for Rosie and Maia but he most certainly also meant the right thing morally, which was to cooperate with the FBI, tell the truth, preserve her own integrity, protect the boys. "We have a bank account at Federal Republic. I have a statement I can give you. And the teller informed me that Russ made the last two deposits of seventy-five hundred dollars apiece…in cash." Irene searches Agent Beckett's face to see if this news startles him as much as it startled her, but he doesn't even blink. Of course, he's in the FBI. He has seen…Irene can't even imagine what. "And I asked my attorney, Ed, Edward Sorley, to find the account that Russ used to pay for this house when we bought it. He has a copy of a cashier's check drawn on a bank—MGST or something like that—in the Cayman Islands."

Agent Beckett's left eyebrow lifts a fraction of an inch. "Sounds about right," he says. "Would you give me Mr. Sorley's contact information, please?"

The FBI agents leave at eight thirty that night. As they're finally heading out the door—with far less evidence than they anticipated, Irene can tell by their dejected demeanors—she suggests that they go to the Wig and Pen for dinner.

"Great wings," she says. "My mother-in-law…" But she can't finish the sentence.

Agent Beckett shakes her hand. "Thank you for your help today."

Irene finds herself uncharacteristically craving validation. She *was* helpful, right? They're aware from how cooperative and accommodating she's been, from the details she's shared, and from her general demeanor that she had no idea what Russ was involved with. *She* is innocent. She should not be held accountable—and yet she fears that she'll see these men again storming her house in the predawn hours with a warrant for her arrest.

Their visit today has taken its toll; she's scared.

"Will you be back tomorrow?" she asks.

"Someone will be by to drop off your phone and your computer," he says. "Here's my card. Don't hesitate to call if you think of anything else you want to tell us."

Irene waits ten minutes, then fifteen. When she's positive the agents are not coming back, she snaps off the porch light and heads for the library.

The house phone rings, startling her.

Should she answer?

It's probably Cash, wondering why she isn't answering her cell phone. *Well, honey, the FBI has it...*

"Irene?"

"Lydia," Irene says. She carries the phone into the library, where she snaps on the Tiffany lamp and collapses in her favorite reading chair. "Hi."

"I got your texts," Lydia says. "But then you didn't answer when I called. You can't...be serious? Russ is not dead! You would have told me right away if you'd found out he was dead. It was just hyperbole, right? You wish he were dead. What did he do wrong? He was away somewhere, right?"

"The Virgin Islands," Irene says. The conversation feels like a hill she doesn't want to climb.

"The...where? Did you *tell* me Russ was in the Virgin Islands? You *didn't* tell me that. I would have remembered."

Irene closes her eyes. This is just as excruciating as she feared it would be. She has made things far worse by waiting for so long. Lydia doesn't believe her; Irene should have called her right away. Irene should have brought her—or someone—in at the beginning. But she hadn't. It had been so sudden and so bizarre, so inexplicable. It was *still inexplicable*—and yet, here they are.

"Lydia," Irene says. "Russ is dead. He was killed in a helicopter crash in the Virgin Islands on January first. He was there on business. The rest of the details are too painful to share right now. His body was cremated and the boys and I flew down to scatter his ashes."

"What?" Lydia shouts. There's a muffled voice in the background. "Brandon and I are on our way over right now."

"No," Irene says. "Please, I was just heading up to bed. We'll talk tomorrow, I promise." She thinks for a second. "Brandon who?"

"Brandon the barista," Lydia says. "We're dating. We've been dating since...that night."

Irene supposes it's too late to ask Lydia to keep the news of Russ's death to herself. "I'll call you tomorrow, really. I...I have to go."

"Okay," Lydia says. She sounds put out, and then she starts to cry. "I'm so sorry, Irene. I'm sure you're destroyed. Russ was...well, you know he was the most devoted husband."

Wasn't he just, Irene thinks. "Good night, Lydia." She punches off the phone, sighs deeply, then turns her attention to the library shelves. Three shelves in from the right, three shelves down from the ceiling, Irene finds the *Oxford English Dictionary* that she lugged to college, *Roget's Thesaurus,* and *Bartlett's Familiar Quotations* in a solid, scholarly stack. She moves the three massive tomes onto the brocade sofa and slides the panel out of the back of the shelf to reveal a secret compartment. And voilà! There's a manila envelope, stuffed full.

Irene had forgotten all about the secret compartment until she started thinking about hiding places. The secret compartment had been original to this room, and even though the library had undergone a complete overhaul, Russ had insisted the compartment stay. It added character and history—they agreed it had probably been used to hide alcohol during Prohibition. It was one of the only aspects of the house Russ had taken a personal interest in.

What will we hide in there? Irene had asked.

Love notes, he'd said.

She remembers that, clear as day. *Love notes.*

She pulls out the manila envelope and empties the contents onto the coffee table. It's a stack of postcards secured with a rubber band. For one second, Irene holds out hope that the postcards are family heirlooms, maybe the correspondence that Milly conducted with Russ's father while he was away in the navy. But once she wrangles the rubber band off, she sees the pictures on the postcards are all of St. John—Cinnamon Bay, Maho Bay, Francis Bay, Hansen Bay.

None of the cards is addressed. On the back of each is

a short, simple message. *I love you. I'll miss you. You are my heart. I'll be here waiting. I love you. I love you. I love you.* All of them are signed with the initials *M.L.*

M.L.? Not Rosie? She thinks of Maia, but these notes feel, almost certainly, like declarations of romantic love. So they have to be from Rosie. M.L. must be a nickname.

These are the love notes Russ was talking about then, years earlier, when he insisted they keep this compartment.

Irene feels a wave of anger and disgust—he kept these *in the house!*—but she also feels implicated. If she had to guess, she would say Rosie tucked these cards into Russ's luggage for him to find once he'd arrived home. Or maybe she slipped them into his jacket pocket as he was leaving. Instead of throwing them away, as Russ certainly knew he should, he'd kept them. He'd wanted—or needed—to save this proof that someone loved him because so little love was shown to him at home.

Irene has heard that love is a garden that needs to be tended. And what had Irene thought about that? She had thought it was sentimental nonsense, the stuff of sappy Hallmark cards. Love, for Irene, was a daily act—steadfastness, loyalty, devotion. It was raising the boys, creating a beautiful, comfortable home, stopping by to see Milly three times a week because Russ was too busy to do it himself. It was ironing Russ's shirts, making his oatmeal with raisins the way he liked it, taking his Audi to the car wash so it was gleaming when he returned from his trips.

She tosses the postcards in the air and they scatter. She would like to burn them in one of her six fireplaces; nothing would give her greater satisfaction than watching

Rosie's declarations of love for Russ curl, blacken, and go up in smoke.

Forgiveness, she thinks. She will save the postcards and give them to Maia someday.

She picks up the landline and dials, and Huck answers on the first ring. "Hello," he says. "Who's calling me from Iowa City?"

"It's me," Irene says, which she knows is presumptive. They haven't been friends long enough for her to be "me."

"Hello, you," he says, and she feels better. "What's up?"

What should Irene tell him first? That she spent all day with the FBI? Or that she found an illicit cache of postcards from his stepdaughter to her husband?

"Adam leaves a week from Tuesday?" she says.

"Yep," Huck says.

"All right," Irene says. "I guess that means I'll be down a week from Monday."

"You serious?" Huck says. She hears him exhale, presumably smoke. "Angler Cupcake, you serious?"

She squeezes her eyes shut. "Yes," she says.

AYERS

Y ou're hiding something," Mick says. It's one of their rare nights off together and they're having dinner at the bar at

Ocean 362, where they can watch the sun set. Ayers spent the afternoon on Salomon Bay by herself; Mick asked to come along but Ayers said she wanted to be alone. It was important, this time around, to preserve her me-time.

I want to lie in the sun and think about Rosie, she said.

You can think about Rosie with me right next to you, Mick said. *You can even talk about Rosie. I'll listen.*

It's not the same, Ayers said. *You'll distract me.* What she didn't tell Mick, couldn't tell him, was that she needed time to read Rosie's journals. She had made it from the year 2000—Rosie at age seventeen—all the way through her tumultuous relationship with Oscar to the weekend in 2006 when she met Russ. Ayers was just getting to the good stuff, the important stuff—but it was tricky, finding blocks of time to read.

"If you're suspicious," Ayers says now, "it's probably because of your own guilty conscience." She digs into the walnut-crusted Roquefort cheesecake.

"What?" he says.

"Don't act offended," Ayers says. She lowers her voice because the bartender, Alex, is a friend of theirs and she doesn't want him to hear them squabbling. "We agreed we wouldn't dance around the topic of your infidelity. We agreed you would own it and that I was free to bring it up at any time."

"Within reason. We said 'within reason.'"

"You're accusing me of hiding something," Ayers says. "Meanwhile, you haven't even fired Brigid."

"I can't fire her just because we broke up," Mick says. "That's against the law." He pulls his phone out because the sun is going down and one of Mick's passions is photographing the sunset every night, then posting it on Instagram as #sunset, #sunsetpics, #sunsetlover. Ayers has forgotten how this annoys her. She enjoys a good sunset as much as the next person, but she finds pictures of the sunset #overdone.

"You can fire her because she's a terrible server," Ayers says. "She's the worst server I've ever seen."

"You're biased."

Ayers carefully constructs a bite: a slice of toasted baguette smeared with the Roquefort topped with the accompanying shallot and garlic confit. "How do you think I feel knowing that she's right there under your nose every single night? The answer is: not great. But do I complain? Do I sniff your clothes or show up at the restaurant unannounced? No. Do I *accuse* you of hiding something? I do not."

"You're right," Mick says. He's distracted by his sunset posting. "I'm sorry."

Ayers lets the topic drop because guess what—she *is* hiding something! She's obsessed with Rosie's journals, and she isn't using that word cavalierly like the rest of the world now does ("I'm obsessed with AOC's lipstick" or "mango with chili salt" or "'Seven Rings' by Ariana Grande"). If Ayers didn't have two jobs and a boyfriend, she would lock herself in a room and binge on the journals until she had the whole story—but there is pleasure to be had in pacing herself. Read, then process.

Of course, it's more difficult to hold back now that Russ has entered the picture.

Ayers and Mick finish dinner and decide to end the evening by going to La Tapa for a nightcap. To an outsider, it might seem pathetic that Ayers can't stay away from her place of employment on her night off, but the fact is, La Tapa is her home and her coworkers are her family. Skip and Tilda finally hooked up—they've been circling each other since October—and Tilda told Ayers that for three days straight, they did nothing but drink Schramsberg, eat mango with chili salt, and have wild sex. But on the fourth day, Tilda woke up at Skip's place and wondered what the hell she was doing there.

It was like the fever broke, Tilda whispered to Ayers as they polished glasses before service. *I'm over him. In fact, looking at him makes me feel kind of sick.*

Human nature being what it is, when Tilda's enthusiasm cooled, Skip's grew more intense, and Tilda confided to Ayers—yes, somehow Ayers and Tilda were becoming confidantes—that Skip followed her home to her parents' villa one night after work. (Tilda's parents are quite wealthy and have a home in Peter Bay. Tilda doesn't *have* to work at La Tapa but she's determined not to "play the role of entitled rich kid," so she hammers out four shifts a week and also volunteers at the Animal Care Center, walking rescue dogs. The more Ayers learns about Tilda's life outside of work, the harder it is not to admire and even like her.) When Tilda explained to Skip in her parents' driveway—she was *not* about to invite Skip in—that she thought maybe they had gotten too close too quickly, Skip had started to *cry.*

Now, apparently, he's venting his anger at the restaurant during service; he's been acting erratically with the customers.

And sure enough, after Ayers and Mick claim two seats at the bar and order Ayers's favorite sipping tequila, Ayers overhears Skip describing a bottle of Malbec for the couple sitting a few stools away like this: "This wine is a personal favorite of mine," Skip says. "It has hints of hashish, old piñata candy, and the tears of cloistered nuns."

"What?" the woman says. "No, thank you!"

Ayers waves Skip over. "You okay?"

"Great, Ayers, yeah," Skip says, scowling. "Seriously, never better." He looks over Ayers's shoulder and his expression changes. "Hey, man, how're you doing? Good to see you! It's...it's...I'm sorry, bud, I've forgotten your name."

"Cash," a voice says.

Ayers whips around. "Cash!" she says. She hops off her stool. It's Cash Steele, here at La Tapa! Ayers remembers too late that she's angry with him. She finds that she's happy, really happy, to see him. She inadvertently checks behind him to see if maybe Baker followed him in.

No. But Ayers finds her heart bouncing around at the prospect of his being here.

"Hey, Ayers," Cash says. He offers Skip a hand across the bar. "Good to see you, man. Just got in on the ferry. I'm starving. Can I get an order of mussels and the bread with three sauces?"

"You got it, Cash," Skip says.

Cash eyes the stool next to Ayers. "This taken?"

Mick clears his throat. Ayers says, "No, no, sit, please. Cash, this is…Mick. And Mick, this is Cash Steele."

Mick raises his tequila and slams back the whole thing. Cash nods in response.

"So what are you doing here?" Ayers asks. "I thought you guys went back to your lives in America." Which is how it always happens, she thinks. Which is why she doesn't date tourists.

"My life in America kind of fell apart," Cash says. "So that text you sent me was pure serendipity."

On the other side of Ayers, Mick sounds like he's choking. Ayers watches Skip set a glass of water in front of him.

"Text?" Ayers says, though she knows exactly what Cash is talking about.

"About the job on *Treasure Island*," Cash says. "Have you filled it?"

"Uh…no," Ayers says. "We haven't. We're pretty desperate, actually. Wade leaves in another week."

Cash slaps some paperwork down on the bar. "I can fast-track my lifesaving certification," he says. "I should be good to go in another week."

"Seriously?" Ayers says. "You want the job on *Treasure Island*?"

"I'd love it," Cash says.

Ayers hears Mick muttering on the other side of her. She would be lying if she said she wasn't taking some satisfaction in his discomfort. She must be angrier at him than she realized.

"Cash!"

Tilda swoops in and throws her arms around Cash's neck, then gives him a juicy kiss on the cheek.

"Hey, Tilda," Cash says.

Across the bar, Skip holds Cash's order of bread with three sauces. He glares at Tilda and Cash, then comes just short of slamming the plate down.

"I thought you were in Colorado!" Tilda says. "I've been trying to figure out how to tell my parents that I'm taking a trip to Breckenridge to ski with you."

"No Breck for the foreseeable future," Cash says. "I'm moving down here. And hopefully working on *Treasure Island* with Ayers."

"'Working on *Treasure Island* with Ayers,'" Mick mimics under his breath.

"Moving down here?" Tilda says. "That's hot."

Skip huffs. "Hot?" he says. "Get back to work, Tilda."

Tilda appears unfazed. "Call me later," she says to Cash. She sashays off to give table eight dessert menus.

Ayers says, "I didn't realize you knew Tilda."

"You sound jealous," Mick murmurs. "How about you let lover boy eat his bread and we get out of here?"

"She gave me a ride home when I was here the last time," Cash says. "She's cool."

"She's *taken*," Skip says. He's holding Cash's mussels and looks like he might dump them over Cash's head.

"She's *not* taken," Ayers says. She waves Skip away. "Get back to work yourself."

"You're not my boss," Skip says.

Mick stands up. "I'm going home. Are you coming?"

Ayers looks from Cash to Mick. It's a standoff, she

realizes. To Cash she says, "Hey, I'm picking up Maia tomorrow morning and we're hiking from Leicester Bay to Brown Bay, then swimming after. Do you want to join us?"

"Do you think Maia would mind?" Cash asks.

"Are you kidding me? She'd love it."

"I'm in," Cash says. "I have Winnie with me. She's tied up outside."

"Winnie!" Ayers says. "This is so great! I'll text you in the morning. How are you getting to the villa? I mean, we can wait until you're finished and give you a ride."

"No, we can't," Mick says. "We have to get home. I have work tomorrow."

"At four o'clock," Ayers says. "Chill."

"Don't tell me to chill," Mick says. "Please."

"No problem," Cash says. "I'll see if Tilda can give me a ride home. If not, I'll take a taxi."

Skip leans across the bar. "How are those mussels?" he asks aggressively.

"I'll see you tomorrow," Ayers says. "Welcome back."

Ayers weaves her way out of the restaurant. Mick is already on the sidewalk, lighting a cigarette. Ayers stops to rub Winnie's head. She seems to recognize Ayers; her tail is wagging like crazy.

Mick takes a deep drag of his cigarette, then exhales. "I guess I'm confused. That's Banker's brother, right?"

"Cash. Right."

"And you guys are buddy-buddy as well?"

"Mick, stop."

"You texted him," Mick says. "You told him about the opening on *Treasure Island*."

"That was a Hail Mary," Ayers says. "He came out on *Treasure Island* a few weeks ago, he was good with the guests."

"The plot thickens," Mick says. "Why am I just hearing about this?"

Ayers shrugs. "Why would I have told you? We were broken up."

Angry exhale of smoke.

"You know we need to hire someone who already has a place to live," Ayers says. "Like Cash. And I think he'd be excellent on the boat. Not okay, not good, *excellent*. He likes people. He's a ski instructor—"

"Did you not hear him say his life fell apart?" Mick says. "Doesn't that send up a red flag?"

"His father died, Mick. He found out his father had this whole other life. That's enough to throw anyone into a tailspin."

"Yeah, but wouldn't you think he'd want to stay as far away from here as possible?"

Ayers inhales the night air. There's guitar music floating down from the Quiet Mon. Across the street, the lights twinkle at Extra Virgin Bistro. "I think he came down here and fell in love with the place," she says. "Just like I did. Just like you did."

"As long as he didn't fall in love with you," Mick says. "But who are we kidding? Of course he did. There isn't a woman in Colorado or anywhere else that's as beautiful and sexy and cool as you."

Ayers climbs into Mick's blue Jeep. She's still bothered by the memory of Brigid sitting in this seat. "Honestly, I barely know him."

"And yet you invited him hiking with you and Maia to-morrow. You didn't invite me; you invited Money."

"Cash," Ayers says, trying not to smile. Mick is good with nicknames and it'll be hard for her now not to think of Baker and Cash as *Banker* and *Money*. "You don't like hiking. And I'll point out that Cash is Maia's brother."

"Half brother."

"Whatever. He and Baker are Maia's only blood relatives, aside from whoever is left on Rosie's father's side."

"I don't want you hiking with him."

"You don't have any say."

"But we're in a relationship," Mick says.

"We're dating. You don't own me. I'm sorry that you don't like it. I don't like it that Brigid still works for you. I didn't like driving down to the Beach Bar at three o'clock in the morning and seeing you—"

"Stop," Mick says.

"I'm going hiking with Cash and Maia," Ayers says. "And Winnie!"

"Great," Mick says. "You're cheating on Gordon as well."

"Just drive," Ayers says. She leans back in the seat, marveling at the unexpected turn the night has taken and how buoyant she now feels. Mick is jealous, but Ayers doesn't care. Cash is here—and tomorrow, Ayers will ask him about Baker.

CASH

His mother called to tell him about her visit from the FBI, so Cash isn't surprised when the taxi turns onto his father's road and he sees a dark SUV parked in one of the dummy driveways.

They're watching the house. Well, he can't blame them.

It's been nearly three weeks since he left. The villa seems basically the same, although Cash can tell things have been gone through. The bed in the guest room he used last time has been hastily made and all of the drawers in the adjacent bath are ajar. Cash does a quick check of the house and this seems to be the case throughout. Irene said they found nothing at the house in Iowa City and Cash imagines the same is true here. There was very little of a personal nature in this house to begin with. When they arrived the first time, reeling from the news of Russ's death, it seemed more like a hotel than someone's house.

It feels good, though, to have the place to himself. It feels better than good; it feels luxurious. Cash stands out on the deck bare-chested while Winnie goes nuts sniffing everything and chasing after geckos. Cash gazes down the lush, leafy hill over the moon-spangled water. He's king of the castle! He wants to howl, he wants to sing. The villa is his!

His exultation is tied to seeing Ayers. He wondered if he'd built her up in his mind—but when he saw her from behind, her curly blond hair hanging loose and crazy down her back and the silhouette of her body in that halter top and white jeans, he felt like he was being swallowed up. She had been so happy to see him, happier than he would have predicted, and she had seemed nearly jealous when Tilda came over to give Cash a hug. The interaction had been great, great, great, everything Cash could have dreamed of.

Today was the first day of the rest of his life, Cash thinks. It's a tired phrase—and yet so true, so true! He has never been more certain of anything: his life began today. He swung down here on a slender filament of hope that a potential job on *Treasure Island* offered and now it looks like it will all work out.

He wants to beat his chest! He has escaped the doom of a lonely winter in Iowa City, shoveling snow and bumping into ex-girlfriends at the grocery store. Tomorrow he has plans with Ayers and Maia, and Monday he starts his lifesaving course, which Irene has given him more than enough money to pay for.

"I'm so happy!" Cash cries out. He wonders if the FBI has bugged the house. Well, if they have, they are going to hear the twenty-nine-year-old son of Russell Steele talking to himself. And maybe it will seem strange or even cruel that Cash is so jubilant only a few short weeks after his father died. Cash misses his father; he's mourning his father, and he's angry and resentful and disappointed in his father. But all of that feels like a pot Cash can pull off the stove for now. His excitement about this island and this girl and this sense of freedom and opportunity win out.

"It's going to be epic!" Cash says. Winnie barks and comes trotting over; she noses around Cash's legs and he bends to rub her soft butterscotch head. "Right, Winnie? Right?"

The next morning Cash winds his way down the hill in one of his father's gray Jeeps, stops at the black SUV, and rolls down his window. "I'm Cash Steele," he says. "Russell Steele's son."

The man sitting in the front seat—shaved head, blond Hulk Hogan mustache—flexes one of his enormous biceps as he brings a cup of coffee to his lips. "I know," he says.

Cash waits a second, thinking maybe there will be more, but the guy looks down into his lap; he's reading the paper. Cash is the one with questions—who is this guy? Why is he watching the house?—but Cash is certain he'll be stonewalled and he doesn't want to be late, so he carries on.

He meets Ayers and Maia in the parking area on Leicester Bay Road. In Cash's backpack are three towels, nine bottles of water, and three sandwiches from the North Shore Deli. He's wearing trunks under his cargo shorts, his Social Distortion T-shirt, and his lightweight hiking boots. Both girls are standing next to Ayers's green truck, tying bandannas around their foreheads.

"Hey," Cash says as he climbs out of the Jeep. Winnie heads straight for Maia, who crouches down to pet her. Winnie is an excellent ambassador; as always, she smooths over a potentially awkward situation. Cash follows, tentatively offering Maia a fist bump. Ayers said that Maia would be cool with Cash joining them, but will she? Cash knows nothing about the psyches of twelve-year-old girls.

"Hey, bro," Maia says. She bumps knuckles with him, then grins. "You came back! And Ayers tells me you're going to work on *Treasure Island*."

"That's the plan," he says. He glances quickly at Ayers in her white tank and light blue Lululemon running shorts; he can see the outline of a bikini underneath.

"Ayers's boyfriend, Mick, is really jealous," Maia says.

"Maia!" Ayers says. "Hush!"

"What?" Maia says. "He is. He's even jealous we're taking this hike."

"Well, he doesn't need to be jealous," Cash says. "Ayers and I are just friends."

"That's what I told him," Ayers says. She drops her blue aviators down over her eyes. "Are you sure you don't mind carrying the pack? It's got to be heavy."

"Please," Cash says. "I hike at eight, nine thousand feet with a pack that's three times this weight."

"Ayers doesn't like hiking," Maia says. "But she's my parent now, so she has to do enriching things with me."

"Mangrove snorkeling is enriching," Ayers says. She looks up at the brilliant blue sky. "And a far more appropriate activity than hiking on an eighty-degree day."

"Next week," Maia says. She strides toward the trail-head. "Come on, Winnie, let's go."

The Johnny Horn Trail has five spurs, Maia explains. The first spur, a flat, sandy walking path, leads to a narrow beach hugging a bay that has a rugged island a hundred yards offshore.

"Waterlemon Cay," Ayers says. "Best snorkeling on St. John. How about I stay here and you guys keep going?"

"We've only been hiking thirty seconds," Maia says. She turns to Cash. "See what I have to deal with?"

The second spur takes them up a steep, rocky incline that requires a fair amount of scrambling and careful foot placement before it levels out, when they reach stone ruins. This is the guardhouse, Maia tells them, built in the 1840s, back when slavery had been abolished in the British Virgin Islands across the Sir Francis Drake Channel but was still legal on St. John.

"There were sixteen soldiers stationed here," Maia says. "And their job was to keep watch for runaway slaves."

Cash is impressed. "You have quite the body of knowledge," he says. "How did you learn all this?"

"My mom," Maia says. "She knew everything about the Virgin Islands."

Cash nods as the peculiarity of what he's doing hits him. He's hiking with a half sister he never knew he had. Maia bows her head and is quiet and Ayers places a hand on the back of her neck and draws her in. They're thinking about Rosie; Cash can feel how much they miss her. A twelve-year-old girl lost her mother, lost both of her parents, and yet here she is, bravely soldiering on with her mother's best friend and a strange man she has gamely decided to accept as "bro."

"Did your mom like to hike?" Cash asks.

"No," Maia says, and she and Ayers laugh. "She was more like Ayers; she preferred the beach. But, I mean, she brought me up here a few times because she wanted me to experience the place we lived."

"I wish I'd been able to meet your mom," Cash says honestly. More than once over the past couple of weeks, Cash has imagined this whole thing unfolding differently. What if, at some point, Russ had just come clean about his life, said that business had taken him to the Caribbean and he'd met a woman and fallen in love. Cash and Baker would have been furious at first, incredulous, resentful on Irene's behalf. They probably would have refused to speak to Russ for a while. But eventually, Cash suspects, they would have come to terms with the situation and flown down to visit Russ here. They could have met Rosie. It might have taken time, but they could have accepted her as part of the family.

Cash shakes his head. *That* is a trail spur that never was; there's no use dwelling on it.

"Shall we go?" Ayers asks. "Get this over with?"

After the guardhouse, they begin to hit their stride. There's not much canopy cover but even so, Cash finds himself slowing down so he can enjoy just being. His breathing steadies. He reminds himself he doesn't need to be anywhere; he has nothing else to do today. Ayers is here, Maia is here. Ayers is right, it's hot, but just then, the sun disappears behind a cloud, so there's a brief respite.

Maia not only knows history, she is also quite the naturalist. She points out a genip tree—in the summer it produces a fruit similar to a lime. Cash has never heard of it.

"In the summer, I eat elk jerky," Cash says.

Maia shoots him a look. "I'm a vegetarian," she says.

"You are?" Cash says. "Ayers told me to get you a pastrami melt."

"I make an exception for pastrami," Maia says. "And Candi's barbecue."

Maia points out wild tamarind, cassia trees, and something called catch-and-keep, which is a cute name for a nefarious pricker bush. They eventually reach a scenic overlook where each of them—Winnie included—sucks down a bottle of water. Maia points across the way to Jost Van Dyke and Tortola.

After the lookout, the trail heads downhill and it's fully shaded. Everyone seems a little happier.

"So I guess I'll address the elephant in the room," Maia says. "How's your brother?"

Cash isn't sure he's heard right. "Is Baker an elephant?"

"I don't know, Ayers, *is* Baker an elephant?" Maia says.

"Stop being precocious for one minute, please," Ayers says. She turns to Cash and he can see the hopeful expectation in her face, even with her sunglasses on. "How is Baker? He…went back to Houston, I take it? I haven't heard from him."

Cash can't look at her. He concentrates on walking, left foot, then right, steady in his boots, moving down the dirt trail over rocks and around the tentacles of catch-and-keep. Ayers likes Baker. She's hung up on him; Cash can hear it in her voice. He can't *believe* it. He'd met Mick the night before, and Mick is who she's with now, but Cash isn't intimidated by Mick. Mick is ridiculous, a clown, a clown who cheated on Ayers once and who would most certainly do it again.

"I haven't heard from him since our grandmother died a few days after we all got home," Cash says.

"Milly?" Maia says. "The one I look like?"

"Yes," Cash says. He chastises himself for being insensitive. Milly was Maia's grandmother too—how weird is that? "I'm sorry. I should have broken the news in a different way. She was really old. Ninety-nine."

They are all silent for a moment, then Ayers says, "So you don't know if Baker is pursuing a divorce or—"

"No idea," Cash says, cutting her off. "If you're curious about Baker, just call him. You have his number, right?"

"Right," Ayers says.

"Uh-oh," Maia says. "Sounds like somebody needs lunch."

When they reach Brown Bay, Maia shows them a little cemetery. "These are the graves of islanders from long ago," Maia says, which is obvious, as the modest headstones are so old and weathered they're barely legible. "But I kind of wish my mom had been buried here. Look at this view, and it's so peaceful and shady under these trees."

"She would have liked it here," Ayers says.

"Where…" Cash starts. He has no idea where Rosie is buried.

"She's with my grandma in the cemetery in Cruz Bay," Maia says. "Or that's where her body is. Her spirit is wherever spirits go when people die."

They march single file onto a ribbon of white-sand beach. It's completely deserted and the water is a clear, placid turquoise. Cash can't recall ever seeing such inviting water. He shucks off the backpack and strips out of his shirt and shorts. Winnie is already splashing in, barking with joy and, probably, relief. Cash follows and soon he's floating on his back, staring up into the cloudless sky. He hears Maia and Ayers get into the water as well. Cash tries to readjust his frame of mind. He's not going to let his brother ruin a perfectly good day when he's a thousand miles away in Houston.

Cash likes Ayers. Ayers likes Baker. It's a classic like triangle. But Cash has the advantage because Cash is here and Baker isn't. Cash has a further advantage because he will soon be working with Ayers. After spending some time with him, Ayers will realize that he's the superior Steele brother. She'll fall in love. He will, somehow, make her fall in love.

After swimming, he joins Ayers and Maia, who are drying off on a flat rock—Picnic Rock, Maia calls it. Cash passes out the sandwiches and gives Winnie the biscuits he brought. Maia slips Winnie some of her pastrami, which makes her Winnie's new best friend. The silence is companionable, Cash thinks, or maybe it's awkward; he can't tell.

It's true that, among the three of them, there are a number of taboo subjects.

"How's Huck?" Cash asks.

"Grouchy," Maia says.

"Yeah?"

"Part of it is that I've started going to town with my friends and he doesn't like it."

"I don't like it either," Ayers says.

"We're just hanging out," Maia says.

"Who's 'we'?" Ayers and Cash say at the same time. They exchange a look and for a second, Cash feels like he and Ayers are Maia's parents instead of her half brother and sort of aunt.

"Me and Joan," Maia says.

"And?" Ayers says.

"And Colton Seeley and Bright Whittaker," Maia says. She licks some mustard off her thumb. "Joan has a crush on Colton."

"And you have a crush on Bright?" Ayers asks.

"No," Maia says. "Bright isn't my type. Plus, he has a crush on Posie Alvarez."

"Do I know Posie?"

"She goes to Antilles," Maia says. "She's friends with a kid named Shane who's a year ahead of us."

"I'm going to take a wild stab in the dark here," Ayers says. "You have a crush on Shane."

Maia shrugs. "I might."

"I can't believe it," Ayers says. "Your first crush! I have to meet this kid. I'm going to come find you guys in town one day before work. And Cash, you have to come with me.

This is your little sister. You need to protect her. You need to be a lieutenant in the cause."

Cash opens his mouth but he's unsure of what to say. *Your little sister. You need to protect her.*

The FBI are staking out the house. Russ was conducting illegal business. He likely got Rosie killed. Do Ayers and Maia know this? If they don't know and they find out, will they hate Cash? Isn't it better to prepare for this eventuality and remain aloof?

Cash focuses on Ayers for a second. She's sitting on Picnic Rock, wearing a white bikini and a towel around her waist. Her blond hair is drying in the sun. She takes a bite of her Cuban sandwich, waiting for him to answer.

They won't hate him, he realizes. They know his heart is pure, that he's as bewildered as they are, maybe more so. He's a good guy. He doesn't know a thing about having a "little sister"—both the phrase and the notion are completely foreign to him—but he wants to learn. He wants some good to come out of the choices Russ made. Their relationship—his and Maia's—can be part of that good.

"I would certainly like to meet Shane before this goes any further," he says.

Maia rolls her eyes theatrically, and although Cash knows exactly nothing about twelve-year-old girls, he can tell that beneath the surface of her exasperation, she's grateful. Her mother is gone, but she's not alone. She has Ayers and now she has Cash, and they're here to pay attention. They're here to care about her.

"Just please, *please,* don't tell Huck," Maia says.

"You have my word," Ayers says.

"And mine," Cash says.

"So I told my secret," Maia says. "Now it's your turn. Cash, who do you have a crush on?"

"Okay," Cash says, standing up. "Time to head back." He whistles for Winnie, who is down on the beach, chasing stray chickens.

He has a crush on Ayers; more than a crush. When they get back to the parking lot, it's difficult to say goodbye. Ayers has to work at La Tapa that night and on *Treasure Island* the next day, and Maia is going fishing with Huck. Then, next week, Maia has school and Cash starts his lifesaving classes. He can begin crewing on *Treasure Island* a week from Sunday; Wade will still be around to train him.

A week from Sunday feels awfully far away.

"Maybe you and I can hike again sometime," Maia says. "I'll take you to the Esperance Trail. There's a baobab tree."

"It's a date," he says. He peers over Maia's head at Ayers. "Thanks for inviting me along today."

"Of course," Ayers says. She and Maia hop in the little green truck and wave. "See ya later."

Cash and Winnie watch them drive away.

There's no reason to feel down, and yet he does. He drives back to the villa, knowing he can crack a beer and spend what remains of the afternoon by the pool, and then he should take a trip to the grocery store because he can't eat at La Tapa every night or he'll quickly burn through the money Irene gave him.

He passes the black SUV in the dummy driveway— different guy, dark-complected. Cash waves.

When he gets up to the house, he hears voices, splashing. Someone is in the pool.

Whoa! Cash's crazy first thought is that it's FBI agent number one. His second thought is that the house has been rented and Paulette forgot to tell Irene, or maybe she thought it wouldn't matter since they'd gone back to the States. That must be it. What is Cash going to do? He doesn't have money for a hotel and his lifesaving class starts Monday. He sends Winnie up the stairs ahead of him. Paulette will have to come up with a solution. Find these people another house.

Cash is nearly at the top step, prepping himself for an uncomfortable confrontation, when he hears a young voice say, "Winnie! Uncle Cash!"

It's Floyd, bobbing in the pool. And Baker, sitting on the edge in just his bathing trunks.

"Hey," Baker says.

"What—" Cash shakes his head. Winnie's tail is going nuts; she barks. "What are you doing here?"

"We're moving here!" Floyd announces. "To live!"

HUCK

Agent Colette Vasco is a serious woman, though not unkind. She has a niece Maia's age, her sister's daughter, and they're very close. Agent Vasco knows that being twelve isn't easy, and she understands how difficult things must be for Maia right now with the sudden loss of her mother. She agrees to come get the money while Maia is at school.

"I'm sorry to say, I have to bring a search team, including a drug dog, but if all goes according to plan, Maia will never know we've been there."

Huck is grateful. A team of four show up, along with a German shepherd named Comanche. Comanche does a quick, frenetic tour of the house, although he's in and out of Huck's room in a matter of seconds, which makes Huck wonder if maybe it *does* smell like rotting fish.

Comanche is tied up in the shade outside while the team comes in to retrieve the money from under Huck's bed. Then they systematically search the rest of Huck's house. Huck would be worried about them invading Maia's room but it looks like it's already been ransacked. There are clothes *everywhere;* supplies for Maia's bath-bomb business are spread across her desk, and hair products and makeup cover the surface of the dresser. There's also a fair amount of trash—wrappers from Clif Bars, half-full cans of LaCroix coconut seltzer.

"Maybe you could clean up while you're in there," Huck jokes. The FBI agents don't so much as crack a smile. They aren't humans, they're robots, Huck thinks. Robots on a mission. Fine; Huck will leave them to it. He peers into Rosie's room—Vasco herself is on her knees, pawing through the dresser drawers—then he goes into the kitchen, does a shot of Flor de Caña, and heads out to the deck, where he smokes three cigarettes in quick succession and keeps an eye on the southern waters for the *Mississippi*.

Adam is taking the charter by himself today; Huck called and told him that something came up and he couldn't get away.

Agent Vasco lets Huck know that they haven't found anything else of interest. They are taking the cash, and Vasco asks for the numbers of Rosie's savings and checking accounts.

"I realize how difficult it must have been to call us about that money," Agent Vasco says. She lays a hand on Huck's arm. Her nails are polished shell pink and she wears no wedding ring; Huck checks out of habit. Agent Vasco is an attractive woman, a redhead like Huck, and she has a salty-sweet aspect that reminds Huck of his ex-wife, Kimberly. And, for that matter, LeeAnn. Huck puts Agent Vasco at about thirty-five, still young enough to want children, which is too young for Huck. He's encouraged that he's even thinking this way; it's taking his mind off Irene.

When he next talks to Irene, he'll tell her how attractive Agent Vasco is. Maybe she'll get jealous.

"That wasn't money I earned and I doubt it was money Rosie earned," Huck says. He hands over the statements from Rosie's bank accounts. "If Rosie is guilty by association of something...well, it's my job to make sure it doesn't affect Maia in any way."

"I understand," Agent Vasco says. "I was really hoping I might find something of a more personal nature in Rosie's room. Letters, or a diary."

Diary, Huck thinks. Rosie kept a diary when she was younger. She used to threaten LeeAnn with it, saying that future generations would someday learn what a mean witch

LeeAnn was, how harsh and unfair she was to her only child. Huck has no idea if Rosie kept up her diary-writing into her adult years. Because she worked nights at La Tapa, most of her downtime was during the day, when Huck was at work and Maia at school.

Letters? Well, there might be letters from Russell Steele if this were 1819 or even 1989, but nowadays people didn't write letters; they wrote to each other on their phones.

"I'm sure Rosie had her phone *with* her."

"Yes," Agent Vasco says. "We've subpoenaed the records."

Subpoenaed sounds serious, but of course, Rosie had a huge amount of cash stuffed into a drawer.

"If you don't mind my asking, what kind of crimes are you investigating?" Huck is thinking drugs, obviously. It's the Caribbean.

"I'm not at liberty to say. Also, we aren't really sure what we're dealing with here." Agent Vasco offers Huck a tight smile. "If we have any further questions, I'll be in touch."

"That's it?" Huck says. "You're leaving me?"

"Yes," Agent Vasco says. "You should be happy." She gathers the goons and they follow her out to the car with two black duffel bags filled with the money.

Easy come, easy go, Huck thinks.

Agent Vasco and company drive down Jacob's Ladder's series of switchbacks; Huck spies the car once, twice, three times—then they disappear. At nearly the same moment, Huck sees the *Mississippi* gliding across Rendezvous

Bay. Today's charter was a couple of state troopers from Alaska. Apparently, these two are famous; they're featured on some reality-TV show, which Huck has a difficult time fathoming. Huck has less than no interest in celebrities; what makes him regret missing today is that these gentlemen really wanted to fish. Huck nearly calls Adam to tell him to turn around and pick him up at the Westin dock, but that's impractical, a waste of time and gas.

It's only ten o'clock and Huck doesn't have to get Maia until three. He could read his book—he still hasn't finished the Connelly—and, he supposes, he could go to the beach. He hasn't been in a long time; whenever Maia wanted to go, Rosie would take her. LeeAnn used to love sitting on Gibney, and Huck loved LeeAnn so he would join her there, though left to his own devices, he would go to Little Lameshur, far, far away from the crowded north shore. Should Huck pack up a fish sandwich and drive out to Little Lameshur? Maybe live really large and stop at the Tourist Trap for a lobster roll on the way? The idea is novel enough to be intriguing, but then Huck thinks about one of Agent Vasco's comments: *We aren't really sure what we're dealing with here.*

Huck isn't sure what they're dealing with either, but he does know one thing: he was relieved when the dog didn't go pawing at the floorboards and they didn't discover blocks of cocaine or heroin to go along with all that money.

Someone on this island must know more than Huck does. The coconut telegraph is real. Huck picks up his phone and calls Rupert.

* * *

Because Rupert doesn't like to leave Coral Bay, he and Huck meet at Skinny Legs. It turns out, it's as good a place as any to have a quiet conversation in the middle of a gorgeous sunny day. Skinny Legs is the quintessential Caribbean bar. It's tucked into a grove of shade trees a few hundred feet from the lip of Coral Bay. The bar itself looks like a lean-to built by Robinson Crusoe after a few rum punches. It's open to the air on one side and features picnic tables thick with paint and a little stage for live music from happy hour until last call. There's an adjacent gift shop that sells souvenirs celebrating all things Skinny Legs; Huck has never set foot in it. In Huck's opinion, Skinny Legs' only fault is that it's gotten so famous. The best way to ruin a place is to make it popular.

One of the things that keeps Skinny Legs authentic is that characters like Rupert still hang out here. Rupert is the prince of the establishment, if you can call a sixty-something-year-old man a prince. He's in his usual spot, corner stool on the right-hand side; he has a Bud Light in front of him. Huck checks the time: eleven fifteen. He still has more than three hours before he has to pick up Maia from school, and for this conversation, he probably needs something stronger than an iced tea. He flags down Heidi, the bartender.

"Painkiller, please," Huck says.

Rupert chuckles. "That's a woman's drink."

"I'm not allowed to say things like that in my house," Huck says. "Don't you know any better?" He takes a stool and rubs the top of Rupert's bald brown head.

They fall into their usual pattern of conversation, which is distinguished by long pauses and subsequent non sequiturs. Rupert doesn't like to be rushed; he's retired now and has earned the right to mull things over, and if his mind wanders in the process, oh, well. Rupert has lived on St. John his entire life; his family goes back generations, and Huck teases him by saying that Rupert's ancestors invented the concept of island time, but Rupert is the one who perfected it.

Huck drinks one painkiller and waves to Heidi for another before Rupert finishes summarizing his list of physical ailments: his back has been giving him trouble, his right toe throbs in the rain, he can't sleep more than three hours without having to get up to take a piss. Then it's Huck's turn to talk about how the fish are running. Better since the new year, he says—meaning since Rosie died, meaning since Irene set foot on his boat and into his life.

"Good to hear it," Rupert says. "And how's Maia?"

Huck tells Rupert about taking Maia to town with her friends and how that bothers him.

Rupert laughs. "It's a goddamned island, Huck. How much trouble can she get in? All the West Indian ladies who grew up with your wife have eyes in the backs of their heads. If Maia takes so much as a puff of a cigarette, you'll hear the crowing all the way up on Jacob's Ladder."

Huck shakes his head. "They don't smoke anymore, Rupert. They vape. It's electronic, thing looks like a pen. They put a pod in it—"

"Don't tell me," Rupert says. "I don't want to know."

"It's all happening so fast. And I don't like the timing, her getting so independent right after her mother dies." This is when Maia would be most vulnerable to vaping and drinking and—Huck can barely let himself think it—*sex.* He has to find a way to make sure she grows up responsibly. Honestly, he could use some help.

They're quiet a few minutes. The song in the background is Warren Zevon's "Lawyers, Guns, and Money." Huck isn't sure Rupert is listening to the music, but it feels like a natural segue. "So I had a visit this morning," Huck says. "From the FBI."

Huck can sense his friend's invisible antennae rising.

"That's why I called you, actually," Huck says. "To see if you know something I don't."

"Funny you should ask," Rupert says. "Because I heard federal officers paid a visit to the Welcome to Paradise Real Estate office."

"Really?" Huck says. "Paulette Vickers—"

"Paulette and Doug Vickers and the little boy are gone," Rupert says. "Rumor has it they left last night on the car barge."

"*Left* as in…"

"*Left* as in *left,*" Rupert says.

Left *as in* left. Paulette and Douglas Vickers, who owned Welcome to Paradise Real Estate, pulled their young son, Windsor, out of school and packed what they needed into Doug's pickup and left twelve hours before the FBI showed up. That was the story Rupert heard from Sadie, one of his many girlfriends, and Sadie's gossip was generally known to be reliable.

On his way home, Huck drives past the office, and sure enough, there's the black SUV parked out front, its presence as ominous as a hearse.

The question that bothers Huck is this: How did Paulette and Douglas Vickers know that the FBI were coming? Did they find out Huck had contacted Agent Vasco? Was Huck's phone compromised? Was there a bug somewhere *in his house?* If so, would the FBI have found it this morning in their search? Huck lights a cigarette. He needs to get a grip. This is the stuff of movies and Connelly novels. This is not daily life in the Virgin Islands.

At three o'clock, he's waiting out in front of the Gifft Hill School when Maia emerges with her cronies Joanie, Colton, and Bright.

Here we go again, Huck thinks.

Maia studies his expression. "You okay, Gramps? You in a bad mood again?"

He meant what he told Agent Vasco. He is determined to keep whatever Rosie was involved with away from Maia. She's a twelve-year-old girl who wants to hang out with her friends. It's a goddamned island. She's safe here.

But really, he could use some help.

"I'm fine," he says. He won't smile because then Maia will *know* there's something wrong, so he adopts the air of a weary chauffeur. "You guys can all hop in."

BAKER

He knows he shouldn't be surprised that his brother came back down to St. John and, apparently, plans to make it his permanent home, sponging off Irene, but he is. He tells Cash as much, though instead of using the word *sponging,* he calls it "taking full advantage of Mom's generosity." It's marginally kinder; after all, Floyd is listening.

"I'm not taking advantage any more than you are," Cash says with what Baker can only assume is a phony smile. "And I found a job."

"So soon?" Baker says. "Where?"

"First mate on *Treasure Island,*" Cash says.

First mate on *Treasure Island*? It takes Baker a second, but he puts it together. *Treasure Island* is the boat that Ayers works on.

"You have got to be"—he swallows the swearword because of Floyd—"kidding me."

"Not kidding," Cash says.

Not kidding; of course not kidding. Somehow Cash weaseled his way onto that boat and into near-daily interaction with Ayers.

"I didn't realize you liked the water," Baker says. "I thought you were more of a mountain guy." He says this with relative equanimity. What he's thinking is this: *You*

hate water unless it's frozen! You're ten thousand feet out of your comfort zone! The only reason you're here is to try and steal my girl! "How did you find out about the job, anyway?"

"Ayers texted me," Cash says. He rubs Winnie under the chin. "Winnie and I just went for a hike and a swim with Ayers and Maia on the Johnny Horn Trail. It was beautiful, but man, was it hot. I was dreaming about this pool the whole way back." Cash pries off his hiking boots and strips down to his swim trunks. Baker tries to look at his brother objectively. Cash is in good shape; he has six-pack abs and really strong legs from all the skiing, but he's not quite six feet tall, so Baker has always discounted him as a possible rival. But now, Baker has all kinds of troubling thoughts. Maybe Ayers is into the short, stocky, and (admittedly) super-cut look as opposed to the tall, broad-shouldered, and (admittedly) dad-bod look. (Baker flexes his arm behind him to see if he still has triceps. Maybe; it's hard to tell.) Cash went hiking and swimming with Ayers and Maia—he's been the recipient of Ayers's smile. It's Baker's fantasy.

He's jealous.

His first instinct is to be a jerk about it. But honestly, he doesn't want to do battle with Cash over Ayers. He doesn't want to do battle with Cash over anything. He finds he's actually psyched—and relieved—that Cash is here. Baker talked a big game about moving down here but he doesn't know a soul except for Ayers and, sort of, Huck, and he has nothing in the way of a support system. He can continue to day-trade and he can accept Anna's offer of financial help, but he needs to see if life here is sustainable—school for Floyd, some kind of job for himself that's part-time with flexible hours that will get him out of the house and into the community. He could even volunteer.

"How's Maia doing?" Baker asks. "Was she...okay seeing you?"

"Surprisingly, yes," Cash says. "She seems great. I mean, don't get me wrong, she had a moment or two where she almost broke down—"

"I'm going down the slide," Floyd announces. "Uncle Cash, are you getting in?"

Cash jumps into the pool and swims over to a spot where he can watch Floyd go down the slide to the lower pool.

"But, I mean, generally, she was okay. She's a smart kid. She was teaching me about the island's history and the plants and trees—"

"Maybe I'll apply for a job with the National Park Service," Baker says.

Cash gives him an incredulous look and Baker thinks it's probably justified. Being a park ranger must require years in forestry school or some such.

"And before you ask, Ayers is still with Mick. I saw them together at La Tapa last night."

"He'll cheat on her again," Baker says.

"Agreed," Cash says. He holds Baker's gaze for a second and Baker can tell they're thinking the same thing: Once Mick cheats on her again, it'll be brother against brother.

Or maybe not, Baker thinks. Maybe Cash will realize

that he and Ayers should just remain friends. Maybe Cash will fall for one of the young, single women who climb aboard *Treasure Island*.

"What's up with Anna?" Cash asks.

"She and Louisa have accepted positions at the Cleveland Clinic," Baker says. "They're moving to Shaker Heights. Floyd will go there holidays and summers. That's why we decided to move down here. There's nothing tethering us to Houston anymore."

"Great minds think alike," Cash says. "I was going to head to Breck to ski but it's too late in the season for me to get a decent job. Then Ayers told me about *Treasure Island*. I start my lifesaving classes on Monday."

Baker is surprised that Cash is so organized; it sounds like he's thought something through for once. Objectively, Baker has to admit that Cash would be great as a first mate on a tour boat. When Baker and Anna visited Cash in Breckenridge, they had a chance to see him in action as a group ski instructor and they had both been impressed. Cash was friendly, engaging, funny, kind, and patient—his patience had been astonishing, in fact.

"What would Dad think," Baker asks, "if he could see us together right now?"

Cash raises his eyebrows. "The more relevant question is, what would *Mom* think? I talked to her yesterday and she didn't tell me you were coming down. Does she even know?"

Baker eases himself into the pool and swims over to Cash. He peers down at Floyd, splashing in the lower pool. "She doesn't."

"Why didn't you *tell* her?"

"I'm not sure," Baker says. "Probably because I didn't want her to stop me."

"Legally, it's *her* house," Cash says. "I'm not trying to be a jerk but my advice is to call her and tell her you're here."

Baker knows Cash is right. "I will," he says. "I'll call her tonight after Floyd is asleep."

Before Cash can respond, Baker hears the strains of "Blitzkrieg Bop," by the Ramones—and Cash pushes himself up out of the pool. He pulls his cell phone out of his hiking shorts, looks at the screen, and says, "Well, guess what, it's Mom."

"Good," Baker says. "Tell her I'm here. She'll like it better coming from you anyway."

Cash says, "Hello, Mother Alarm Clock, what's up? Good, yeah...I saw Maia today. Ayers and I took her on a hike, or she took *us* on a hike, actually...yeah, I start Monday, they said I'll be good to go in a week. Hey, listen, I have some news...oh, all right. No, you go first."

There's a pause during which Baker can hear the tinny sound of Irene's voice over the phone and Baker grows hot and uncomfortable. He just wants Cash to spit it out already! Baker checks on Floyd, who is splashing around, happy as can be, like a model only child. Baker will check out preschools for Floyd.

When Baker phoned Anna and told her that he and Floyd were considering moving down to St. John on a somewhat permanent basis, Anna had accepted the news the way she accepted everything he said: with indifference.

"It's nice there," Anna said. "I'll have to see what Louisa thinks—"

"It doesn't matter what Louisa thinks," Baker said. "She doesn't get to weigh in on my decisions."

"But Floyd..." Anna says. He recognized her distracted tone of voice; she was probably writing in someone's chart while she was talking to him.

"Louisa isn't Floyd's mother," Baker said. "You are. Now, assuming I find a suitable school for our child, do you have any objections to Floyd and me spending some time in St. John? The vacation schedule will be the same. Nothing changes except he won't be in Houston. Do you object?"

"No," Anna said. "I guess not..."

"Wonderful, thank you," Baker said, and he hung up before she could change her mind.

Baker is yanked back into the present moment when he hears Cash say, "A week from *Monday?*"

A week from Monday what? Baker wonders.

"Well, you're in for a nice surprise," Cash says. "Because guess who else is here—Baker and Floyd!"

Pause. Baker hears his mother's voice, maybe a little more high-pitched than before.

"Yep, I guess Anna took a job in Cleveland and so Baker and Floyd are...yep, they're here now. Yes, Mom, I think that's the plan." Cash locks eyes with Baker and starts nodding. "Yes, it *will* be so nice, all of us together."

All of us together? Does this mean what Baker thinks it means?

"Just text to let us know what ferry you'll be on," Cash

says. "And one of us will be there to pick you up. A week from Monday."

That night, they grill steaks and asparagus and Baker makes his potato packets in foil and he and Cash and Floyd devour everything and Baker remembers that it's nice cooking for people who actually appreciate it. Floyd goes inside to watch *Despicable Me 3* for the ten thousandth time and Baker and Cash stare out at the scattering of lights across the water.

"So Mom is coming a week from Monday," Baker says. He's not sure how he feels about this. "There are obviously pluses and minuses to this situation."

"Agreed," Cash says. "On the plus side, we have been through a family crisis. If Mom stayed in Iowa, I would worry about her."

"I can't believe she quit her job," Baker says.

"She wants a change, she says."

"But working on Huck's fishing boat? Mom? She's a fifty-seven-year-old woman. She must have been kidding about that."

"Don't you remember the way she used to wake us up at dawn on Clark Lake to go out on Pop's flat-bottom boat to fish for bass? Mom took us, not Dad. Mom baited our hooks. Mom taught us how to cast."

"Yeah, I do," Baker says. He hasn't thought of it in eons but suddenly he has a vivid picture of being out on Clark Lake before the sun was even fully up, Irene yanking on the starter of the outboard motor, then Irene driving the boat to the spot where the smallmouth bass were biting.

Irene had indeed taught both Baker and Cash to cast. She had shown them how to reel in a fish after they felt a tug on the line. She had deftly worked the hook from the fish's mouth, using one gloved hand to hold the fish and one hand to maneuver her Gerber tool. Irene could snap fishing line with her teeth. She could fillet a bass or a perch so expertly that there were no bones to worry about when it came off the charcoal grill that evening at dinner. Baker had forgotten that his mother liked to fish, but even now that he remembers, he wonders if this is really what she wants to do for a living. Maybe she needs a break, a respite, a time to recharge and reset.

Maybe that's what they all need.

"On the minus side," Cash says, "we'll be grown men living with our mother."

"Sexy," Baker says.

"But the house is big," Cash says.

"The house *is* big," Baker says. And it'll be nice to have an extra person to watch Floyd. He won't mention that, however, lest Cash call him a self-involved bastard.

Later that night, Baker wants to go out. The dishes are done and Baker has read to Floyd and tucked him in. Baker also showed him how their bedrooms connect; the house feels more familiar this time around.

Baker finds Cash collapsed in a heap in front of a basketball game. He considers slipping out the door—he needs to go to town; he needs to see Ayers—but he can't just leave with Floyd asleep upstairs. "Hey, Cash?"

"Yeah." Cash doesn't move his eyes from the TV.

"I'm going out for a little while, man," Baker says. "Or I'd like to. If you could just…keep one ear open in case Floyd wakes up?"

"Yeah, of course," Cash says.

Baker lets his breath go.

"Are you going into town to see Ayers?" Cash asks.

Baker considers lying, but what can he say? That he's going to the grocery store? Out for a nightcap? Cash will know better.

"Yeah," Baker admits.

"She asked about you today on the hike," Cash says.

Baker's heart feels like a speeding car without brakes. "She did?"

"She said you didn't call her after you left." Cash pauses. "Were you really that stupid?"

Yes, Baker thinks, he was. There had been dozens of times when Baker thought to reach out, but, honestly, he hadn't seen the point. He had been stuck in Houston…until Anna announced she was leaving. "I was that stupid," Baker says.

"My guess is she has a thing for you," Cash says. "Don't mess it up."

Cash's tone indicates that he fully believes Baker *will* mess it up. It's true that Baker's track record with women hasn't been great. He chose to marry a woman who didn't love him, who may or may not have liked men at all. But Ayers is different. It's as though Baker had been on a quest without even realizing it—until he found exactly what he was looking for.

He's not going to mess it up.

Baker wonders why Cash is being so cool about Ayers. He seems relaxed and at ease in a way that is very un-Cash-like. Maybe it's some kind of trap. Or maybe the island is working its magic.

"Thanks, man," Baker says. "I mean it, Cash. Thank you."

"Good luck," Cash says.

Good luck. Baker turns up the radio in the Jeep; the excellent station out of San Juan—104.3 the Buzz—is playing the Red Hot Chili Peppers. Baker sings along, woefully off-key, but who cares; he's got the windows open and the sweet night air is rushing in. Baker hasn't felt this sense of freedom, this sense of *possibility,* since he was in high school. He's nervous. He has *butterflies.*

He drives into town at ten thirty and things are still lively; it's Saturday night. He worries that to see Ayers, he'll have to go to La Tapa for a drink—he really wanted to be sober and clearheaded tonight—but then he spots her leaving the restaurant, wearing cutoff jean shorts and a T-shirt and a pair of Chucks, a suede bag hitched over her shoulder.

She reaches up and releases her hair from its bun. She is so strong and composed and self-possessed. Baker is dazzled. He has been dazzled by women before, of course—when he watched Anna pull a splinter out of Floyd's foot with one quick, precise movement; when his old girlfriend Trinity knotted a cherry stem with her tongue (Baker still doesn't understand how people *do* that)—but Ayers is different. She's flawless.

Baker drives up alongside her and rolls the window down. He thinks about trying to be funny—*Hey, little girl, want some candy?*—but there's no way he'll be able to pull it off.

"Ayers," he says. "Hi."

She stops, ducks her head to peer into the car. They lock eyes.

"Baker," she says. She holds his gaze and the two of them knit together somehow. He can't speak so he nods his head toward the passenger seat. She runs around the front of the car, opens the door, climbs in, and fastens her seat belt.

"Wow," she says. "I can't believe I'm doing this."

"Where to?" he asks.

"Hawksnest Beach," she says. "I'll show you the way."

ROSIE

February 22, 2006

I'm afraid to write down exactly what happened with Russ but I'm afraid not to write it down because what if I forget and my weekend with him is washed away like a heart drawn in the sand?

There was sex, a lot of sex, and it was the best sex of my life, but I have only Oscar to compare it to and if there's one thing I can say about Oscar, it's that he's selfish and greedy and arrogant and any time I opened my mouth to ask him to change his style, he took offense and kept on doing things the same way because in his mind, he knew the path to my pleasure better than I did.

I faked a lot with Oscar. I faked so much that I got quite skilled at it and I assumed I would have to fake it with Russell from Iowa City because, well, let's just say he was older and grayer and not at all in shape. But, man, was I surprised at how…good he was to me. He was gentle and firm and confident when he touched my body and he was also appreciative, maybe even reverent. The sex was so sublime that I started to feel both jealous of and guilty about his wife, Irene.

At one point I said to Russ, "I hope your wife knows how lucky she is to have you."

Russ laughed. "I doubt she would describe herself that way. And not that you asked, but my wife and I don't have sex like this. We don't have sex much at all. Like I said, in Irene's eyes, I'm a day late and a dollar short in nearly everything I do. Her main attitude toward me is weary disappointment. Which kind of kills the magic."

On Saturday night I sneaked out of his room at three o'clock in the morning and got back to Jacob's Ladder at three thirty. I somehow managed to get in the house without waking Mama, who is a very light sleeper.

Russ and I had planned to spend the day together on Sunday but I had to be careful, so careful, because the island has eyes and very loose lips. Turns out, Russ's friend and po-

tential new boss, Todd Croft, had left behind the skiff from the yacht for Russ to use, although Russ admitted he didn't feel comfortable navigating in unfamiliar waters. "Leave the driving to me," I said. I was off all day Sunday and Sunday night, so I went to church with Mama, which normally I hated, but I needed to ask forgiveness for the sins I had already committed as well as the ones I was about to commit. I told Mama I was going to Salomon Bay for the day, then straight to a barbecue, and I'd be home late.

Mama said, "You got home late last night, mon chou.*" (She uses the French phrases that she picked up in Paris when she's displeased; it's a signal I alone understand.) "I want you to tell me right now that you are not back involved with Oscar. I've heard he's been sniffing around."*

Estella must have been talking to Dearie, who did my mother's hair. I faced her on the stone walk outside the Catholic church and said, "Mama, I am not involved with Oscar."

Her expression was dubious but my words contained conviction. "Better not be," she said.

Even though we were traveling over water, which was a lot safer than land, I had to be sneaky. I left my car at the National Park Service sign as though I had indeed headed to Salomon Bay, but instead I hiked down to the public part of Honeymoon Beach and cut through the back way so that I popped out of the trees in a place where I could wade to the skiff, which I did, holding my bag above my head. Russ was waiting for me with a cooler and a picnic basket he'd asked the hotel to pack. I started the motor on the first try, and we were off.

It was an idyllic day. The water sparkled in the sun; the air had a rare scrubbed-clean feel, as though it had just received a benediction. It was as fine a performance by planet Earth as I had ever seen. Russ had on bathing trunks, a long-sleeved T-shirt, and a baseball cap that said IOWA CITY ROTARY CLUB, which made me chuckle because, really, what was I doing with this guy? And yet I liked him. Just as I thought I had him pegged as one kind of person—he had just ended his second term on the Iowa City school board; he was encouraging his mother, Milly, to move into a retirement community but she was having none of it—he would pull out a surprise. Like the way he stroked behind my knee in a spot so sweet and sensitive, I had a hard time concentrating.

We anchored off of Little Cinnamon because the cliff above was undeveloped so no one would be spying on us with binoculars for voyeuristic purposes. Russ unpacked the cooler—there was a nice bottle of Sancerre for me, the Chavignol, which I loved, and a couple of cold beers for Russ. There were slender baguette sandwiches with duck, arugula, and fig jam, and as I ate one, all I could think of was Remy the chef preparing them, having no idea that one was for me. There was also a container of truffled potato salad and a couple of lemon tarts, and I thought of how nice it was to be on the receiving end of Caneel's hospitality for once.

We puttered along the north shore as far as Waterlemon Cay, where we stopped again because, although we hadn't brought snorkeling gear, you could watch turtles pop their heads above the surface for air and Russ loved that. It was *hot enough that we both decided to jump in for a swim and Russ held me in the water, his arms incredibly strong for a corn-syrup salesman or whatever he was. We kissed, and I thought,* What are we doing here at Waterlemon Cay when we have a perfectly good hotel room?

I said, "Do you think you'll take the job?"

"It's hard to say no. The signing bonus is nearly as much as I make in a year right now."

"If you take the job, will you spend more time down here?" Unfortunately, my voice betrayed what I was really asking: Would I ever see him again? *I was afraid the answer would be no; I was afraid the answer would be yes. What we were doing was wrong. He was married with two sons in high school and he must have been trying not to imagine what they would think if they could see him at that moment. But...it was as if we were living in a sealed bubble. One weekend in February in the sixth year of the new millennium, this happened. I had a vague idea that affairs like this could actually improve a marriage. Russ would return to Iowa City with not only a big job offer but also a sense of power and virility, and Irene would see him in a new light. They would renew their vows, go on a second honeymoon.*

And for me—well, things wouldn't be awful for me either. I had faith in men again. The ghost of Oscar was permanently banished; every time I thought of him helpless and whimpering in Russ's grip, I thought, How pathetic. *I would venture forth with my self-esteem and self-worth restored. I would meet someone like Russ—kind, thoughtful, secure, adult—and that would blossom into the relationship that this could never be.*

Our affair would be almost excusable if this all turned out to be the case. But even as I had these pretty and nice thoughts about us both going our own ways after this without any looking back, I felt my heart stirring up trouble. Maybe Russ was experiencing the same thing, because he looked genuinely crestfallen as he said, "You know, I'm really not sure. I know there will be travel with this job but I think it'll be in dull places like Palm Beach and Midland, Texas. I think Todd just brought me down here to woo me."

"Okay," I said, trying to keep my tone light and unconcerned. "Let's go back to the hotel, then, and properly enjoy the time we have left."

We did just that, and it was wonderful—not only the sex, but also falling asleep in that luscious bed with our limbs intertwined.

When I woke up, he was staring at me just like the leading man in the movies looks at his leading lady—right before he betrays her or kills her or carries her off into the sunset.

"You're exquisite," he said. "And just now, watching you sleep, I felt so… privileged. Like I've been granted a private viewing of the Mona Lisa.*"*

"Everyone says the Mona Lisa *is so beautiful," I said. "But frankly, I don't get it."*

This made Russ laugh and he reached over to the nightstand and plucked a pale pink hibiscus blossom out of a water glass. He tucked it behind my ear.

"You're right," he said. "You're far prettier than the Mona Lisa.*"*

I swatted him to downplay how happy that made me—

show me a woman who doesn't like being compared to a masterpiece—then said, "I'm starving."

It was dark outside. The bedside clock said twenty past nine. It was too late to get dinner anywhere on this sleepy island, besides which I was basically in hiding. So we ordered room service, lavishly, recklessly, like we were rock stars on the last leg of a world tour—one bacon cheeseburger, one lobster pizza, French fries, a Caesar salad, the key lime pie, a hot fudge sundae, and, of course, conch fritters, because now that was our "thing." I would never see Russell Steele again but every time I put in an order of conch fritters, I would think of him. I told him this and he threw me down on the bed and said, "God, Rosie, how can I ever leave you? I'm…different now, in such a short time. I'm changed." He was putting words to what I felt as well. I had tears in my eyes as I tried to control my crazy, runaway heart.

Don't leave me, I nearly said—which would have been pathetic after a relationship of only twenty-four or forty-eight hours (depending on how you looked at it)—but I was saved from myself by a knock at the door.

It was room service with our food, which I knew would be delivered by Woodrow, so I had to go hide in the bathroom while Russ answered the door.

I stayed overnight Sunday; Todd Croft and the other guy, the company lawyer, Stephen, were due to pick Russ up at noon. I had been up since dawn worrying about how the goodbye would go and I even brazenly wandered out to the beach where I saw my donkeys, Stop, Drop, and Roll, eating grass at the edge of the beach. I decided to take their presence as a positive omen. This is my home, this is where I belong, and I need to find someone who calls St. John home as well. The reason that getting involved with a married man is wrong is that it hurts. I knew that if it continued one minute past noon today, it would be destructive. What did I want Russ to do? Go home and tell his wife that he was leaving her for some woman half his age with whom he'd had a fling in the Caribbean?

Hell no!

We lay in bed together until the last possible minute. Then Russ showered and dressed and I thought, What can I give him to remember me by? *I wished I'd dived down at Waterlemon and picked up a shell or a piece of coral—some island token—but I hadn't. And so I rummaged through the desk in the room and found a postcard with a picture of the Sugar Mill on the front, and I wrote,* I'm going to miss you. *I signed it with the initials* M.L., *for Mona Lisa. I wasn't sure he would figure that out, but I enjoyed imagining him puzzling over it. I stuck the postcard in the side zip pocket of his bag and right as he was gathering up his things to go, I told him I'd left him a surprise in that pocket that he should look at before returning home. The last thing I wanted was for Irene to find it.*

He held my face in his hands. Out the window I could see the yacht anchored and a crew member pulling the skiff around (it fit, somehow, underneath the boat or inside of it). Russ kissed me hard and deep. It was the kiss you give someone when you're absolutely, positively never going to see her again.

"I don't have anything to leave you with except for that," he said. Then he turned and left the room and I was so addled, so undone, that I hung in the doorway and watched him trudge through the sand. He raised an arm to Todd Croft, who was standing on the deck of the boat.

Bluebeard was the yacht's name. I hadn't noticed that before.

I saw Todd Croft see me; his head tilted and his smile grew wider, and I disappeared into the shadows of the room, cursing myself. I was wearing my swim cover-up. If Todd asked, Russ could say we'd struck up a friendship and I'd come to say goodbye. It didn't matter, I would likely never see Todd Croft again, but I regretted not leaving first. I should have headed for home an hour or two earlier, but that would have meant losing time with Russ, and I hadn't wanted to do that. For my greed, then, I was punished. I became the one who was left behind.

As I drove home, I thought of how the weekend had been a Cinderella story, minus the part with the glass slipper. I was returned to my ordinary self, in my proverbial rags, facing my scullery work. The only part of that magical story I could claim was that I had enjoyed a night (in my case, two nights) of bliss. I had successfully charmed a prince, only the prince was a midwestern corn-syrup salesman. A married corn-syrup salesman.

Mama was at work when I got home, despite the holiday, and I was momentarily relieved. Now I'm locked in my room, writing this down, because supposedly "getting it out" is a kind of catharsis. I have an hour left to get ready before

I have to go back to Caneel, where I will work and pretend that everything is just fine.

February 23, 2006

I've decided that Bluebeard *is an appropriate name for the yacht that delivered Russ to me and then took him away.*
He was a pirate.
He stole my heart.

March 30, 2006

Mama was the one who noticed that I looked peaked and that I wasn't eating much. When had I ever said no to her blackened mahi tacos with pineapple-mango salsa? Never was the answer. But they just didn't seem appealing. Nothing seemed appealing.

She said, "Do you want to come to the clinic at lunchtime tomorrow and I'll slide you in?"

I couldn't tell her that I was suffering from a broken heart, and there's no cure for that except time, and for all the technological advances going on in the world, no one has figured out how to speed time up or slow it down—or stop it. Whoever figures out that trick is going to be rich. "Nah," I said.

"No, but thanks for offering," Mama prompted.

I retreated to my room. I needed to put less energy into pining for the pirate and more into saving money so I could get a place of my own.

Then, a couple of days ago, I woke up feeling dizzy and

nauseated and I thought, Damn it, I really am sick. *I had
planned to go to Salomon Bay—the best thing for me to do
was get back into a routine—but it looked like it would be
the clinic instead.*

*I raced to the bathroom and puked into the toilet. I heard
Mama knocking on my bedroom door, asking if I was all
right, and then I heard Huck say,* "LeeAnn, leave the poor
girl alone, no one likes to be bothered when they're praying
to the porcelain god."

And Mama said, "You're right, handsome. I'll leave her
be. She'll be okay as long as it's not morning sickness."

Morning sickness, *I thought.*

*It was off to the Chelsea drugstore for a test, but I had to
wait until my mother's friend Fatima left for lunch because
Rosie Small buying a pregnancy test would win Fatima a gold
medal in the Gossip Olympics.*

I hurried home, praying, praying, *and then I peed on the
stick.*

I'm pregnant.

April 30, 2006

*Today a package addressed to me was hand-delivered to the
house. The package contained ten thousand dollars in cash.*

I'm being bought off.

*There wasn't a note but I don't have to be a wizard to
know the money is from Todd Croft. But has Todd Croft told
Russ that I'm pregnant?*

Let me go back.

When I found out I was pregnant four weeks ago, all I could think was that I needed to tell Russ. I was pretty sure he would offer to help. And by help, *a part of me was thinking he would leave his wife, move to St. John, and raise this baby with me. It was a long shot, I knew, but not impossible. Maybe instead of making Russ's marriage stronger, the weekend affair (I'm shying away from the word* fling) *had been a breaking point. Maybe Russ would say yes to the job and goodbye to Irene and start a whole new life. The boys were teenagers; the older boy was headed to college in the fall and the younger one was only a year or two behind, so they were nearly out of the house. If anyone was poised for a second act, it was Russ.*

Or so I let myself momentarily believe.

I called Iowa City information and asked for the phone number for Russell or Irene Steele.

"Irene Steele," the operator said. "Hold for the number."

I hung up the phone. The listing was under Irene's name. She paid the bills. She was in charge of the household. She intimidated me—indeed, scared me—even from afar. I would never call the house, I decided. I wasn't that desperate.

I had to somehow circumvent Irene. I needed an e-mail. I knew there was probably an e-mail attached to the room reservation at Caneel. I had worked at Caneel long enough to know that all reservations were kept in a database, but that database couldn't be accessed on any of the restaurant computers.

So I would have to ask the restaurant manager, Estella, to get it for me.

I said to her, "Please don't tell my mother"—Estella rolled her eyes as if to say, Rosie-child, no matter how you implore me, you know I could never keep a secret from LeeAnn—"but a gentleman who stayed here over Presidents' Day weekend begged me for the conch-fritter recipe. He wants to give it to the chef at his country club so they can serve them at his wife's surprise birthday party and I promised him I'd send him the recipes for the fritters and the aioli. He gave me his e-mail, but I lost it, Estella. And I feel terrible. I remember he said his wife's birthday is May twenty-third because that's a day after mine and so time is of the essence. Can you help me find the man's e-mail, please, Estella? I want to provide the kind of service Caneel is famous for."

Estella huffed for a minute. Didn't I know that accessing the guests' personal information was forbidden?

I said, "But he already gave it to me and I lost it! It's his wife's fortieth birthday!"

Estella hesitated, then she ushered me into the back office, and together, we looked. The name Russell Steele didn't turn up in the system, which was perplexing. Had he used a fake name? Was he not only a pirate but an impostor?

Then I said, "Let's check the name Todd Croft." And it popped right up—room 718 for two nights, total bill $1,652. There was an e-mail, but it was Todd's, and my heart sank, though I did think it was encouraging that it was a BVI e-mail address.

I copied it down and thanked Estella, who closed the file and hurried us out of the office, saying, "That was the easy part. Good luck convincing Chef to hand over his recipes."

I wrote to Todd Croft, explained who I was, and said merely that I would like an e-mail address for Russ so that I could send him the conch-fritter and aioli recipes that he'd requested.

But I guess Mr. Croft saw right through my ploy because here I am, holding ten large.

I know I should feel insulted but all I feel is relieved. Because if Mama kicks me out, and she very well might, I'll have money to get a place for me and the baby.

I'm telling her tomorrow.

May 1, 2006

I was so nervous that I got out of bed early after barely sleeping all night. I couldn't wait another hour, another minute. Once I heard both Mama and Huck in the kitchen, I walked down the hall, comforted by the idea that in thirty seconds, the secret would be out. They could holler; they could scream, call me names, and cast me out, but all of that would pale against the relief of speaking the truth.

When Mama saw me, she was shocked. "Rosie? What are you doing awake? Is everything all right?"

In that second, everything was *still all right. Mama was dressed for work in her raspberry scrubs and her white lab coat, her towering bun wrapped in a brightly patterned scarf. She'd had her nails done—she was vain about her nails, and they were the same shade of raspberry—and I noticed her fingers against the white porcelain of her coffee cup. Every morning, Huck makes her coffee, one poached egg, and a piece of lightly buttered wheat toast. Huck was stand-*

*ing at the stove tending to the egg. He was wearing cargo
shorts with a lure hanging from the belt loop and a long-
sleeved T-shirt advertising the* Mississippi. *He had a bandanna wrapped around his neck and was ready for a day of
fishing. I didn't dread Huck's anger; what I dreaded was his
disappointment in me. We'd had a rocky start to our relationship. When he started courting Mama seven years ago,
I resented him. I thought,* He sees a single woman and her
wayward daughter and thinks they need to be saved—but
we *don't* need to be saved. *But I quickly grew to love Huck
and, yes, to count on him. I remember one time when he'd
told me to help myself to twenty bucks from his wallet so
I could go into town to meet my friends, I found a folded-
up, faded picture of Huck with another woman. The picture
was obviously old, from the seventies or eighties. In it, Huck
was a young man. He had a full head of strawberry-blond
hair and a mustache but no beard; he wore jeans with what
looked like a white patent-leather belt and a Led Zeppelin T-
shirt. The woman was in a crocheted chevron-print dress and
had on white patent-leather boots. Her blond hair was feath-
ered and she wore too much black eyeliner.*

*I took the picture to Huck and said, "Who's this?" Huck
had had a sister who had died of cancer and I thought maybe
this was her; he rarely talked about her but I knew her name
was Caroline.*

*"Her?" Huck said. I thought he might be angry that I'd
snooped in his wallet for more than just the twenty, but he
didn't seem angry. "That's my first wife, Kimberly."*

I was shocked *by this. I didn't know Huck had been
married before. I felt affronted, maybe even betrayed—for*

Mama's sake, but also my own. He and Mama had been married a year or two when I found this picture and the three of us had become a happy family. I didn't like the idea of sharing Huck with anyone. "I didn't realize you'd been married before." *I swallowed.* "Does my mother know?"

"Yes, of course," *he said. He smiled sadly.* "Sorry, Rosie, I should have told you. There just never seemed to be an appropriate time and it doesn't matter anyway."

"If it doesn't matter, why do you keep the picture?" *I asked. I handed it back to him, though really I wanted to tear it to shreds.*

"Well," *Huck said. He thought about it for a minute. One thing I love most about Huck is that he's a straight shooter. He doesn't candy-coat the truth or brush it away because he doesn't want me to see it.* "Kimberly ended up being a disappointment to me. She was an alcoholic, a really, really mean drunk, and that destroyed our marriage. It destroyed just about all of her relationships, actually. But in this picture, we were happy, so I keep it as a reminder that my time with her wasn't all bad." *He slipped the picture back into the wallet.* "In even the bleakest situations, there's usually some good to be salvaged."

Facing Mama and Huck to tell them I was pregnant was a bleak situation. Would any good be salvaged from it?

"I'm pregnant," *I said.*

Huck turned from the stove.

"What?" *Mama said.*

"I'm pregnant."

She set down her coffee cup and stood up. Her face was unreadable. Shock, I suppose. Huck was watching her.

"Oscar?" she said.

"Not Oscar," I said. "It was a man at the hotel, someone you don't know. I was stupid. He's gone now and I don't know how to reach him."

There was a moment of such profound silence that I felt like the world had stopped. She was probably deciding whether or not to believe me.

Then, finally, she opened her arms, and I entered them.

PART THREE

The Soggy Dollar

IRENE

Before she leaves for St. John, Irene has some loose ends to take care of.

A death certificate issued by the Department of Vital Statistics of the British Virgin Islands arrives in the mail in an unmarked envelope. Is it authentic? It seems so, though Irene has no way of knowing for sure.

So, obviously, Paulette received her message. There's no note, no invoice, no mention of a fee. Irene has assumed that Paulette is the one who pays to maintain the villa—taxes (do they *have* taxes in the Virgin Islands?), insurance, landscapers, repairs, et cetera—probably out of a fund that Russ or Todd Croft set up...with cash.

She takes the death certificate to Ed Sorley's office and drops it off with the receptionist, then leaves before Ed appears with questions.

She withdraws eight thousand dollars from the account at Federal Republic, using the drive-through window. The cash and the postcards from M.L. go right into Irene's suitcase.

* * *

At Lydia's insistence, Irene puts an obituary in the *Press-Citizen,* and she phones her close friends and neighbors to invite them to the house for a memorial reception. She tells them that Russ was killed in a helicopter crash; lightning was the cause. He was down in the Virgin Islands for work. He's been cremated and the ashes scattered. This is a small gathering so his friends can pay their respects.

"No food and no flowers," Irene told them. "I'm taking some time away, leaving Monday. If you feel you must do something to honor his passing, you can donate to the Rotary Club scholarship fund. It always goes to some terrific kid who really needs it."

Lydia arranges for the Linn Street Café to cater the reception and Irene is grateful. Under normal circumstances, she would insist on doing everything herself—but these aren't normal circumstances. The people from the café will drop off sandwiches, quiche, salads, and urns of coffee. Irene chills wine and rolls her drinks trolley into the parlor. With so many people in the room, it will be too warm to light a fire and Irene will be so busy visiting that she won't have time to tend it.

Irene is anxious about facing everyone. She doesn't want to be the recipient of sympathy or to be asked any probing questions. She nearly succumbs to the temptation of taking an Ativan right before the reception begins. She has the prescription bottle in her hand, but the doorbell rings and Irene hurries downstairs.

It's Lydia, attended by Brandon the barista, who looks

far more distinguished out of his leather apron. He's holding Lydia's hand, and with his other hand he offers Irene a platter of cookies.

"Homemade," he says. "Lemongrass sugar."

Irene tries out a smile. Lydia looks radiant. She and Brandon are delirious with infatuation, and Irene is, of course, happy for her friend. Brandon and Lydia take charge of setting out the food and cups for coffee and filling buckets with ice, leaving Irene idle to steep in her dread and count the minutes until she boards the plane.

The doorbell rings again. Irene mentally pulls herself up by her bootstraps. Compared to what she's been through already, this is nothing. This is easy.

And for a while, it's not so bad. The Kinseys arrive, followed by the Dunns; Ed Sorley and his wife, Anita; Dot, the nurse from Brown Deer; and some of the neighbors. Nearly everyone from the magazine attends, including Irene's boss, Joseph Feeney, Mavis Key, and the receptionist, Jayne, who brings her newly retired husband, Rooney. Rooney is something of a blunderbuss. He's always the first to get drunk and obnoxious at the holiday party. He speaks without thinking, he's a know-it-all; honestly, Irene can't stand him. Thankfully, he leaves Jayne to gush out the condolences.

"I'm so sorry, Irene, none of us had any idea! But it was unusual for you to be out for an entire week without any notice. Of course, once we learned that Milly had passed, it all made sense...none of us knew that Russ...I mean, you've had *such* a double whammy!"

A little while later, Irene notices Rooney pouring himself a scotch at the drinks trolley. She needs to find

Lydia and tell her to keep an eye on him. But she's too busy. She has to spend time with everyone, nodding her head and lying by omission.

Why is it the people you'd like to leave the party first are always the last to go? The party has thinned out to just Irene, Lydia and Brandon, Dot, Ed and Anita Sorley, and Jayne and Rooney. Irene finally allows herself to eat something— a lemongrass sugar cookie—and Brandon, ever the barista, steeps her a tea that he thinks will complement the cookie. Irene nearly laughs at the absurdity of the notion. *It's a cookie, Brandon,* she wants to say. Irene hasn't tasted anything since Russ died—except the fish that Huck grilled. That had been delicious.

Her thoughts are interrupted by Rooney, who raises his voice above the others and says, "Russ worked for a hedge fund, right? You're aware, I assume, that the Virgin Islands were recently added to a blacklist of tax havens by the EU? What kind of business was Russ involved in? Are you sure it was aboveboard?"

Brandon, possibly attempting to head Rooney away from the topic, makes things worse. "What does that mean, a blacklist of tax havens?" He looks around the room and shrugs. "I can explain the difference between a latte and an Americano, but tax havens confound me."

"What does it *mean?*" Rooney asks in a way that makes it clear he isn't sure what it means. He's sitting in the velvet-upholstered bergère chair, holding court now. "It means they conduct business without obeying the tax code. We're

talking money-laundering, numbered accounts at banks in Switzerland and the Cayman Islands, shell companies, dark money, terrorists, drug dealers, human traffickers..."

Irene shoots a look at Ed Sorley. *The Cayman Islands?*

Jayne emits a nervous laugh. "Rooney, *stop,*" she says. "You knew Russ. He was...well, he was the nicest man in the world is what he was."

"I second that," Dot says.

"Sometimes it's the nice guys who are the worst criminals," Rooney says. "Because they're the ones you'd least suspect of anything."

Irene stands up. "I'm feeling a little worn out," she says, and everyone takes the hint.

Monday afternoon, Irene's ferry pulls in among the powerboats and catamarans moored in Cruz Bay, and Irene scans the crescent of white sand that's home to a string of open-air restaurants backed by palm trees. She feels like she can breathe again. It's bizarre that the place her husband conducted his wild and massive deception has become her refuge. Irene doesn't want to overthink this and she doesn't want to fight it. She's now experiencing the emotions one *should* feel upon arriving on St. John: anticipation and joy.

Both of her boys are here, and her grandson. It feels like an embarrassment of riches, all of them choosing to be together this time, choosing to be in the paradise Russ unwittingly brought them to.

Cash had texted Irene the night before to let her know that today was his first day as a crew member aboard *Trea-*

sure Island. He thought he'd be back in time to pick Irene up, but if not, he'd send Baker. However, when Irene steps off the ferry and grabs her luggage—two rolling suitcases that contain sundresses, sandals, plenty of bathing suits, and some old fishing shirts that she used to wear out on Clark Lake—she doesn't see either Cash or Baker, and she's annoyed. Have they forgotten her?

"Irene!"

Irene looks around. Huck is in the parking lot, standing in front of his truck. Irene can't believe the feeling that overcomes her. She ducks her head so he can't see her smiling.

Get a grip! she thinks. *It's just Huck*. "Oh, hi," she says. She grabs her luggage and starts rolling it over to his truck. "Are you here for me?"

"Baker took Floyd to the Gifft Hill School and Maia wanted to show them around," Huck says. "So that left me free to pick you up."

Things are really happening, then—Cash started a job, Floyd will go to school. Irene opens the passenger door to Huck's truck.

"Wait a minute," Huck says. He strides over and puts his hands on her shoulders and looks her in the eye. "It's good to see you, Angler Cupcake. I'm glad you're back."

Irene feels herself reddening. "Stop it," she says. "You're embarrassing me."

On the way to Russ's villa, Irene thinks it best to fill Huck in on what's been happening.

She says, "I've had a visit from the FBI."

Huck says, "I'm afraid that might have been my fault.

I had a call from an agent down here right after you left to let me know that they'd opened an investigation into the crash—"

"Yes," Irene says. "The boys and I received calls as well—"

"And then I contacted Agent Vasco myself last week to let her know that...well, we found money in Rosie's room."

Irene gazes out the window, trying to focus on the views. The vista of the neighboring islands across the turquoise water is nothing short of spectacular. Less than a month ago, Irene made the same drive but she saw nothing, noticed nothing.

Money. "How much?"

"A lot."

"How much, Huck?"

"A hundred and twenty-five grand."

A hundred and twenty-five grand. A hot, nauseating panic rises in Irene's chest. "In cash, you mean?"

"Yes, in cash. Bricks of it."

"And they took it?"

"They took it," Huck says. He lights a cigarette and blows the smoke out his window. "And I heard they paid a visit to Welcome to Paradise Real Estate."

"Dear God," Irene says. "Paulette?"

"She left the island. Her husband and her son too."

"She left the island?" Irene says. "I called and left a message asking for a certified copy of the death certificate and she never returned my call, but then, voilà, a copy came in the mail."

"Well, that's good," Huck says. "Right?"

"I thought Russ was still alive somewhere," Irene says. "I had these dreams where he was so...*vivid,* so present, so whole. He was there, three-dimensionally, in my mind. And when I'd wake up, I'd think, *He made it out of that helicopter and Croft plucked him out of the sea and whisked him away.*" Irene is mortified when her voice breaks. "I thought he was just hiding somewhere. I thought I'd see him again."

Huck takes Irene's hand. Irene looks down to see their fingers intertwined, her hand slender and wrinkled and white, his large and wrinkled and brown.

"The FBI didn't find anything in Iowa," Irene says. "Did they find anything in your house, other than the money? Did they find anything in Rosie's room?"

"Not that I know of," Huck says. "I had Ayers go through Rosie's things while Maia was at school. Ayers was the one who discovered the money."

"But not anything else?" Irene says. "No clues? No...explanations?"

"No," Huck says.

"And we can trust Ayers?" Irene asks. "We don't think she knows more than she's saying, do we?"

"I trust her," Huck says. "She's just as in the dark as you and me."

"But she was Rosie's best friend," Irene says. "Her confidante. Surely..."

"Where the Invisible Man was concerned, Rosie was a brick wall," Huck says. He signals to turn up Lovers Lane. "Sorry—I mean Russ."

"It's okay," Irene says. "The nickname fits."

When they get to the house, they see both Jeeps are gone; the boys must still be out. Huck brings Irene's luggage up the stone steps to the deck.

"Will you stay for a beer?" Irene asks.

"I should go collect Maia," he says.

"No, of course," Irene says. She needs to shower and unpack. The news of the FBI, the cash, and Paulette *leaving the island* has Irene rattled. "Are you *worried,* Huck? Does it feel like the fire is getting a little close?"

"I'm concerned," Huck says. "I want to remain informed and aware, but I'm not going to let this whole mess control me. This has nothing to do with us, AC. I have a clean conscience and I know you do as well."

"I do," Irene says.

"I'll tell you if we ever have reason to worry," he says. "Will you trust me on that?"

Irene nods. It's remarkable how much better she feels knowing Huck's on her side. If he's not going to worry, she isn't either.

"I'll take a rain check on the beer," Huck says. "I promise. And hey, we have an afternoon charter on Wednesday. Two couples from Wichita."

"So you haven't had second thoughts?" Irene says. "You still want me to be your first mate?"

"I *need* you to be my first mate," Huck says.

"I'll come on Wednesday and we'll see how I do, okay? But I promise I won't be offended if you want to hire some young guy." She winks at him. "Or young woman."

"Agent Vasco was quite attractive," Huck says. "I nearly offered *her* the job."

"Oh, *was* she," Irene says. She sounds jealous to her own ears.

"Are you jealous?" Huck asks.

"Are you trying to make me jealous?" Irene says.

"I dunno. Maybe."

"Well, maybe it worked," Irene says. She's afraid to look Huck in the eye so she busies herself by rolling her suitcases over to the slider. "Thank you for coming to get me. I'll see you Wednesday."

Huck smiles at her, shaking his head, and she thinks, *What? What?*

She shoos him away and he heads down the stairs. Only once he's gone can Irene get a clear breath. She is so keyed up when he's around, both agitated and happy.

Agent Vasco was attractive. Bah!

Before she goes into the house, Irene stands at the stone wall and inhales the sight of the sea and the verdant island mountains and the lush hillside below. It's the prettiest place she's ever seen, but what is she doing here? It's truly insane, this decision to move down to work on a fishing boat. Has she lost her mind?

Well, yes, Irene thinks. She probably has. And good for her.

AYERS

On Tuesday night, Mick announces that he's going over to St. Thomas the next morning and he won't be back until late, so he can't meet Ayers after her charter with a smoothie.

"I guess the honeymoon is over," Ayers says. "I knew it wouldn't last. What's happening in St. Thomas?"

"Picking up some stuff for the bar," Mick says.

"Really?" Ayers says. "Like what, from where?"

"Stuff, from places," Mick says. "Paper straws, for one thing. I have to take all the plastic straws to recycling and replace them with paper straws. Which, although environmentally friendly, disintegrate once they come in contact with liquid, thereby providing a poor straw experience."

"And what else?"

"What's with the third degree?" Mick asks.

She didn't sleep with Baker. When he pulled up alongside of her out of the blue, she thought, *Is this really happening?* And then, without thinking twice, she'd climbed into the car with him and directed him to Hawksnest. She thought they would just sit in the parking lot and talk but that wasn't very romantic, so she led him down the path toward the beach, which was deserted, and she thought, *Is that what I want? Romantic?*

The truth is, she hasn't stopped thinking of him since he left. She doesn't want to like him, but she does. And reading Rosie's journals is screwing with her head. *Rosie willingly had an affair with a man she knew was married.* Ayers's own dear, sweet friend, a person Ayers admired and respected, did that. The story in the diary is, at least, providing some context. Russ was unhappy, at a crossroads career-wise, and he'd been dropped into paradise for the weekend, where he'd met Rosie, who even on her worst day was achingly beautiful. Something had sparked between them—then ignited. It's the spark and the flame that intrigue Ayers. Did two good people do something they knew was wrong because there was some kind of magical chemistry involved? Or was it plain old human fallibility, weakness in the face of temptation?

Ayers isn't sure. What she is drawn to in Rosie's journal is the rawness of Rosie's desire for Russ and her pain when he leaves.

Has Ayers ever felt that way about *anyone?* Does she feel that way about Mick? She was hurt and angry— really angry—when she found Mick with Brigid, but that pain might simply have been the blow to her self-esteem and the sting of being rejected. The truth is, the way she feels about Mick now has changed. She still loves him but she doesn't trust him and she doesn't trust herself, and sometimes she thinks she went back to him only be- cause it was comfortable and familiar, whereas the idea of embarking on a whole new relationship with Baker Steele is terrifying. And unrealistic. He's still married. He lives in Houston.

Once they were on the beach, Baker reached for Ayers's hand, but she batted him away, then turned to confront him. There wasn't a moon; it was really dark. Ayers could barely see Baker, but despite this, there was an instant pull of attraction. He was so tall and broad; she loved having to crane her neck to look up at him. He had a fresh haircut, she'd noticed; it looked good with his chiseled features and his dimple. He'd gone soft around the middle and there was something dad-like and a little nerdy in his demeanor. But these things set her at ease.

"I didn't bring you here for that," Ayers said. "I want to talk."

Baker nodded. "Yeah, me too. Sorry, it's a beach, we were walking, I've been thinking of you every second of every day since I left, so believe me when I say that reaching for your hand was something I did instinctively."

"I need to know a couple things," she said. "One, are you still married?"

"Legally, yes," Baker said. "It's only been a few weeks. But Anna, my wife, accepted a surgical post at the Cleveland Clinic with her girlfriend, Louisa, so they're moving and giving me physical custody of Floyd."

"Have you started divorce proceedings?" Ayers asked. "Have you spoken to a lawyer?"

"We're using a mediator," Baker said. "And yes, I've spoken to her. This is happening. There's no going back. I actually had dinner with Anna and Louisa a few days ago, and, wow, they're *together*. Two peas in a pod. An intimidating pair."

Intimidating, Ayers thought, because they weren't sexually attracted to men. Ayers let Baker's typical attitude slide because she had a more pressing question. "How long are you staying down here?"

"We're moving here," Baker said. "I have Floyd with me. I want to put him in school."

This wasn't the answer Ayers was expecting. "So you packed up all your stuff and shipped it down here?"

"Well..." Baker said.

No, she didn't think so. It would have been too good to be true.

"We're here for two weeks. Then I have to go back to Houston for this event at Floyd's school."

Which he was supposedly pulling Floyd out of.

"And then I'll take care of packing up the rest of what we need."

"So it's your *intention* to move down here," Ayers said. "But if after two weeks you aren't feeling it, you'll go back to Houston."

"It's my intention to stay," Baker said. "Cash is staying. And tonight I found out my mother is coming down. So I'll have a built-in support system."

Irene, Ayers thought. She had a whole new set of feelings about Irene now that she'd read Rosie's journals—mostly fear that she, Ayers, could someday be duped and blindsided as badly as Irene had been. It was so important to stay vigilant where your heart was concerned. Why didn't they teach you that in school?

"What about a job?" Ayers said. "Cash has a job, with me." Even in the darkness, she could see Baker wince. "I won't believe you're staying until you have something tethering you to this island."

"I'm going to look for a job," Baker said. "I day-trade for money, I can do that anywhere, which is how I'm able to pick up and leave Houston. But I want something part-time here, something flexible so I can still be around for Floyd. I admit I don't have any leads yet. I just got here today. The first thing I wanted to do was find you."

"I'm still with Mick," Ayers said.

"I know," Baker said. "Cash told me." He reached out and touched a strand of her hair. "I'm not going to put any pressure on you. I just want you to know that I'm here because of you."

Against her wishes, this affected her. "I'm with Mick," she said again, weakly.

"Well, if things don't work out with Mick, I'll be here waiting." He grinned. "Like a complete idiot. An utter fool."

She laughed, then they stood smiling at each other and she thought, *He's going to try and kiss me.*

He bent down toward her—but stopped. "Come on," he said. "I'll take you back to town."

Wednesday morning, Ayers drives down to *Treasure Island* and Mick follows behind her in his blue Jeep with Gordon hanging his head over the side. They're on their way to the ferry; Mick honks as he peels off.

They have a full boat today, twenty people, six of them kids, and handling that is a tall order, especially because it's only Cash's third day of work, his first without Wade there to train him. But Cash seems to be a natural when it comes to managing groups of strangers all keyed up for an adventure. He's courteous and convivial, he has the gift of gab, and it's clear that he takes his procedural responsibilities—the passport paperwork, tying up at the docks, cleaning and prepping all the snorkel equipment, and assisting with any young, old, or infirm guests—very seriously. Of course, this job offers a different roll of the dice each and every day; that's one of the things Ayers likes about it. Occasionally there are mechanical issues with the boat or the weather isn't great, but that's for Captain James to deal with. Ayers and Cash handle the humans.

Ayers goes to the top deck to put out the seat cushions. Six kids is a lot, she thinks, especially if the parents start drinking. She decides to tell Cash that she'll manage the kids and he'll be in charge of the adults.

Adults are easier. Most of the time.

From her perch, Ayers spies Mick on the top deck of the ferry, Gordon with him on a leash, garnering attention from every dog lover on the boat. Mick took Gordon with him because, with both Ayers and Mick gone all day, there'd be no one to let him out. Still, Ayers suspects Mick also brought Gordon because Gordon is a chick magnet. And sure enough, a girl with long brown hair in a cute white sundress takes the seat next to Mick. The girl puts her arm around Mick and lays her head on his shoulder, so it must be someone they know. Ayers squints; the girl lifts her head and turns.

It's Brigid.

To get some stuff for the bar, Ayers thinks. *Paper straws.* This is such bullshit, Ayers can't believe she bought it! Well, she didn't quite buy it, did she? She'd had a funny feeling because Mick *hated* going to St. Thomas. If there was a reason to go, he'd send one of his employees. But when Ayers asked follow-up questions, he'd accused her of giving him the third degree, and she hadn't argued the point because she was feeling guilty about the journals and about seeing Baker.

Brigid! Where is he going with Brigid? To the recycling center and the restaurant-supply store? Or to the Tap and Still for a long boozy lunch followed by...what? Not back until late, he said. What a jerk!

Gordon puts his paws up on Brigid's knees and starts licking her face, and Ayers turns away; if she watches any longer, she's going to be sick. She pulls her phone out of her shorts pocket and as she's wondering what to text to Mick—what can she say that will make him feel as nauseated as she feels right now?—Cash calls up the stairs.

"Paperwork is ready," he says. "Permission to board?"

"Permission granted," James says from the wheelhouse.

Ayers's phone says it's ten past eight. Time to get everyone on so they can leave. She shoves her phone back into her shorts pocket, then whips it back out and shoots a quick text to Mick: I saw you with Brigid. Please don't ever call me again. It's over.

She feels triumphant, but it lasts only an instant.

Brigid!

The six children are all in the same family, the Dresslers, and they're all boys, towheaded and tan, ranging in age from fourteen to six. They all have D-names: DJ, Danny, Damian, Duncan, Donner ("Like the reindeer," the mother says), and Dougie.

Who names a child after a *reindeer?* Ayers wonders. She's in a foul mood.

The kids seem relatively well behaved, and the parents—Dave and Donna—are a striking couple, tall and superior-looking. Donna carries a bag (as big as Santa's!) that holds the entire family's snorkeling equipment.

You just never know what you're going to get, Ayers thinks. Today it's a cross between the von Trapp children and Russian matryoshka dolls.

She finds Cash in the cabin; he's setting out the platter of fruit and the sliced coconut-banana bread. The greatest thing about Cash is he doesn't mind the menial jobs. He thinks it's a privilege! And Cash is clearly skilled with a knife. The fruit is uniformly sliced and spread out in an appetizing pinwheel.

Ayers pulls Cash aside. "I'll keep a close eye on the boys. You take the so-called grown-ups."

"Got it, boss," he says. He turns from Ayers and smiles at a young woman who is hanging by the counter. "What can I get for you?"

"When does the bar open?" the young woman asks.

Ayers has to wait a beat before she answers. This happens every day, but Ayers is in no mood right now for someone whose sole reason for coming aboard *Treasure Island* is to get shitfaced.

"No alcohol until we're under way," Ayers says. "And even then, I'd urge you to be prudent until the snorkeling portion is over."

"Prudent is my middle name," she says. "But snorkeling is quite a while from now, isn't it?"

"Yes," Ayers says. "Baths first—including travel, that takes two hours—then the captain will pick a snorkeling spot. We should be finished snorkeling by eleven or eleven thirty."

"That's a long time to be prudent," the woman says.

Ayers feels herself about to snap. "Once we are on our way to Jost, you can drink as much as you want."

Cash says, "If Prudent is your middle name, what's your first name?" He sticks out a hand. "I'm Cash."

"I'm Maxwell," she says.

"That's your *first* name?" Cash asks.

"'Fraid so," she says. "It's kind of confusing, but don't worry, I'm *very* female." She sticks her chest out at Cash, and Ayers notices a tattoo of a keyhole between her breasts. Ayers gets it—she's waiting for the person who holds the key to her heart.

Cash must notice the tattoo at the same time—how could he not; it's nestled right there between her boobs, which are straining against the green cups of her bikini—because he says, "Cool tattoo."

Maxwell glances down at her chest as if she has no idea

what he's talking about. "Oh, thanks," she says. Over the bikini, she's wearing a sheer green paisley peasant blouse. She gives a tiny shrug, and the blouse slips down off her shoulder. This girl has all the moves and she has her bright gaze trained on Cash. "I hope you don't mind my hanging around. It's just that I came on this trip by myself. I'm visiting a friend of mine from high school who lives here but she said she has a lot of errands today because she works at night—"

Ayers can't stop herself from jumping in. "Is your friend named Brigid, by any chance?"

"No," Maxwell says.

"Long shot, I know," Ayers says. "You just remind me of someone."

"Anyway," Maxwell says, now showing Cash one creamy shoulder, "she encouraged me to come out on this tour. She said it's the *best*." She beams at Cash, as though *Treasure Island*'s sterling reputation is all Cash's doing. "I think she was trying to get rid of me. I can be a lot."

"*You?*" Ayers says.

The boat engine starts. Cash says, "I have to go tend to the ropes. Excuse me, Maxwell."

"Just call me Max," she says. "When you're finished, will you come back and make me a painkiller, extra strong?"

"You got it," Cash says. He gives her a wink and shoots out a finger like Isaac, the bartender from *The Love Boat,* a cultural reference Ayers suspects is lost on Max.

Ayers wrestles with her wandering mind. She told Cash she would keep an eye on the kids and let him handle the adults, but by now, all six of the boys might have drowned.

Ayers puts on her headset. "I'm about to give the safety talk," she says to Max. "You should listen."

The ride to Virgin Gorda is smooth. Ayers makes herself notice how glorious the water, the sky, and the emerald-green islands are. She is so lucky to live here, to have this job and her job at La Tapa, her friends, her community, Maia and Huck. Rosie is gone, but at least while Ayers is reading the journals, it feels like she has Rosie back. It feels like Rosie is, finally, telling her everything.

But then she succumbs to the red, hot, itchy temptation of thinking about Mick and Brigid. *Brigid!* If Ayers had seen Mick with anyone else—Emily Ratajkowski, Scarlett Johansson with her tongue in Mick's ear—it wouldn't have sickened Ayers the way seeing him with Brigid has. Why did he even bother getting back together with her? Because she was hurting? Because he felt *sorry* for her? Because her apartment was far more homey and comfortable than the rat hole where he and Gordon lived? Is he using her? Preying on her pain and her wobbly judgment? She's actively mourning the loss of her best friend and she has been trying to hold it together so she can be whole and strong for Maia. How *dare* Mick go behind her back *again* after all Ayers has just been through. That is what makes this unforgivable.

She scans the boat, looking for anyone who seems to be suffering from seasickness, but the passengers look calm and happy, their faces turned toward the sun, hair blowing back in the breeze. The six boys are sitting on a bench be-tween the statuesque bookends of their parents, and there isn't a single electronic device among them, which Ayers finds impressive.

She leans toward the mother, Donna, and says, "Your boys are so well behaved."

Donna wraps her arm around the youngest, Dougie, who is sitting next to her, and kisses the top of his head. "Believe me, this is a rare moment of peace. We told them if they behaved today, we'd rent a dinghy tomorrow and go to the pizza boat in Christmas Cove."

"Good bribe!" Ayers says. "I love Pizza Pi." Mick had said something the night before about borrowing his boss's boat so they could raft up in Christmas Cove on Monday— eat pizza, listen to live music.

Maybe now he'll take Brigid.

"How do you manage six boys?" Ayers asks. Because she's an only child, she has always been fascinated by big families and she still harbors a fantasy of having a bunch of kids herself someday. Which will probably never happen, seeing as how she can't even sustain a relationship. (She has to lasso her psyche! Stay in the moment!) "Isn't it a lot, to keep track of their sports and activities and their dental appointments and haircuts and stuff?" Just looking at the Dressler family brings up visions of reminders written on a chalkboard in the mudroom, a color-coded calendar, baskets labeled with each boy's name to hold hats and gloves and rainboots.

"They're all swimmers," Donna says. "I just drop them off at the Y on Saturday morning and collect them at the end of the day. I go to some of the meets, though I've learned to pick and choose. I used to go to every single one and my hair turned green just from sitting in the pool balcony for so long." She laughs. "They aren't interested in impressing me, anyway. They want to impress their coach, their teammates, and each other. They all swim freestyle and do the IM, so it's pretty intense competition." She looks down to the end of the bench and whispers, "DJ has just committed to swim at Stanford."

"That's so cool," Ayers says. "Where are you guys from?"

"Philadelphia," Donna says. "The Main Line."

Sure, of course, Ayers might have predicted that. The Dresslers probably live in an old stone house that has a creek running behind it. The husband, Dave, probably takes the train downtown to work, and Donna probably makes enormous dinners—Taco Tuesdays!—that the boys devour, exhausted from a day of school and swimming the fifty-free in under a minute. Ayers feels herself falling in love with the Dressler family. *Adopt me, please,* she thinks.

But maybe there are secrets, like soft spots on a seemingly perfect apple. Maybe Donna is having an affair with the kids' swim coach; maybe Dave is a degenerate gambler who has lost the college savings; maybe the oldest boy got his girlfriend pregnant, which he'll reveal the day they get home from this vacation, and suddenly, Stanford will be called into question.

Ayers shakes her head. What is *wrong* with her today? She suspects it's a combination of the diaries and seeing Mick and Brigid together. It feels like the whole world is hiding something.

Ayers lifts her gaze from Donna to the cabin of the

boat. The past two days, Cash has circulated around the boat and introduced himself to the guests, but there he is, behind the bar, making that chick Max another drink.

In the seven years that Ayers has been working on *Treasure Island,* she has seen a spectrum of eye-popping outfits, which she and Wade have put into three categories. Category one, the most popular, was the Siren. This included teensy bikinis and wet T-shirts. Category two was the Riviera Gigolo, a gentle way of describing men who wore, instead of trunks, European-cut briefs—nut-huggers, grape-smugglers, banana hammocks. Category three was the Vampire. These folks showed up in head-to-toe Lycra— usually black, for some reason—because they couldn't risk exposure to the sun. (The Lycra suits were always accompanied by wide-brimmed floppy hats.) Ayers was all about SPF but in her opinion, if exposure to sunlight was *that* verboten, then a day trip on *Treasure Island*—hell, a vacation on a Caribbean island in general—probably wasn't for you.

Once Max takes the paisley peasant blouse off and slides out of her jean shorts, Ayers sees that the green bikini consists of only three tiny triangles of iridescent material (possibly meant to reference fish scales) and some string. It's a dental-floss thong, leaving the pale orbs of Max's buttocks exposed. Ayers notices a tattoo on the right cheek—a pair of lips.

Kiss my ass, Ayers thinks. *Got it.* Max's body is a living rebus.

Ayers is dismayed that Max chose to wear such a revealing suit on a family-oriented boat trip. What must the six boys think? At least half of them will be ogling her all day; it's impossible *not* to ogle her.

Donna gives Ayers a sympathetic smile. "If you've got it, flaunt it."

That's a generous perspective, Ayers thinks. She will bet anyone the keys to her truck that Max is going to lose her bikini when she jumps off the boat to swim into the Baths.

Ayers puts on her headset and runs through the drill: Jump in, swim to shore, here are the life vests, and does anyone need a noodle?

Everyone does just fine—including six-year-old Dougie—and then Max climbs up to the edge of the bow and turns around in a panic. "Where's Cash?" she says. "I want Cash to go with me."

"He's onshore already, Max," Ayers says. "See him there?" Cash is standing on the small golden beach herding everyone toward the entrance of the Baths. He's going to lead the tour today and Ayers is bringing up the rear. "Just jump in and swim right for him, okay?"

"Oh, okay," Max says. She waves both arms overhead. "Cash! Cash!" She loses her footing and falls in. Ayers peers over the edge, checking to see whether Max can swim or if Ayers will have to save her.

To be safe, Ayers jumps in a few feet away. "You okay?"

Max is busy doing the doggie paddle, eyes squeezed shut, and because she is, actually, making forward progress, Ayers lets her be, swimming behind her just in case.

She can't believe this chick isn't a friend of Brigid.

"Looks like you have a barnacle on your boat," Ayers says to Cash once they're all back aboard *Treasure Island*. Max had trailed Cash through the Baths so closely that whenever he stopped, she bumped into him. At Cathedral, she jumped off the ledge into his arms and clung to him far longer than was necessary.

"Huh?" Cash says. "Oh, yeah. She's harmless." They both turn to see Max standing at the bar, waiting for Cash so he can make her another drink and she can show him her chest.

James anchors off the coast of Norman Island for snorkeling because there are already three boats parked over at the Indians. Cash helps everyone with equipment, and Ayers goes to see how the Dressler boys are faring.

"They're all set," Donna says. "But thank you."

Ayers finds herself with a free minute and she's in a spot that has reliable cell service. Should she check her phone? See if Mick responded?

No, she decides. If he knows what's good for him, he'll ditch Brigid and be waiting at the dock for Ayers, smoothie in hand.

Is that what she wants?

She checks her phone despite herself. There are two texts from Mick, but Cash has started sending people into the water. She has to go.

Ayers snorkels with the Dressler boys and encourages two of the middle ones to follow her over to a rocky outcrop of Norman where the spotted eagle rays like to hang out. She can hear the boys oohing and aahing through their snorkels, and as always, this makes her happy. Some things are more important than her romantic trials and tribulations. Things like wonder.

Ayers raises her head and sees everyone heading back to the boat. She lets the boys swim ahead and she brings up the rear, scanning the water for the fluorescent orange tape on the tips of their snorkels.

When she climbs up to the deck, she says, "Everyone accounted for?"

"Yes," Cash says.

Ayers signals James, who starts the engine, and Cash goes to pull the anchor, which makes his muscles pop in a way that is undeniably attractive. Ayers can't believe Max isn't right beside him, taking pictures for her Instagram account: #coldhardcash.

When the anchor is up and they're moving, Ayers says, "Where's the barnacle?"

"Wait," Cash says. "What?"

Panic in the form of absolute stillness seizes Ayers. "Stop the boat!" she yells.

Max is not dead and Max is not lost. Ayers repeats this like a mantra, though for the first thirty seconds after Ayers realizes Max isn't on the boat (how can she not be on the boat? And why did Cash say everyone was present? Did he not do a head count?), these are Ayers's prevailing thoughts, that Max is dead or Max is missing and will turn up dead.

James cuts the engines and Ayers races up to the top deck with the binoculars, trying not to exude any sign of the sheer terror she is feeling. But the rest of the guests realize something is wrong. Ayers overhears Cash say, "We're missing someone, the woman in the green bikini." Then everyone starts looking. They spread out around the port side and starboard side and the bow. Ayers's main concern is that Max is *under* the boat, that they unwittingly ran over her when they lifted anchor and started toward Jost Van Dyke.

Max is not dead and Max is not lost, Ayers tells herself.

Cash appears next to her. "I'm so sorry, I thought—"

"There's no *time* for sorry!" Ayers says. She mentally breaks the water into a grid and starts scanning it square foot by square foot. In seven years, she has never lost a swimmer. She has had to do only five rescues—five, in seven years. Today will be her sixth rescue, she tells herself. Today, she will rescue Max.

Someone calls out, "Over there!"

Ayers follows the pointing arm of Mr. Dressler. Yes, she sees a piece of fluorescent tape about two hundred yards away. Before Ayers knows what's happening, someone dives off the lower deck of the boat and starts swimming toward the snorkeler. It's the oldest Dressler kid, DJ, Ayers realizes. She strips off her shorts, and, although it's forbidden, she dives off the top deck, hits the water with so much force that her nose and ears flood with water, and swims after him. A second later, she feels the concussion of someone else plunging in nearby and she envisions everyone on the boat trying to be a hero.

She raises her head in order to get her bearings. Cash goes thrashing past her. He's moving so fast he nearly catches DJ. Ayers sees DJ and then Cash reach the snorkeler and Ayers hears shouts. She swims closer, and only then does she realize that the snorkeler isn't a she. The snorkeler isn't Max. It's some guy from another boat who has also gone rogue.

"Go back to your boat!" Ayers yells to the other snorkeler. She casts about helplessly. Where is Max?

She hears the air horn and swivels her head to see Captain James on the top deck windmilling his arm to beckon her back.

What? Ayers thinks. *We can't just leave her here.* Or…has Max turned up? DJ and Cash are already swimming back to the boat and Ayers puts her head down and powers forward with everything she's got left, thinking, *Please let her be okay, please let her be alive.* If she's injured, they can get her to Schneider Hospital on St. Thomas in half an hour.

When Ayers is only a few yards from the boat, James calls out, "She's aboard."

"She is?"

"She was in the head," James says. "Why didn't you guys check?"

In the head. Max was using the bathroom. Why didn't Ayers check?

Sure enough, Max is sitting on the stairs to the upper deck (which isn't allowed) drinking what's left of a painkiller when Ayers hauls herself up the ladder.

Ayers can't bring herself to say anything to the girl. What would she say? *We thought we'd lost you. We thought you drowned.* At which point, Max would say, *I went to the bathroom. Sorry, I didn't know I needed to report in. I wanted to change my swimsuit.* Because, yup, Max is wearing a new bikini, white, which Ayers will (again) bet the key to her truck becomes completely see-through when wet.

Ayers climbs past Max without a word and goes into the wheelhouse to apologize to James.

"I'm sorry," she says. "I should have checked the head. I…" Ayers tries to explain what made her jump to the conclusion that Max was still in the water. All Cash had said was *Wait. What?* Ayers was the one who had panicked. "She'd been drinking. More than everyone else combined. I guess my mind supplied the worst-case scenario, that she went out snorkeling while drunk and she drowned."

James gives her the eyebrows. He's a man of few words, though he's been blessed with wisdom beyond his years—he's thirty-five; he went to high school with Rosie—and a dry sense of humor. "If I didn't know you better, I'd say you were jealous."

"Jealous of Max?" Ayers says. "Please give me some credit."

"She's been hanging on your boy," James says. "And we both know it's not like you to fly off like that."

"First of all, he's not my boy," Ayers says. "Is that what you think?"

James starts the engine.

"I'd like permission to cut her off," Ayers says. "She's had enough to drink."

"She didn't do anything wrong," James says. He leaves it unspoken that this whole event was Ayers's fault. Ayers can only imagine what kind of dramatic retelling the fourteen adults will provide on TripAdvisor.

"I'm sorry," Ayers says again. "I'm having a bad day."

James nods. "You're allowed," he says. He laughs. "Tell you what, though—your boy sure can swim."

Ayers puts on the headset. "Sorry about that, folks," she says. She notices that the Dressler kids are all lined up at the railing seeing who can spit the farthest and there's now a queue at the bar three-deep.

Right, she thinks. Crisis averted, people are getting bored, time to drink. "We're on our way over to Jost Van Dyke, named for the man who discovered it in the early seventeenth century. It became a center of custom shipbuilding, but now, however, Jost is most famous for its world-class beach bars, including Foxy's, One Love, and…the Soggy Dollar!"

Everyone claps. She's forgiven.

There's no happier place on earth than White Bay on a sunny day. The stunning crescent of powder-fine sand is lined with palm trees and funky, bare-bones beach bars. *Treasure Island* slips in among a flotilla of boats. There are people splashing in the shallows, tossing a football; there's reggae music and the smell of jerk chicken and the low buzz of blenders making Bushwackers and piña coladas.

"Please get yourself some lunch," Ayers says. "And try not to wander off. We'd like you back on the boat at two thirty sharp."

Ayers counts the Dressler kids as they jump off the boat in succession. There's a bit of a wade required, which the boys don't seem to mind. To DJ, Ayers says, "Thank you for your help. You're a fast swimmer."

DJ shrugs and Donna Dressler puts a hand on Ayers's shoulder and says, "That was some unexpected drama, huh?"

Ayers spies Max walking down the beach—with Cash, of course—toward the Soggy Dollar. "I don't know if I should feel angry or relieved."

"Sounds like being a parent," Donna says. "You're not sure whether to ground them or hug them."

Grounding sounds good, Ayers thinks.

Lunch isn't a bad idea, and Ayers is a big fan of the Soggy Dollar lobster roll, so she walks down the beach and into the bar. Her favorite bartender, Leon, is pouring something pink and fruity out of the blender and into two cups, which he delivers to Max and Cash, who are sitting together at the end of the bar.

Cash says, "I'm on the clock," and passes his drink to Max.

"Awwww," she says. "Thanks." She leans her head on Cash's shoulder and closes her eyes.

Did Ayers give Cash "the talk" about not fraternizing with the guests? She knows she didn't. It never occurred to her that it would be a problem. Cash had been so earnest, so eager to please—please her, Ayers—that she hadn't realized that many if not all of the available women (and maybe even those who weren't necessarily available) would find Cash sexy and attractive and throw themselves at him as inelegantly as moths beating themselves against a screen.

Cash nudges Max's head off his shoulder and orders a Coke and a blackened mahi sandwich with coleslaw. He says, "So what do you do for work?"

"I sell drugs," Max says. She waits a beat, then honks out a laugh. "Not what you're thinking! I'm a pharmaceutical rep."

"Did you grow up in the Midwest?" Cash asks.

"Peoria," she says, diving nose-first into her pink drink.

"I'm from Iowa City!" Cash says.

Ayers isn't eavesdropping; she's just waiting to get Leon's attention. It's like she's invisible today. She debates interrupting the happy couple to remind Max to eat something, but she's not the girl's mother and she's afraid of sounding like a schoolmarm or a scold.

Max says something under her breath and Cash laughs. *Is* Ayers jealous? Maybe she is. She had thought Cash was in love with *her*. She thought Cash had taken the job on *Treasure Island* because he wanted to work with her. And yet he hasn't looked over at her even once. He's completely entranced with Max!

Ayers can't believe she's having these thoughts. She doesn't like Cash in that way—does she? She didn't think so, but right now, there's no denying she's jealous.

No, Ayers thinks. She enjoys being the object of Cash's affection. It's flattering, a boost to her ego. What's really going on is that she's upset about Mick and Brigid and confused about her feelings for Baker. Baker, who is maybe staying on St. John but also maybe not staying. Ayers would bet the keys to her truck *and* her apartment that Baker will go back to Houston for the school fund-raiser and never return. He'll find relocating too complicated. He'll spend two weeks on St. John and become bored; without a job to do, it's just sun, sand, and water. There are no museums or movie theaters, there are no professional sports teams or shopping malls. There isn't even any golf.

He won't stay. The schools won't be good enough for Floyd. Baker won't be able to find a fulfilling job; St. John isn't Wall Street. There will be some solid reason why he has to go back to the States. St. John is paradise when you visit, but when you live here, it becomes very real very quickly.

Ayers can't risk getting involved with Baker.

"Ayers," Cash says suddenly, yanking her out of her mental quicksand. "Would you like to join us?"

Ayers assesses her options. Cash's sandwich has now arrived and he offers some to Max, who slowly, *slowly,* shakes her head. She's slipping down her stool, melting like a candle.

Leon finally gives Ayers a wave. "I see you, darling. Just gonna be a minute."

"That's okay, Leon," Ayers says. "I'm not staying." She steps back out onto the sand. She'll head down to One Love, she decides, and get some jerk pork.

At a quarter after two, Ayers is feeling a little better. She has eaten and taken a ten-minute chair nap, and now she combs the beach for her guests, urging everyone to head back to the boat. If they get out of here at two thirty, there will be less of a line at customs.

Ayers has never so badly wanted a charter to end.

Coming toward her down the beach are Cash and Max. Max is stumbling and bent over; she's so drunk she can barely walk. Cash has to take her by the hand once they're wading back to the boat. If she fell over, she would drown in only two feet of water. Ayers wants to say something to Cash, something like *Why did you let her get so drunk?* She wants to point to Max and say to James, *We should have cut her off after snorkeling!* But instead, Ayers helps Cash get Max up the three-step ladder and onto the boat. Max heads toward starboard and Ayers thinks maybe she's going to the bar for another drink, but she bypasses the cabin, pushes little Dougie Dressler out of the way, and starts puking over the side of the boat.

Ayers bows her head. It would be very unprofessional to let the others see her smirking.

CASH

He's not sure how he got saddled with the drunk, and now crying, young woman named Maxwell—well, yes, he does know, he enabled her drinking and indulged her little crush on him because she's attractive and flirtatious, and both of these things seemed to bother Ayers, which was, he thought, a very good sign—but now he's responsible for making sure she gets home safely.

"Find her friend, her people, whoever," Ayers says. "I'll clean the boat by myself."

"But—"

"And, please, Cash, don't let this happen again. These are our guests, not our friends."

"You're right," he says. "It won't happen again."

He half leads, half carries Max off the dock and into the streets of St. John. As they pulled into port, he'd asked Max the name of her friend from high school, but all she'd said was *I dunno,* and then she groaned and started vomiting again.

It hadn't been a good look for her, for him, or for *Treasure Island,* though everyone else on the boat seemed to take it in stride. The parents of the six boys used it as a cautionary tale. "That," Cash overheard the father whisper to the Stanford-bound DJ, "is what happens when you decide three shots of tequila sound good after midnight."

There was a couple on the boat, keen snorkelers who'd brought a checklist of fish they were hoping to see, and the man said, "I could have told you how this was going to end up, but she was having so much fun, I hated to put a damper on it."

"We've all been there," his wife said. "For me, it was the Sig Ep house at West Virginia University in 1996."

Cash tended to agree; many people at some point in their lives had overdone it like Max. Cash had sampled his father's scotch and smoked one of his cigars when he was a week away from graduating high school, and that had ended badly. And he had taken care of Claire Bellows after she drank Jägermeister from a flask in the bathroom during their junior prom.

The town is teeming with people. All of the tour boats have just disgorged their passengers and it's happy hour at nearly every bar in Cruz Bay. Cash has no leads on who he should hand this chick off to. No one seems to be waiting for her. Cash then tries to imagine bringing Max home to the villa, where Baker, Floyd, and his mother will all be waiting.

Nope. No chance.

"Cash!"

Cash cranes his neck, trying to figure out who's calling his name. Then someone appears under his nose.

It's Maia. With a boy in tow—a handsome young man with dark hair that has been highlighted in the front. He's a couple inches taller than Maia.

"Hey," Cash says. He's more than a little uncomfortable bumping into...well, his little sister...with Max draped over him like a fur coat. "What are you doing?"

Maia shrugs. "Hanging out." She nods at the boy next to her. "This is my friend Shane. He goes to Antilles."

"Hey, Shane," Cash says. Shane is the kid that Maia has a crush on; Cash remembers this much. It's nice that they're hanging out together—alone, from the looks of it; is that okay?—and Cash feels honored to be introduced, but he really wishes it wasn't under these circumstances. Any minute, Max might projectile-vomit onto Shane's shoes.

"What are *you* doing?" Maia asks, taking an appraising look at Max.

"I'm...well, this woman was a guest on the boat and I'm trying to find her friend. She has a friend who lives here, she said, but I have no idea who it is or what to do."

"Is it Tilda?" Maia asks. "She was just here, looking for her friend who was visiting...from Chicago." Maia turns to Shane. "Did she say Chicago?"

Shane nods. "Definitely Chicago," he says. "But I thought her friend was a boy."

"Was she looking for a Max?" Cash asks. "Maxwell?"

"Yes!" Maia says.

"*Tilda* is her friend?" Cash says. "Really? The Tilda that I know? Tilda from La Tapa?"

"Yeah," Maia says. "She worked with my mom."

"Right, yes, yes," Cash says. He's forgotten that everyone on this island is connected. "I'm going to sit with Max on this bench. Can you guys go find Tilda and tell her where we are?"

"Come on," Shane says, clearly energized by this mission. He takes Maia's hand and leads her across the street toward the docks. Is it okay that they're holding hands? Cash wonders. They look pretty darn cute.

"This way, Max, easy does it, here we go," Cash says. He sighs. He would give anything to be twelve again.

"I am *so* sorry about this," Tilda says. "I'm mortified. I told her to behave herself. I told her I worked with Ayers. And I'd forgotten that you were working on the boat now too. That makes it so much worse!"

"You don't have to apologize," Cash says. "It's not your fault." Cash offered to help Tilda get Max settled at home, and now he leans back into the soft leather seat of Tilda's Range Rover and enjoys the air-conditioning blowing full blast. Max is lying across the back seat, moaning. Tilda laid a beach towel across the floor of the car in case Max throws up again, although she's been at it for so long that Cash doesn't see how there could be anything left in her stomach. "I think maybe she was just nervous about going on the trip by herself."

"She should have made some friends," Tilda says.

"She sort of...attached herself to me," Cash says.

"Of course she did," Tilda says. "You're superhot and you're her type. You look *exactly* like her boyfriend in high school. Freddy Jarvis."

Cash isn't sure how he feels about being the reincarnation of high-school boyfriend Freddy Jarvis. If he'd seen a woman who looked like Claire Bellows, he would have steered clear. "I don't think Ayers was too happy about it."

"Oh, please," Tilda says. "As if Ayers isn't hit on herself every single charter."

"Is she?" Cash says. "She wasn't today."

"That's rare," Tilda says. "But Ayers is used to it. She never succumbs to temptation because she loves Mick." Tilda pauses. "Did you hear me, Cash? She loves Mick."

"I heard you," Cash says.

Tilda pulls up a steep incline called Upper Peter Bay and they go up, up, up until they can't go any farther. There's a gate; Tilda punches in the code and then they shoot down a driveway that's so steep Cash feels like he's on a luge or a log flume in the amusement park. They arrive, finally, at the villa, which is absolutely stunning. It's three separate buildings in the Spanish-mission style attached by arched, columned walkways.

"Um...okay?" Cash says.

"It's my parents'," Tilda says. "As is this Rover. They only come three times a year, and I have the west wing to myself." She parks the car. "Max is staying in the guest wing."

Cash follows Tilda through the main entrance into a foyer that's two stories high. Everything is white, with accents of palm green and the palest blue. To the right is a sweeping curved staircase; above it hangs a long, dripping chandelier that looks like crystal rain. In front of them is a white and pale blue living room and a white kitchen with a very cool curved bar around which are pale blue suede stools. Beyond the kitchen are floor-to-ceiling sliding doors that open out onto a patio and a T-shaped pool.

"That pool," Cash whispers. He's carrying Max like a bride over the threshold. She's snoring.

"The pool is for Granger, my dad," Tilda says. "He's very intense about his swimming. About everything, actually." Tilda sighs. "The only person who makes him seem relaxed is my mom. Now, *she's* a maniac."

Cash wants to hear more but Max is getting heavy. "Which way?"

They head out a side door and down one of the covered walkways into the guest wing. It's two stories, complete with its own garden and plunge pool. They are so high up that Cash can see all of Jost Van Dyke and Tortola.

The bedroom is on the first floor. Tilda throws Max's bag down and hurries to sweep back the white sheers from the side of the mahogany four-poster bed so Cash can set Max on it. It's like they're in some kind of weird fairy tale.

Max rolls onto her side and continues to snore.

"She needs to sleep it off," Tilda says. "Wanna go get a drink?"

"Yes," Cash says. "As a matter of fact, I do."

They go back to town and Tilda picks a place called the Lime Inn, where they sit at the open-air horseshoe-shaped bar. Tilda orders them each a cocktail called the Danger, which is probably the exact opposite of what Cash needs right now, but he rolls with it.

"So your parents..."

"Run an international headhunting firm," Tilda says. "Specializing in IT. My mother is the owner and CEO and my father is the CFO. I'm proud of them. When I was young, my mother worked in HR at a software company in Peoria and my father was a financial adviser for a lot of the top execs at Caterpillar. Then, when I was eight, my mother had an idea for this business. We moved to Chicago right before I started high school and by the time I was a freshman at Lake Forest, their company was everywhere—India, Australia, Eastern Europe, South Africa."

It's not so different from Cash's own story. Russ took the job with Ascension when Cash was sixteen and life changed—for the better, he'd thought at the time.

"My parents want to invest in a business for me," Tilda says. "But I'm not sure what I want to do yet. So I'm living down here, waiting tables at La Tapa, and I volunteer at the animal shelter."

"You do?" Cash says.

"I love dogs," Tilda says. "But I can't have one because...a white house."

"I have a golden retriever named Winnie," Cash says. "She's my world."

"I'd love to meet your world sometime," Tilda says. "Should we have one more Danger or do you have to go?"

Cash thinks about it for a second. "Let's have one more," he says.

Tilda is cool. And she's really smart. She has a degree in economics from Lake Forest. She gave business school some thought, but she's grown attached to St. John.

"I'm thinking about starting an eco-tour company here," she says. "Hiking, kayaking, snorkeling. But I'd want to provide lodging too, I think, so I've been checking out real estate. I'm not going to jump into anything."

"I wish I'd been as savvy as you," Cash says. He taps his fingers alongside his glass, wondering how in depth he wants to get with Tilda. "You know that my father was killed in the helicopter crash with Rosie?"

"You told me," Tilda says. "A few weeks ago, when you were hitchhiking and I picked you up. You remember that night, right?"

"Kind of," he says. He remembers Tilda picking him up; he hadn't recognized her as working at La Tapa until she reminded him. That was the night he'd gotten drunk at High Tide after his fight with Baker. He can't recall a thing that he and Tilda talked about. At that point, Tilda had been a minor character, someone in the background. But now that Cash is getting to know her, he's intrigued. It's enough of a plot twist that she's a child of enormous wealth, but it's an even greater twist that, despite this, she works her ass off and volunteers and is researching business ventures. "So what did I tell you about my dad?"

"That he had been killed in the copter crash, that he was Rosie's lover, and that he'd bought you two outdoor-supply stores in Denver that went under."

"I told you that? Ouch. I can't believe you're still sitting here with me."

"You invited me to Breckenridge to ski!" Tilda says. "You made me promise I would come."

Cash laughs. "Did I?"

"And…" Tilda fiddles with the straw in her drink. "You told me that both you and your brother were in love with Ayers."

Cash drops his head into his hands. "Idiot," he says. "I'm an idiot."

They decide to stay at the Lime Inn for dinner. Tilda gets the grilled lobster, which she says is the best on the island, and Cash gets the guava pork ribs, and when their food comes, they push their plates together and share.

"Eco-tourism, huh?" Cash says. "Do you like to hike?"

"Obsessed," Tilda says. "I'm trying to do every hike on the island this year."

"I told Maia I'd do the Esperance Trail with her," Cash says.

"To see the baobab tree?" Tilda says. "I haven't done that one yet!"

"Well, let's plan a time and you can come with us," Cash says.

"Are you asking me on a *date?*" Tilda says. She leans into him, much like Max did at lunch, but instead of being irritating, it feels nice. Tilda smells good. She's tomboyish, which he finds sexy. Her short hair draws attention to her light brown eyes.

"A date?" Cash says. "Aren't we on a date now?"

"Are we?" Tilda says.

"I don't know, aren't we?"

"Maybe we shouldn't examine it too closely," Tilda says.

"Maybe you're right," Cash says. "The hike would be with Maia. So I don't know how romantic it would be."

"No kissing under the baobab tree?" Tilda says.

Cash puts his hand over Tilda's. "I wouldn't rule it out."

Tilda turns her hand so that it's clasping his. Cash feels a rush. Does he *like* Tilda?

"Just do me one favor," Tilda says.

"Okay?" Cash says.

"Don't use me as a substitute for Ayers."

"What?" Cash says. "I know what I supposedly told you in the car, but I was very drunk. Ayers and I are just friends."

"I'm not stupid, Cash," Tilda says. "And I don't blame you. I get it. Ayers is a queen. She's the complete package. I know you and your brother both have a thing for her—"

"Baker might," Cash says. "But I—"

"You do too," Tilda says. "Trust me, I get it. If I were still in my lesbian phase, I'd go after Ayers."

Cash takes a deep breath. This has been a very long, very strange day. "Lesbian phase?"

"High school," Tilda says.

"Max?" Cash asks.

Tilda swats him. "Come on, let's get a nightcap."

They walk hand in hand over to La Tapa.

"It's kind of a thing we do," Tilda says. "Whenever we're out on our nights off, we stop in for a drink."

"I would think it'd be the last place you'd want to go," Cash says.

"Except we all love it," Tilda says. "It's so gratifying to watch everyone else work."

"Ohhhhkay," Cash says. He wonders if Ayers will be there and, if she is, what she'll think when she sees him with Tilda. Will she be jealous? She had been jealous of Cash's attention to Max, that's for damn sure.

Cash worries that he *is* using Tilda. But he likes Tilda and he doesn't want to stop holding her hand.

Maybe he shouldn't examine it too closely.

By the time they reach La Tapa, service has ended. Ayers is nowhere to be seen, though there are still a few people sitting at the bar. Cash and Tilda take seats on the corner and Skip, the bartender, looks between the two of them and glowers.

"Hey, Skip," Cash says.

"So, what, are you two *together* now?" he asks. He glares at Tilda.

"I'll have a glass of the Schramsberg, please," Tilda says.

"Beer for me," Cash says. "Island Hoppin'. Please."

"I'm helping these people right now," Skip says. He holds up a bottle of wine for the couple sitting next to Cash to inspect. "This is the Penfolds Bin Eight Cab. It has notes of imitation crabmeat, hot asphalt, and a one-night stand."

Nervously, the couple laughs.

Tilda says, "Don't do this, Skip."

Skip opens the bottle with a flourish and pours some in the woman's glass. She brings it to her lips. "I can definitely taste the one-night stand," she says. "The asphalt is harder to detect."

"He's a maniac," Tilda whispers.

"What's going on with you two?" Cash asks.

"Nothing," Tilda says. "And I do mean *nothing*."

"But something did happen, right?" Cash says. "Let me guess. You had a thing, then you broke it off and he's pissed. That's the vibe I'm getting."

"A very *short* thing," Tilda says. "A very *insignificant* thing."

Cash puts his hand on the slender stalk of Tilda's neck and pulls her in close. "Tell you what," he says. "I promise not to use you as a substitute for Ayers if you promise not to use me as revenge for old Skippy here. Deal?"

Tilda pantomimes picking up a glass—her champagne has not yet, and may never, arrive—and raises it to Cash. "Deal," she says.

HUCK

At the end of his first week of fishing with Irene, he writes down the following in his ledger:

Monday: 3 adults, 1 child; last name Ford; Calabasas, CA. 2 hardnose, 1 blue runner, 2 blackfin (1 keeper)

Tuesday: 2 adults; last name Poleman; Winchester, MA; 2 mahi (2 keepers)

Wednesday: 2 adults, 3 children; last name Toney; Excelsior, MN; 2 barracuda, 3 wahoo (3 keepers)

Thursday: 2 adults, 4 children; last name Petrushki; Chapel Hill, NC; 4 wahoo (4 keepers), 2 barracuda; 1 mahi (keeper)

Friday: 4 adults; last name Chang; Whitefish Bay, WI; 3 barracuda, 3 mahi (3 keepers), 1 wahoo (keeper)

These are the usual details that Huck records, along with the credit card numbers or a notation that the client paid with cash. He used to include where the clients were staying on the island and how they'd heard about his charter, but then he decided it didn't make any difference. Nearly everyone finds him one of two ways: word of mouth or the GD internet. Huck pays a computer whiz named Destiny over in St. Thomas to make sure that when someone types in *deep-sea fishing* and *St. John USVI,* the *Mississippi* is the first link to pop up. Destiny also runs the cards and sends Huck a brief text the night before a charter so he knows what he'll be dealing with the following day.

What Huck doesn't write down is the way that having Irene on the boat has changed the experience of going to work. Adam was good. Adam was great. He was technically sound with the rods and the gaff, he was excellent when driving the boat, and he was usually pretty friendly with the clients—some more than others, of course, but that's true of Huck as well. Huck doesn't need to be friendly; he's the captain. His only responsibilities are keeping everyone safe and putting people on fish.

If Huck had any reservations about hiring Irene—and yeah, there had been a couple moments when he'd wondered if he was making a giant mistake—they were erased on the very first day. Irene showed up at the boat even before he did, bringing two cups of good, strong, black coffee and two sausage biscuits from Provisions. She was wearing shorts with pockets and a long-sleeved fishing shirt and a visor and sunglasses; her hair was in that fat braid of hers and she looked every inch like the fisherwoman of Huck's dreams. He had forwarded Destiny's text to Irene so she knew they were expecting three adults and one child from Calabasas, wherever that was, someplace in California.

"Los Angeles suburb," Irene said. "The Kardashians live there."

"I don't know who that is," Huck said gruffly, though he did, sort of, because he lived with a twelve-year-old girl.

The three adults turned out to be a gay couple, Brian and Rafael, and a drop-dead gorgeous Swedish au pair who wore only a bikini and a sarong. They wandered down the dock with an eight-year-old boy who was crying.

Irene looked at Huck and said, "We'll stay inshore?"

I love you, Huck thought. "You bet," he said.

The charter—one Huck and Adam might have written off as a bad blind date due to the crying child and uninterested nanny—had been a big success. Brian was an interior designer to the stars who had zero interest in fishing. Rafael was Brazilian and had grown up fishing in Recife, so he was enthusiastic. The au pair lay across the bench seating in the sun and Irene—somehow—worked magic with the kid, whose name was Bennie. She not only got him casting but helped him when he got a bite. Together, Irene and Bennie reeled in a blue runner; it wasn't a keeper but it was a good-looking fish in pictures. Rafael caught two hardnoses and a blackfin that was too small to keep, but all that action made him happy. While checking everyone's lines, Irene chatted with Brian about restoration glass (whatever that was) and epoxy floors (whatever those were). The coup de grâce, however, came near the end of the trip when Irene encouraged the au pair, Mathilde, to cast a line and she caught a nice-size blackfin that they could take home. It was big enough for a sushi appetizer.

"That's the first useful thing she's done all week," Brian whispered. Huck watched him slip Irene a hundred-dollar bill.

Huck figured that was beginner's luck. However, the entire week had gone smoothly. No matter who walked down the dock, Irene was ready, friendly but not too familiar (Adam would have fallen all over himself with the Swedish au pair). After the first day with Bennie, Irene made a habit of bringing snacks—boxes of cheese crackers, bags of hard pretzels. On Friday, Irene showed up with two dozen lemongrass sugar cookies and after Huck tasted one, he took the whole bag from her and said, "These are too good to share."

Irene laughed and tried to take the bag back and soon they were in a tug-of-war and Irene shrieked, "Huck, you're going to turn them to crumbs!" Her tone was playful and the delight on her face made her look even younger and more beautiful than the Swedish au pair and Huck had relented because at that moment, all he wanted to do was kiss her.

He didn't, of course. He couldn't—not on the boat, not while she was working for him.

That wasn't the first time he realized he might be falling in love with Irene. The first time it hit him was Thursday, when they had the family from Chapel Hill on board. The Petrushkis were a mixed-race couple—husband a big white dude, wife a dark-skinned lady—and they had four children: twin fourteen-year-old girls, Emma and Jane, a ten-year-old son, Woody, and a four-year-old son named Elton. Huck had no opinion, really, when it came to children; all he wanted to know was whether they were interested in fishing and, if not, whether they were able to sit on a boat for six or eight hours without causing trouble. If a child was "cute" or not didn't enter his brain. All children were cute, except for Maia, who was exquisite. But even Huck would have had a hard time saying that Elton Petrushki wasn't the cutest child he'd ever seen. He had café-au-lait skin, like Maia, big brown eyes, and chubby cheeks, and as soon as he climbed aboard the boat, he attached himself to Irene and started asking, "We gon' fish? We gon' fish?"

Irene said, "Yes, yes, Elton, we gon' fish."

"We gon' fish!" Elton announced to Huck.

Elton sat with his mother for the trip offshore. Huck was always worried about taking children offshore but Mr. Petrushki assured him that the kids had grown up on the water. The Petrushkis owned a vacation home on Wrightsville Beach on the North Carolina coast and they boated around Cape Fear.

When they slowed down to troll out at Tambo, the fertile spot where Huck and Irene had had such phenomenal luck just after the new year, Huck ran through the drill with Mr. Petrushki and the older kids. He was extra-kind and solicitous—maybe he was trying to show off for Irene—while she dealt with little Elton, who was dead set on catching a fish of his own.

"He gets a fish on, you hold his rod," Huck said. "Wahoo gets a hold of that line, kid's going in. Shark bait."

"Understood, Captain," Irene said. "Nothing is going to happen to this child in my care."

The Petrushki family had, in fact, enjoyed a banner day. Mr. Petrushki got a fish on first—Huck was secretly relieved because plenty of time, he had seen grown men bitter about being shown up by their own children—then Huck tossed chum into the water and they got more hits. Mister brought in a wahoo, then one of the twins brought in a smaller wahoo, then a few minutes later, the other twin brought in a wahoo exactly the same size. It was almost eerie. With the appearance of each fish, Elton Petrushki would jump up and down and yell, "Got fish! Got fish!" He stood over the hold staring down with wide eyes as Huck tossed the fish in.

There was a little bit of a lull at one point but Huck

saw birds diving and directed the boat over. Sure enough, the ten-year-old Woody caught a barracuda, and then Mr. Petrushki caught a barracuda.

Mrs. Petrushki was reading a book bigger than the Bible, the *Collected Works of Jane Austen*.

"I love Jane Austen," Irene said.

"So do I!" Mrs. Petrushki said. "I'm a professor at UNC. I teach the Austen survey course."

"Oh, I get it now," Irene said. "The children's names! Emma, Jane, Wood for Woodhouse, and Elton."

"Yes, I did my thesis on *Emma,*" Mrs. Petrushki said. "I'm a bit obsessed, as my girls like to say."

Huck was in awe at the same time that he felt like an illiterate dummy.

Mrs. Petrushki closed her book and beamed. "Looks like wahoo for dinner."

Elton gazed up at Irene. "We gon' fish?"

"We gon' fish," Irene said. She got a determined set to her mouth. "Elton is taking the next fish."

A few minutes later, they had a bite. Irene steered Elton to the port rod. "We have a bite, Elton," she said. "We are going to reel in your fish. But you have to do exactly what I say."

"Listen to Miss Irene," Mrs. Petrushki said.

Irene showed Elton how to spin the reel; meanwhile, she had her hand firmly on the rod. Huck could see the tight clench of her fingers and he was glad. The rod bowed dramatically; this was a big fish.

"Irene," Huck said.

"We've got it, Captain," she said. "This is Elton's fish."

The fish put up a terrific fight, Huck thought, and by *terrific,* he meant terrible. Irene could maybe have brought the fish up alone but she had Elton squeezed between her legs and her hand over his hand on the reel. Huck was about ready to suggest she pass the kid off to his mother when he saw the flash of green-gold under the surface. He grabbed the gaff and brought up a gorgeous bull mahi that was nearly as big as the one Irene had brought up their first time out.

The other kids were impressed and Elton was beside himself. "My fish! My fish!" As soon as Huck yanked the gaff out and extracted the hook, they all watched the fish flop on the deck while Elton danced alongside it, yelling his head off with joy.

Elton decided he wanted to sit next to Irene going home and it was then, as Huck caught a glimpse of the two of them—Irene with her face raised to the mellow late-afternoon sun, Elton Petrushki tucked under one arm—that he realized he was in serious danger of falling in love with the woman. When Huck looked at Irene, he could see the future. That could be her, fifteen years from now, with Maia's child.

After their charter on Friday with the Changs (who had wanted to stay inshore and fly-fish), Huck and Irene clean the boat (the boat was never this spick-and-span when Adam did the cleaning), and then Huck hands Irene her first paycheck, which he wrote out that morning at home, and says, "Good job this week, Angler Cupcake."

She looks at the check, raises one eyebrow, and says, "I had so much fun, I feel bad taking your money."

"You earned it," Huck says. He wants to tell her how different work was this week compared to every other week of the past six years since LeeAnn died, but he finds a lump in his throat. "I couldn't ask for a better mate."

"Really?" she says.

Huck fears if he gives her any specific compliments, all of his feelings will come tumbling out and he'll embarrass them both. "Next week, we have driving lessons."

"I signed up for the online marine-safety class," she says.

"Good girl," Huck says. He unties his neckerchief and wipes off his forehead. The sun is starting its descent and Huck can already hear the hooting, hollering, and steel-drum music that characterize Cruz Bay on a Friday night. "So, do you have big plans for the weekend?"

"I'm going to sleep in," she says. "Go for a swim or two. Read. Spend time with the boys. And check in with my attorney at home."

"You...haven't heard any news, have you?" Huck asks.

"No." She pauses. "Huck, I have to say it. I'm haunted by all that money in Rosie's dresser."

"That makes two of us." Huck is uncomfortable talking about the Russ-and-Rosie mess at all, and he's glad they've avoided it all week.

"Cash said there were FBI agents watching the house when he got here, but I guess they've decided we're harmless because they haven't been back."

"I told you, AC, nothing to worry about," Huck says. "Hey, listen, Maia is with Ayers tonight. Do you want to go to dinner? Say, Morgan's Mango?"

Irene sighs. "I'm just not ready to go out," she says. "It's too soon."

"I get it," Huck says. "I have some of that wahoo from yesterday and I hid those cookies. Why don't you come to my place and I'll cook for you?"

"I should probably go on home," Irene says. "But thank you."

He nearly offers to grab some barbecue from Candi's—enough for everyone—but then he thinks, *She's telling you no, Sam Powers.* And can he blame her? She's just spent five days straight trapped with him out at sea on a twenty-six-foot boat. Is it any wonder she wants to get away and have some time to herself?

This is what Huck should want as well. After all, the last person he'd wanted to spend his free time with during the past three years was Adam. When he bumped into Adam at Joe's Rum Hut or the Beach Bar—which happened plenty of times—they would wave and not say a word to each other.

But what Huck wants now...is to see more of Irene. In fact, he feels bereft at the idea of an entire weekend without her. Maia is with Ayers tonight, which means Huck will be home alone. He can, in theory, crack open a cold beer and try to finish his damn book. Or he could wander over to the Rum Hut, then to the Beach Bar, then go up to the Banana Deck—he hasn't been up to the Banana Deck since the new year. *Well, yeah,* he thinks. Because Rosie died.

Maybe Irene is right; maybe it *is* too soon to go out to dinner and have a nice time. Maybe they should just stay home and reflect, confer with their attorneys, and wonder what the hell happened.

Then Huck remembers that Maia and her little friend who goes to Antilles, Shane, are planning to see the baobab tree with Cash.

"I heard Maia is planning a hike with Cash," Huck says.

"That's nice," Irene says. "They're forging a relationship."

It *is* nice, Huck agrees. He notices that Irene doesn't suggest *they* forge a relationship outside of work, off this boat, and what can Huck conclude but that Irene isn't interested in him? Somehow, he never considered this. Somehow, he'd let himself believe that her interest in him matched his interest in her.

Was it strange as all get-out that Irene's husband and Huck's stepdaughter had been in a secret relationship and had a love child? Hell yes.

Too strange, maybe. Huck should just forget about it. He should be grateful that he and Irene are friends and now coworkers and that they don't hate each other and aren't in litigation over God knows what—money or the villa or Maia.

Huck watches Irene as she strolls off the dock carrying her reusable shopping bag filled with snacks.

He scratches his face. Maybe he should shave his beard. Or read some Jane Austen.

* * *

The next morning the phone rings, and Huck assumes it'll be Maia asking to stay with Ayers a little longer. If that's the case he might see if Irene wants to take a drive out to the East End. He'll offer to bring Floyd and Baker along if they're looking for something to do.

He's making a nuisance of himself; he's aware of this, but he can't help it.

It's not Maia calling, or Ayers. It's Rupert.

"Huck."

"Rupert."

"You been drinking yet today?" Rupert asks.

"No," Huck says. "Not yet." His eyes graze his trusty bottle of Flor de Caña up on the shelf. Is he going to need it? Or is Rupert about to invite him to meet for lunch at Miss Lucy's—an invitation Huck just might take him up on?

"You remember talking the other day about Paulette Vickers?"

"Yes," Huck says warily. The Flor de Caña, then. He brings the bottle down to the counter.

"She and her husband were arrested over on St. Croix. You know how Doug Vickers has a sister there? FBI, two, three cars, pull into Wilma Vickers's driveway in Frederiksted and Paulette and Doug get led away in handcuffs."

"This reliable?" Huck asks.

"Sadie went to school with Wilma," Rupert says. "Wilma called Sadie herself. She has the little boy. Parents went to jail."

"Did they say why?" Huck asks. "What were they charged with?"

"Conspiracy to commit fraud, Wilma said. Real estate fraud. Financial fraud." Rupert pauses. "The guy they were in business with, and the Invisible Man, too, were doing laundry."

"Laundry?" Huck says.

"They were cleaning money," Rupert says. "Head honcho had a yacht, *Bluebeard,* and Wilma told Sadie that she knows for certain that boat used to pull into Cruz Bay with a hold full of cash. From guerrilla groups in Nicaragua, Wilma said. And the Marxists in Cuba and Argentinean soccer stars trying to avoid taxes and God knows who else. And Paulette and Douglas Vickers were helping them."

When Huck hangs up with Rupert, he calls Agent Vasco but is shuttled immediately to her voicemail. It's Saturday, so maybe she's off duty—but who is he kidding; she's probably waist-deep in the Vickers morass.

Huck has known the Vickerses for twenty years—not well, he's never been invited to their home, never done any direct business with them, but he knows them. Croft must have made them an offer they couldn't refuse; they must have thought they would never get caught. Huck understands what it's like to live here as a local person and see the big boats roll in and watch the enormous villas go up and wonder, *Why them and not me?* Maybe Paulette let herself get into a compromising spot with her family's business; God knows, real estate is risky everywhere. Huck could call some of LeeAnn's friends—Dearie and Helen come to mind—and ask what they've heard. But it's possible that what they heard came from Sadie via Wilma as well, and it's possible that Dearie and Helen haven't heard a thing but will start jabbering as soon as they realize it's a topic of interest. The Vickerses got mixed up with Russell Steele and his boss, Todd Croft, and they were helping to launder the money.

Huck's next instinct is to call Irene. He's been looking for a reason and now he has one. Paulette and Doug Vickers arrested on St. Croix. That much he could share. The rest of it—the laundering and *Bluebeard*—that all sounds suspiciously like gossip. Still, Huck feels the seed of fear that has been in his gut since Rosie died start to grow. Russ was involved in illegal and dangerous business dealings. Guerrillas in Nicaragua?

What Huck wants to know is if he or Maia—or Irene—will somehow be implicated in a crime.

We didn't know anything, Huck thinks. Surely the FBI realizes this. Huck has done nothing wrong, Maia has done nothing wrong, and Irene has done nothing wrong. They're innocent—but does that mean they're safe?

Getting Paulette and Doug Vickers can't possibly be the FBI's endgame, Huck thinks. They want to find Todd Croft. And Paulette will sing—of this, Huck is certain. She has her child to think about.

From this perspective, maybe Irene would be intrigued by the news, possibly even happy to hear it. They're tracking down answers. What were Croft and Russell Steele doing? Where was all that money coming from?

No, it will *not* make Irene happy, Huck decides. It will make her agitated, especially since all they can do until they get official word from Agent Vasco is speculate. And so Huck decides *not* to tell Irene until he's had a conversation with Agent Vasco.

Huck sets the Flor de Caña back up on the shelf. He heads out onto the deck to have a cigarette. He imagines Irene lying on the beach in Little Cinnamon, thinking about little Elton Petrushki or about how cold it is back in Iowa City or about what she's going to make for dinner. But she will *not* be thinking about Paulette Vickers sitting in an interrogation room and giving the FBI who knows what kind of information about her husband. Huck's silence is a gift. Irene is sure to find out at some point; hell, maybe she'll find out tomorrow. But at least she has today in peace. At least she has right now.

BAKER

Baker is so excited after their meeting and tour at the Gifft Hill School that he texts Anna from the parking lot.

Found a school for F. They ran assessments, he can start kindergarten now. V. advanced, they said. Happy to have him and he loved it.

"Bye!" Maia calls out. She's staying at the school to hang out with friends and then someone's mother is taking them to town.

"Thank you, Maia!" Baker says.

"Thank you, Maia!" Floyd says, waving like a maniac. Then he turns to Baker. "Daddy, how do we know Maia?"

"Oh," Baker says. Floyd is probably confused because Maia introduced Floyd to the head teacher, Miss Phaedra, as her "sort of nephew," a phrase that elicited an expression of surprise and suspicion from Miss Phaedra. Apparently, the phrase didn't get past Floyd either. Baker was glad Maia threw the *sort of* in there because it could be explained any number of ways; they wouldn't have to tell Miss Phaedra that Floyd is, in fact, Maia's actual nephew, the son of Maia's brother Baker.

Sometimes Baker wishes Floyd weren't so "advanced."

"She's our friend," Baker says. Not a lie.

"I like her," Floyd says. "I like the Gifft Hill School. Why are there two Fs?"

"No idea, buddy," Baker says. He checks that Floyd's seat belt is fastened, then heads for home.

He doesn't hear back from Anna until two days later, Wednesday.

K, the text says.

K? Baker thinks. He hadn't expected a fight, necessarily, or even a debate, but he *had* anticipated something more than just *K*. They're talking about Floyd's education! Baker was armed with the school brochure and the notes he'd taken in the margins, and he has the website for backup as well as his own impressions, which he'd spent the past two days organizing into a sales pitch. The school is nurturing (but not indulgent), inclusive, tolerant, and forward-thinking. (Anna will love all of this.) The sky is the limit for Floyd! The classes are small and they have an island-as-classroom initiative that gets the kids outside studying nature and history and Caribbean culture.

But...Anna doesn't care. Anna is relocating to Cleveland, learning the ropes at a new hospital, meeting her colleagues, reviewing protocols, buying furniture, and maybe even getting excited for Louisa to become pregnant.

Baker tries not to feel like he and Floyd have been brushed off, forgotten.

He doesn't bother telling Anna that he also got good news during the visit to the Gifft Hill School—he'd received a job offer. The upper school, Miss Phaedra said, desperately needed someone to coach basketball and baseball as well as do some administrative work for the athletic department. She mentioned this because Baker was so tall and "fit-seeming" (the "seeming" being key) and she wondered if maybe he had any background in either sport and might want a chance to get involved in the community, seeing as how he was new to the island. It was like she'd read his mind. Baker said that he did indeed have some background in both sports; he'd played basketball and baseball in high school and in college at Northwestern on the intramural level.

"Which means, essentially, that I haven't used my skills in almost ten years. I've been waiting for Floyd to be old enough so I could coach his teams."

"The job does come with a stipend, and the hours would be after school during the respective seasons," Miss

Phaedra says. "I'd love to be able to pass your name on to the head of school, and she can talk with you more about it."

It's exactly what Baker is looking for, and yet he doesn't commit right away because he still has to go back to Houston for the auction this coming weekend. There's a quiet but persistent voice in Baker's head telling him that it's crazy—and, worse, irresponsible—to move to the Caribbean with Floyd.

He came down here for one reason only and that's Ayers. But Ayers is with Mick. And Ayers was clear that she wouldn't even entertain the possibility of a relationship with Baker until he had a job or an opportunity here on St. John.

The whole thing is risky. Baker can leave Houston, take the job at Gifft Hill, and move here, but Ayers might still stay with Mick.

The evening that Anna responds with *K,* Irene comes home from work with some fresh wahoo steaks from her charter. She grills them for Baker and Floyd, and because Cash is out somewhere, it's just the three of them eating dinner on the deck. It's nice. Irene is in a good mood; her frame of mind seems better now that she's working on Huck's fishing boat, though she's not her old self by any means. Baker tells her that Floyd liked the school but he doesn't say anything about the job offer yet. He reminds his mother that he and Floyd are headed back to Houston on Friday for the auction.

"Right," Irene says, though it's clear she's forgotten about it. "But you're coming back, yes?"

"Yes?" Baker says. "I think so. I mean, yes." He wants to sound definitive but the truth is, he's not sure. He's packing everything they brought down, just in case.

"When?" Irene says. "When will you be back?"

"I don't have return tickets yet," Baker says. "Though I can get them, of course, at a moment's notice. I have to figure some stuff out when I get to Houston. What to do about the house, my car, that kind of thing."

"Of course," Irene says. "No one expects you to drop everything and move down here. Though that's what I did." She laughs—at her own crazy spontaneity, maybe. "And that's what your brother did."

"Where *is* Cash tonight?" Baker asks. He suddenly gets a bad feeling. Cash didn't come back after *Treasure Island*. Did he go somewhere with *Ayers?* Out to dinner? This is what Baker has privately feared about Cash and Ayers working together, that they would become chummy, that Cash would, somehow, manage to charm her.

"He had an incident on the boat today, I guess," Irene says. "Passenger got drunk and Cash was called on to help get the girl home. Turned out the girl had a friend that Cash knew. From that restaurant you both like so much?"

"La Tapa?" Baker says.

"That must be it," Irene says. "And I think he went out with the friend. Something like that."

Baker pushes his chair away from the table. "Was it Ayers, Mom? Is he out with Ayers?"

"It wasn't Ayers," Irene says. She throws Baker an exasperated look. "You boys, honestly. No, it was some other name. British, unusual..."

"Tilda?" Baker says.

"Yes!" Irene says. "He went out with Tilda."

"Who's Tilda?" Floyd asks.

"A friend of your uncle's," Irene says.

Baker can't describe his relief. He tousles Floyd's hair. "You want some ice cream, buddy? They had red velvet cake at the Starfish Market."

Baker puts Floyd to bed, then decides to turn in himself, mostly because there's nothing else to do. Cash is still out and Baker has no other friends. If he were at home in Houston right now, he would smoke some weed and crash out in front of the TV—he needs to catch up on *Game of Thrones*—but he can't watch *that* with Irene around.

His phone rings. This, he thinks, will be Anna, just getting home from work at nine o'clock at night. He steels himself. It would be just like Anna to have glanced at his text distractedly and responded with *K,* but then, after running the whole thing past Louisa, suddenly have a list of objections.

Baker should have texted Louisa.

But his display says Ayers.

"Ayers?" he says.

"Hey." Her voice sounds funny—sad, trembling, like she's been crying. "Are you busy?"

"Not at all," he says. "I just put Floyd to bed so I can talk. What's up?"

There's a pause. "Can you get out? Is Cash there? Or your mom? To watch Floyd?"

"Uh…yeah. Cash is out but my mom is here." Baker stands up and checks himself in the mirror. He hasn't shaved—or showered, for that matter, unless swimming in the pool counts as a shower—since the day he went to Gifft Hill, Monday. He does have a nice tan now, but he looks like a Caribbean hobo. "Do you want to meet somewhere?"

"Can you just come here, to my place?" Ayers asks. "There's something I want to talk to you about."

"Your place?"

"Fish Bay," Ayers says. "It'll take you fifteen minutes if you leave right now."

"Right now?" Baker says. And before he can explain that he needs to shower and change, she's giving him directions.

Unlike the rest of the island, Fish Bay is flat. And really dark. Ayers said she lived past the second little bridge on the left, but Baker would have missed her house if he hadn't caught a flash of green, her truck, out of the corner of his eye.

She's standing in the doorway, backlit, hugging herself. He doesn't need to feel bad about not showering, he sees. She's still wearing her *Treasure Island* uniform and her hair is wild and curly.

"Hey," he says. "You okay?"

She moves so that he can step past her, inside.

Her place is small, cute, bohemian. There's a tiny kitchen with thick ceramic dishes on open shelves. There's a papasan chair, a bunch of houseplants, a glass bowl filled with sand dollars, and a gallery wall of photographs from places all over the world—the Taj Mahal, the Great Pyramids, the Matterhorn. Ayers is in every picture; in many, she's a kid.

"Have you *been* to all these places?" Baker asks.

"Story for another day," she says. "Come sit."

Baker picks a spot next to Ayers on a worn leather sofa draped with a tapestry. There's a coffee table with three pillar candles sitting in a dish of pebbles, and lying across the pebbles is a joint.

Are they going to smoke?

"Would you like a glass of water?" Ayers asks.

"Maybe in a minute," Baker says. "Why don't you tell me what's going on."

Ayers folds her legs underneath her. How is it possible that even when she looks awful, she's beautiful?

"This morning—" She laughs. "Which now feels like three days ago." She picks up the joint and lifts a barbecue lighter off the side table, then seems to think better of it and sets both down. "It's been a very long day."

"Some days are like that," Baker says. "Start at the beginning."

"Last night Mick told me he had to go to St. Thomas to get restaurant supplies today," Ayers says. "Whatever, I found it a little strange, but I didn't question it. Too much." She throws her hands up. "Anyway, then this morning, I saw him on the ferry with Brigid."

Baker makes a face like he's surprised. But he's not surprised. He knew Mick would screw it up. He actually wishes Cash were here to listen to this. Baker leans in. "You're kidding."

"Not kidding. I saw them sitting together and I was...pissed. Livid. Suspicious."

"I bet."

"So I sent him a text telling him never to call me again."

Baker spreads his palms against the cool, cracked leather of the sofa. This is real? He didn't fall asleep in bed next to Floyd? Ayers is telling him exactly what he's been waiting to hear, only much sooner than he had hoped. Her timing couldn't be better.

"Then Cash and I had this weird, awful thing happen at work."

"Yeah, I heard, sort of."

"This girl got really drunk, and I thought she'd tanked while snorkeling. We stopped the boat, I dove off, your brother dove off, this other kid who's probably going to be in the Olympics dove off, it was a total circus, and in the end the chick was in the head changing out of one inappropriate suit into a second, even more inappropriate suit, and this was all before we even got to Jost. The girl continued to drink and then puked off the side the whole way home." Ayers sighs. "And I left your brother to handle it because guess who was waiting for me at the dock."

"Mick," Baker says, and he suspects that maybe this story isn't going to have the ending he wants it to.

"Mick," Ayers says. "He just left here a little while ago. Right before I called you. We broke up."

"You broke up?" Baker says. He's afraid to go back to feeling optimistic. "What did he say? Why was he with Brigid?"

"He *said* they bumped into each other. Unplanned. A coincidence. She was headed over to St. Thomas to get a tattoo of the petroglyphs."

"Okay?" Baker says.

"I just got a tattoo of the petroglyphs a few weeks ago," Ayers says. She holds out her ankle so Baker can see the tattoo; it's a curlicue symbol in dark green. "We're hardly the only two people in the universe with a petroglyph tattoo. Rosie had one. But still, I was chafed."

"Understandably," Baker says.

"Mick says they only talked for a couple of minutes, then Mick took Gordon, that's our dog, *his* dog, up to stand at the bow and he didn't see Brigid again."

"Do you believe him?"

"I don't want to believe him," Ayers says. "But I do."

"You do?"

"I do."

"So…why did you break up?"

"Two reasons," Ayers says. "Both are secrets that I'm keeping from him. One is this…project that I'm working on. I can't tell him about it, and I can't tell you about it yet either. Maybe in the future, once I'm finished, but not right now."

"Secret project," Baker says. "I won't ask."

"Please don't," Ayers says. She seems to shrink under her *Treasure Island* T-shirt and when she gazes at him, her eyes appear robbed of their pigment. They are very, very pale blue. "The second reason is…that I have feelings for you."

"For me?"

"For you," Ayers says. "I haven't been able to stop thinking about you."

"You haven't?" Baker says.

She shakes her head and presses her lips together like she's embarrassed.

"So, wait," Baker says. Is this really happening? Him and Ayers? Does she want him to kiss her? Does she want him to—finally—make proper love to her? Baker can't find the words to ask, he's too overwhelmed, but it turns out it doesn't matter.

Ayers stands up, takes his hand, and leads him to her bed.

He wakes up in the middle of the night; 4:20 a.m., his phone says. Ayers is naked in bed next to him. He's in love. He's beyond in love.

But he has to get out of there. He can't have Floyd waking up and finding his dad gone.

Baker eases out of bed and uses the bathroom. He sees a clothbound book balanced on the edge of the sink. Ayers's journal? Baker is, of course, tempted to open it and read Ayers's innermost thoughts, presumably about how she's stuck with crappy cheater Mick but can't get Baker Steele out of her mind. However, back when Baker was in college, he read his girlfriend Trinity's diary and all hell broke loose. That was why they'd split. Trinity had called it a "devastating breach of personal trust."

If you learn one thing from me, Baker Steele, she'd said, *I hope it's never to read a woman's private thoughts without her express permission.*

No matter how tempting, she'd added. *And, oh yes, it will be tempting.*

It *is* tempting—the journal with the red floral cover, demure and innocent with the look of a colonial-era recipe book.

But Baker leaves it be.

In the end, Trinity taught him a lot. He must remember to hit her up on Facebook and thank her.

Back in the bedroom, he runs a finger down the length of Ayers's spine and she shivers awake and opens one eye. "You leaving?"

"I have to," he whispers. "Floyd."

"Okay," she says.

Baker clears his throat. "And, uh, you remember that I'm leaving tomorrow for Houston? I have that thing on Saturday? But I'm coming right back. So you don't have to worry."

"What day?" Ayers asks. "What day are you coming back?"

Baker does a quick calculation. The benefit auction is Saturday night. Sunday he's on cleanup duty. He needs at least two additional days to get the move organized, maybe three; honestly, he could use a week, but now that this has happened, all he can think about is how to get back here as quickly as possible. But then again, he has a life to dismantle—Floyd's medical records need to be transferred (to where?); Baker needs to forward his mail (to where?) and figure out what to do about his income taxes. There's stuff. "Wednesday," he says. "Thursday."

"Wednesday or Thursday?" she asks.

248 • *Elin Hilderbrand*

"Thursday," he says. "Week from today."

"I'm working at La Tapa Thursday night," she says. "Come by after work. We can celebrate your move."

He kisses her temple. "You got it," he says. He puts his clothes on and runs both hands through his hair. "Oh, by the way, the chick who got drunk on your boat was a friend of Tilda's."

Ayers rolls over and squints at him. "Really?"

"Yeah, that's what my mother told me Cash said. I guess Cash and Tilda went out last night."

"They *did?*" Ayers says, sitting up.

"Yeah," Baker says. "I think so." He wonders if hearing this bothers Ayers for some reason.

She smiles. "They're perfect for each other." She falls back into her pillows. "When you get back, we can double-date."

"Great," Baker says sardonically—although, actually, it sounds like fun.

The theme for the Children's Cottage benefit auction is Monopoly. This was Debbie's idea. She was in charge of dreaming up something to top Oh, the Places You'll Go!, which was last year's theme. Although Baker was skeptical about the appeal of Monopoly—it evoked nothing so much as the rainy afternoons of childhood, trapped in a never-ending game of being sent to jail, paying other people rent, and eventually going bankrupt due to real estate failures— the execution is brilliantly done. Baker has dressed up as Rich Uncle Pennybags, in a vest with a pocket watch, and people are chattering with anticipation as they leave the school parking lot. (FREE PARKING signs abound, which is cute, even though parking is always free at the Children's Cottage.)

The event is being held in the school gymnasium (built back in 2000 by one of the owners of the Houston Rockets), but the board of directors, naturally, have created a path that takes attendees through the school so that they can see where their donations will be going. Baker, with Ellen at his side, walks through the reading nook filled with picture books, the numbers room with boxes of manipulatives, the science room where kids study birds' nests and leaves and different kinds of rocks, the social studies room, festooned with flags of the world, and last, and most popular, the water-table room. They then pass through the courtyard with the outdoor playground into the gym, which has been transformed into a Monopoly board for the evening.

At the front table, everyone picks up a plastic top hat and mustache on a stick (each stick has a number printed on the back; it doubles as an auction paddle) and proceeds to one of the tables, all of which are named for Monopoly properties and sheathed in tablecloths of the corresponding colors. Baker and his school wives are, naturally, at Boardwalk, with a tablecloth of Columbia blue. The centerpiece is a flour-sack money bag filled with pebbles and holding a bouquet of gold dahlias. The photo booth is decorated to look like the Jail square, so once Baker's friends choose seats, he suggests they get their pictures taken, then go find glasses of the event's signature cocktail, the Chance Card, which is a lurid orange.

They're being served by Vicki Styles, who likes to expose her cleavage whenever she can.

"That was a good choice," Becky says. "The Chance Cards are being served by the Community Chest."

Baker loves his school wives. How will he ever leave them?

The event swims along. People drink, eat hors d'oeuvres, bid on silent-auction items. Baker really wants to get Floyd tickets to the first Texans game, but then he remembers that he's not going to be around for it. Wendy wants them all to chip in on a house in Galveston in May— but Baker won't be here for that either. He needs to tell his friends about his plans, and soon; the only person who knows is Ellen.

Standing in the strobe-lit school gym surrounded by people he has known for years—and even psycho Mandy in her little black dress with her satin Justin Verlander team jacket on top seems endearing tonight—Baker has a hard time believing that he was in Ayers's apartment only two days earlier. He has switched worlds. Which one of them is real?

He could easily make the argument that this world is real. This is Houston, a real place; the Children's Cottage is a real school. Baker is a part of this community. He is known. He's Floyd's dad. No one misses Anna, though they all know that she's a big deal, if not a particularly hands-on mother. Baker's friends are real friends, there when he needs them. He's giving up a lot by leaving—his house, his autonomy. There's a way in which moving to St. John feels like regressing. He'll be back living with his mom and brother.

All of this is on one side of the scale—and Ayers is on the other.

Dinner is served. It's boardwalk food, which sounds iffy but ends up being delicious: jumbo hot dogs with a variety of toppings, skinny truffle fries, and Mexican street corn. Then the live auction starts and Baker zones out, thinking he'll tell Debbie, Becky, and Wendy his plans after the auction but before the dancing. They'll be upset initially but then one of them will request "We Are Family" from the DJ and they'll all cluster together to dance and all the married parents will be jealous. Nothing new there.

Baker perks up only when the auctioneer announces a superspecial item, added at the last minute by an anonymous donor. It's one week in a villa on St. John with 180-degree views over the Caribbean Sea. Nine bedrooms, dual-level pool, private beach and shuffleboard court, outdoor kitchen, and the use of two 2018 Jeeps. July or August dates only.

Ellen nudges Baker's leg under the table. "This is you?"

He gives the slightest of nods.

The bidding is robust. It starts at five thousand and skyrockets from there—ten, fifteen, twenty thousand dollars. July or August is the perfect time of year to escape the beastly heat of Houston, and when Baker ran the idea past Irene and Cash, they'd agreed that July or August would be an ideal time to take a break from St. John and fly to Door County (Irene) and Breckenridge (Cash).

Twenty-five thousand dollars. Thirty thousand.

"Jeez, Baker," Ellen murmurs.

"It's Nanette's husband bidding," Wendy says. "Oil."

"Against Beanie O'Connor's grandmother," Becky says. "Oil."

Thirty-five thousand. Forty thousand.

"That's going to buy a lot of manipulatives," Debbie whispers.

Forty-five thousand.

Fifty thousand. Going once, going twice…sold, for fifty thousand dollars.

"Are you going back?" Ellen asks. "For good?"

Baker sighs. He hasn't even told Ellen about his night with Ayers. He hasn't told anyone. "I am," he says.

"Good for you," Ellen says.

The auction is over, the DJ gets warmed up with "Celebrate," and all of Baker's friends go to the ladies' room, leaving him sitting at the table alone.

First order of business on getting back to St. John: Find some *male* friends. Other than Cash.

When the ladies reappear, they envelop Baker in a group hug. Wendy is crying. Baker gives Ellen a quizzical look and she shrugs as if to say, *Sorry, not sorry*. The thing that Baker has long suspected happens in ladies' rooms has happened. The truth has come out.

"I'm going to miss you guys," Baker says.

Turns out that when Nanette's husband, Tony, lost out to Beanie O'Connor's grandmother in the auction, it lit a fuse. Nanette and Tony have a raging, alcohol-fueled fight in Free Parking (though, thankfully, no one ends up dead like in that book all Baker's friends read three or four years ago), and Nanette announces that she wants a divorce.

"The auction was just an excuse," Debbie says when she comes over the next day to help Baker get organized. "She's been sleeping with Ian for years." Ian is Wendy's ex-husband.

Yes, true, everyone knows this.

Nanette sends Baker a text less than an hour later: I hear you have a place for rent?

He texts back, Just so happens, I do.

On Sunday, Debbie helps Baker clean out his fridge and cabinets. Becky helps him figure out his tax returns. Wendy comes over with her daughters, Evelyn and Ondine, and they play with Floyd while Baker packs Floyd's suitcase.

Ellen stops by with a goodbye present, a Rawlings alloy baseball bat for his new coaching duties.

"You won't hit the ball if you don't swing," she says.

Baker books tickets for Wednesday. Debbie drives a minivan; she's going to take Baker and Floyd to the airport after she drops Eleanor and Gale at school.

Monday after school, Baker and Floyd sit in the kitchen eating pizza because Baker doesn't want to dirty any dishes. It's ironic that they're eating pizza, Anna's favorite meal, when Anna is so far away.

Baker decides to reach out to Anna. He snaps a selfie of himself and Floyd and the sausage and pepperoni pie from Brother's and texts it to her with the words Miss you, Mom!

She'll probably respond to the text sometime next week, Baker thinks.

A few minutes later, Baker's phone beeps and he checks it, expecting Anna's response to be *Okay* or *Sounds good* or maybe even *Miss you 2.*

The text isn't from Anna, however. It's from Cash. Baker reads it, then drops his phone.

ROSIE

July 31, 2006

I should have known that telling Mama and Huck had gone too easily.

Mama read my diary and found out about Russell and found out about Irene—and one night after work, I walked in the door expecting to find her asleep or, possibly, waiting up with a plate of chicken, beans, and rice—she was concerned that I wasn't eating enough for two—but instead she was in the doorway, my diary in her hand, her eyes popping.

"A married man?" she said. "Have you no shame, Rosie?"

I grabbed the diary from her. "Have you no shame?" I asked. I went into my room and slammed the door behind me, my heart cowering in my chest because I had left it exposed and my mother had found it.

I'm going to set the diary on fire, *I thought. And if the whole house goes up in smoke, so be it.*

There was a light knock on the door and I figured it was Huck, there to try and fix what my mother had broken. But when I opened the door, it was Mama herself. I tried to slam the door in her face but she pushed back—for a second, our eyes locked, and it was a test of strength. I was younger but pregnant; Mama was Mama. Then she put a finger to her lips and I relented.

She entered, closed the door quietly behind her, sat on my bed, and patted the spot next to her.

I shook my head, lips closed in anger.

"I'm sorry," she said. "I had to be sure."

What she meant was that she had to be sure the baby wasn't Oscar's.

I wasn't naive. I knew there was talk across the island. Who is the father of Rosie Small's baby? *The odds were on Oscar. It was possible that Oscar had even claimed it was his, though we hadn't been together since he'd been out of jail.*

"My word isn't good enough?" I said.

"It's not," Mama said. I gave her a look, which she brushed off. "You're young, you're afraid, you might have said anything to keep a roof over your head."

"I don't need this roof," I said. "I have money saved."

"Oh, that's right," she said. "The ten thousand dollars. Where is it?"

She knew about the ten thousand dollars, of course. She

knew everything now: Vie's Beach, the sex, the room service, the wife and sons in Iowa, the name of the boat—Bluebeard.

"I kept a thousand in cash," I said. "The other nine I deposited a little at a time along with my paychecks."

She nodded like she approved. "Good."

"I haven't contacted him," I said. "I have no intention of ever seeing him again, Mama. Like I said, it was a mistake."

"Your voice is saying it was a mistake but your face is telling a different story."

I almost broke then. I almost said that it wasn't a mistake, that I didn't regret being with Russ, that there had been something between us and that something was real. But my mother was Catholic; she believed in the sanctity of marriage. A married white man having a baby with an island girl was no good. I could tell, however, by her mere presence in my bedroom that it was far, far better than me being pregnant by Oscar.

"What does Huck think?" I asked. I wondered if he might be more sympathetic to my situation. He had been married, then divorced. He, maybe, understood that relationships didn't always fit into neat boxes—though it would be very unusual for him to battle Mama.

"Huck doesn't know."

"You didn't tell him?" I said. It was even more unusual for my mother to keep a secret from Huck.

"I told him the man was white. A pirate."

Pirate *had been the word I used in my diary.*

"That's the story from here on out," Mama said. "Pirate came in on his yacht, you had relations, then he left, never *to be seen again." She clasped my hand. "Do you understand me, Rosie? Never to be seen again. You see this man again,*

I phone the wife. Irene Steele from Iowa City. I called Information. I have the number."

Hearing Irene's name come out of my mother's mouth gave me chills. I knew she was serious. I could never see Russ again, even if he did someday return.

August 22, 2006

It was as though we'd conjured him. Three weeks after my mother confronted me, I was at work—still cocktail waitressing, even though my belly was enormous and my ankles swollen—when Estella tapped me on the shoulder and said, "There's a man at the bar who wants an order of the conch fritters."

"Isn't Purcell on the bar?" I asked.

"He is, child, but this gentleman asked for you."

I was punching in an order and I had a table with food up and a table still waiting to order drinks and Tessie was taking a leisurely cigarette break as always and I was about to snap. The restaurant was closing September first for two and a half months—hurricane season—so I only had to make it through another week. I gathered my wits, delivered one table their meals, took the drink order, ran quickly to the ladies' room, and then, feeling relieved and refreshed, I lumbered over to the bar to see which gentleman at the bar wanted the conch fritters.

Honestly, I didn't even think.

Russ was sitting at the corner seat.

I was torn between running straight into his arms and running for the parking lot.

His eyes became round as plates when he saw my belly.

He knew, Todd Croft must have told him, but maybe he didn't believe it or maybe he was overwhelmed to see evidence of his child with his own eyes.

"Mona Lisa," he said.

"Stop," I said.

"Mine?" he said.

"Don't insult me," I said. I turned and gazed out at the water in front of Caneel, but I didn't see the yacht.

"Bluebeard is on Necker Island today," he said. "I came over in a helicopter. We have . . . a client . . . with a helicopter." He seemed proud to be telling me this, like I would care about a helicopter, of all things.

"Must be nice," I said. My voice was stony, nearly icy, but my insides were molten. He came back. He was here. As discreetly as I could, I checked his left hand—ring still in place. At least today he was dressed appropriately. He wore stone-white shorts and a navy gingham shirt, crisp and expensive-looking, turned back at the cuffs. A new watch, a Breitling. He had a tan, a fresh haircut; he had lost twenty pounds. He looked great; there was very little trace of the sweet, bumbling man I had known. I was even more drawn to this sleeker, more confident version.

"What time are you off?" he asked. He nodded down the beach. "I got our room."

Our room, 718. I had avoided going anywhere near the hotel rooms since he left.

"I can't," I said.

"Why not?"

Why not. I thought about telling him that my mother had read my diary and was threatening to call Irene, but

I didn't want him to know how much control my mother had over me. I thought he'd be angry that I'd written about our relationship and been stupid enough to leave the diary in a place where Mama could find it. I thought he'd think poorly of my mother for blackmailing me—and I couldn't bear that. Mama was looking out for me.

"You're married," I said. "To Irene. You have children already. I'm not going to disrespect that. You can't ask me to. It's not fair."

"Rosie…" he said.

"It happened," I said. "But it can't continue."

He nodded at my midsection. "Except it is continuing. You're having my baby."

I nearly surrendered to him right then and there. My baby. Here he was, willing to claim the child so that I wasn't alone in all of this. And in the months since he'd left I had felt very, very alone. Mama and Huck would help me. I would live with them and bank the money that Todd Croft had given me to get me through the first year.

"I have to get back to work," I said. I left Russ and put in an order for conch fritters.

He stayed until service ended. His mere presence at the bar—he was watching the Braves-Phillies game—made my pulse quicken and my breathing get shallow and I feared this reaction would affect the baby so I tried to stop and rest, drink plenty of ice water, and get to the ladies' room often to splash my face.

Finally, I was finished. It was time for me to leave. I walked over to him.

"*I'm going home,*" I said. "*It was nice to see you again.*"

"*Please, Rosie,*" he said. "*Just come to the room.*"

I wanted to, if only for the air-conditioning and because I knew he would order me whatever I wanted from room service. But then it occurred to me that Russ might have been after sex and sex alone; maybe he saw me as a girl in a port, an island wife. I was nobody's island wife.

"*No,*" I said. "*I'm sorry. You're married.*"

He nodded. "That I am."

It pained me to hear him say it, but it also gave me resolve.

"*Please don't come back here,*" I said. "*Unless you get divorced and you have bona fide legal documents to prove it. It's difficult for me to see you.*" I spread my hands across my stomach. "*I had feelings for you.*"

"*Had?*"

"*Had, have, it doesn't matter because you don't live here and you aren't mine.*"

"*I'd like to support the baby,*" he said.

"*I received money already,*" I said. I wasn't sure if this would come as news to him or not.

He said, "Todd showed me your e-mail last week. He told me he sent you money back in May. He told me he came down to Carnival in July and that he checked in on you and that his hunch was correct: you were pregnant. The instant he told me, I made plans to come down here. I'm here only to see you, Rosie."

Todd Croft had come during St. John's Carnival and had spied on me? I didn't like that one bit.

Russ had found out only last week?

"I have everything I need," I said. "But thank you."

"You don't have to forgive me but you do have to let me support that child," Russ said.

"I don't, though," I said, and I walked out of the restaurant, past the Sugar Mill, and into the parking lot, where I climbed in my car and cried.

The following week, a package arrived containing five thousand dollars in cash. An identical package came the week after that. And the week after that.

October 29, 2006

Today at 5:09 a.m., Maia Rosalie Small entered the world weighing six pounds and fourteen ounces and measuring twenty inches long. She is the most beautiful creature I have ever laid eyes on.

The nurse brought me a form to fill out so she could make the birth certificate. On the line where it asked for the father's name, I wrote Unknown.

November 1, 2006

Maia is three days old. Today, I sent an e-mail to Todd Croft at Ascension letting him know that I'd had a baby girl and that her name was Maia Small.

September 4, 2012

Today is Maia's first day at the Gifft Hill School. She marched into the classroom, head held high, shoulders back, with *barely a wave to me and Mama and Huck, all of us standing in the doorway, watching her go.*

Huck had a charter and Mama was due at the health center and I thought, What am I going to do now? Then I realized this was the perfect time to start journaling again. Because if you don't write down what happens in a day, you forget—and that day becomes a blur and that blur becomes your life.

If I had to describe what has happened in the past six years, what would I say?

I quit my job cocktail waitressing at Caneel and got a job waiting tables at La Tapa, but only four nights a week because of Maia.

I have a best friend named Ayers Wilson, who's another waitress at La Tapa. She's like a sister to me and an auntie to Maia. She dates Mick, the manager at the Beach Bar, so we stop by there after our shift and sometimes there are cute guys and a live band and sometimes I dance and a date comes out of it—but there has been no one special because the first thing I say is that I have a daughter but the father isn't in the picture and the second thing I say is that I was born and raised on the island and will never leave.

This scares everyone away. Everyone.

On the first day of each month, cash arrives in a package and I put it in the bank for Maia. It's how I can pay for Gifft Hill. I won't say I'm not grateful, but receiving the packages also fills me with anger, shame . . . and longing.

Unbelievably, after all this time, I still think about Russ. I wonder how he's doing. I can only assume he's still married to Irene, trying in earnest to make the marriage work.

I hope he's happy—because if he's not happy, then what's the point of staying with her?

February 9, 2013

Journaling is like exercise; it's hard to keep it up. You have to make yourself do it, and ultimately, I don't see the point of Went to work, played Tooth Fairy, went to bed.

Tooth Fairy because Maia lost her first tooth, bottom front left. It popped out when she bit down on a piece of breakfast toast, then it skittered across the floor and Huck found it.

I sometimes wish I had an e-mail or a cell phone number for Russ. I would tell him: Your daughter lost her first tooth. *What would he do with that news? I wonder. He has no one to share it with.*

February 13, 2014

Two things happened today, almost at the same time. One, I was on Salomon Beach, finally reading Eat, Pray, Love, *the book that Ayers holds above all others. (She has been to Italy, India, and Bali, so it resonates with her.) Anyway, I was in the midst of the India section when I looked up and saw that yacht,* Bluebeard, *sailing past Salomon toward Caneel.*

No, I thought. But then I remembered that it was this time eight years ago that I met Russ.

I stood up. I was wearing a white bikini, just like I had been when I met Russ at Hansen Bay. I wondered if Russ was on the boat and, if so, whether he could see me. I was tempted to drive to Caneel to check if Bluebeard had anchored out front, but while I was in my car, debating, my phone rang and it was Huck.

It was midafternoon. This was very unusual.

"It's your mother," he said. "She's sick and I'm taking her over to Schneider."

"What do you mean?" I said. My mother didn't get sick. My mother was a nurse practitioner who, after years of treating everything from head colds to herpes, had developed a force field around her. Nothing got through.

"She's being admitted," he said. "It's her heart. It's failing. You and Maia should plan to come over and see her after school lets out. I'll handle today, get her settled, talk to the doctors, see if it's better for us to go to Puerto Rico or the States."

I could have told Huck then and there that Mama would never agree to be treated in the States, but I didn't want to start a health-care debate.

Her heart failing? It seemed impossible. My mother had the strongest constitution of anyone I knew, and that didn't even take into account her iron will.

For years I would have said it was impossible for my mother's heart to fail—because she didn't have a heart.

March 3, 2014

My mother, LeeAnn Small Powers, died at home with Huck and me by her side. We'd let Maia have her first sleepover, an overnight with her little friend Joanie. We explained the sit-uation to Joanie's parents and they were very kind.

We'll tell Maia in the morning.

March 10, 2014

My mother is dead and, now, buried in the Catholic cemetery. We had a service, led by Father Abrams, my mother's fa-vorite, followed by an enormous reception on Oppenheimer Beach. The community center was open, everyone brought a dish to share, the men got the grill going, my mother's friends sang some gospel hymns followed by some Bob Marley. There were children running in and out of the water and down the beach. It was as much a celebration of life as it was a memorial.

When the sun set, the rum came out and a steel band set up, and once I made sure Maia was safe, under the watchful eyes of her aunties, I found Huck and he poured some Flor de Caña and we did a shot together.

"We're going to make it," he said.

"Are we?" I said. I knew it was the right time for me to find a home of my own. I had plenty of money in the bank to rent a nice place, maybe even buy, but I knew that if I moved out, my heart would break and so would Huck's. My mother was gone. We needed to stick together.

I found Ayers and Mick sitting on the beach together and I joined them and Mick's dog, Gordon. We were such good friends that we didn't have to speak; we could just be.

Mick whistled, snapping me out of my daydream. "Would you look at that," he said. "Bluebeard."

*I made a sound, words trying to escape that I caught
at the last second. Bluebeard? I stood up and, sure enough,
there was the yacht, cruising across the horizon in front
of us. Headed away from Tortola, it looked like, and
toward…well, toward Caneel. Where else?*

*I stayed on Oppenheimer until the very end, helping
to clean up until every trace of the celebration was swept
away. Ayers and Mick offered to take Huck and Maia home.
I wanted to stay there and hang out by myself for a while.
They hugged me. They said they understood.*

*They did not understand. Ayers was my confidante but I
hadn't even told her the truth. I feared she would tell Mick,
and Mick would tell someone who worked at the Beach
Bar, and the next day, the whole island would know. Ayers
thought Maia's father, someone I called the Pirate, had come
in on a yacht one weekend and then left, never to return.*

*Ayers hadn't given a second thought to a yacht called
Bluebeard.*

*By the time I got to Caneel, it was very late. I still
knew people who worked there—Estella, Woodrow, and
Chauncey, the night desk manager. I knew that Chauncey
had grown complacent at his job. Absolutely nothing happened at Caneel between the hours of midnight and five a.m.
Chauncey slept in the back on a cot.*

*I parked in the lot and sneaked across the property in
the shadows, going past the Sugar Mill, the swimming pool,
and tennis courts, across the expanse of manicured grass, to a
string of palm trees that lined the beach.*

Bluebeard was anchored offshore.

Honeymoon 718. I stood in front of the room trying

to summon my courage. If I knocked and it wasn't Russ's room, whoever was in there might call security—and what would they think, seeing me there? They'd escort me off the property or they'd call the police or ... Huck. Maybe someone would know me and realize I'd just lost my mother. They would chalk it up to grief.

The worst outcome would be if Russ did answer the door and he had a woman in there.

Irene.

Someone other than Irene.

I knew it was naive, but for some reason, I didn't think Russ would take Irene or another woman to our room.

I stepped up and knocked.

Nothing. No rustle, no voices, no footsteps.

I knocked again, louder—and then I turned to look at the boat. Bluebeard. I could swim out to the boat, climb up the ladder at the back, ask for Todd Croft. I laughed. I was losing my mind.

The door to 718 opened.

It was Russ standing before me, blinking, befuddled.

"Rosie?" he said.

"Hi."

"You're real? I'm not dreaming?"

"My mother died," I said. "Today was her service."

"Oh, Rosie," he said. "I'm so, so sorry." His voice was thick with sleep.

I peeked behind him. The room was dark, the bed empty. "Can I come in?"

"Yes," Russ said. His eyes filled and I could see my own emotions reflected back at me. For eight years I'd told my-

self that staying away was for the best, that denying what we'd shared was for the best, that sacrificing this man was for the best.

I had lived with agony, with sadness, with longing.

I had been such a fool.

I stepped inside.

PART FOUR

Christmas Cove

IRENE

Lydia sends Irene a text asking how things are going.

Irene replies: As well as can be expected.

This is a flat-out lie.

Things are going *far better* than could have been expected. It's unsettling, almost, how well Irene is adjusting to life in the islands.

To start with, she loves her job on the *Mississippi*. She loves being out on the water; she loves the clients; she gets a rush every single time someone gets a bite. She has mastered stringing the outrigger and using the gaff. Huck has promised to teach her how to read the GPS and drive the boat. Irene bragged about her ability to fillet a fish, though Huck isn't ready to relinquish that duty yet. Still, Irene tried to buy a proper fillet knife on Amazon but her credit card was declined and a call to Ed Sorley confirmed that now that Russ was "officially dead," her account at Federal Republic would be frozen until they sorted out his estate. Her account at First Iowa S & L in her own name is still active, but it has less than three thousand dollars in it.

272 • Elin Hilderbrand

Just as Irene was about to fret, she received an e-mail from Mavis Key asking where Irene would like her final check and year-end bonus sent.

Year-end bonus? Irene thought. They never received bonuses at the magazine.

"It's a gift from Joseph Feeney," Mavis said. "As a thank-you for all your years of hard work. You built *Heartland Home and Style* from the ground up."

Irene asked Mavis to send the check to St. John. It was twelve thousand dollars! Irene still had seventy-two hundred of the eight thousand in cash she'd brought from Iowa City, plus a check from Huck on her dresser. She decided to open an account at FirstBank next to Starfish Market—with the Lovers Lane address printed on her checks.

"I'm becoming a local," she told Huck.

"Can't be a local if you don't show your face around town," Huck said. "Come to dinner with me tonight at Extra Virgin."

Irene declined. She wasn't ready.

Against all odds, Irene loves the villa. She has locked the door to the master suite where Russ slept with Rosie, even though it's the best-appointed room with the most dramatic views. Frankly, Irene would like to lop it right off the house, though this isn't an opinion she shares with the boys.

The boys—Cash, Baker, and Floyd—have all chosen bedrooms and Irene is comfortable at the opposite end of the hall, next to Maia's room.

She thinks about redecorating the entire house. The décor now is functional but uninspired. It needs brighter colors, some original and surprising elements; it needs personality. Once Russ's estate is settled and she has access to some funds, she plans on turning the house into a tasteful, tropical dream home.

Maybe when it's done she'll pitch it to Mavis Key for the magazine's Escapes feature. *Irene Steele, editor emeritus of* Heartland Home and Style, *opens up about redecorating the St. John villa that her late husband, Russell, shared with his mistress and love child.*

Irene also toys with the idea of turning the house into an inn, just as she'd considered with the Iowa City house in the minutes before she found out Russ was dead. What if she "rented" rooms free of charge to women who, like herself, had discovered a husband's infidelity or who, like her cousin Mitzi Quinn, had lost a husband and were having a challenging time bouncing back. Irene and these women could bond over iced coffee, papaya smoothies, and wine. They could gain strength from one another here in paradise, make it a sort of emotional convalescent home.

Irene loves the idea, though she knows it will never come to pass. She enjoys having the boys here. They have developed an easy routine and the house is big enough that they can all do their own thing without stepping on one another's toes. Irene is still Mother Alarm Clock; she rises before the sun and makes sure Cash is up in time for his charters. When Baker and Floyd went back to Houston, Irene was sad to see them go, but Baker assured her they'd be back the following week.

Overall, Irene is far happier than she should be. It's not lost on her that, ultimately, this is because of Huck. He's a wonderful, kind, supportive boss and he's becoming a better friend each day. Irene assumes that they share the same emotional space; they're still in mourning, still dealing daily with the shock of their situation. But because they are also mature adults, they soldier on.

And then on Monday, the beginning of Irene's second week of work, things fall apart.

It starts with the text that Irene receives Sunday evening about the next day's charter. It says: 1 adult, 2 children, last name Goshen, New York, NY—D!

Irene texts Huck. What does "D" mean? She wonders if it was just a typo or maybe Destiny's new sign-off.

Huck texts back: "D" for difficult. She must have been a real humdinger on the phone because Destiny is tough.

Great, Irene thinks. *D* for *difficult.*

She starts the day with a positive attitude. The Goshens are from New York City. Possibly, they're caught up in the rat race that is Manhattan. The father works in finance or advertising, maybe the mother is a fashion editor. Do people in New York have other kinds of jobs? Irene tries to think of characters in movies she's seen— architect, elite private-school headmaster, museum curator, bohemian artist, editor in chief, publicist, restaurateur, Broadway actress.

Irene gets two coffees and two sausage biscuits from Provisions. Meredith, the owner, has seen her enough times that she now waves. Irene stops there as a show of kindness toward Huck—he makes breakfast for Maia every day but many times forgets to eat himself—and besides, the sausage biscuit is delicious. Irene is starting to gain back some of the weight she lost.

The boat is tied up at the dock before Irene arrives, which has never happened before. Huck is watching her as she approaches. She figures he's here early because of the difficult clients. He takes the coffee and biscuits from her, then helps her down into the boat.

"There's something I need to tell you," he says.

Something about the clients? She raises her eyebrows.

"My friend Rupert called over the weekend to tell me that Paulette and Douglas Vickers have been taken into custody by the FBI."

"What?"

"They were on St. Croix with Doug's sister," Huck says. "The FBI tracked them down and arrested them."

"On what charges?"

"Real estate fraud," Huck says. "Financial fraud."

Well, yes, Irene thinks, *of course.* She wonders if the Vickerses were somehow responsible for the helicopter crash. Was Paulette Vickers the kind of person who could kill three people, then pick up one of the men's widows at the ferry and describe the delights of the island?

"They'll find out what she knows," Huck says. "She'll likely lead them to Todd Croft."

"Real estate fraud," Irene says. She thinks about the dummy driveways on the way up to Russ's villa. "Financial fraud."

"I didn't want to tell you anything until I heard back from Agent Vasco," Huck says. "She left me a message late last night, after I was asleep. I thought it might be time to start worrying..."

"Is it?" Irene says. Her wheels are spinning. Of course it is! Real estate fraud, Todd Croft, the money in Rosie's drawer. Paulette knows far, far more than she's saying, although likely she's just a pawn manipulated by Todd Croft and maybe Russ as well.

"No, AC," Huck says. "No. Agent Vasco told me it's an ongoing investigation and if she has any other questions, she'll be in touch."

"So there's nothing we should do?" Irene says. She wonders if the FBI knows she's working with Huck. And if so, what do they think about *that?* Does it seem suspicious? Does it seem like Huck and Irene are part of the conspiracy with Russ and Paulette Vickers? Should Irene quit? She doesn't want to quit. She takes a breath of the morning air and tries to calm down. She has done nothing wrong; Huck has done nothing wrong. The FBI agents know this.

"Nothing we should do, nothing we can do," Huck says. "We just have to wait until they find Croft. But I wanted you to be aware."

"Yes, thank you," Irene says. She takes Huck's left hand, the one with the missing pinkie, and squeezes it. "Please tell me everything you know. Don't spare me because you think I can't handle it. I'm tough."

"That you are, Angler Cupcake," Huck says. "But I'm happy to give you today off if you want to go home and mull this over."

"Don't be ridiculous," Irene says. "If I do go home, I

will mull this over, and what good will that do? I'd much rather be on the boat."

"I feel exactly the same way," Huck says. "Even if these people *are* difficult."

Irene holds the ropes, smiling, as the Goshens approach. What she told Huck is true: She is tough. This family can't throw anything at her that she can't handle. But when she sees them, her heart sinks. There's the mother, a pretty but sour-looking woman—blond, thin, midforties. She's followed by a teenage daughter, a younger, prettier, angrier version of the mother. Trailing behind them with a bounce in his step is the son. He's maybe thirteen or fourteen years old and he's completely bald.

The mother's name is Galen Goshen, the daughter is Altar, and the son is Niles; Niles, Galen announces, has just finished eighteen rounds of chemo. He has leukemia, Galen informs Irene, and this last round of chemo is either going to put him in remission or it isn't. She says this right in front of Niles, who shrugs.

"I want to catch a fish," he says. "A big one. Something I can hang on the wall."

"He's frail," Galen says.

Yes, Irene can see that. He's white as chalk and his arms and legs are like sticks. His blue eyes are sunken on his face but they're bright and lively and he hasn't stopped smiling.

Huck says, "Four to six feet today."

Four to six feet isn't terrible, but going into the wind, it will be a jarring ride. Even Irene hasn't gotten used to the teeth-rattling that occurs when the boat smacks the trough of a wave. More than once she has gone home sore from tensing her muscles for so long. She can't imagine this kid surviving the ride to the drop-off six miles south. He'll be broken into pieces by the time they're ready to cast a line.

But if they stay inshore, they won't catch a big fish. Nothing big enough to mount, anyway.

"Four to six feet is too big for an offshore trip," Irene says. "We'll stay inshore today and catch plenty of fish."

Niles seems happy with this and Galen and Altar look like they couldn't care less.

Galen says, "Certainly you have a life preserver for Niles?"

"Life preservers are under the seat behind me," Huck says. "We have one to fit the boy, though for an inshore trip, we won't go faster than ten knots, so he probably won't need it."

"I was clear with the woman on the phone—" Galen says and before she can finish her sentence, Irene is pulling out a life preserver for Niles. *D* is for *difficult.*

Niles sits next to Huck at the wheel as Huck explains the dash, shows Niles the fish finder, and points off the port and starboard sides, identifying the other islands. Irene checks the light tackle rods, then sits on the stern bench next to Galen and Altar, who are whispering angrily back and forth. Irene doesn't want to eavesdrop—as Huck told her early on, family drama rarely stops because people are out on a fishing charter, and it's absolutely none of their concern. However, it's impossible not to overhear. The daughter, Altar, is turning eighteen sometime after the family returns to New York, and Altar wants her mother to allow her to throw a party in the—house? Apartment?—for a hundred people with a DJ and a keg.

"No, no, and no," Galen says. "It's me saying no but it's also building security saying no. A DJ won't work, a hundred kids dancing to a DJ won't work. We'll get evicted."

"What about Pineland?" Altar says. "She had that exact party on the fourth floor two years ago."

"Pineland's father bribed Mr. Soo," Galen says.

"So there's the answer," Altar says. "*You* bribe Mr. Soo."

"I have neither the desire nor the spare cash," Galen says. "Your brother's treatment."

"I knew that was the real reason," Altar says. "It's Niles's fault I can't have a party."

"Well, what exactly are Niles and I supposed to do while you throw this party in our home?"

"I don't know," Altar says. "Check into a hotel?" She laughs. "Niles will probably be in the hospital anyway, and you'll be at his bedside, so what does it even matter?"

Irene can't stand to hear another word. She moves to the captain's seat. Niles is now on his knees on the bow banquette, earbuds in. He's as still and majestic as a figurehead.

The earbuds, she supposes, are useful for blocking out his mother and sister.

Irene leans in to Huck. "They're fighting back there."

Huck nods to let Irene know he's heard her, but he doesn't seem to care. Maybe he's thinking about Agent Vasco. Or, more likely, he's trying to pick a good spot to anchor and cast. The engine noise makes most conversations impossible and yet the mother and daughter's discussion has escalated to a screaming match. It's impossible to ignore them.

"I'll just ask Dad to pay for it, then!"

"Be my guest! See how far that gets you!"

"...bitter because Misty is way cooler than you..."

"Misty is twenty-six years old. She *should* be cooler than me..."

"I'm calling him now and telling him to book me a plane ticket home. I don't want to be here! The only reason we're here is because of Niles!"

"...selfish little..."

"...I have children, I'm going to love them all equally..."

"...*sick,* Altar..."

"I don't care!" Altar screams. "I hate you and I hate Niles!"

Finally, Huck leans over to Irene. "I know it's difficult, but you have to let them go. They obviously have things to work through."

Irene wipes away the tears that are rolling down her cheeks. She's crying for them but also for herself and for all families that have been broken.

Turns out, she's not as tough as she thought.

When it sounds like Galen and Altar might actually come to blows—Galen grabs Altar's phone and holds it over her head, threatening to throw it overboard—Irene moves up to the bow with two light tackle rods. She touches Niles on the back.

When he turns to see Irene holding both rods, his face lights up. Irene feels more tears building behind her eyes but she'll be damned if she's going to cry in front of Niles.

This last round of chemo is either going to put him in remission or it isn't.

It's going to put him in remission, Irene thinks. And right now, she's going to put this kid on a fish.

A higher power must be with them because on his third cast, Niles gets a bite, and Irene can tell just by the bow of the rod that it's something big—but what? There aren't too many big fish to be found inshore, at least not that Irene has experienced firsthand.

Niles has a natural instinct for what to do. He reels with surprising tenacity and lets the spool go when the fish runs. He keeps the rod tip up and the handle pressed into his jutting hipbone. "What's it gonna be?" Niles asks.

"I'm not sure," Irene says.

Huck comes to check on them. "Tarpon, from the looks of it," he says. "Big one."

Sure enough, a little while later, Niles Goshen reels in a tarpon that is a big fish by anyone's standards.

"I didn't think it was the season for tarpon," Irene says.

"It's not, really," Huck says. "But once in a while, the universe throws you a favor."

They're going to take the tarpon home. Huck gives Galen the card of a taxidermist who can stuff and mount it. Galen looks relieved and defeated. Altar is either asleep or pretending to be asleep behind her sunglasses.

Galen pulls Irene aside. "You have a good man there,"

she says, nodding at Huck. "It's clear how much he cares about you. I hope you don't take that for granted."

Irene can't think of how to respond. *He's not my man? We're not together? I'm just the mate on his boat?* What if Irene were to tell Galen that, back on the first of the year, she had been a married magazine editor living in Iowa City, but then her husband was killed in a helicopter crash, and his secret life was revealed. Galen wouldn't believe it. But if she did believe it, she might understand that everyone has her baggage and her sad stories. What differentiates people is how they choose to deal with them. Irene has done pretty well, she thinks, assuming the FBI aren't waiting on the dock when they get back.

"I take nothing for granted," Irene says.

On the way back to Cruz Bay, the sky darkens and there's one loud thunderclap, followed by a torrential downpour. Irene hands the Goshens a couple of waterproof ponchos to hold over their heads; they are squeaking and squealing like they're going to melt. As Irene stands under the canvas Bimini with Huck, she catches sight of Niles kneeling on the bow. His arms are open, his head back. He's embracing the earth and all of her aspects.

It's just rain, he seems to be saying. *I will survive it.*

The Goshens disembark early—they've barely been on the water for two hours—and Irene feels a strange melancholy, watching them go. She realizes she'll never know what happens to the Goshen family. Will Altar have her birthday party? Will Niles live to be an adult? Will he hang the tarpon he caught off the coast of St. John in his home and gaze on it with pride in his fifties, in his sixties? Irene will be forgotten, lost, as soon as tomorrow or the next day. He will never know how hard Irene was rooting for him.

"Wow," she says to Huck. She's wet—and cold for the first time since she's been here.

"D," he says. "For *difficult.*"

"There's no charter tomorrow, correct?"

"Correct," Huck says. "You get a day off, unless something comes up at the last minute, which has been known to happen."

Irene nods and wraps her arms around herself. She's shivering.

Huck notices and holds his arms open.

She stares at him.

"I'm just offering you a hug," Huck says. "That was tough on you and the news I greeted you with was no picnic either."

Irene takes a tentative step toward him. He wraps his arms around her. It has been…well, a *long* time since a man held her like this. Russ, before he left for his "business trip" after Christmas? Had he hugged Irene or kissed her goodbye?

No, she remembers. She had been in Coralville returning some Christmas presents for Milly. She had been angry at Russ for leaving over the new year, and as punishment, she had denied him a proper goodbye.

She tries to remember what Christmas had been like. It was just the two of them in the morning in front of the tree, opening gifts. They had talked to each of the boys on the phone and they had joined Milly for the Christmas lunch served at Brown Deer.

Had they been intimate? Had they hugged and kissed? They'd held hands, she remembers, during the Christmas Eve service at First Presbyterian.

That had been nice, Irene supposes, but it hadn't offered the comfort or the rush of this hug. Irene fits into Huck's arms perfectly. His body is solid and warm. Can she trust him? She feels like the answer is yes—but she would have said exactly the same thing about Russell Steele. She would have said Russ was beyond reproach.

"Let me take you to dinner tonight," Huck says in her ear. "Maia is with Ayers and I have an idea. We'll go over to St. Thomas."

St. Thomas is bigger, and they can be anonymous. For some reason, this suits Irene better than being seen out in Cruz Bay, where everyone knows Huck and might guess who Irene is.

"Okay," she says.

Irene meets Huck back at the dock at six thirty. He told her to dress up and so she's wearing a spring-green linen sheath with a belted middle, a dress she bought for Baker's high-school graduation thirteen years earlier—right around the time that Russ met Rosie, although she tries to put this thought out of her mind.

Huck is wearing a blue button-down shirt, ironed khakis, and if Irene isn't mistaken, there's a navy blazer folded across the back of the captain's seat.

This is a real date.

Huck has wine on the boat. He pours her a glass of Cakebread chardonnay—she can't believe he remembered what kind of wine she likes—and he opens a beer for himself.

"We aren't going far," he says. "Just over to the yacht club in Red Hook. Fifteen minutes."

They cruise out, nice and easy, across Sir Francis Drake Channel as the sun sets. Irene considers sitting in the bow and letting the wind catch her hair—it's out of its braid tonight—but instead, she sits next to Huck where she can listen to the music, Jackson Browne singing "Running on Empty." The sky glows pink and blue and gold; Huck is humming; Irene's wine is crisp and cold. There is nothing wrong with this moment.

The world is a strange and mysterious place, Irene thinks. How is it possible that Russ's web of deceit and his secret second life led Irene here? She laughs at the absurdity of it. Huck never met Russ but Russ certainly knew that Huck existed. What would Russ think if he could see Huck and Irene now? It turns Irene's mind into a pretzel just considering it.

They pull into a slip at the St. Thomas Yacht Club and a cute young man in white shorts and a green polo hurries over to help with the ropes. He offers Irene a hand up to the dock.

"Captain Huck," he says. "Good to see you again, sir. It's been a while."

"Good to see you, Seth," Huck says. "Are we all set inside?"

"Yes, sir," Seth says. "They're ready for you. Enjoy your dinner."

Huck offers Irene his arm and walks her down the dock. He's wearing his blazer now and Irene is soothed by how at ease he seems and how gentlemanly he is as he opens the door to the club and ushers Irene inside.

The hostess, a stunning young West Indian woman, greets Huck with a kiss and introduces herself as Jacinda to Irene, then leads Huck and Irene to a table by the front window that overlooks the docks and the water. Irene can see the twinkling lights of St. John in the distance.

Theirs is the only table set. They are the only people in the dining room.

"Is it...always this empty?"

"The kitchen normally isn't open tonight," Huck says. "But they owe me a favor."

So they are having a private dinner. The whole club, all to themselves.

"The prime rib is very good here," Huck says. "I don't know about you, but I'm sick of fish."

They eat like royalty: Warm rolls with sweet butter, organic greens with homemade papaya vinaigrette, prime rib, baked potato with lots of butter and sour cream, and, for dessert, sabayon and berries. Huck and Irene drink wine with dinner, then end with a sipping rum, a twenty-five-year-old El Dorado that is even better than the Flor de Caña, Huck says.

They do not talk about the Vickerses' arrest or what it might mean. They don't talk about Russ or Rosie or real estate fraud or Todd Croft or frozen accounts. Irene pushes all that away, though during the natural lulls in the conversation, it feels like she's holding an unruly mob behind a door. It feels, as they finish up dinner, like Agent Vasco has just taken a seat at the table; that's how badly Irene wants to talk about it.

Instead, she says, "The mother on the boat today thought we were married. She said, 'You have a good man there.' She said she could tell how much you cared for me." The instant these words are out, Irene feels her cheeks burn.

"I hate to break it to you, AC," Huck says. "Everyone who gets on that boat thinks we're married." He reaches for Irene's hand. "And everyone can see how much I care for you."

They head back to the boat, hand in hand. There are stars overhead and it feels like there's a bright, burning star in Irene's chest. What is happening?

Huck helps Irene down into the boat. Before he turns on the running lights, he takes Irene's face in his hands and he kisses her. The kiss is sweet but intense—and there is no room for thoughts of anything or anyone else, not even Agent Vasco.

AYERS

There's no such thing as a clean breakup, Ayers thinks.

When she and Mick hashed it out, Ayers told him

exactly how she felt—his infidelity with Brigid was insurmountable. Mick said that he had bumped into Brigid on the ferry and Ayers believed that—but she still didn't trust him, with Brigid or with anyone else.

"I can't do this anymore," she said.

Deep down, she acknowledges that the fault is not entirely Mick's. Ayers wanted a chance to be with Baker and she refused to sleep with him while she was still with Mick. She had only gotten back together with Mick as a way to exact revenge on both Baker and Cash for withholding the truth about who they were, and then once she and Mick—and Gordon—were back in their routine, Ayers was comfortable, if not particularly happy.

Now that she has slept with Baker—and without protection, like an irresponsible idiot—and now that Baker has left to go back to Houston, Ayers is neither comfortable nor happy.

She had meant to take it slow and steady with Baker. She had vowed to wait until he came *back* from Houston to consummate their relationship. But passion and high emotion had ruled and although their night together had been unforgettable—at least for her—now the anticipation is gone. Baker might decide Ayers isn't worth returning for.

Monday morning, there's a knock on her door. Ayers is in bed. Mondays she's off from both jobs, though she has Maia tonight. Ayers is picking Maia up in town at six and they have plans to get takeout from De Coal Pot.

Ayers doesn't like unexpected knocks at the door. Who could it be at nine thirty in the morning? Her landlady? Jehovah's Witnesses?

She pulls a pillow over her head. The door is locked. *Whoever you are,* she thinks, *please go away.* Monday is her day of rest.

"Hello?" a voice says, loud and clear. "Ayers?"

It's Mick. He still has a key. Why didn't she ask for her key back?

A second later there's a flutter of footsteps as Gordon comes running into the bedroom and jumps up on Ayers's bed. Mick is no dummy, she thinks. He sent his goodwill ambassador in first.

But Mick soon follows. "Get up," he says.

Ayers flips over and partially opens one eye. "What are you doing here?" Does she need to remind him that they've broken up? What if she had company?

"It's Monday," Mick says. "We're going to Christmas Cove. The boat is anchored in Frank Bay. I have rum punch, I have water, I have snacks, I have your snorkel and fins."

"It's over, Mick," Ayers says. "We're through."

Mick sits on the bed and brushes Ayers's hair out of her eyes. "We're not through," he says. "We'll never be through."

He looks unreasonably good, for Mick. He has a day's worth of scruff, which is how she likes him best, and he's gotten some sun on his face, making his eyes look very green. Gordon has already snuggled against the curve of Ayers's back. Ayers closes her eyes for one second and travels back in time to before the disgusting discovery of Brigid, back when Mick and Gordon were "her boys," back when life was calm and happy.

But she can travel backward only in her mind. In real time, she has no choice but to move forward. Baker. And Floyd too, she supposes. Assuming they come back.

"I slept with Baker last week," Ayers says. "The night we broke up."

Mick's eyebrows shoot up in an expression of surprise, and then a split second later, Ayers sees the hurt, which was her aim. "Banker? Wow. You wasted no time."

Ayers props herself up on her elbows. "I like him," she says. "He's a grown-up. He doesn't *lie* to me."

"Doesn't he?" Mick says. "He didn't tell you who he was. And his father"—Mick whistles—"didn't exactly serve as a role model in the honesty department."

Ayers should never have told Mick anything about Baker. "He's not his father," she says. "I'm nothing like my parents. You're nothing like yours."

"Point taken," Mick says. "I'm sure you want me to be angry or jealous about your tryst with Banker, and I am." He takes a couple of deep breaths and Ayers can see his Irish temper eddying beneath the surface. Baker is bigger than Mick, but Mick is fiercer; if they ever came to blows, Baker would lose. "But I'm glad you got it out of your system. I had my fling and now you've had yours—"

"It doesn't work like that, Mick," Ayers says. "I didn't do it for revenge. This isn't a tit for tat. And by the way, I *waited* until we were broken up—"

"You waited, what, an hour? And we aren't really broken up. We had a misunderstanding, and you overreacted. Bumping into Brigid on the ferry doesn't warrant a breakup. Check the relationship rule book. Ask your friends."

"I don't have any friends," Ayers says.

"That's what this is really about," Mick says. "Banker, Money...they're attractive to you because it's a connection to Rosie."

"Baker is in love with me," Ayers says.

"Oh, really?" Mick says. "Well, where is he now? Is he here with a pineapple-banana smoothie, waiting for you in the Jeep? Has he planned the best day off imaginable, complete with a new Jack Johnson Spotify playlist and a solemn promise that we can order the carbonara pizza *and* the bloomin' onion pizza *and* the chocolate-banana Pizza Stix? Did he arrange for Captain Stephen from the *Singing Dog* to play his guitar for three hours this afternoon? Did he make a reservation for tonight at the Longboard?"

"I have Maia tonight," Ayers says.

"I know," Mick says. "I made the reservation for three people."

Ayers has to give him credit for that. Maia will die of happiness, eating at the Longboard with Mick. She loves the lobster tacos.

"It's over, Mick," Ayers says, though even she can hear that her voice lacks conviction. "Go to Christmas Cove by yourself and when everyone asks where I am, tell them we broke up. Or better still, take Brigid with you so they figure it out on their own."

"I called Bex at Rhumb Lines," Mick says. "I begged her to take Brigid off my hands, but she says she's fully staffed. Then I heard Robert and Brittany at Island Abodes were looking for someone to help out with the villas. Brigid has an interview with them on Thursday."

"Poor Robert and Brittany," Ayers says. They're one of the nicest, coolest couples on island, and they have a cute baby. "But it'll be good for Brigid to get a different kind of job. She's a terrible server."

"Agreed," Mick says. "I wish I'd never hired her. I wish I'd never met her. But what's done is done. She'll be out of the Beach Bar by next week."

Ayers can't deny it—this news pleases her.

"Back to Banker," Mick says. "Does he know that you're ticklish right here?" Mick digs his fingers into Ayers's ribs. She shrieks and soon they're tussling in bed and Mick crawls on top of her and she lets him rest on her for a couple of seconds before pushing him off.

"I have a surprise for you," Mick says. "Two surprises. One for now and one for later. Does Banker know how much you love surprises?"

Ayers *does* love surprises. "Okay," she says. "I'll come."

It's a swan song, she tells herself, *a last hurrah.* Because she has Maia tonight, there's no danger of her *sleeping* with Mick. There's no reason they can't go out together in public as friends.

The second Ayers sits in Mick's Jeep with Gordon perched in her lap, she feels happy about her decision. The day is crystal clear, sunny, and hot—and what else would Ayers have done with her time? She would have holed up at home and read Rosie's diaries. She has been so engrossed in the story about Russ, she's on the verge of becoming addicted. She has finally gotten to the part where they're reunited. Russ knows about Maia. Rosie knows about Irene and the boys.

They're going to be together.

It's good for Ayers to leave the diaries alone for a while. She sips the smoothie Mick got her from Our Market and sings along to Chesney on the radio. This is what a day off is supposed to feel like.

Mick turns onto Great Cruz Bay Road and Ayers says, "Where are we going?"

"Surprise number one," Mick says. Great Cruz Bay Road is one of Ayers's favorite places; it has views northwest over the Westin toward St. Thomas and Water Island. Mick follows the road almost to the tip of the point, then he signals and turns into a driveway marked with a sign that says PURE JOY. This leads to an adorable white cottage with bright blue shutters. It reminds Ayers of the months that she and her parents spent living on Santorini.

They climb out of the car. "Follow me," Mick says. He steps up onto the wraparound porch that has an uninterrupted water view.

"What are we doing here?"

"This is my new place," Mick says.

"You bought it?"

"Renting," Mick says. "Long-term. But it's mine. You want to see the rest?"

He leads her inside, and everything is picture-perfect. There's a bedroom, living room, dining nook, kitchen, and a brand-new, sparkling-white-tiled bathroom; every room in the house has a view of the water. On the deck is a grill and a hot tub, and around the corner is an outdoor shower painted the same blue as the shutters.

It's a real *place*. Not a hole-in-the-wall like where Mick lives now, which meant that he was always crashing at Ayers's in a way that felt like he was infringing on her space. For years, Ayers has been begging him to find someplace better. And now he has. This cottage—Pure Joy—is a dream.

"This is amazing," Ayers says. "You'll be much happier here."

"*We* will be happier here," Mick says. "I got it for us. See those chairs?" He points to two stools, upholstered in blue, in front of a bar counter. "Those are what convinced me to take it. I pictured the two of us coming home from work late at night and having a drink there together—and can you imagine the sunset from here?"

"Hashtag sunset," Ayers says. "Your Instagram account will blow up."

"We can have our coffee out here in the mornings," Mick says.

We broke up, Ayers thinks. But Mick's expression is so earnest that she doesn't have the heart to say it.

"It's nice," she admits.

One last hurrah, she tells herself again, though Mick is slowly but surely wearing down her resistance. Her night with Baker—which had seemed so vivid and unforgettable right after it happened—is now fading from her mind.

Has she merely fallen prey to the sexual attraction she feels for Baker because it's bright, shiny, and new? Her relationship with Mick is deep and long and intense. Mick is the person Ayers tells things, even the small, inconsequential things, because he's the one who has shared her history. He has context.

If she starts something new with Baker, she would have to go back to square one. The thought is, frankly, exhausting.

Ayers wades through the crystal water of Frank Bay and climbs into the boat. Mick is borrowing *Funday,* a thirty-two-foot Grady-White, from his boss for the day, something he normally does only on special occasions. Mick loads Gordon in and turns up the music and they go zipping across the surface of the water at breathtaking speed. Ayers loves nothing in the world more than being out on a boat—*Treasure Island* included—though the experience is much better when she isn't working. She fills a Yeti cup with rum punch—Mick makes the best—and belts out, *"Save it for a rainy day!"*

It's well known that Monday is the weekend for people in the service industry. La Tapa closes on Monday nights after the holiday rush, as do a bunch of other restaurants, so when Mick and Ayers arrive in Christmas Cove, it's a Who's Who of St. John hospitality all rafted together on either side of the Pizza Pi boat. The guys from 420 to Center are there and so is Bex from Rhumb Lines and Mattie the bartender from the Dog House Pub with his girlfriend, Lindsay, who works at the Beach Bar with Mick, and Colleen from Pizzabar in Paradise and Jena from Extra Virgin Bistro. Alex the bartender from Ocean 362 is on a catamaran—with Skip. From the looks of things, Skip is pretty far along in the partying department. When he sees Mick and Ayers pull in, he raises his arms over his head and hollers at the top of his lungs, "They're here!" As though Mick and Ayers are the king and queen of this particular St. John prom.

Ayers grins at everyone and waves. This is her family.

Mick and Ayers tie up to a sleek, black Midnight Express that has a woman on board who looks familiar. She's wearing a tropical-print bikini and enormous sunglasses. She waves and says, "Hey, Ayers!" and then she helps Mick with the ropes and the bumpers while Ayers racks her brain for how she knows this woman.

She leans over to hug Ayers. "I suppose you've heard that Brent and I are getting a divorce?"

Who's Brent? Ayers thinks. The woman pulls a cigarette and a lighter out of a pair of teensy white shorts lying at her feet and Ayers realizes the woman is Swan Seeley, the mother of Colton Seeley, Maia's little friend. Swan has traded in her reusable shopping bags and sustainable vegetable gardening for day-drinking and lung cancer.

Ayers laughs. This is fabulous! She always liked Swan best when she was breaking the rules anyway. But a divorce is sad, right? "I'm sorry to hear that," Ayers says.

Swan waves the sentiment and her exhale of smoke away. "Don't be," she says. "He's got a gambling problem. I had to cut bait before he sank us."

"Good for you, then."

Swan smiles. "There are eligible men *everywhere,*" she says. "Just look at this place!" Her eyes scan the now-impressive raft of boats. "What about Skip? He's single, right?"

"He's single," Ayers says. "But I'm not sure he's your type." *Or anyone's type,* she thinks. Although who's to say that Skip, who's coming off his weird thing with Tilda, and

Swan Seeley, freshly separated, wouldn't be a good match for each other?

"There's the hottest new dad at the school," Swan says. "He's brand-new to the island, relocating from Houston. I saw him last week when I was picking up Colton. Maia seemed to know him, though of course I couldn't ask who he was with Colton in the car."

Hottest new dad. That would be Baker. Ayers feels herself *bristling*. Naturally Swan Seeley and all the other Gifft Hill mothers will pant over Baker. Ayers wants to inform Swan that Baker is *taken,* by *her,* but she can't very well do this when she's here with Mick.

At that moment, who should step onto Swan's boat but Skip, holding a chilled bottle of Dom Pérignon and a bouquet of plastic flutes.

"Champagne, ladies?" He pours some for Swan and some for Ayers. "This storied bubbly has notes of Canadian pennies, your dad's Members Only jacket, and..." He glances over Ayers's shoulder. "'We Are Never, Ever, Ever Getting Back Together.'"

Why does he keep *doing* this? Ayers wonders, but Swan laughs. "Ha! You can say *that* again!"

Ayers turns to see a cute little speedboat pull up. Tilda is at the wheel and Cash is next to her.

Ayers is seized with panic. *Cash* is here? What's *Cash* doing here? It's obvious, hello, that he came with Tilda, that's her parents' little runabout, though they also have a sixty-two-foot single-hull sailboat. Tilda and Cash? Yes, Baker told her this the other night. It's good, it's great, Tilda and Cash together isn't the problem—except, maybe, for

Skip. The problem is that Cash will see Ayers here with Mick and report back to Baker.

Ugh! Arrgh! What can she do? Can she pretend she's here with Swan? Maybe Cash and Tilda won't stay; there are a lot of boats here already, maybe they want privacy, maybe they'll head over to Mermaid's Chair where they can be alone. Or to Dinghy's on Water Island.

Go to Dinghy's! Ayers thinks.

But Tilda has earned her place at this party; she works just as hard as everyone else. Ayers notices she gets a sadistic grin on her face when she sees Skip. She must want to gloat.

Cash and Tilda raft up with Mick. Ayers watches Mick and Cash shake hands. Ayers offers a lame little wave.

Captain Stephen starts playing the guitar and singing "Southern Cross."

Think about how many times I have fallen…

Mick's hand lands on the back of Ayers's neck. He knows how much she loves this song.

The pizza arrives—one carbonara with lobster, one bloomin' onion drizzled with lemon aioli, and Ayers's ultimate splurge, the chocolate-banana Pizza Stix. She drinks her champagne—Skip has, generously, left the bottle for her and Swan to split—and she eats some pizza, plays tug-of-war with the crust with Gordon, and dives off the boat for a swim.

Tilda and Cash have noodles. They're floating in the water, interested in no one but each other.

Mick is gone somewhere. Ayers cranes her neck to see if, by chance, Brigid has arrived on any of the boats. Captain Stephen stops playing and there's the spine-chilling shriek of microphone feedback, then she hears Mick's voice.

"You guys, can I have your attention please? Hey! Everyone, please quiet down."

Ayers sees Mick heading toward her with the microphone. Is he going to sing to her or ask *her* to sing, maybe something from the Jack Johnson Spotify playlist?

It all happens so fast. A hush blankets Christmas Cove, and all eyes are on Mick, now standing in the bow of *Funday* in front of Ayers, who is dripping wet in her bikini.

He drops to one knee and only then does Ayers get it: the second surprise.

"*This* is why I went to St. Thomas," he whispers. He pulls a box out of the pocket of his swim trunks and says into the microphone so that every single person they work and live with on the tiny island that is St. John USVI can hear, "Ayers Wilson, will you marry me? Will you be my wife?"

Ayers isn't sure where Cash is, but she can feel his eyes boring into her. Swan Seeley claps a hand over her mouth and then everyone starts chanting, "Say yes! Say yes! Say yes!"

Gordon, who never barks, is pressing his flank against Ayers's leg, barking.

A public proposal is never a good idea, Ayers thinks. Or is it? She can't say no. She can't dive off the boat and seek asylum on Little St. James Island. She could, she supposes, beg Cash and Tilda to take her back to Cruz Bay. Yes, that's what she should do.

But what a buzzkill. What a depressing end to such a well-executed surprise. Ayers realizes that a good number of these people must have been in on it. Nobody knows that Ayers and Mick broke up and that Ayers embarked on a new relationship. They're all caught up in the theatrics.

Rosie? Ayers thinks with a glance skyward.

But there's no answer.

Ayers presents her left hand to Mick and he slips the ring on her finger, then stands and pulls her in for a kiss.

The crowd cheers. Ayers studies the diamond. It's a beautiful ring; she has to give him that. The stone sparkles so brightly that Ayers is, temporarily, blinded.

CASH

Cash takes a picture of Mick down on one knee, holding out a ring to Ayers. He sends it to Baker with a caption that reads She said yes, dude. Sorry.

Maybe, just maybe, it was all for show. Cash always wondered about guys who thought it was a good idea to propose during the seventh-inning stretch of a Colorado Rockies game or up on the stage during a Jason Aldean concert. Was it to guarantee a yes because most women wouldn't say no in front of twenty thousand people? But then, later, was the ring pulled off the finger, put back in the box, and taken to the nearest pawnshop? Ayers looked surprised but not necessarily *happy*.

On the boat ride home, he asks Tilda for her opinion.

"She looked dazzled," Tilda says. "In the best possible way. And who can blame her? Those two have been together *forever*, they've had their issues and come out the other side. They'll get married and have kids. They'll be great parents. They dote on Mick's dog, Gordon."

"Okay," Cash says.

"Please don't tell me seeing that *upset* you," Tilda says. "If it did, I'll drop you off at the National Park Service dock right now and you can walk home. Or find another unsuspecting woman to pick you up hitchhiking."

"It didn't bother *me* in the slightest," Cash says. Which is true. His feelings for Ayers have changed dramatically in the past few days. "I'm worried for my brother. He really likes her. Maybe I shouldn't have sent him that text."

Sure enough, as soon as they get back to Cruz Bay, Cash's phone starts ringing. Baker.

Cash sends him to voicemail. He and Tilda are going to her villa to "hang out," then they're heading into town for dinner.

La Tapa is closed so they decide to go to the Longboard—Tilda is in the mood for their frozen rosé—and who should they happen across but Ayers, Mick, and Maia, who are enjoying more champagne and platters of tacos.

When Maia sees Cash, she jumps to her feet. "Bro!" she says. "Did you hear the news?"

"I did," Cash says. He smiles at Mick and Ayers. "Congratulations, you two."

Mick puts an arm around Ayers and squeezes her. "I should have done this a long time ago."

Ayers's expression can only be described as dazed. Or maybe she's just drunk. "I meant to text you," she says. "The boat has a mechanical issue and we had to cancel the charter for tomorrow."

"She wouldn't have been able to go anyway," Mick says. "I want to keep her in bed all day."

"Really?" Maia says. "We're eating!"

Yeah, Cash thinks. The idea of Mick and Ayers in bed is enough to turn his stomach as well. He can feel his phone buzzing away in his pocket. Baker. Baker. Baker.

"Well, if I don't have work," Cash says, "that means we can finally hike to the baobab tree."

"After school?" Maia says. "Can we leave at four so my friend Shane can come?"

"Works for me," Cash says.

"And me," Tilda says.

"Pick us up at the ferry dock, please," Maia says. "And bring plenty of water."

"Yes, ma'am," Cash says.

"She's a force," Ayers says. Her eyes mist over. "Just like her mother."

At four o'clock the next day, Cash and Tilda pick up Maia and Shane in Tilda's Range Rover, which both kids find impressive; immediately, they start taking pictures of themselves in the back. Cash has probably overprepared for the hike. In his backpack, he has eight bottles of water, two of them frozen, as well as trail mix, four Kind bars, two spare clean bandannas, and a first-aid kit. He and Tilda are both dressed in hiking shorts and boots. Tilda has six bottles of water in her pack, plus sunscreen, bug spray, peanut butter–filled pretzels, a selfie stick, and a paper map from the National Park Service.

"You guys are so…gung ho," Maia says. She holds her phone over her head and snaps a photo of herself making a fish face. "We're just gonna hike in our Chucks."

"Yeah," Shane says. They all climb out of the Rover and Shane gives Cash and Tilda the once-over. "But when I climb Everest, I'm bringing you guys with me."

"Smart aleck," Tilda says.

Chucks aren't really the proper footwear for a hike but Maia and Shane have youth and exuberance on their side. They bound down the trail, and in a couple of minutes, they're so far ahead, they're out of sight.

"Hey, wait up!" Cash calls out. "It's not a race!" He would like to look around, take in the scenery, maybe stop to identify some plants—though that clearly isn't happening.

"So this company I want to start," Tilda says, "would provide guides for every hike on the island. You wouldn't need a map, and you'd have someone there to point out the pineapple cactus and the catch-and-keep, and someone to explain the historical significance of the ruins. The National Parks just aren't staffed to keep up with demand."

"I should quit *Treasure Island* and come work for you," Cash says. "I'm much more comfortable on land."

"We should be partners," Tilda says.

"I have no money," Cash says. "I might get some once my father's estate is settled." This isn't something Cash lets himself think about often, but it's always there, twinkling like a star in the distance—a possible inheritance.

"Sweat equity," Tilda says, then she nods down the trail. "Look."

Maia and Shane are up ahead, holding hands. Cash says, "I saw them holding hands last week in town. It's cute, as long as that's all they're doing."

"Don't be naive," Tilda says. "Do you *think* that's all they're doing?"

"Yes," Cash says, because he can't stand to think otherwise. "I'm new at this big-brother thing, but my natural instinct is to be overprotective. If he tries anything more, he'll have me to deal with."

"You're adorable," Tilda says. She turns, stops in the middle of the trail, and gives him a kiss.

Because they're losing daylight and the mosquitoes are coming out, once they reach the baobab tree by the Sieben plantation ruins they decide to turn around—but first they give the tree the reverence it deserves. The tree is extraordinary in breadth and height. It's the only one of its kind on the island.

"The seeds are edible," Maia says. "They were brought over from Africa by Danish slaves."

They use Tilda's selfie stick to take a picture of the four of them standing at the base of the tree. After Maia inspects the picture, she turns to Shane. "We're a cute couple," she says. She looks over at Cash and Tilda. "And so are you guys." She pauses a beat. "You two *are* a couple, right?"

"Uh..." Cash says.

"Right," Tilda says, and they all head back up the hill.

When they reach the Range Rover, both Cash's and Maia's phones start going nuts. Cash ignores his—it's Baker, of course. Maia does not ignore hers.

"Would you guys please drop us in town?" she asks after she checks her texts.

"Are you sure?" Tilda says. "I'm happy to take you all the way home."

"I live on Jacob's Ladder," Maia says. "Trust me, you do *not* want to drive the Rover up Jacob's Ladder."

"You're probably right," Tilda says. "Town it is."

"And how will you get home from town?" Cash asks.

"You're being overprotective," Tilda murmurs.

"I'm being responsible," Cash says. "She's twelve." He looks at Maia in the rearview mirror. "How are you getting home? Shane's parents?"

"Huck is coming to get me," Maia says. "His charter ran late."

"Okay," Cash says. Reluctantly, he pulls his phone out. He has two missed calls from Baker and one missed call from Ayers, which he hopes is work-related. He shoots her a text: What's up?

A second later, she responds: I need your advice.

No, Cash thinks. He's not getting in the middle of this.

As soon as the kids climb out at Powell Park, Cash reaches over and pulls Tilda in for a kiss. "So we're a couple, huh?"

"Yes," Tilda says. "We are."

Cash becomes so light-headed thinking about this that

they get all the way to Jumbie Bay before he realizes that Maia was lying to him. Huck's charter didn't run late. Huck didn't *have* a charter today. Irene told Cash that this morning. She was home all day.

"Turn the car around," he says to Tilda.

They head back to Powell Park, where they dropped Maia and Shane off, but of course the kids are gone. Cash calls Maia and gets her voicemail.

"What do you want to do?" Tilda asks.

"Loop around, please," Cash says. He hangs out the window of the Rover scanning the ferry dock, which is packed with workers headed back to St. Thomas. Did Maia and Shane get on the ferry? The thought makes Cash ill. They pass the jewelry store, the timeshare office, Slim Man's parking lot. Then Tilda has to make a decision— right toward Drink and Gallows Point or left past the Lime Inn and De Coal Pot?

"Arrrgh, I don't know," Cash says. "I should never have let her get out of the car in town. It's just, I knew she and Shane had hung out in town together before, but now it's dark and she lied to me, so she must be doing something she doesn't want Huck to know about."

Tilda turns left. They pass the Dog House and the Longboard and Our Market and Cap's, then Tilda takes a right and says, "Maybe they went for pizza. Let's check Ronnie's."

Yes, Ronnie's Pizza, bingo, brilliant, Cash thinks. They're twelve.

Tilda pulls up out front and Cash runs in, looks around. No Maia, no Shane.

"She likes Candi's Barbecue," Tilda says. "I remember Rosie telling me that. Let's swing by and if she's not there, we'll call Huck."

"I don't have Huck's number," Cash says. "I'll call my mother if she's not at Candi's."

Maia is not at Candi's. Cash climbs back into the Rover and stares at his phone. He calls Maia's phone again and again, it goes directly to voicemail.

"She's ghosting me," he says.

Tilda laughs. "Maybe. Or maybe her phone died. Or maybe she turned her phone off because she wants to kiss Shane in peace."

"You're not making me feel any better," Cash says.

"Sorry, sorry," Tilda says. "Okay, let's think. Do you want me to take you home or run you up to Huck's?"

"Home," Cash says. "The last thing I want to do is face Huck."

When Cash and Tilda arrive at the villa, Irene is sitting at the kitchen table, paging through a *House Beautiful*.

"Cash," she says, standing up. "And you must be…"

"Tilda. It's nice to meet you, Mrs. Steele."

"Are you kids hungry? I haven't given a single thought to dinner, though I probably should, it's getting late—"

"Mom," Cash says. He's not sure why he feels so panicked. Maia has probably already made it home. Shane's parents probably came and picked them up. But what if they didn't? Cash should have insisted on taking Maia straight home. She acted like a full-blown teenager but she's only twelve. Twelve! "We hiked the Esperance Trail with Maia and her friend Shane."

"Oh, that's nice," Irene says.

"Then she asked us to drop her off in town," Tilda says.

"She told us Huck would pick her up," Cash says. "She told us it wouldn't be an inconvenience because his charter was running late..."

"Wait," Irene says. "What?" Cash watches Irene snap into parenting mode and it's like being transported back in time fifteen years. "Let me call Huck." Irene fishes her cell phone out of her bag and dials. Cash can hear her reach Huck's recording.

"He's not answering," she says. "And I don't want to leave a message and panic him. Maybe Maia is home and they're sitting down to dinner."

Maybe, Cash thinks. He pictures Huck and Maia at a table, Maia describing the baobab tree.

Cash needs her to be home, to be safe. He can't handle losing anyone else.

HUCK

When he gets out of the shower, he sees Irene has called. *Prayers answered,* he thinks.

It was bad luck that there had been no charter today— or maybe it was good luck. Huck isn't sure.

Huck has done nothing all day but think about kissing

Irene. He kissed her on the boat, then he kissed her in his truck, and finally he walked her up the steps to the villa and kissed her next to the sliding glass door. He thought that maybe, just maybe, he'd get an invitation to come inside, upstairs—but eventually, Irene had put her index finger to his lips and slipped inside alone.

He understood. It was too soon to go any further. She was newly widowed and so much still remained a mystery.

But he had hoped.

If they'd had a charter, would they have gone back to their normal, pre-kiss selves? Would it have been like the kiss never happened? What torture. Huck wouldn't have been able to focus on fishing for one second. Who cared about fishing? Love was the only thing that mattered.

He prefers to think there would have been a new energy between him and his first mate, barely sublimated. Huck would brush against Irene, their hands would touch, she would sit next to him behind the wheel of the boat. He would count the hours and then the minutes until the clients were walking away down the dock so that he could kiss Irene again.

People would assume they were newlyweds.

It's been so long since Huck has felt this way about a woman that he hardly recognizes himself. He feels twenty-five again.

But they hadn't had a charter and so Huck was left in a vacuum of solitude. He wanted to call Irene and invite her to do something. There was a new floating taco bar in the East End called Lime Out. They could drive to Hansen Bay, rent a kayak, and paddle out for tacos. Would Irene like that? Or maybe a simple lunch would be better, at Aqua Bistro in Coral Bay. Huck could introduce Irene to Rupert—but no, Rupert would be smitten immediately and Huck would have to beat him back.

In the end, Huck lay in his hammock and finally finished the Connelly book. After enjoying a brief sense of accomplishment, he'd stared at his damn phone, willing it to ring, willing it to be Irene inviting him to the villa for a swim in the pool.

Three o'clock didn't even provide its usual respite because Maia was going hiking with Cash so she didn't need a ride home from school.

Huck figured Maia would be hungry when she got home and so at five thirty, he went to Candi's for barbecue, then he got the text from Destiny about the next day's charter and he assumed Irene had received it too. They would be together tomorrow on the boat.

Huck tried Maia to get her ETA but was delivered straight to her voicemail. She always let her phone run down at the end of a day; it was frustrating. He decided to take a shower—and now that he's out, he can see he has two missed calls, both from Irene, which at this time of day is strange—and maybe troubling.

"Maia?" Huck calls out, but there's no answer. Huck pokes his head out into the hallway. The house is quiet; Maia's bedroom door is open. She's not home yet, but she should be any second, so his privacy is limited. He closes the bedroom door and prepares to call Irene back, but something stops him.

She has called twice without leaving a message, so

clearly there's something she wants to tell him in person. He fears—he can barely say the words in his mind—that the kissing changed things for the worse and that Irene no longer feels she can work on the boat. He'll be crushed. He has relived the kissing so many times in the past twenty-one hours that it has taken on the quality of a dream. Irene *was* enthusiastic about kissing him back, right? In his mind, she has her hands in his hair; she's pulling him closer, wanting the kiss to be deeper. But Huck had been drinking and he has seen far too much on the news not to have doubts about even the most consensual-seeming of acts. Huck shouldn't have gotten so carried away. There was a moment at the villa where he'd wanted very badly to press his body against hers, but he hadn't done it. There had been the impulse and then maybe the start of a movement but he'd stopped himself in time. Still, he worries she read his mind, sensed the power of his urges, and now is afraid and maybe even repulsed by him and thinks that working together is no longer a good idea. In fact, it's inappropriate. In fact, the friendship has to go as well.

As Huck is spiraling down into bleaker and bleaker depths, his phone rings. It's Irene.

Hard things are hard, he thinks. He'll just have to apologize and promise to be a gentleman from here on out. But he cannot, *cannot,* let her quit.

"Hello?" he says, as jolly as Santa Claus.

"Huck," she says. "It's Irene."

"I already knew that," he says. "The marvel of cell phones."

"I'm calling to see if Maia has made it home?" Irene says.

"What?" Huck says. He's confused. "Not yet, no. Why? I thought she was with Cash."

"Oh, dear," Irene says.

Huck hangs up the phone, calls Maia, gets her voicemail, then climbs into his truck and slams the door so hard his ears ring.

Late charter? Since when has Huck ever, ever come home *late* from a charter?

Never, that's when.

He wants to wring Cash Steele's neck!

Put your son on the goddamned phone! Huck had shouted at Irene. *I need to know exactly where he dropped her off.*

Irene gave the phone to Cash. Cash sounded worried and kept apologizing; he should have brought her straight home, he said.

You're goddamned right you should have brought her home! Huck said. *You should have checked with me. I'm her family. I'm her only family!*

You're not, though, Cash had said. *I'm her brother. You can't possibly be accusing me of intentionally putting her in danger.*

I'm accusing you of being thoughtless, Huck said. *And negligent. She was a child in your care.* Huck slammed down the phone; he was livid. The Steele family, one and all, are pirates, he decides. And now they're trying to steal Maia. Well, Huck won't allow it.

He sits in his car, fuming, wondering who to call. Joanie's mother? Shane's parents?

As he's wondering about this, his phone rings. Irene, it says.

"What?" he barks.

"Huck, please, calm down," Irene says. "Whatever you said to Cash really upset him. You and I both know it was an innocent mistake. Why don't you come pick me up and we'll look for Maia together? Or I can take one of the Jeeps and meet you in town?"

"How about you and your family stay away from my granddaughter?" Huck says. "Assuming I can even find her. Your numbskull son dropped her off at Powell Park when it was nearly dark. She's twelve years old, Irene. Twelve! That is called gross negligence in my book. Now, I'm going to hang up and find my granddaughter. She's mine, Irene. Not yours, not Cash's—mine. Goodbye." Huck ends the call and feels much better for one second, then much, much worse. He dials Joanie's mom, Julie.

"I hate to bother you," Huck says.

"Oh, Huck," Julie says. "I was just about to call you. We're frantic. We can't find Joanie."

Julie is an organizer, so with a few calls, she discovers that they're all missing: Maia, Shane, Joanie, Colton, and Bright Whittaker. But Julie doesn't have eyes and ears the way Huck does. He calls Rupert, tells him Maia and her little friends are at large, probably somewhere in Cruz Bay, and asks him to alert his lady friends.

Meanwhile, Huck drives into town and checks first at the little beach in Chocolate Hole and then at the basketball courts across from the gas station.

No Maia.

As Huck is heading into the roundabout, his phone rings. It's Mick. Huck heard from Maia that Ayers and Mick got engaged—which, Huck has to admit, he found startling—and he wonders if Mick is calling to give him the news. Huck nearly sends the call to voicemail, but at the last second, he answers. "Hey, Mick, what's up?"

"Hey, Huck," Mick says. "Just thought you should know that Maia and her friends are hanging out on the edge of Frank Bay. I . . . was taking a little walk, and I saw them down there. It's pretty late, so I thought—"

"Yes, thank you," Huck says. "I'm on my way."

Huck drives to the Beach Bar, double-parks, and strides out onto the sand. He doesn't see Maia. He heads to the left, spies a couple of kids—it's pretty far away from the Beach Bar, Huck wonders what Mick was doing all the way down here—and whistles. Even in the dark, he can see Maia jump to her feet. She comes running through the sand toward him.

"Uh-oh," she says.

"Uh-oh is right," he says. "Follow me. We're going home." Over Maia's head, Huck calls out, "Party's over, kids. I'm calling everyone's parents."

Maia sits in the truck while Huck leans against it. He really wants a cigarette right now, but he can't set that kind of poor example until every child is claimed. This gives Huck a chance to calm down and second-guess himself.

Did he overreact? No; it's nearly nine o'clock on a school night and they were having a kumbaya sit-in on a deserted section of beach. God only knows what they were doing.

"What were you doing?" Huck asks Maia once he gets behind the wheel. "Other than trying to send me to an early grave."

"Talking," Maia says. "And I know I was wrong and I know I owe you an apology. I'm sorry. I also know it's not going to make any difference and that I'm grounded. But we had a crisis."

"Crisis?"

"Colton's parents are getting a divorce," Maia says. "He needed us."

Huck sighs and lets the rest of his anger go. One of the things he likes best about St. John is exactly what Maia is describing: in times of trouble, people come together. That was true when LeeAnn died and even more true when Rosie died. Why should it be any less true for Maia and Colton just because they're kids?

"You should have called me," Huck says.

"My phone was dead."

"Not everyone's phone was dead," Huck says.

"I didn't want to call," Maia says, "because I thought you'd make me come home. We all made a vow we wouldn't tell our parents where we were until we knew Colton was going to be all right."

"Colton is going to be just fine," Huck says. He nearly points out that Maia just endured something far worse and she's okay, but Huck doesn't want to bring up Rosie right now, even though he misses her very, very much at this moment. Rosie would have been far more understanding than Huck about this little powwow. Rosie might have invited all the kids to pile into her car and then taken them all home herself, encouraging them to share their feelings as she drove. "He has two parents who love him."

"Facts," Maia says. "Unfortunately, while we were on the beach, I discovered another problem."

"Oh, really."

"I saw Mick," Maia says. "He walked all the way down from the Beach Bar."

Huck nearly says, *Yes, he was the one who called me*—but he doesn't want to reveal his sources.

"And he was with Brigid. Brigid was crying hysterically. Mick had his arms around her trying to comfort her—this was before he noticed me sitting with my friends…"

"Yeah?" Huck says.

"And then they started *kissing!*" Maia says. Her voice is shaky. "I'm so disgusted with him. He pulled away after a minute, but not soon enough. As soon as I get home and charge my phone, I'm calling Ayers."

For Pete's sake, Huck thinks. *Does the drama never end?*

"They're adults, Nut," he says. "I think maybe you should let them work it out."

"He'll never tell her," Maia says. "Ayers will never know if I don't say something."

"Maybe that's for the best," Huck says. He lights a cigarette and takes a long, much-needed drag. "Maybe he and Brigid needed closure."

"Closure?" Maia says, and she laughs like a full-grown woman. "Spare me."

When they get back to Jacob's Ladder, Huck says, "Grounded for a week. No town for two weeks."

Maia nods.

"You lied to Cash," Huck says. "You told him I had a late charter. So then I turned around and ripped him a new one for believing you. Now your own brother can't trust you."

"I'm sorry," Maia says.

"Your mother hid a lot of things from me," Huck says. He hadn't wanted to bring up Rosie, but here she is, showing up anyway. "Probably because she didn't think I could handle the truth." Huck clears the lump in his throat. "I've learned my lesson. You promise to tell me the truth, whatever it is, and I promise to handle it. Understand?"

"Yes, sir," she says.

"Go inside, please. There's Candi's on the table with extra comeback sauce. Then straight to bed."

"Where are you going?" Maia asks.

"I have some apologizing to do myself," Huck says.

He drives to the villa even though it's late and Irene might be in bed. Both Jeeps are in the driveway, which Huck supposes is a good thing. He needs to apologize to Cash; he shudders when he thinks how hard he was on the poor guy.

But it was Maia. When Cash has a child of his own, he'll understand.

Huck trudges up the stairs and sees a light on in the kitchen. Cash is sitting at the kitchen table with his phone in front of him.

Huck knocks on the sliding door and Cash jumps, then hurries to let Huck in. "Did you find her?"

"I did," Huck says. "She's safe." He can see the relief wash over Cash's face and Huck feels ashamed. He's so afraid of losing Maia, even of sharing her, that he's ignoring the best part about her newfound family: there are more people who care about her. "Listen, I'm sorry."

"*I'm* sorry," Cash says. "I've been beating myself up since I dropped her off, wondering how I could have been so gullible—"

"You trusted her," Huck says. "That's a good thing. I had no right to speak to you the way I did, and I hope you can forgive me."

"My mom gave me your cell number," Cash says. "If you ever let me hang out with Maia again, I promise I'll follow the rules and drop her only at home."

"She's grounded for a week," Huck says. "But I'm sure she'll be bugging you as soon as she's a free woman."

"I hope so," Cash says. He offers Huck his hand. "Thanks for coming all the way up here to apologize, that was above and beyond. But I have an early morning tomorrow..."

"Right," Huck says. He turns toward the door, then stops. "Is your mom still awake, do you think?"

"Probably," Cash says. "She just headed upstairs a minute ago. Do you want me to check?"

Huck hesitates. He could just wait and talk to Irene on the boat tomorrow.

"I'll get her," Cash says. "I'm sure she wants to know about Maia."

Cash disappears up the stairs, and a moment later, Irene comes down. Her hair is out of its braid, wavy over her shoulders. She's wearing gym shorts and a gray Iowa Hawkeyes T-shirt. Huck feels himself trembling.

"I owe you an apology, AC," he says.

Irene points at the door. "Let's go outside."

This is a good sign, he thinks. He holds the door open for her and she heads out to the railing at the edge of the deck, where they can look out over the water. The pool is gurgling to their right and glowing an ethereal blue.

"Maia is okay?" she asks.

"She was at the beach with her friends," Huck says. "I'm sorry I lost my temper."

"It was understandable," Irene says. "She's your girl."

"That she is," Huck says. "I vowed she would be my first and only priority. I can't let anything happen to her."

"She's lucky to have you," Irene says.

Huck throws caution to the wind and gathers Irene up in his arms. She allows this, but he can feel tension in her body.

"What's wrong?" he says.

"The other night was magical…" Irene says.

Huck loosens his hold on her. "But?"

"Meeting you, becoming friends with you, has been nothing short of miraculous. That first day of fishing…it saved me."

And me, he thinks.

"I love working on the boat. Not just because I like the work but because I enjoy your company—"

"Did I mess things up by kissing you?" he asks. Meeting him was miraculous, he saved her, she enjoys his company...but that doesn't mean she feels romantic about him.

"Yes and no," Irene says. Without warning, tears pool in her eyes. "When we kissed...I never thought I'd feel that way again." She sniffs. "There's a way in which I've never felt that way before, ever."

"That's good, right?" Huck says.

"It's too soon, Huck," she says. "This whole situation is still so fresh. I know you don't think we need to worry about the authorities hauling us off to jail like they did the Vickerses, but I do anyway."

"I'm not going to let anything happen to you," Huck says. "I care for you."

Irene reaches up to touch his face. "And I care for you. But I need more time. I just...I need time." She rests her hand on the side of his neck. "I want you to promise you won't give up on me."

Huck isn't sure he can speak. He's disappointed. Crushed. Can she not feel the chemistry here? The love? He's not sure how he'll be able to hold himself in check. And yet he's also relieved. Irene is nothing if not a woman of her word. She does have feelings for him. She's not ready. Is Huck going to give up on her? Hell no.

"You have my word, AC," he says.

She pulls him close and rests her head on his chest for a moment. "We have an early day tomorrow," she says.

"You're right," he says. "I should go." It's difficult, but he releases her. "See you tomorrow, AC." He strides across the deck without looking back, but he hopes it's like the movies and Irene is staring after him with longing, telling herself she's made a mistake, that she is in love with Huck and should chase after him and let him know.

Huck is halfway down the stairs when he sees a pair of headlights winding up the hill toward the villa. Then he sees another pair, and another and another. Four vehicles are winding their way up Lovers Lane.

BAKER

On Tuesday, he calls an emergency breakfast meeting at Snooze. Once his friends are assembled and they all have coffee—he can't expect them to provide any kind of decent advice without coffee—Baker passes around his phone.

On the screen is a picture of Mick on one knee, proposing to Ayers, with Cash's text: She said yes, dude. Sorry.

Debbie says, "Wow, she's hot. I know you said she was hot, but...wow."

"Wow," Wendy echoes when she gets the phone. "Debbie's right."

"That's not helpful," Baker says morosely.

"Can we talk about the manipulative nature of public proposals in general?" Ellen says. "Why do people do it?"

"Insecurity?" Becky says. "Fear? Or is it the opposite—hubris."

"I think it's romantic," Wendy says. "And fearless. Don't you think it takes courage?"

"You're off topic," Baker says. "I'm now moving myself and my four-year-old son down to a remote Caribbean island for a woman who just agreed to marry someone else."

"This is Mick, right?" Ellen says. "The guy who cheated on her?"

"Yes."

"Ew," Debbie says.

"He's not bad-looking," Wendy says. "But he's not you."

"Cool dog," Becky says. "Is that Mick's dog? Or Ayers's dog?"

"Mick's," Baker says. "He has a cool dog but I have a cool kid."

"That's a pizza boat in the background?" Ellen says. She looks at the others. "A pizza boat! We need to plan a trip to St. John."

"We'll come visit you," Debbie says. "The villa has room, right?"

"Nine bedrooms," Baker says. "But again, off topic. Should I even go? Or should I stay here?"

"Wearing my human-resources hat, here's what I think," Becky says. "I like this move for you. It's not necessarily permanent. You go down there, you coach at the school, you get Floyd situated. He's a bright, perceptive, resilient kid and he's a sponge. I think it'll be good for both of you to live somewhere else for a while. You're renting your house, not selling it, so you can always come back. Think of it as a sabbatical of sorts. And then if Ayers sees the light and you two get together, you can make it more permanent."

The other women nod their heads.

"What did I tell you before?" Ellen says. "You won't hit the ball if you don't swing."

Baker appreciates his friends' advice, but there's no way he's making such a huge leap of faith without talking to Ayers.

But first, Baker tries Cash. He would like some intel. Has his brother talked to Ayers about the engagement? What does he know? Cash doesn't answer his phone; either he's very busy or he doesn't want to get involved. Baker assumes it's the latter, but why did he send the photo, then? To be informative or to be a jerk?

Baker tries Ayers on Tuesday evening, a full twenty-four hours after he received the photo. It doesn't seem quite as horrific now that some time has passed. Engagements get broken every day, right?

She doesn't answer either, which could be a bad sign—she's with Mick, she's finished with Baker, she wants him to go away—in which case, Baker will just stay in Houston.

He doesn't leave a voicemail—no one ever listens to

them—but he does shoot her a text. Any chance I can talk to you tonight?

A little while later, there's a response. I'm at work. I'll call on my way home.

Baker stares at the words for a long time, trying to imagine what Ayers is thinking.

Well, he'll know in a few hours.

He feeds Floyd and reads him three stories, but Floyd is keyed up because they're supposed to leave in the morning. Floyd has already said goodbye to his friends and his teachers. He's excited to live on an island.

"Dad," he says. "Islands are surrounded by water."

"That's right," Baker says.

"Gramma has a job on a boat," Floyd says. "Catching fish. And Uncle Cash has a job on a boat, giving tours to people from other places." Floyd closes his eyes. "I want to work on a boat."

"Okay, buddy," Baker says, ruffling Floyd's hair. "We'll get you a job on a boat."

Floyd's eyes fly open. "Really?"

Baker laughs, and he thinks of what a unique and amazing experience it would be for Floyd to grow up on a Caribbean island. He'll learn to sail and navigate; he'll become familiar with the natural world. And maybe he will grow up to be a person who contributes so much to the island that it makes up for his grandfather's wrongs—whatever those turn out to be.

Baker indulges in some red velvet–cake ice cream but resists the temptation of marijuana.

At nine fifteen, his phone rings. It's Ayers.

"Hey," she says.

"Hey."

"You heard?"

"I did. Cash sent me a picture of Mick slipping the ring on your finger." Baker pauses. "I guess the breakup didn't last long."

"I was taken by surprise," Ayers says.

"But you said yes, right?" Baker says. "And it was still a yes once you were alone with him? I mean, I understand the manipulative nature of public proposals..." He shakes his head; he's parroting Ellen.

"Yes," Ayers says. "It was manipulative. Good choice of words."

Ellen has never steered him wrong, he thinks. "You're going to marry Mick? Even though he cheated on you? Even though you said yourself that you can't trust him?"

"Do you have time for a story?" Ayers asks. "This is something I've never told anyone—not Mick, not Rosie, not anybody."

"I have all night," Baker says.

She takes a breath. "When I was Maia's age—younger even; ten or eleven—I lived in Kathmandu with my parents."

"Kathmandu." Baker remembers all the photographs on Ayers's wall. *Story for another day.* "In Nepal?"

"Yes," Ayers says. "Kathmandu used to be this frenetic, dirty, dusty, poverty-stricken place where emaciated cows roamed the streets along with the cars and the motorbikes. My parents and I lived in a backpacker hostel. My mother, Sunny, tended bar at an expat pub, I can't remember the name, only that it had a snooker table, and while my mother worked, my father would try to teach me to play, but my arms were too short to hold the cue stick. Anyway, the manager of the pub was this guy named Simon and he was the most handsome man I have ever seen in my life—and he liked my mother. Even at my tender age, I figured out that was why my father kept me in the pub playing snooker rather than exploring the city." She sighed. "But my father couldn't keep me there too late, so eventually every night we'd go back to the hostel. One night, something must have happened with Simon because my mother didn't come home. For three days, we didn't see her."

"What did your dad do?" Baker asks.

"He moved us to this place called the Hotel Vajra, which looked like it was pulled out of a fairy tale. The beds had crimson silk spreads and the doors were made of carved teak. At night they lit pillar candles up and down the hallways, and my father and I would go to the rooftop terrace restaurant and eat lamb *momos*. It was a big change for me, having a hotel room to myself and eating out in a fancy restaurant, and I knew, somehow, that we were doing it only because my mother wasn't there. I think I even knew that we were doing it to get back at her." Ayers sighs. "Anyway, one morning as we were headed over to Mike's, this place that served a real American breakfast, we saw my mother sitting in the front garden, waiting for us. She linked her arms through ours and we all went to Mike's and ordered big stacks of pancakes."

"Did she say where she'd been?"

"No," Ayers says. "Nothing was ever mentioned about it to me. My mother quit the job at the pub and we moved to Vietnam." She pauses. "Now, as an adult, I can only assume my mother had a fling with Simon and my father waited it out."

"Are your parents still together?" Baker asks.

"Yes," Ayers says. "They're very happy. To my knowledge, nothing like that has ever happened again, on either side. It was like a hiccup."

"A hiccup," Baker says. "And that's how you see Mick's behavior with Brigid? As a hiccup?"

"Mick took a detour," Ayers says. "But he found his way back to me. And I truly believe it was a one-and-done. He knows what he lost and he won't risk it again. I've asked him for years to find a better place to live, and on our way to the boat yesterday, he drove me past this house he rented. It's gorgeous."

"Where is it?" Baker says. "I'll buy it right out from under him."

"Baker," Ayers says.

"You said you have feelings for me," Baker says. "You said you couldn't stop thinking about me."

"That's true," Ayers says. "Even on Monday before Mick proposed, one of the mothers from Gifft Hill was talking about this hot new dad, and I knew it was you and I was...*jealous*."

"Think about that," Baker says.

"I have been thinking about it!" Ayers says. "But Mick and I have been together a long time. He knows me. We have a life here that we built together, month by month, year by year. I can't just throw that away for something new."

"You can, though," Baker says. "Because I'm moving to St. John tomorrow and I'm going to stay. I got a coaching job at Gifft Hill. I'm going to take scuba lessons..." He doesn't know where this idea comes from, it just pops into his head, but it sounds good. "I'm going to work on getting my real estate license down there. I'm going to build a life, month by month, year by year, and I want you to be in that life. When I first saw you, I felt like *I* was the one who had been struck by lightning—only instead of dying, I came to life." Is this corny? He can't tell. "I made a decision then and there that I was going to marry you. So you can hang up with me now thinking you're going to marry Mick. But I promise you, I *promise you,* Ayers, that I can do better than Mick. I will be true and steadfast and devoted and crazily in love with you until the day I die. I will never have any hiccups. Ever."

Ayers is quiet.

"If a proposal is what you want, then you have one from me. I want to marry you as soon as I'm legally able."

"You barely know me," she says, but her voice is softer. He's getting to her, maybe.

"We can worry about that later."

Ayers laughs, but her laugh is cut short. "Oh, hey," she says. "Maia is calling in on my line, and I should take it. It's late and she never calls me this late. She never calls me at all, she only texts."

"By all means, take it," Baker says. "I hope everything is okay."

"Me too," Ayers says. "I'll let you know. Bye."

Baker stares at the blank screen of his phone. If Floyd weren't asleep, he would play the Clash's "Should I Stay or Should I Go?" at top volume. What the hell—he finds his AirPods and cranks the song up.

If I go, there will be trouble.

And if I stay it will be double.

Repeat song, repeat song, repeat song.

During his fourth time through—Baker is still waiting for the answer to be revealed—he sees a text from Anna. What does she want? he wonders.

Louisa and I have some concerns about you uprooting Floyd, the text says. Please hold off on your move until we talk. I should have some time for a conference call next week.

"Ha!" Baker says to the empty living room. "That's rich. That's *really* rich!" 'Louisa and I have some concerns' means that *Louisa* has concerns, because Anna said she was 'K' with it last week."

Baker knows the text should persuade him to stay put, but it does exactly the opposite. Louisa has concerns about Baker uprooting Floyd to take him to St. John, but Anna and Louisa uprooting Floyd to take him to Cleveland was fine?

Ha!

Ha!

Another text comes in, and Baker assumes it's Anna burying herself even further—she doesn't even have time to talk about it until next week!—but the text isn't from Anna.

It's from Ayers.

Maia saw Mick kissing Brigid on the beach tonight. I'm giving the ring back.

Baker shuts the music off and heads upstairs to bed. He has an early flight in the morning.

ROSIE

January 1, 2015

Love is messy and complicated and unfair.

I see Russ when he's here, which is every few weeks for a couple of days. I'm elated for forty-eight hours before he arrives and devastated for forty-eight hours after he leaves. Actually, the leaving part is getting worse.

I see him often enough that it's getting hard to keep secret. I have to lie to Huck, say I have friends from the States in town and would he mind watching Maia for a couple of days? Huck is always happy to do this. I think being with Maia helps get his mind off Mama. He's started taking Maia out on the fishing boat. Even though she's only eight, he says she's a natural, and it's important for her to get her sea legs. Huck asked the names of my "friends from the States," and I said Rachel, Monica, and Phoebe. He didn't pick up on my joke—I knew he wouldn't—but he must be getting suspicious. Since when do I have friends from the States, or friends at all except for Ayers? I'm sure he suspects it's a man.

Russ and I can't go anywhere or do anything; he doesn't even want to risk a trip back to Miss Vie's on Hansen Bay. I visit him in room 718 at Caneel, which requires me to sneak in the back way from the parking lot, or, if Russ has the yacht to himself, I visit him there.

I show him pictures of Maia. He wants to meet her but I'm not allowing that. Every time he leaves, I know I might never see him again.

Once you prove to me you're staying here, I said, you can meet her.

June 24, 2015

Russ is leaving right before Carnival and he says he won't be back again this summer, which means the earliest I'll see him is September, but September is hurricane season and Caneel is closed, so it'll most likely be October or possibly even November.

I considered traveling to the States for the summer. Lots of people here do it. But Russ says that he has some meetings with clients in Grand Cayman and Miami and then he and Irene are spending two weeks in Door County, Wisconsin.

I had never heard of Door County, Wisconsin, so I looked it up on my computer and what I found were photographs of lakes and barns and orchards and cute little towns with church steeples, ice cream parlors, and antiques stores. It looks like America in the 1950s. When I asked Russ what he and Irene did there, he said they hung out on the lake—fishing, water skiing, swimming. And then in the evenings they played cards, attended fish boils, listened to the loons.

He asked me how I would spend the summer and I tried to explain about Carnival—it's a week of music, food, and dancing when nobody sleeps—and then the entire island needs a week to recover. I explained that Huck fished for blue and white marlin in the summer, which brought in a different kind of fisherman. And then in September, Maia would go back to school and everyone would pray there were no storms.

I told him four months was a long time to be apart. He said he knew that. Then he took me in his arms and kissed me and said that he realized our "arrangement" was unfair to me and he would understand if I wanted to find someone who could give me all the things I deserved—an engagement ring, a home, a future.

I said, "Yes, I should find someone else." But I knew I wouldn't. Because I love Russ. I didn't tell him that. I want him to say it first. He didn't say it, however, and what could I think but that he only loved Irene?

I kissed him goodbye and told him to have a wonderful summer. Enjoy the fish boils in Door County, Wisconsin, and the sound of the loons. I did slip another postcard into his duffel bag saying I would miss him. I didn't warn him about it. If Irene happened to discover it, oh, well. Russ would have to explain or lie about who M.L. was.

I'm glad I didn't allow him to meet Maia. My heart is in danger, but at least hers is safe.

November 9, 2015

Russ came back and he had good news, such good news that I'm almost afraid to believe it. His company, Ascension, was looking for investment opportunities and they partnered with a "local real estate concern" (he wouldn't tell me which one) to buy a hundred and forty acres in west Cinnamon, an area known as Little Cinnamon. They plan to develop the hillside, hire someone to build luxury villas. But the even better news was that the local real estate concern had built one home on spec and lost a lot of money on it, so Russ had bought the villa himself.

I had questions. Why had Russ been the one to buy it and not Todd or Stephen?

"They don't want a house," Russ said.

"Really?" I said. Then I thought: Who *doesn't want a house?*

"Really," Russ said. "They have homes elsewhere. They offered it to me because they know I have interests here."

"Interests?" I said. "You mean me."

"Yes."

"They know about us."

"They do."

"How?" I said. "Did you…tell them?"

"No," he said. "But they're not naive, Rosie."

They weren't naive; I'd never thought that. In fact, I'd always worried about it. This was a holdover from years earlier, the first time I laid eyes on the three of them, when it seemed like Russ was a sheep running around with a couple of wolves.

"The bigger news is that we're doing more business down here. In both the USVIs and the BVIs. Maybe we could even go to the BVIs together."

"You mean...Jost?" Jost Van Dyke was a party island. That was true when I was growing up but it's even more so now. Everyone loved Foxy's and the Soggy Dollar.

"I mean Anegada," he said. "Have you ever been?"

I had been to Anegada once, long ago. Before Mama met Huck, she had briefly dated a lobsterman who took us to Anegada for the day on his fishing boat. Anegada is the most remote of the British Virgin Islands and unlike any of the others in that it's just a spit of flat white sand. There are a few businesses, a few bars, a few homes, hundreds of flamingos, thousands of lobsters, and not much else. I hadn't been impressed with it at thirteen, but now, as a lovers' getaway, it held enormous appeal.

"When can we go?" I asked.

December 18, 2015

Russ and I celebrated Christmas and New Year's rolled into one during our three days on Anegada. We went over on Bluebeard on Monday and the captain said he'd be back for us on Thursday. We stayed in a simple white clapboard cottage on the most pristine beach imaginable. I thought the sand on St. John was white but it looks positively dingy compared to Anegada's. The cottage had a big white bed and a tiny kitchen that Russ had arranged to have stocked with provisions. Our mornings consisted of sleeping in, followed by coffee, fruit, and toast on the balcony overlooking the sea.

Unlike on St. John, there were no other islands on the horizon. It was a bizarre feeling, even for me, to stare out at nothing but water. At least on St. John, I felt connected to a larger whole, seeing St. Thomas, Water Island, Little St. James, and St. Croix in the distance. Here, we might have been perched on the edge of the world.

We made love, we walked on the beach, we fell asleep in the sun. In the late afternoons, our supper was delivered: lobster fritters; lobster bisque; baked, stuffed, or boiled lobster with butter. We drank champagne with our lobster; it seemed only fitting, and there were a dozen bottles of Krug in the refrigerator.

I used to drink champagne with Oscar and I had forgotten how tipsy it made me.

"Now that you've bought the villa in Little Cinnamon," I said, "will Irene come down?" This was my biggest fear. I could handle the idea of Irene but I could not handle the reality of Irene coming to stay on my island.

"No," he said. He went on to tell me a story about an ill-fated trip to Jamaica when the boys were young. They had wandered off, gotten lost in a shantytown near the hotel. Irene had been frantic; the trip left her scarred. She hated the Caribbean.

"Besides, she's consumed with our project at home," Russ said. He cleared his throat. He knew I disliked it when he used words like *we* and *our* to describe him and Irene. The project he was referring to is a Victorian fixer-upper that Irene had begged him to buy; she was desperate to restore it "to period."

I sipped my champagne and thought about Irene im-

mersed in a home-renovation project in Iowa City. How vastly different that life was from my own. I suppose that's part of the appeal for Russ, part of the point. He has a wife and a mistress—I'm not sure what else to call myself—and I suppose that we nourish different parts of him. I'm sex and lobster and champagne-drinking under a blanket of stars. Irene is home and hearth, mother of the boys, keeper of the traditions that make a family.

Can I lure Russ away from her? Can I make him feel his family is here? I can try.

In the new year, I decided, I'm going to introduce him to Maia.

February 11, 2016

I told Maia she was going to meet a friend of mine but that it was a secret and she wasn't to talk about this friend to anyone, including Huck.

Then I hated myself.

But I can't have it both ways. I can let Maia meet Russ and make sure she keeps it quiet, or I can not introduce them at all.

Maia said she understood. She looked at me with her wise-child eyes and repeated what I'd told her: Russ was a friend of mine but I didn't want the whole island talking about it and I didn't want Huck to know because he wouldn't like it.

Why wouldn't he like it? Maia wanted to know. I could see her backing away from any situation that Huck might not approve of. Maia is devoted to Huck. He is God, Santa Claus, and Justin Bieber rolled into one.

"He would *like it*," I said. "He wants me to be happy. But I'm not ready to tell Huck about it, only you. Russ is a person for just you and me, okay?"

"Okay," she said.

We visited Russ at the villa in Little Cinnamon. When he shook Maia's hand, he slipped her a cherry lollipop, which she accepted only after I said it was okay. He asked her if she wanted to play Chutes and Ladders. She said yes, then added, "But just so you know, I always win."

I won't go so far as to say it was an instant success. Maia didn't care about any old white guy except for Huck. But I will say they got along fine. Russ was charmed, maybe even smitten, and as I watched them play their game—Maia won handily, landing on only ladders while Russ's rolls put him on only chutes—it struck me how much they looked alike, how their mannerisms were similar, their earnest, goofy enthusiasm matched.

She is his daughter. No doubt about it.

April 8, 2016

Maia and I went back to the villa in Little Cinnamon last week.

Russ asked Maia if there was anything he could add for her at the villa and she said a shuffleboard court.

Russ said, "I will tell the architects tomorrow to add a shuffleboard court, as long as you promise to play with me."

Maia said, "I'll play with you, but just so you know, I always win."

May 23, 2016

Love is messy and complicated and unfair.

   Russ's grandson, Floyd, is getting baptized in Iowa City, which is something of an issue because Baker's wife, Anna, isn't religious and has only grudgingly agreed to the ceremony.

   "Anna is a doctor," Russ said. "A real smart cookie."

   "Smart cookie?" I said. "Please promise me never to use that term in front of her."

   "I already did," he admitted. "It didn't go over well."

   I don't know anything about the baptism except that it is happening. I imagine a church full of people with Russ and Irene sitting up front, holding hands. Everyone gazes on them with admiration, not one soul guessing that Russ has a mistress and a daughter in the Caribbean.

   Does he think about us? I wonder. Or does he have a vault in his brain where he locks us, and all the feelings he has for us, away?

May 30, 2016

The villa needs some sprucing up, and Russ asked me to make the decorating decisions.

   "I have no taste," he said. "At home, Irene handles these things." As soon as he said this, he knew it was a mistake.

   The at home bothered me more than Irene. His home is in Iowa. This is . . . well, I'm not even sure what to call it. His second place, I guess. I live in second place.

   I told Russ I want no part of any decorating decisions. It's his villa, not mine. In truth, I don't want to pick things and then have him compare my taste to Irene's. Russ asks Paulette Vickers to handle the decorating. It's Paulette and Douglas from Welcome to Paradise Real Estate who built the villa in the first place, and just as they were about to lose it to the bank, Todd Croft and Russ swung in on a vine; Russ bought the villa and Ascension the hillside. They asked Paulette and Douglas to stay on as property managers. I know them both but I'm not worried about Huck finding out because Paulette is a distant cousin of my father, Levi Small, and the Smalls did not speak to Mama, and they do not speak to Huck.

I was concerned about what would happen once the other houses were built and sold and suddenly we had neighbors watching my car coming and going from the best villa.

When I shared this concern with Russ, he said, "We won't have any neighbors."

"We won't?"

He clammed up then, which is something he's been doing more and more frequently, every time I ask him about his work. He'd told me early on that Irene didn't have the first idea what his work entailed. She couldn't care less, he said. All she cared about was the money.

"She wouldn't care if I were a paid assassin," he said.

To differentiate myself from Irene, I tried to understand what Russ does for work. He is executive vice president of customer relations for Ascension, which means, essentially, that he does exactly what he'd done in college when Todd Croft was selling beer in the dorms—he lends him his trustworthy face, his cheerful good-guy demeanor, and his sterling personal reputation. Ascension invests in "high-risk, high-yield" investment opportunities for very wealthy clients, many of them foreign.

"Why won't we have neighbors?" I asked. We were down on the private beach—I had decided to leave Maia with Huck so we could have some alone time—sitting together on one of the brand-new chaise longues that Pauline had bought. We were drinking champagne, the Krug. "Russ?"

I was leaning back against Russ, tucked between his legs, and he murmured into my hair, "We sold those lots to fictional entities. Shell companies that we set up…"

"So, wait," I said. "Is that legal?"

"People do it all the time down here," Russ said. "To clean money, to hide money."

"That wasn't my question."

Russ squeezed me tight. "This is the Caribbean, Rosie," he said, as if it weren't the only home I'd ever known.

Russ is in the business of money-laundering and tax evasion. I said I didn't believe him capable of it, and once I pried a little more, he admitted that he'd taken the position at Ascension thinking it was 100 percent aboveboard, but once he'd figured out it wasn't (in addition to everything else it did, the company invested money for some bad people—bad both morally and politically), it was too late. He was in too deep to protest.

"Then there's the fact that both Todd and Stephen know about you," he said.

Without a word, I got to my feet and bent down to kiss Russ on the cheek. "Be right back," I said. I ascended the eighty steps to the villa, got in my car, and drove home.

I hate that I now know Russ is cheating the system—

and yet, what did I expect? He's cheating on his wife. I'm an integral part of the grand deception. I'm a lie. Maia is a lie. Mama was right, so *right, to tell me to stay away from him. But had I listened? No. Three days after she was gone, I was back in his bed.*

It's over, I've decided.

When I kissed Maia as she lay sleeping, I thought, I am going to find a man who deserves to be your father.

February 14, 2017

The money still arrives in packages, only instead of depositing it in a bank account for Maia's college, I've started stacking it neatly in the bottom drawer of my dresser. If the money is illegal, someone will trace it to my bank account eventually. Cash is safer.

Then, this weekend a text came to my phone from a foreign number. It said: Please come to the villa. I want to see you. Things will change, I promise.

I blinked, read the text again, read the text a third time. Russ had never texted me before. We'd both agreed cell phones weren't safe.

Things will change, I promise. *It wasn't a text saying he had left Irene, but I gave in anyway. I ached with missing him.*

March 2, 2017

Love is messy, complicated, and unfair.

Things have not changed in any way except that the villa

is newly redone and Maia has been allowed to decorate one of the rooms as her own. Also, I finally came clean with Huck and Ayers and told them that, yes, there was a man—I even said his name out loud once—but my relationship was nobody's business but my own.

Huck and Ayers disagreed. Huck wants to meet the guy and so does Ayers; I've put them both off, saying that when the time is right, introductions will be made. When the time is right will be when Russ leaves Irene. He says he's getting closer to making a clean break. They live separate lives. Baker and his family are happy in Houston, and Russ has just set his son Cash up in an outdoor-supply business in Colorado. Once Irene finishes working on the house in Iowa City—it still isn't done—he'll move down here full-time.

He doesn't talk about work and I know enough not to ask. He spends a lot of time in the Cayman Islands as well as the BVIs—in Anegada, specifically. He asked me if I wanted to go back to Anegada; it's the one place he's not afraid to be seen with me.

"Maybe?" I said the last time he asked. I worry that he has business interests in Anegada, and I can't risk getting mixed up in them.

Huck calls Russ the Invisible Man, and I don't object. That's exactly what he is.

November 3, 2018

I haven't written in ages, and usually when I take breaks like this it's because too much is going on for me to stop and write about it. But life has been relatively placid, if also topsy-turvy.

When Russ is away, I work at La Tapa, live with Huck, hang out with Ayers, and take care of Maia, who is growing into a very cool young person. When Russ is here, I live with him. Sometimes Maia comes with me; sometimes she decides that she would rather stay home.

"It's not that much fun watching you guys kiss all day," she said. *"Even if there is shuffleboard and SpaghettiOs."*

We didn't tell Maia that Russ was her father; she told us. One day when it was pouring rain and there was nothing else for Maia to do, she deigned to come to the villa with me, and while she and Russ were playing Scrabble (they had graduated from Chutes and Ladders), Maia looked up and said, "You're my father, right?"

Russ had searched my face in wild panic. "Uh…"

"Right," I said. "How did you know?"

"How did I know?" Maia rounded the table and put her face cheek to cheek with Russ's. "Come on, Mom. Really?"

I'm writing now not because of any great upheaval in my life but because Ayers and Mick broke up. What happened was that Mick hired a girl named Brigid to work at Beach Bar and something about Brigid set off warning bells with Ayers. Sure enough, a couple nights ago, at three in the morning, Ayers drove into town and caught Mick and Brigid together. Mick was basically living at Ayers's place in Fish Bay, but Ayers threw him and his dog, Gordon, out. For the past two days I've had to listen to what a disgusting liar and cheat Mick is and what an unforgivable harlot Brigid is because Brigid knew Mick was in a committed relationship and still she fooled around with him. While I do agree that Mick is weak and Brigid doesn't deserve to have another female friend as long as she lives, this situation has also led me to some painful introspection.

I am Brigid. I know Russ is married and still I am involved with him. Deeply involved.

Russ showed up a few days ago—hurricane season is now officially over and the island is gearing up for the holidays—and I told him about Ayers breaking up with Mick because she had caught him cheating. Russ nodded distractedly.

I said, "These aren't fictional characters from a book I'm reading or a show I'm watching, Russ. These are my friends. You don't know them because you can't meet anyone in my life, but they're real to me, they're important to me."

"I know, Rosie," he said. "I've been hearing about them for years. They're real to me too."

"I want an engagement ring," I blurted out. "By the new year. Otherwise I'm done for good. Maia just turned twelve. She's a young woman, Russ. She's been very accepting of our arrangement, but someday soon she's going to start asking the hard questions."

"I know," he said. "And believe me, I want to give you an engagement ring. Things are tough at work right now…"

Tough at work. That old chestnut.

"I'm thinking about quitting," he said. "I love my income, but if I left, I'd have a shot at getting my integrity back. The things we're doing…they aren't right, Rosie."

"Don't tell me!" I said. I have this notion that if I don't know any particulars, I'll be safe. I have almost a hundred

and twenty-five thousand dollars in my bottom drawer. It's a lot, but is it enough to live on for the rest of my life? I thought about Maia going to high school—I want to be able to send her to Antilles on St. Thomas—and then to college in the States. Russ must have savings, right? If not, we could sell the villa and move someplace smaller. We don't need nine bedrooms; we never have guests. Seven of the bedrooms have never even been slept in.

Russ said, "If I quit, things will change. For the worse, initially, and then for the better."

"Quit," I said.

November 19, 2018

My hand is shaking as I write this. I'm thinking about calling the police, but the police here on St. John won't be able to do anything. I need to call the FBI. But if I do that, I might get Russ in trouble.

I was waiting tables at *La Tapa* tonight when Tilda told me there was a one-top, a man, who had asked for me specifically. This was the downside of being mentioned by name so frequently on TripAdvisor. Complete strangers pretended they knew me.

"He's ridiculously hot," Tilda said. "In a Clooney-meets-Satan kind of way."

That description should have tipped me off but it was a busy night and I didn't have time to think. I approached the table and noted only that Tilda's description was accurate; the guy was attractive but scary-looking. Sharply dressed, too sharp for the Virgin Islands.

"Hello," I said. "Welcome to La Tapa." I handed him a menu and the wine list. "Can I get you started with sparkling, still, or tap water?"

He looked up. "Hello, Rosie," he said.

"I'm sorry," I said. "Do I know you?"

In the split second before he spoke, it clicked: Todd Croft.

"Todd Croft," he said.

I wanted to scream. I did a quick survey of the restaurant. Who could help me? Skip was behind the bar. There was no way he could handle this. Ayers could, maybe. Or Tilda.

Or me. I could handle this.

"What are you doing here?" I said.

"How old is your daughter now?" he asked. "Twelve?"

The mention of Maia made me bend down and get in his face. "Get out of here," I whispered. "This is my island. Mine, not yours. If your intention was to come in here and threaten me or threaten my family, I would think again. I know people."

He seemed amused by that. "Do you?"

"Yes," I said. "I do." I was thinking of Oscar. If I took twenty or thirty thousand dollars from the drawer, could I get Oscar to board Bluebeard in the middle of the night and shoot Todd Croft, or at least scare him to death?

I half feared Todd would try to hire him. They were both pirates.

"Russ is finished with you," I said.

"He's not, though," Todd said. He pushed back from the table and stood. "That's what I came to tell you. Russ isn't fin-

*ished with me. He doesn't seem to see it that way, however, so
I need you to talk some sense into him." He gave me a tight
smile. "There's big money in it for you if you're persuasive."*

*"If you want a burger," I said, in a voice loud enough to
draw attention from nearby tables, "you should try the Tap
and Still across the street. Thanks for stopping in."*

*With that, I snapped up his menu, corralled Ayers from
table 11, and dragged her into the kitchen to do a shot of beer.*

"Who was that?" she asked. "He was hot."

*I longed to tell Ayers the truth. She's my best friend and
she doesn't know the first thing about me. By choosing to be
with Russ, I'm hiding from everyone else.*

"Some creeper," I said. "I sent him packing."

December 31, 2018

*Russ came back the day after Christmas with a leather and
black pearl choker for me—not an engagement ring. I gave
him a framed photograph of me and him in the hammock
that I had taken with Maia's selfie stick. He was happy with
his present. I was less happy with mine, which he could tell.*

*"I have until the new year, January first," he said.
"Right? That was the ultimatum?"*

I didn't like the word ultimatum *or the fact that I had
issued one, but I nodded.*

*I'd told him about Todd Croft coming to La Tapa, and
Russ had assured me that everything was going to be all right.
He'd had a confidential talk with Stephen Johnson, Todd's
partner, and he'd told Russ that he would smooth things over
with Todd. There was no reason Russ couldn't make a seam-*

less exit as long as he signed a confidentiality agreement and a noncompete.

This came as a relief to me, and it made sense. Stephen was an attorney.

"Let's celebrate New Year's Eve at the villa," Russ said. "And then go over to Anegada on the first. Stephen has offered to take us by helicopter."

"I've always wanted to ride in a helicopter," I admitted. "Should we take Maia?"

He kissed my nose. "Next time," he said. "This trip is just for us."

Just for us; I liked the way that sounded. He would extract himself from Ascension with the help of coolheaded, legal-minded Stephen Johnson, and we would go to Anegada to stay in the pristine white clapboard cottage—where, maybe, oh please, a diamond ring would be waiting for me.

When I went home to pack, I heard Maia and Joanie giggling in Maia's room. I tapped on the door.

They were sprawled across Maia's bed, both on their phones, which I didn't love, but what I did love was the evidence of their bath-bomb business strewn about—the Epsom salts, the food coloring, the citric acid, the tropical fragrances.

I chatted with the girls for a minute—they were starting to have crushes on boys—and then I gave Maia a squeeze and a kiss and wished her a happy New Year.

"I love you, Mama," she said.

I left the room but then I peeked back in. I wanted very badly to tell Maia the truth: I was going to Anegada with Russ because he planned to propose! We were going to be a real family!

But instead, I simply caught her eye and mouthed, I love you.

And I closed the door.

IRENE

Irene watches Huck's back as he leaves. What is she doing? She's asking for more time because she's scared. She has never felt so drawn to a man in her life and it's terrifying; she doesn't like the sensation of losing control.

But what did Russ's accident teach her? What is the number-one thing?

She's alive.

She, Irene Hagen Steele, has today and God knows how many days after. Why not spend those days falling headlong in love with Captain Sam Powers?

"Hey, Huck?" she says.

But he has disappeared down the stairs.

She shakes her head. *Go to bed, Irene,* she thinks. *You can talk to Huck in the morning.*

Yes, that's a smart idea—but even as she decides this, she's walking toward the villa stairs, envisioning kissing Huck through the open window of his truck.

And then she sees a flash of light. Headlights, more than one pair, are coming up the hill.

"Huck?" she calls out.

The headlights get closer, and before Irene can process what's happening, four black SUVs pull into the driveway.

What must be ten people climb out of the cars and start up the steps. Irene's instinct is to back up all the way to the far railing of the deck.

The first person to arrive at the top is a woman, red-haired, attractive. She flashes her badge and a piece of paper that could be a shopping list for all Irene can tell; she'd need her glasses to read it.

"Hello?" Irene says. "Can I help you?"

"I'm Agent Vasco, and as of right now, this villa, one Lovers Lane, is the property of the United States government." She looks at Irene, not unkindly. "Mrs. Steele?"

Irene nods.

"Your husband, Russell Steele, bought this property as well as the property at thirty Church Street, Iowa City, Iowa, with illegally acquired funds. We've arrested Todd Croft and charged him with one hundred and seventeen counts of fraud, money-laundering, and tax evasion for a total of over three point five billion dollars. He named your husband, Russell Steele, as a coconspirator, and he has documentation to prove it. I'm afraid we have to seize both properties."

"Wait," Irene says. "You're taking this house?"

"This house, yes," Agent Vasco says. "And there are federal agents at your home in Iowa City right now."

"But that's my *home*," Irene says. "I invested six years restoring it. I *live* there."

"You may pack one suitcase of personal effects," Agent Vasco says. "But I'm afraid you have to vacate the property."

"But my boys," Irene says. "My grandson." Irene can't think. Baker and Floyd are in Houston, but they're on their way back. Cash is asleep upstairs.

"I'm sorry," Agent Vasco says. "I'm afraid I'll have to oversee your packing."

"But I've done nothing wrong," Irene says. "I met with Agent Beckett in Iowa City. I was very forthcoming. I told him everything I knew. I *helped* him."

"I wish it were different," Agent Vasco says. "But it's not. This is no longer your property, I'm afraid."

For one suspended moment, Irene mentally leaves the scene. She's back on the unnamed beach, naked. She hears Russ say, *The storm is coming. It will be a bad storm. Destructive.*

This is the storm. It's here. The villa. Her home in Iowa City. What is she going to do? Where is she going to go?

"Huck?" she cries out.

She sees him running up the villa stairs toward her.

"I'm here, AC," he says. "I'm here."

ACKNOWLEDGMENTS

Every year for the past eight years, I have been lucky enough to spend five weeks on the island of St. John in the U.S. Virgin Islands. While I consider it a home away from home, it is not my main residence, nor do I own property there. It is for this reason that I am so grateful to and humbled by the people of St. John, all of whom have been so kind, welcoming, helpful, and supportive.

I have to start by thanking my St. John family: Julie and Matt Lasota and their wonderful children. I'd also like to thank Beth and Jim Heskett for giving me "a room of my own" at the St. John Guest Suites for four idyllic years.

Shout-outs to those people who assisted with my research by either talking to me or providing me with valuable experiences. In no particular order: Karen Oscar Coffelt and head of school Liz Morrison from the Antilles School; Captain Stephen and Kelly Quinn of Singing Dog Sailing; Bridgett and Jimmy Key of Palm Tree Charters; Heather and the whole staff on Pizza Pi (the pizza boat!); Matt Atkinson, who was literally my first friend on St. John in 2012; Peter Bettinger; Chester of Chester's Getaway; Colleen from Pizzabar in Paradise; John Dickson from the Pink Papaya; Jorie Roberts; Sarah Swan; Richard from Lime Inn—thank you for saving Maxx's life (story for another day); Jerry and Tish O'Connell from the Soggy Dollar (and you too, Leon!); and huge, enormous thanks to Alex Ewald for the wonder that is La Tapa.

Last and most important, thank you to my partner in crime, Timothy Field. Here's to many, many more days of being the last people left on Oppy.

ABOUT ELIN HILDERBRAND

Elin Hilderbrand is the mother of three 3-sport athletes, an aspiring fashionista, a dedicated jogger, a world explorer, an enthusiastic foodie, and a grateful four-year breast cancer survivor. She spends part of every winter writing on St. John. *What Happens in Paradise* is her twenty-fourth novel.

KEEP READING FOR
A PREVIEW OF
TROUBLES IN PARADISE

Travel to the bright Caribbean one last time in the dishy and satisfying conclusion to the nationally bestselling Paradise trilogy. At last all will be revealed about the secrets and lies that led Irene Steele and her sons to St. John—and to their new lives in the Caribbean.

ST. JOHN

The gossip recently has been as juicy as a papaya, one that gives just slightly under our fingertips and is fragrant on the inhale, the inside a brilliant coral color, bursting with seeds like so many ebony beads. If you don't fancy papaya, think of a mango as we crosshatch the ripe flesh of the cheeks with a sharp knife or a freshly picked pineapple from the fertile fields of St. Croix, deep gold, its chunks sweeter than candy. Like these island fruits, the talk around here is irresistible.

The drama began on New Year's Day with tragedy: a helicopter crash a few miles away, in British waters. One of our own was killed, Rosie Small, whom some of us remember back when she was in LeeAnn's belly. Because LeeAnn's first husband, Levi Small, left the island when Rosie was a toddler, we'd all had a hand in raising her. We sympathized with LeeAnn when the cute Rosie girl we doted on turned into the precocious Rosie teenager LeeAnn couldn't quite control. At the tender age of fifteen, Rosie dated a fella named Oscar Cobb from St. Thomas who drove the Ducati that nearly ran our friend Rupert off Route 107 right into Coral Bay. We were all overjoyed when Oscar went to jail for stabbing his best friend. *Good riddance!* we said. *Throw away the key!* A group of us took LeeAnn out for celebratory drinks at Miss Lucy's. We thought we'd dodged a bullet; Rosie would not waste her life on a good-for-nothing man with shady business dealings like Oscar Cobb.

The man Rosie ended up with was far more dangerous.

After LeeAnn died, five years ago now, Rosie took a secret lover. We called him the "Invisible Man" because none of us had ever caught more than a glimpse of him. But while Paulette Vickers was under the dryer at Dearie's Beauty Shoppe, she let something slip about "Rosie Small's gentleman." Then Paulette clammed up and it was the clamming up that made us suspicious. Paulette was a little uppity because her parents had started the successful real estate agency Welcome to Paradise. She liked to talk. When she stopped talking, we started listening.

The Invisible Man's name was Russell Steele. He was killed in the helicopter crash along with Rosie and the pilot, an attorney from the Caymans named Stephen Thompson. They were on their way to Anegada. The callous among us commented that they should have taken a boat like normal folk, especially since there were thunderstorms. The perceptive among us noted that, while there were thunderstorms on New Year's morning, they were south and west of St. John, not northeast, which was the direction the helicopter would have been flying to get to Anegada.

Both Virgin Islands Search and Rescue and the FBI had reason to believe that the helicopter exploded. Maybe an accident—an electrical malfunction—or maybe something else.

If you think this is intriguing, imagine hearing of the arrival of the Invisible Man's family. For, yes indeed, Russell Steele was married, with two grown sons and one grandchild. And did his wife and sons stroll right down the St. John ferry dock on January 3 and climb into the car belonging to Paulette Vickers, who then whisked them off to whatever grand, secluded villa Russell Steele owned?

Yes; yes, they did.

Would the family of Russell Steele find out about Rosie?

Yes; yes, they would.

It was one of the taxi drivers, Chauncey, who witnessed a determined-looking woman marching down the National Park Service dock calling for Captain Sam Powers (we all know him as Huck), LeeAnn's devoted second husband and Rosie's stepfather, and then talking herself right onto Huck's boat, the *Mississippi*. Chauncey remembers whistling under his breath because he had seen women on a rampage like that before and they always got what they were after.

The two sons appeared out and about in Cruz Bay, going to the usual places tourists go—La Tapa to enjoy the mussels, High Tide for happy hour. We saw these young men (one tall and clean-cut with a dimple, one stocky with bushy blond hair) in the company of two young women we were all very fond of (charming and lovely Ayers Wilson, who had been Rosie's best friend, and Tilda Payne, whose parents owned a villa in exclusive Peter Bay), and that set us speculating, even though we knew that beautiful young people find one another no matter what the circumstances.

When we learned that one of the sons, Baker Steele, took his child on a tour of the Gifft Hill School and that the other son, Cash Steele, had joined the crew of *Treasure Island,* we began to wonder: Were they *staying?*

When we discovered that the Invisible Man's wife, Irene Steele, was working as the first mate on Huck's fishing boat, we thought: *What exactly is going on?*

We couldn't run into one another at Pine Peace Market or in line at the post office without asking in a whisper: *You heard anything new?*

Sadie, out in Coral Bay, was the one who learned that the FBI had come looking for Paulette and Douglas Vickers, but Paulette and Douglas had taken their six-year-old son, Windsor, and fled by the time the FBI arrived. They went to St. Croix to hide out with Douglas's sister in Frederiksted. Did one of *us* tell the FBI where they were? No one knew for sure, but Paulette and Douglas were arrested the very next day.

We'd barely had time to recover from this shocking news when the FBI sent agents in four black cars along the North Shore Road to whatever secluded villa Russell Steele owned to inform Irene Steele that the villa and the entire hundred-and-forty-acre parcel we called Little Cinnamon was now the property of the U.S. government, since it had been purchased with dirty money.

Whew! We woke up the next morning feeling like we had gorged ourselves. We were plump with gossip. It was, almost, too much.

We feel compelled to mention that this kind of scandal isn't typical of life here in the Virgin Islands.

What is typical?

"Good morning," "Good afternoon," or "Good evening" at the start of every conversation.

Sunshine, sometimes alternating with a soaking rain.

Wild donkeys on the Centerline Road.

Sunburned tourists spilling out of Woody's during happy hour.

Silver hook bracelets.

Hills.

Swaying palm trees and sunsets.

Hikers in floppy hats.

Rental Jeeps.

Turtles in Salt Pond Bay.

Full-moon parties at Miss Lucy's.

Mosquitoes in Maho Bay.

Iguanas.

Long lines at the Starfish Market (bring your own bags).

Cruise-ship crowds on the beach at Trunk Bay.

Steel-drum music and Chester's johnnycakes.

Snorkelers, whom we fondly call "one-horned buttfish."

Driving on the left.

Nutmeg sprinkled on painkillers (the drink).

Captain Stephen playing the guitar on the *Singing Dog.*

Eight Tuff Miles, ending at Skinny Legs.

A smile from Slim Man, who owns the parking lot downtown.

Nude sunbathers on Salomon Bay.

Rum punches and Kenny Chesney.

Afternoon trade winds.

Chickens everywhere.

St. John has no traffic lights, no chain stores, no fast-food restaurants, and no nightclubs, unless you count the Beach Bar, where you can dance to Miss Fairchild and the Wheeland Brothers in the sand. St. John is quiet, authentic, unspoiled.

Some people go so far as to call our island "paradise."

But, we quickly remind them, even paradise has its troubles.

IRENE

Cigarette smoke. Bacon grease. Something that smells like three-day-old fish.

Irene opens her eyes. Where is she?

There's a blue windowpane-print bedsheet covering her. She's on a couch. Her neck complains as she turns her head. There's a kitchen, and on the counter, a bottle of eighteen-year-old Flor de Caña.

Huck's house.

Irene sits up, brings her bare feet to the wood floor. A suitcase with everything she owns in the world is open on the coffee table.

She hears heavy footsteps and then: "Good morning, Angler Cupcake, how about some coffee?"

She drops her face into her hands. How can Huck be thinking about coffee? Irene's life is…over. This time yesterday she'd been steady and stable, which was *no small feat* considering only a little over a month has passed since her husband, Russell Steele, was killed in a helicopter crash and Irene, who'd believed Russ was in Florida playing *golf* and schmoozing with *clients,* discovered that Russ had a secret life down here in the Virgin Islands complete with mistress, love child, and a fifteen-million-dollar villa. Irene handled that news *pretty damn well,* if she does say so herself. Another woman might have had a nervous breakdown. Another woman might have set the villa on fire or taken out a full-page ad in the local paper (in Irene's case, the *Iowa City Press-Citizen*) announcing her husband's treachery. But Irene adapted to the shocking circumstances. She found that she liked the Virgin Islands so much that she's returned here to live—maybe not forever, but for a little while so she can catch her breath and regroup. Just yesterday she was looking around Russ's villa, thinking how she would redecorate it, how she might turn it into an inn for women like herself who had survived cataclysmic life changes.

Just last night, Irene felt like a teenager falling in love for the first time, because, in a plot twist that happens only in novels and romantic comedies, Irene has developed feelings for Huck Powers, the stepfather of Russ's mistress. The universe did Irene "a solid" (as Cash and Baker would say) when she met Huck. He's an irresistible mix of gruff fisherman, devoted grandpa, and teddy bear. What would Irene's situation look like if she hadn't become friends with Huck? She can't imagine.

But entertaining notions of a love life is a luxury she can no longer afford. Last night, FBI agents seized Russ's villa. It's now the property of the U.S. government.

If Irene was painfully honest with herself, she would admit that, once she got down here, she'd realized there was no way the business Russ had been involved in was aboveboard. From the minute Irene set eyes on the villa, it had a bit of a magic-carpet feel: Was it real? Would it fly?

It was a tropical...palace. Nine bedrooms, each with its own en suite bath. The outdoor space featured an upper pool and a lower pool connected by a curvy slide, a hot tub dropped into a lush gardenscape, an outdoor kitchen, a shuffleboard court (which Irene had never used), and, eighty steps down, a small, private sugar-sand beach (which she had). The view across the water to Tortola and Jost Van Dyke was dramatic, soaring. The villa was so over-the-top *luxurious* that Irene was able to get past the fact that it had been the home of Russ and his mistress, Rosie, and their daughter, Maia. She had been looking forward to putting her own stamp on the place— choosing lighter, brighter fabrics, redoing a bathroom in an under-the-sea theme for her four-year-old grandson, Floyd, creating a custom window seat where she or Maia could read or nap.

The far bigger, more devastating development is that, as Agent Colette Vasco of the FBI informed Irene, the authorities were, at that very moment, also seizing her home on Church Street in Iowa City, an 1892 Queen Anne–style Victorian that Irene had spent six years renovating. The Church Street house is Irene's *home*. It's where her photo albums, her cookbooks with the sauce-splattered pages and handwritten notes, her clothes, her teapot, and her Christmas ornaments are. She has the idea that maybe, with luck, some of these items might be returned to her, but how is she to accept the loss of, say, the third-floor landing, paneled in dark walnut with the east-facing stained-glass window, or the mural of Door County on the dining-room walls? Those moments in her house are priceless and irreplaceable. Irene thinks longingly of her amethyst parlor, the velvet fainting couch, the absurdly expensive Persian rugs, the Eastlake bed in the Excelsior suite, the washstand, the sepia-toned photograph of Russ's mother, Milly, as a child in 1928.

Thinking about that photograph brings Irene to her feet.

Huck, it turns out, has been watching her every move. "Coffee?"

She casts her eyes around the room and finds her phone plugged into the far wall. That's right; Irene remembers being methodical about packing her suitcase and double-checking for essentials like her phone charger. Agent Vasco had looked on suspiciously, as though she thought Irene might try to slip in a stash of cocaine or blocks of hundred-dollar bills.

When Irene got to Huck's house, they each did a shot—or two? three?—of the Flor de Caña, and Irene only barely recalls plugging her phone in before sleep. She remembers so little about the end of the night that she supposes she should be grateful she woke up on the sofa and not in Huck's bed.

He's a gentleman.

"I need to make a phone call," she says. "Do you have any...aspirin?" She points to her head. "Good morning," she adds, because she has learned the number-one rule of the Virgin Islands: "Good morning," "Good afternoon," or "Good evening" begins every conversation.

"Two aspirin coming right up," Huck says.

"Three," Irene says. *Four,* she thinks. "Please."

"The best reception is out on the deck," Huck says.

Irene slips through the sliding glass door, going from the pleasant air-conditioning of Huck's house (though she gathered last night that he turned it on only because she was there) to the mounting heat of the day. Her phone says seven o'clock, which means it's five o'clock in Iowa City.

Five a.m. Will Lydia be awake at five a.m.? She is going through menopause and complains that now she never sleeps, so maybe. Even if she is asleep, Irene needs to wake her up. Dr. Lydia Christensen is her best friend; she claims she is there for Irene no matter what. The bonds of best-friendship get tested infrequently, especially as Irene prides herself on being self-sufficient.

Today is a different story.

"Hello?" Lydia says. She's laughing. Irene hears the whisper of bedsheets and, in the next instant, a deep male voice. This would be Brandon the barista, Lydia's new boyfriend. Irene doesn't want to imagine what the two of them are doing up so early.

"Lydia, it's Irene." She stops herself. "Good morning."

"Irene?" Lydia says. "Is everything *okay?* Did something happen? Something *else?*"

"Yes," Irene says.

Lydia is there for Irene no matter what. No matter that it's five a.m., no matter that it's negative ten degrees with the wind chill in Iowa City, no matter that Irene interrupted pillow talk. Lydia and Brandon are going to put on their parkas and drive directly over to Church Street to see what's what. She'll call Irene when she gets there.

Inside, Irene accepts the three aspirin and a glass of ice water. The Flor de Caña bottle has been tucked away, and in its place is a cup of coffee that Irene understands is for her. There are eggs cooking on the stove.

"I don't want to seem ungrateful, but I just can't eat," Irene says.

"The eggs are for Maia," Huck says.

Right, Irene thinks. Maia has school. For everyone else, it's a normal day. It's Thursday.

"We have a charter," Irene says.

"That we do," Huck says. "I'm going to take it alone. I thought about passing it off to *What a Catch!,* but it seems like now we could probably use the money. You stay home and figure out what you need to figure out, and I'll be back this afternoon to help you in any way that I can." He gives her a tentative smile. "Maybe with fresh mahi."

Irene bows her head. She notices his use of the pronoun *we,* which she finds both sweet and confusing. What he doesn't understand is that there is no *we.* Irene has lost her house here and her home in Iowa City. She feels like Wile E. Coyote in the old cartoons: suspended over a canyon, running on air, and then looking down and realizing there's nothing beneath him. Irene's problem can't be fixed. It can't be made better by fresh grilled mahi for dinner. Irene's problem is that her husband of thirty-five years, in addition to keeping a mistress and fathering a child and lying about his whereabouts, had been evading tax laws and laundering money.

"Did I ever tell you that Russ sent me flowers on New Year's Day?" Irene asks. "Calla lilies, a beautiful bouquet. He must have arranged it with the florist ahead of time and paid extra because of the holiday. And do you know what I thought when I got them? I thought, *What a lovely man Russell Steele is. I am so lucky to have him.*"

"AC," Huck says. He turns off the heat under the eggs and takes a step toward her, but she holds up her palm to warn him away.

"He was dead by the time the flowers arrived."

"Irene," Huck says. "You're allowed to be upset."

Apparently Irene hasn't avoided the nervous-breakdown stage after all because what she wants to do is scream, *You're damn right I'm allowed to be upset! It's a good thing the man is dead because if he were alive, I'd kill him!*

But Irene holds her tongue, and a second later Maia walks into the kitchen. She's wearing pink shorts, a gray T-shirt with a hand-painted iguana on the front, and a pair of black Converse.

When she sees Irene, she does an almost comical double take. "Um... hi? Miss Irene?"

"Good morning, Maia," Irene says. She turns the corners of her lips up, which physically hurts. Then, as a demonstration that everything's okay, everything's fine, she takes a sip of her coffee. It's strong. One small mercy.

Maia looks from Irene to Huck and back with raised eyebrows. "Did you... stay here last night?"

Irene nearly laughs. She has no idea what to say. Part of her wants to claim she's here just to pick up Huck for their charter, but in another second, Maia is going to notice Irene's suitcase open on the coffee table.

"I did," Irene says. "Huck was kind enough to let me sleep on the sofa."

"Okay..." Maia says.

Huck spoons some eggs onto a plate and pushes the button on the toaster. "Irene and the boys lost the villa, Nut," he says. "There's some... tax trouble."

Tax trouble is a useful phrase, Irene thinks. It'll put everyone to sleep.

Maia takes a seat at the table. "So you guys can't stay there anymore?"

The toaster dings. Huck pulls butter and jam out of the fridge and sets them on the table along with the plate of eggs and toast. "I have to get ready," he says, and he disappears down the hall, leaving Irene to explain the unexplainable.

"We can't," Irene says. Cash called his friend Tilda and spent the night at her house. Irene asked Cash to call Baker and let him know what happened. Baker was planning on moving down to the island from Houston with his son, Floyd—though these plans will certainly have to change. Hopefully, Baker hasn't done anything that can't be undone. "The villa belongs to the government now. Because Russ...your dad...he owed the government money for taxes, and since he's not here to pay them, the FBI took the house instead." This isn't quite true, but it's close enough.

"So none of us can stay there?"

"No," Irene says. "They let me leave with only one suitcase. Just my clothes. So the stuff in your room...might be difficult to get back."

Maia's fork hovers over her breakfast. She looks so much like Russ's mother, Milly, in that moment that Irene wants to hug her. Those eyes. Milly's eyes.

"Are you guys leaving, then?" Maia asks in a wavering voice.

"Oh, Maia," Irene says, and her eyes fill with tears. "No? I don't know? The FBI also took my house in Iowa City."

"They did?"

"They did," Irene says. She can no longer stand, she's shaking too badly, so she takes the seat next to Maia. "That house is what's called a Victorian, and it had been a dream of mine since I was a young girl to restore and live in a real Victorian house. When Russ and I were first married, I kept clippings in a file folder of paint colors I liked, sofas, wallpaper, old sinks, light fixtures, doorknobs."

"Like Pinterest?" Maia says.

"Yes, like Pinterest," Irene says. "And once Russ… your dad…took the job down here, I had the money to buy a real Victorian house in a style called Queen Anne, which has elaborate gingerbread fretwork trim…" She looks at Maia. "Do you know what that is?"

Maia shakes her head.

"It looks like a house in a fairy tale, with a deep front porch and a turret and some stained-glass windows."

"Cool," Maia says. Irene thinks maybe Maia is indulging her, but it *is* cool, the definition of *cool*.

"It was as if my entire Pinterest board came to life," Irene says. "The house is filled with antiques and hand-knotted silk rugs. There are built-in cabinets and salvaged fixtures and stained-glass windows and murals on the walls and chandeliers, and I have a doorbell that used to ring in a convent in Italy." She needs to stop. What is she doing, unloading all this on a twelve-year-old? "I would have loved for you to see it." This is true, Irene realizes. She wanted both Huck and Maia to see the Church Street house someday. It was her life's work. In a way, it was an incarnation of Irene herself. "But they're taking it. I'm losing my swimming pool and my rose garden with all my heirloom varietals and my two cars. It'll all be gone. They're taking it because of Russ. And now I have nothing left."

Maia stares at Irene, and Irene is just sane enough to feel ashamed.

"You have Cash and Baker and Floyd," Maia says. "You have Huck. He really likes you...he was in a terrible mood when you went back to the States, you know. And you have me." She picks up her toast, butters and jams it, and holds it out to Irene. "And you have this papaya jam from Jake's, which is one of the best things I've ever eaten. Try it."

Irene accepts the toast—how can she not?—and takes a small bite. The jam is...well, it's delicious.

"Good, right?" Maia says.

Irene nods and takes another small bite.

"You can start a new Pinterest board," Maia says. "And the first thing on it can be the papaya jam from Jake's."

If only it were that easy, Irene thinks. She knows Maia is right; Irene still has what matters. Her family. Her friends. Her health. Her good sense, sort of.

"We aren't going to leave," Irene says. She doesn't add *because we have nowhere to go.* This isn't strictly true, anyway. Baker still owns a house in Houston that is untouched by Russ's tainted money. And Irene's elderly aunt Ruth has their family summer home in Door County. But the thought of moving to Houston or living with her eighty-something-year-old aunt isn't at all appealing. "We'll figure something out."

"You can stay here," Maia says. "And you don't have to sleep on the couch—we have an extra room. My mom's room." She takes a bite of eggs and seems to realize what she has just offered.

"The couch is fine for now," Irene says quickly. "And I'll find something. I'm not completely penniless."

Maia swallows. "Gramps told me I could move into my mom's room. That means you can have my room."

"Oh, Maia…"

"It's a mess, I know," Maia says. "But I'll clean it after school. I'm grounded anyway."

That's right; Maia is grounded. She'd pulled a disappearing act last night after lying to Cash to get him to drop her off in town. That drama now seems extremely minor, like running out of dinner rolls on the *Titanic*.

"You don't have to move on my account," Irene says, though there is obviously no way she's going to sleep in Rosie's room. "The couch is fine."

"I want to move," Maia says. "You being here is a good impetus." She scrunches up her eyes. "Did I use that word correctly?"

Irene can't help herself; she halfway smiles. "You did."

"So you'll stay?"

It's not in Irene's nature to accept help from anyone, but she can't turn down such a sweet offer—besides which, she is the definition of *desperate*. "I'll stay until I get back on my feet."

Suddenly, Huck is before them, dressed in his sky-blue fishing shirt and his visor, a yellow bandanna tied around his neck. "I'm glad that's settled," he says.